the trouble with wanting

JILLIAN LIOTA

Love Is A Verb Books

Book Cover Design and Layout by Blue Moon Creative Studio

Cover Photo by Madison Maltby

Editing by C. Marie

ISBN 978-1-952549-03-8 (paperback)
ISBN 978-1-952549-04-5 (eBook)
ISBN 978-1-952549-05-2 (kindle)

to all the girls who struggle to believe
they are worthy of being loved

it's a long road to unlearn that belief
but it is worth every damn step

chapter one
boyd

"Paging Boyd Mitchell. Passenger Boyd Mitchell, please see the closest Summit attendant. Thank you."

The sound of my name over the intercom pulls my eyes from where they've been focused on my phone, my attention briefly drawn away from the work that dominates my focus at all hours.

I quickly scan the crowded seating area at Gate C21, taking in the host of cranky, agitated passengers waiting to board the flight, as if one of them might be able to confirm that I did, in fact, hear my name announced throughout the terminal.

I don't know why I do that, especially considering the fact that I'm usually traveling alone, but coming from a family as large as mine, one that is always in my business and full of a bunch of know-it-alls, I can't help but believe I'm never alone, no matter how much I wish it were so.

Grabbing my carry-on and tucking my jacket into the crook of my arm, I carefully make my way through the extended legs and belongings of my fellow travelers.

Boston Logan International Airport is always a busy place, but today it seems especially so with families and groups trying to squeeze in last-minute summer vacations before the weather on the east coast begins to turn crisp and school starts back up.

It's the reason I'm traveling today as well, even though I don't really have the time to take off from work to spend two weeks in Cedar Point.

But it's tradition, and my mother would absolutely pitch a fit if I were the one Mitchell child who bucked the tradition I had such a large hand in creating.

The last two weeks of August are *officially* Mitchell family time, and the idea that this two weeks on the calendar could belong to anyone or anything else is unjustifiable, work be damned.

It started when I left for college then continued when my sister Briar followed a year later. Originally, it was just a chance for us to catch up and reconnect with our family after long, boring summer jobs before starting school again.

My parents took that idea and cemented it into stone, turning those two weeks every summer into a non-negotiable family exclusive. Work doesn't matter. Significant others don't matter. Everything in life gets planned around those two weeks. Period.

A few times, my mom has even turned the end of August into a family reunion of sorts, inviting aunts and uncles and cousins back to the very town that grew them, our lakefront home and guesthouse turning into a glorified hostel with air mattresses galore and family members sleeping on couches.

I resent the obligation every year, wishing I were somehow brave enough to tell my mother I simply cannot take off of work this year, bold enough to tell her my employers are unwilling to be flexible.

But I don't think any of us Mitchell kids have ever had the

heart—or the balls—to break free from what's expected, or to let down my mother.

"Boyd Mitchell," I say when one of the Summit Airlines attendants finally nods me over to the counter. "I was called up just a minute ago."

Her head bobs once but her eyes never leave the screen in front of her as she types furiously. She must be writing a dissertation, because I can't imagine any airline computer program needing as much information as she's providing.

"Can I see some identification?"

I slide my driver's license forward, having already had it in my hand. The woman in front of me—Kimmy, her nametag says—takes a look at it, looks at me, and looks back at the ID before returning it.

Seems I've passed the test.

Suddenly, a wide and completely disingenuous smile covers her face. I almost want to ask her to go back to ignoring me.

"You've been upgraded to first class, Mr. Mitchell. Let me just print you up a new boarding pass and we'll get you all settled."

I usually hate flying Summit. It's the airline my job partners with, and I have to fly regularly for work. It does come with some nice perks like getting upgraded here and there, but the number of times my flight has been canceled or delayed due to mechanical issues is ridiculous.

I always wonder if I'm actually going to get to travel when I arrive at the airport, or if I'm going to be hanging out in the terminal for hours while I get booked on a new flight.

Most of my travel for work keeps me moving on short-leg flights around New England and the east coast, an hour here, two hours there, so when I'm stuffed into an economy seat, I don't stress over it. My flight to the west coast this morning, however, is an almost-7-hour doozy, so this upgrade couldn't have come at a more perfect moment. I can feel my broad shoulders and long legs silently thanking the upgrade gods for their gift.

As Kimmy makes the necessary adjustments, I turn and take another look around the gate.

City life is perfect for me. I'm an eyes down, nose to the grind kind of guy, and I don't make it a habit to pay attention to what is going on around me.

Having grown up in a small town, I know what it's like to have people paying attention to my every move at all hours of the day, and I remember what it was like to wish those eyes weren't watching and setting town tongues wagging. In Boston, if you give someone a little too much eye contact in a public space, you're likely to get a stream of foul language shouted in your face. You're supposed to keep your gaze down and stay out of other people's business.

Like I said, it's perfect for me.

But my therapist has been encouraging me to keep my head up, so I try to remind myself to take a look around a few times a day. Apparently, paying attention to the world around me will provide me with a 'new perspective.'

I don't know what she's hoping I'll find by watching a woman pick a wedgie then grab a French fry to put into her mouth, but I'm assuming there's a lesson to be learned in there somewhere.

"Hi, how are you?"

The bright voice next to me has my focus shifting down the counter to the short brunette approaching the attendant standing next to Kimmy.

This woman has her dark hair in a messy knot high on her

4

head and doesn't look to be wearing a lick of makeup, but damn if I'm not knocked on my ass by the most breathtaking smile I've seen in my entire life.

If only it were directed my way.

I shake my head and let out a quiet huff of laughter at myself, wondering where in the hell that thought came from. When was the last time I hoped any woman looked my way outside of a bar?

Apparently, my little laugh wasn't quiet enough, because the woman's eyes flit to mine for just a second, the tiny wrinkles next to her lids crinkling slightly as she acknowledges me. Then she turns back to talk with the woman at the desk.

"Here you are, sir."

I drag my eyes away from the brunette with the bombshell smile and look back at Kimmy. I blink once, feeling like I've missed something while I was staring, then take in the fact that she's slid my new boarding pass forward on the counter.

"Thanks." My response is quick as I retrieve the slip of paper and tuck it into my wallet.

"Absolutely. Can I do anything else for you?"

I shake my head, giving her a tight smile, and I'm turning to walk away when the brunette's words penetrate my mind.

"...never flown before and I'm a little nervous. Is there anything really important I need to know or be prepared for?"

Her voice, while upbeat and melodic, has the hint of nerves behind it, and it takes an effort to hide my smile. I don't think I've ever met an adult who has never been on a plane before. I wonder what that's like, to enter into a situation that's completely out of your control and totally unfamiliar.

Sounds horrible.

Truth be told, I also struggle with fear when it comes to flying. You can explain it to me a million different ways, but I still have trouble with the concept that something weighing close to 350 metric tons can just *float* in the air.

And yes, I know it doesn't actually float. Obviously. But that's what it feels like.

With the job I have working with startup tech companies and app developers across the Eastern Seaboard, though, saying I'm afraid of flying isn't an option. So, I've had to suck it up and rack up those frequent flier miles.

Thankfully, it has gotten easier over the years, the gripping panic as we lift off the ground easing to more of a mild anxiousness that passes as soon as I've had my first drink.

And whether I'm seated in first class or not, there is *always* a drink when I'm flying. Because whiskey just makes everything better.

I'm lucky enough to come from a family that did a lot of traveling when I was growing up. My parents wanted us to see the world and all the differences and opportunities that exist. My sweet mother, hoping to calm my troubled mind, always had a bible verse for me when we'd fly. *Blessed is the one who trusts in the Lord* or *He is a shield to those who put their trust in Him.*

I again take a seat in the gate area and stretch my long legs out in front of me, settling back in to wait until we're called to board.

I have no problem trusting in a higher being, whoever that is. I grew up in the church and believe in a greater plan, a God-like figure who loves us and wants us to have good lives and be good people.

What I *don't* trust is human ability. We are innately fallible, and technology created by fallible humans is literally designed to be imperfect. As a person who does not enjoy the state of *not* being in control, I find it difficult to put complete trust in something so precarious other than myself on this great earth.

Or, I guess, in the open air.

Thirty minutes later, I'm walking down the jet bridge, first class boarding pass clutched like a lottery ticket in my hand, when my phone starts to ring. The soft notes of the familiar ringtone echo down the corridor for a few seconds as I change my jacket from one hand to the other and dig my device out of my right front pocket.

I let out a disgruntled sigh when I see the name on the screen.

Thing 1 would like to Facetime...

Instead of ignoring him like I should, I swipe right and watch while the call connects, moving slowly behind the handful of other passengers boarding the plane in group one.

When the call goes from 'connecting' to 'connected,' Bishop's face appears and he gives me a big, childish smile.

"Hey, dickface."

The sound of my brother's voice booms out of my phone and fills the mostly silent walkway, my cheeks heating as I give an embarrassed wave to the elderly couple who turns to glare at me.

I quickly shuffle around to plug my headphones in, popping

one in my right ear before giving Bishop a nasty look.

"Thanks for that. It's not like I'm in public or anything."

His face morphs into that shit-eating grin that says he knows exactly what he's doing, and it makes me want to hang up on him.

"It's your own fault, Boy," he says.

"Boyd," I correct him for the millionth time since we were children, my tone firm.

I hate that obnoxious nickname. It's not even a real nick-name as much as it is my brother enjoying his relentless antagonism. I've never fully understood his fascination with Boy, though, since *he's* the one who couldn't pronounce his Ds until he was ten.

"Oh. *Really?* I never knew your actual name before today. Thank you, *kind sir*, for enlightening me so that I might serve at your every request." He bows his head, and I roll my eyes at the horrible British accent.

"What do you want?"

I step through the open plane door when the couple in front of me moves forward then stop again in the galley to wait for the people in front of me to take their seats.

The flight attendant in a purple and tan uniform gives me a big smile, and I manage one in return.

"I'm getting on the plane," I grumble, hoping he'll take that as a clue that he should get to his point, and quickly.

"Bell wants me to remind you that you promised to do the Kilroy hike with us this year. You know, since you manage to find an excuse every year not to go."

I let out a sigh, wishing I'd just put my phone in airplane mode a few minutes early.

The much-dreaded—at least by me—Kilroy hike is an overnighter that requires lugging a massive pack into the mountains just outside our hometown. I enjoy a good run or swim and make frequent use of the gym by my house, but hiking long distances has never been my thing, something my younger siblings have never seemed to care about since they demand I go with them every year.

"It can be a new family tradition," my sister Bellamy said five years ago, excitement in her voice at the idea of all of us going together and pitching tents at the campground near the top.

It sounds like a miserable time to me, but as the only voice of dissent for most things in our family, my opinion rarely matters.

Luckily, I've always had an excuse, and it's getting to the point where I'm actually impressed by how long I've managed to get out of it.

Five years.

That's quite the record of evasion.

Last year, I had an emergency company teleconference that coincided with the date that worked for everyone. The year before that I hurt my knee playing a pickup rugby game with some friends from college. One year I even used a crazy hangover to my advantage, faking a cold that kept me bedridden, though how I was feeling after splitting a full bottle of whiskey with my friend Rusty wasn't any kind of a lie.

So. I'll tell them whatever they want, but I'm not gonna be dragging my ass up a mountain any time soon.

"Yup. No worries."

I finally reach my row, lifting my carry-on into the overhead compartment. Picking up the pillow and blanket provided on my seat, I plop down, letting out a rush of breath as the people behind me surge past like a wave.

I love first class. Being 6'4", it is quite the squeeze to sit in economy. The extra width of an upgraded seat is wonderful for my broad shoulders, but it's the legroom that makes all the difference.

Summit Airlines seats are pretty snug in the main cabin, and I usually have to manspread my legs so I don't punch a hole through the seat in front of me. I always feel like shit as I apologize profusely to the people sitting next to me, knowing I'm not going to be able to change the fact that my legs are seriously encroaching on the tiny bit of real estate they've paid for.

Flying is bad enough, and I'm a firm believer that everyone should interact as minimally as possible. My rules of the air are as non-negotiable as this trip home at the end of every August.

Don't make small talk. Don't touch me. Don't sneeze on me. Don't ask me to move to go to the bathroom more than once. Don't set your things on my tray table. Don't hog the armrests. Don't kick my chair.

It's a give and take, and everyone has to be on board with it, which is rarely the case in economy, where the mentality is more like cattle jockeying for room to breathe.

First class, though? Everyone's in a completely different mood. Nobody is bothersome. Everyone is considerate. We get a drink and a meal and enough space for our limbs and torso. Most of the time, you're left alone instead of stuck sitting next to some overly verbose crazy person who wants to share their life story.

Having the ability to sit here in silence with my noise-canceling headphones and all the room I need for my long-ass legs on this long-ass flight?

I'm overjoyed.

No one would be able to tell by looking at my face, of

course, since my default expression is the male version of resting bitch face.

What would that be called? Resting dick face?

Sure. That works.

"You get bumped to first?" Bishop's voice in my ear reminds me that I'm still on the phone with him, and I tilt the screen toward me to just in time to see him stuff a handful of Cheetos in his mouth.

"How could you tell?"

He shrugs. "There's always that weird pad behind your head when you're in first."

I turn to look and there is, in fact, a pad that rests on the seat.

When I look back at my brother, I see that he's set his phone up on a table and taken a few steps back, getting comfortable on a couch I would know anywhere. The tan walls and deep blue accents of my mom's living room are as familiar to me as the lines on my hands.

"You're already home, then?" I ask, doing a quick mental calculation of when my brother might have traveled to town.

"We got in a few days ago," he responds. The *we* can only be referring to himself and his twin sister, Bellamy.

The two of them drive each other—and the rest of us—bonkers, but I am certain there has never been a set of twins who were more of a *we* than Bishop and Bell.

"I bet Mom was thrilled you showed up early."

He doesn't catch the sarcasm in my voice.

Patty Mitchell normally loves surprises, but she's also a very planned person, and balancing those two parts of her personality can be…a challenge, to put it delicately.

So, having two of her kids show up a few days earlier than

she planned—before the house is ready, *good gracious*—was probably enough to send her into some sort of tizzy.

But Bishop just shrugs, his youth reflected in that *whatever* kind of look he always seems to have on his face. It wouldn't occur to him that showing up early would aggravate our mother, because he struggles to think past his own opinion and needs.

"She seemed a little irritated at first, but she came around."

Of course she did, because her love for her kids took priority over the fact that she probably hadn't set up their rooms or stocked the fridge or any of the hundred other things she likes to do before we come home.

I might keep my nose down a lot, but that doesn't mean I don't pay attention, and I know my family, particularly my mother. That woman is nothing if not the ultimate host, even to her brood of selfish children.

Before I can say anything that might attempt to clue Bishop in on why our mom was cranky with him, a pair of green leggings stops right next to me.

"Excuse me."

I let my eyes trail up the short but toned legs, over sweet hips and lush curves before I finally meet the eyes of the woman who was standing next to me at the counter earlier.

A soft blue I've never quite seen before twinkles back at me.

"I think I'm sitting right there," she says, pointing to the empty seat next to me by the window.

"Who's that?" Bishop barks into my ear, and without another word, I close out the screen, ending the call.

"Sorry about that," I say, unbuckling my belt and standing up, moving into the aisle to let her pass by me.

"No problem." She gives me that smile again as we both settle down and buckle in.

"I'm Ruby," she says, her eyes bright and cheery, that smile looking to be permanently locked onto her face but still managing to be genuine. "I saw you earlier, at the counter, right?"

I nod but don't answer.

Part of me is kicking myself, because the gorgeous girl from the counter is sitting next to me and I should *absolutely* talk to her.

But the minute I say anything, I'm breaking one of my cardinal flying rules, which just opens the door to needless conversation I'm never in the mood for.

And yet, damn if I don't feel more than tempted to break that rule just to hear that lovely voice of hers again or have an excuse to look at her.

I waffle back and forth for a moment as I stare at the black screen of my phone. Ultimately, logic wins out, and I stay silent.

Seemingly unaware of my internal dialogue, Ruby is focused on the small bag she has in her hands. It's a backpack, I guess, made entirely out of patches. She unbuttons the top and sticks her hand inside, pulling out a green Moleskine notebook and placing it in the seatback pocket in front of her. Then she rebuttons the bag, drops it on the ground, and kicks it forward.

Rapid-fire texts from my brother begin to pop up, and a quick glance confirms he's asking about 'the hot girl' and wondering if I'm bringing someone home.

Instead of responding, I swipe it over to airplane mode and tuck it into the pocket in front of me.

My eyes scan the entering passengers, hoping to distract myself from the woman sitting next to me, but for some reason I can't seem to explain, I'm hyperaware of her. Her scent—jasmine—and the soft noises she makes as she explores her seat. Opening and closing the window. Her legs swinging slightly like a child's in a chair that's too big for them.

"What's your name?"

Her voice takes me by surprise and I look in her direction, finding her beautiful blue eyes twinkling at me, a small smile on her face.

"Boyd," I reply, my name popping out of my mouth, almost without my consent.

Since when do I give my name to the people I sit next to on planes? Since when does someone even *ask*?

Something moves in my peripheral vision, and when I look down, I see she's extended her hand.

In the first ten seconds of sitting next to me, she's broken one of my important flying rules by making unnecessary small talk even though I assumed my silence a few minutes ago would communicate that I'm not much for chatter.

And now she wants to break another rule by shaking my hand?

I look from her hand back to her eyes, finding her still wearing that same brilliant smile, before I feel compelled to place my hand in hers.

She gives it a firm squeeze, and damn if I don't feel that squeeze rush through my whole body, especially when she leans toward me just slightly.

Her voice is perky and happy and full of the qualities I typically find irritating in anyone giving me their attention.

But not today, apparently. Today, I find myself drawn in by her sweet smile and kind eyes, and I realize I'm leaning forward as well, mimicking her body language.

She lowers her voice, almost as if she's about to tell me a secret—a secret I desperately want to know.

"Nice to meet you, Boyd."

chapter two
ruby

I hate everything about this tin can the second my foot crosses the threshold and I'm enclosed within the interior of the plane taking me to California.

I hate the stagnant air.

I hate the way the buckle feels pressed against my abdomen.

I hate that my roommate told me the entire flight is just everyone farting the entire time and breathing in each other's gas, so now I'm consumed with worry about breathing through my nose because the idea of inhaling particles from someone else's butt is making me want to gag.

But mostly? I hate how much I hate this.

I don't usually hate *anything*.

I'm the girl who claps for the performers on the T, even though they're in everyone's way. The girl who dances to the music in my headphones as I walk home from work. The person who looks people in the eye as I walk down the street and always has a smile.

I'm a massage therapist, for goodness sake. My whole job is to create a relaxing and peaceful environment for people and then work their bodies over so they let go of the mental worries that are causing them physical stress.

Even though I'm maintaining my composure and calm at the forefront of my mind, I can feel this tiny vein of toxic, sludgy pessimism and negativity slowly churning through my body.

I don't want to be on this stupid plane, going on a trip that was a stupid idea in the first place, to spend time with a stupid person I don't even want to see.

I let out a slightly shaky breath and tuck my hands under my thighs.

Okay, so none of that is actually true. I'm just nervous.

I've never flown before. I'm the only person I know who has never been on a plane, and that includes my neighbor Fiona's kids, who are 2 and 5 years old and have apparently flown "a skillion times" if you ask them.

It makes me feel like a bit of a crazy person, willingly buckling myself into a big metal machine that's supposed to defy gravity, but I figure millions of people do it every year and the number of times you hear about people dying in a plane crash isn't often enough to warrant hysteria.

Right?

Right.

Still, that doesn't help the fact that my stomach has decided to turn itself inside out.

I let out another breath, trying to steady my emotions and focus my mind on something soothing. I need to find a happy place, need to channel the calm I seek in my weekly yoga class and the peace of my daily meditations.

Taking in another deep breath, I remind myself that I have a reason for this trip, and I'm not going to back down from it just because I'm afraid of falling from the sky.

Fuck do I hate this.

I glance over at my seat buddy.

Boyd.

Such a strong, masculine name. It sounds like something out of a movie.

Even the way he said it, with that rich baritone striking a chord somewhere deep in my body, made him sound like he belongs on the silver screen. He could be a voiceover artist or someone who reads audiobooks. It wouldn't surprise me if I found out he was someone famous, or at least social media famous.

I mean…he's gorgeous.

It's not the kind of boyish charm I normally find attractive. It's much more serious, like he's got real-life responsibilities. The kind of guy who has an accountant and a barber and a favorite grocery store. A guy who drinks whiskey neat and smokes cigars and can fix his own dishwasher when it stops working.

A man kind of man.

As he stares at the phone in his hand and the flight attendants wander around finishing up their last checks, I allow myself a moment to study his profile.

Clean-shaven strong jaw, thick brows that slash across his face, and a prominent nose. Warm, chestnut eyes help to soften his otherwise harsh features, though even just based on the brief moment we spoke, he seems like the type of man who would *never* want to be described as *warm*.

When he stood up earlier to let me pass, I was overwhelmed by his size. He's probably an entire foot taller than I am, though that isn't very hard to do since I clock in at 5'3" at the start of the day when my spine hasn't fully compressed yet. I only get shorter from there.

I've always had a thing for tall guys. Call it genetics or hormones or some sort of subconscious, antiquated notion of wanting a big strong man to protect me, but damn if I don't have a thing for them big boys.

Tall and lanky has been my thing in the past—a common body type in the yoga world—but I can definitely get behind the more filled-out, muscular frame Boyd is carrying around.

Sure, I can pretend I was just being friendly when I introduced myself. I *do* love chatting with people I've never met before, but the truth is that I couldn't imagine anything better on a horridly long flight than chatting with the stud next to me—especially if it means I get to listen to that sexy-as-sin voice rumble my way.

I just wish he would smile or something, let that softness in his eyes translate onto his face a little bit.

He glances over at me and I realize I've been staring at him for way longer than is probably socially acceptable, so I smile and return my attention to the back of the seat in front of me, taking a deep breath through my nose and letting it out through my mouth, willing my body to calm itself.

This trip is going to be fine.
This trip is going to be fine.
This trip is going to be fine.

I click around on the little TV screen a bit, picking a few movies and marking them as favorites so I can watch them later. Fiona told me I should watch a movie the second I get on the plane so I can distract myself from takeoff, but as the plane lurches backward, away from the gate and out onto the tarmac, I let out a startled squeak. There is no way in hell my attention will be diverted.

The man sitting next to me shifts in his seat, and I settle on the thought that there *is* a way to distract myself. Boyd might be the strong, silent type, but I bet if I can find the right topic, he'll loosen up in no time.

"So, Boyd, are you from Boston, or are you connecting from somewhere else?"

He turns to look at me, and there's this little flutter in my chest when his eyes connect with mine.

It happened earlier, too, at the counter. When his gaze turned my way, it felt like I was in an elevator that suddenly dropped a foot. My stomach shot up and shoved my heart into my throat, punched a hole in my mind, and made my tongue trip over itself.

Thankfully, he doesn't seem to be aware of the way my internal organs are having seizures.

"I'm from California," is all he says. Then he returns his attention to his phone.

"Oh, cool," I say, resting my elbow on the armrest between us and plopping my chin in my hand. "Were you in Boston for business or pleasure?"

He clears his throat, taking his time before he responds.

"I originally came to Boston to go to college. I like it here, so I just never left."

"Wow," I say, impressed at that mentality of wanting to brave the world at such a young age. "How amazing are you to venture off on your own when you were just figuring things out? I don't know if I could have ever done something like that when I was eighteen. I mean, this is my first time on a plane and I'm twenty-four, so clearly the great adventurer I am not." I snicker. "So where did you go to school?"

Another pause. "MIT."

"Oh, wow!" I exclaim again, my eyebrows shooting up. "You must have a huge brain. I have a friend who's getting his PhD there and he's like, an absolute genius and a part of Mensa. So, yeah. That's amazing."

He looks like he enjoyed my compliment, but he doesn't say anything else. Maybe he's one of those men who struggles with knowing how to continue a conversation? I can help with that, definitely.

"So you graduated? What do you do now?"

He clicks his phone screen to black and lets out a sigh, resting his head against the seat and closing his eyes.

"I work with app developers, startup tech companies, stuff like that."

I nod, even though he can't see me.

"It must feel great to be doing something you're so good at. Well, I guess I'm making an assumption that you're good at it," I add, laughing at myself. "But I'm also assuming you wouldn't have a job doing it if you sucked. Is that what you always hoped to do? Is it, like, a dream come true to work in the tech field?"

His eyes open and he glances over at me then turns his attention to the screen on the seat in front of him. "Not really a dream come true, no, but it pays well."

He pushes some buttons and the screen lights up, but I'm stuck on what he said: *but it pays well.*

"Well, at least there's that," I say. "So, if you weren't doing a job just because it pays well…what would you do if you could do anything?" I ask, my voice kind of a whisper, my eyes wide with hope that he'll share with me.

I know he's technically a stranger. Well, okay, so not just technically. Literally—he is *literally* a stranger. And maybe it's weird that I'm asking such a personal question when I just met him ten minutes ago, but one of my favorite things is hearing about people's hopes and dreams, the things they want to accomplish that they worry are too big or too much for them to handle.

My roommate tells me all the time that I should be a professional encourager, although I'm not sure that's a real job. If it were? I would be so great at it. My favorite part about hearing people share their ambitions is that I can encourage them, build them up, tell them they're smart and amazing and worthy and they definitely have it in them to be and do whatever they want.

When Boyd looks back at me, I think I'm going to get that from him, this beautiful man I've just met on my very first plane ride. Maybe this will be a lifechanging moment where I can encourage him and believe in him.

"What would I do if I could do anything?" he asks, and I nod, a smile planted firmly on my face. "I'd watch a movie."

My smile drops slightly when he picks up a pair of noise-canceling headphones and plops them on his ears, turning his eyes away from mine.

"Can I get you something to drink before we depart?"

I tear my eyes away from Boyd's profile and look up at the flight attendant, who is hovering over us and waiting for a response. I glance once more at Boyd and see his eyes are glued firmly to the screen in front of him.

"Nothing for me, thanks," I say to the attendant, doing my best to give her a smile.

She looks to Boyd, who says he wants a whiskey neat—I *knew* it—and then she moves on to the next row of passengers.

I watch Boyd for a moment longer, feeling oddly wounded by his actions. Scanning back, I guess I could have paid more attention to the clues that he didn't want to talk to me instead of assuming he was hoping for a seat buddy to chat with.

Maybe I was being too nosy.

That's what my mom used to say about me, that I was a nosy parker, but she always said it with affection, like it was a part of me that I should be proud of, or at least not feel the need to apologize for.

I guess maybe some people don't see it that way.

I shift back from where I was leaning against the armrest, making sure I give Boyd his space, and stare blankly ahead, my fingers fiddling with my seatbelt.

Unable to distract myself, I pull out my notebook and flip to the next blank page, staring at it for a few minutes, willing my mind to create something for me to doodle so I can ignore the fact that I probably annoyed my seat neighbor.

I hate when I'm annoying.

It's the one thing I really do hate, for the most part. I'm a person who can stand up for herself, a person who has a drawer full of confidence and plenty of sass and happiness to spill over onto the floor in most instances.

But the last thing I want to be is annoying. A nuisance.

And this Boyd guy...the last thing I want is to make him uncomfortable, or for him to be upset with me. If I'm gonna sit next to him for the next seven hours, I should apologize or something.

I tap his shoulder lightly. When he doesn't react, I tap it again, a bit more firmly.

He takes his headphones off and looks at me.

"Sorry."

I want to slap my hand over my mouth as soon as I say the word, mostly because I shouted it at him and now several people are looking at us.

I lean forward and lower my voice.

"I'm sorry if what I said was nosy. I'm just...one of those people. You know? My mom always said I never met someone who wasn't a friend, probably because I talk their ear off and they don't get a choice whether they're my friend or not, but"—I shrug—"anyway, just...sorry if I did or said something that bothered you."

The silence between us is deafening, and all I can hear are the sounds of people shifting around in their seats and the airplane engine revving up then revving down again.

Is revving down a thing? I'm not sure, but that's what it sounds like.

He just stares at me, his jaw clenching and unclenching. Then he lets out a sigh and tucks his headphones into the pocket in front of him.

"Aeronautics," he finally says, his rich voice expanding and filling all the empty space around me, making my heart flutter wildly in its cage.

"Huh?"

"If I could have done anything, I'd have gone to school for aeronautics. My dream was to be a pilot, or at least someone who works for an airline, maybe streamlining services or finding new ways to advance the technology that improves flight." He shrugs. "But I'm afraid of flying, so my dad told me to major in something else."

I'm stunned silent, which doesn't happen to me often.

I thought maybe I'd get a polite nod from him in a best-case scenario, a glare and a grouchy retort in the worst case.

But he just spoke several sentences in a row to me. I wasn't expecting him to suddenly word-vomit and share his actual dream, and the sound of his voice has my heart moving just a bit faster, causing my tongue to trip over itself again.

When the silence stretches for a beat too long, I finally manage to spit something out.

"But you're flying today," I say. "Does that mean you've overcome your fear? Maybe you could go back for aeronautics now?"

He scrunches up his nose a little bit and shakes his head, accepting his drink and a napkin from the flight attendant.

"I'm just as afraid of flying today as I was when I was a kid. I understand lift and propulsion and engines and all the stuff you're supposed to understand when it comes to how an airplane flies." He shakes his head again. "It still doesn't sit well with me."

I laugh. "Oh thank *god*." And then I keep laughing.

He gives me a questioning look.

"I'm just thankful that other people are afraid too, that I'm not some sort of freak who is completely irrational. It's what everyone I know made me feel like before I left for this trip, and let me tell you—implying someone is stupid for being afraid doesn't ever take away their fear."

I didn't appreciate the people who tried to make me feel like I was an idiot for being afraid. Fear is fear, and shaming someone does nothing but make you an asshole.

"You're definitely not a freak, and you're not alone in being afraid," Boyd says. "Most people are afraid of flying to some degree. It's all about the unknown. That's what most fear is. My mom has always said fear is just rooted in a lack of understanding."

I play his words over again in my mind, letting them percolate. The idea has merit, but I don't think that's what drives my fear.

He must see my disagreement on my face. "You don't agree?"

I shake my head.

"I mean, I think what your mom said is true to some degree, but I don't think fear is caused by a lack of understanding. We feel fear because of love."

The face he makes when I say it has me laughing.

"That is…one of the strangest things I've ever heard," he says, lifting the tumbler of whiskey to his mouth to take a sip.

"Why? Is it so implausible to believe we are afraid because we have something to lose?"

He looks like he's about to refute my opinion but pauses, and I can tell by his expression that he's mulling it over.

"Sure, it sounds ridiculous when I use a word like *love*, but look at you—you *just* told me you understand how planes work yet you're still afraid. If you're afraid to fly, it's probably less about not understanding how flying works and more about not wanting to die, right?"

He's silent, so I barrel on.

"And why don't you want to die? Because you love your life, or your kids or your spouse, or your job or your church or whatever else that matters. That fear builds because you imagine what life would be like without you for your family, or the things you would miss out on with the ones you *love*."

He's quiet for a moment. I've never seen someone so clearly working a thought over in his mind, his brows pressed together until they're almost one long caterpillar.

I assume he's gearing up to disagree with me, but what he says is a surprise.

"Let's say I agree with you—how would you explain that a lot of people are *not* afraid of flying?" Then he smirks. "A lack of love?" he tacks on, sarcasm in his voice.

I shake my head with a smile. "It's not a *lack* of *love*. It's about the *existence* of *logic*. Think about it this way: Some people

25

believe there isn't a reason to be afraid because of data or science or whatever other argument that exists about safety. Other people ignore legitimate reasons to be afraid and choose not to be because they've accepted that death is inevitable and sometimes weird things happen."

He nods, his lips pursed, and I think I've won the argument—although I don't think we were in an actual argument as much as we were just debating something. My mom says there isn't a difference, but there totally is.

"So which one are you?" he asks, leaning closer.

"What do you mean?"

He grins. "Are you afraid because of love? Or are you afraid because you lack logic?"

I burst into laughter, enjoying the look of surprise on his face, his eyes wide and his own grin growing.

"Definitely both," I reply, enjoying the rumble of laughter that slips out of his own mouth, the two of us laughing together.

It's a good feeling.

"Sorry for rambling," I say, giving him another smile. "It's way too early in the morning to be debating something so highbrow. So, how 'bout them Sox, huh?"

Boyd looks at me with a twinkle in his eyes, a kind of friendly charm I wasn't expecting from him, regardless of how well we got on with our chat.

What I wouldn't give to look at that kind of handsome joy every day for the rest of my life.

A stupid thought, sure, but still true.

"I bet you ten dollars you can't name a single player on the team this year."

I narrow my eyes, trying to hide my smile as I shake my head. "I'm not a gambling girl."

"You'd gamble if you knew you were probably going to win." His response is as quick as lightning. "People only choose not to gamble when they're afraid they'll lose."

"That is so not true." I giggle. "Some of us poor folk don't gamble because we can't take the risk. Not all of us are first class aficionados with money to throw around willy-nilly."

"Nobody says *willy-nilly* anymore."

I snort. "Clearly that's false, because I just did."

He bites his lip and shakes his head, and I can't help the little thing that keeps bouncing around in my chest.

We like him, it tells me. *We like him a lot.*

Is this flirting? We are definitely flirting, right? I hope so, because it has been far too long since I've enjoyed a good flirt sesh with someone as handsome as Boyd.

That's a lie.

I've *never* flirted with someone as handsome as Boyd. He is in a league of his own.

Before I can say anything else, the plane lurches forward, and it feels like my stomach is going to fall out of my body.

My eyes slam shut and my throat closes up, my hands gripping the armrests for dear life as the plane barrels down the runway, all the good feelings from my talk with Boyd rushing out of me with a surreal quickness.

It's going to be okay.

It's going to be okay.

It's going to be okay.

I'm like that for who knows how long before I feel a hand on top of mine, the warmth and roughness surprising me enough that my eyes fly open, taking in the man sitting next to me.

He lifts my hand and twists his fingers in mine, the sensation robbing me of my voice—and maybe my sanity.

27

For the rest of my life, I'll remember exactly what he says to me. Not just the words, but the soothing tone of his voice and the earnest caring in his eyes, so surprising from someone I was expecting to ignore me for the entire flight.

"It's okay to be afraid," he says. "I can't take that feeling away from you, but I can hold your hand until it's over so you know you're not alone."

chapter three
boyd

Ruby's eyes stay shut for the entire time it takes for our plane to rise into the sky and level off. I know because I stare at her the entire time, until I see those beautiful blues finally open back up and look at me.

Watching her sitting next to me…it's the first time I've ever been distracted enough to ignore the feeling in my chest when we lift off the ground, that heart-in-your-throat kind of feeling that always takes me a good fifteen or twenty minutes to shake off once we've leveled.

Focusing on Ruby kept me calm, my attention strictly on her facial expressions and the way the loose strands of her hair drift around her chin and long neck, the softness of her hand in mine.

When she peeks one eye open and looks at me, I'm catapulted out of my reverie and slammed back into my seat on this plane, holding the hand of a woman I don't know.

I think we realize it at the same time, both of us releasing our grip at almost the exact same moment.

"I can't believe we're in the air."

Her voice is soft, but I can still hear the nervousness underneath.

Ruby reaches out to lift the window shade but then returns her hand to her lap, leaving it firmly closed and giving her head a few shakes.

"Maybe I'll watch as we land," she says, talking mostly to herself. Then her eyes look over at me. "Thanks for that. You helped distract me, which I seriously didn't know was possible."

She gives an awkward chuckle and looks away.

Instead of responding—because, really...what am I going to say?—I take a final sip of my whiskey, hoping the last remnants in my glass can help drown out the strange sensation this girl seems to elicit from within me.

I don't know Ruby at all, and within 20 minutes of sitting next to each other, I'm talking to her about things like love and fear and holding her hand so she's not as scared?

I don't do things like that.

Who does? Who *actually* has conversations like that?

We sit in silence for a little while, and I have a chance to think back to what we were discussing before takeoff.

All that talk about fear being about love?

Can't say I agree with her entirely.

My sister is afraid of small spaces. I don't know how that can possibly be rooted in love unless it's her love of refusing to get into her dickbag fiancé's tiny bullshit car.

And what I said to Ruby as we took off...I don't even know where those words came from. I just know I was looking at her and she looked so terrified and small in her seat. I couldn't *not* do something, couldn't manage to keep my words to myself.

Another first.

Now that we've reached cruising altitude, the flight attendants begin their breakfast service, stopping by our seats to help us pull out our tray tables and lay out a tablecloth. I order another whiskey and Ruby gets a sparkling water.

There's a little voice inside of me that's saying I should look over and talk to her, engage in the conversation she so clearly wants to have.

But the me who has been me for a long time can't seem to get on board. Just because I feel this insane urge to talk to her doesn't mean I'm actually comfortable enough to do it.

So I grab my noise-canceling headphones and pop them on, selecting one of the newer *Mission Impossible* movies to watch during our meal.

I've already seen this one, which is what I prefer on flights. I put on a movie I've seen before so I can have part of my attention on work or other passengers or food or just general mental wanderings and not have to worry about missing something crucial to the plotline.

Which ends up working out perfectly, because twenty minutes in, I realize I'm not watching the movie at all. My attention stays focused almost entirely on the little movements in the seat next to mine as Ruby takes sips of her drink. Sets her phone on her tray then tucks it under her leg. Reaches over to open the window then pulls back, changing her mind again.

Her little ditherings have snagged my attention in a way I can't remember having happened before, and it is both amusing and maddening.

When the flight attendant brings over our trays, I give up on the movie and tuck away my headphones, accepting that conversation with the woman next to me is not only plausible, but very likely—desirable, even, if I'm honest with myself.

Sure enough, the minute our trays are dropped off, Ruby begins to chatter.

"Did you know Tom Cruise broke his ankle filming a scene in that movie?"

I can't say that's where I thought she'd begin the conversation, and my response reflects my surprise. "What?"

"Tom Cruise?" she says, as if I've never heard of him before. "I went on a date to see *Mission Impossible* with a guy who was *obsessed* with Tom Cruise. Knew his birthday and his weight and his dog's name and all this stuff."

She shifts in her seat as she mixes the blueberry yogurt and granola in the bowl in front of her.

"It was super creepy. I won't be accepting a date from him again any time soon, that's for sure. So, anyway, he told me Tom Cruise was running across a roof or something and totally shattered his ankle when he had to jump from one building to another one, and apparently he just kept filming like it was no big deal until they got the shot. Crazy, right?"

I keep my attention on my own plate of food, trying to hide my smile at the very strange conversation we're having.

Or rather, the one she's mostly having with herself.

"Crazy," I say before stuffing a bite of food into my mouth so I don't have to say anything else.

If I can safely indulge her desire to talk without having to speak much, maybe I can convince myself I'm not breaking my own rules.

"I'm not a really big movie buff. If it's up to me, I'd much rather be outside doing things than sitting inside watching a movie. Hiking, biking, swimming—anything, really. Which should have been my first clue that this guy wasn't the right one for me, you know? I mean, when your friends refer to you as your online gamer handle in person, I think it's safe to assume you spend a lot of your time indoors. And that's just not for me."

I keep eating, listening to her babble on about whatever seems to come to mind, and I have to work to keep the smile off my face.

"But that's just the life of someone committed to wellness, you know? I'm a massage therapist, and I see so many people coming through who have these aches and pains, and most of them are from stress, obviously, but also from sitting around in front of the TV or staying hunched over laptop keyboards or phones. I tell them to get outside and enjoy nature and spend time doing things that are good for their minds and bodies, a. And if I tell *them* to do it, I have to be doing it myself, or else I'd just be a big old phony. And nobody likes that."

There's an extended pause, and I glance over to make sure she isn't choking, only to find her nibbling happily on her breakfast.

I almost laugh. She was able to have this entire one-sided conversation with me about *Mission Impossible* and some guy she dated and her job and enjoying the outdoors, and I didn't have to say a word.

In most circumstances, I'd be miserable, clambering out of my seat, trying to find a way to avoid the incessant prattle from an annoying seatmate.

But instead, I'm feeling...charmed? Is that the right word? I don't even know, really, because it's such an unfamiliar sensation. A kind of low buzz warms my chest and collarbone, loosening my muscles. I want to relax in my chair and listen to her ramble on some more.

And then, just when I wonder if I should say something to

her because suddenly I'm fascinated by the things coming out of her mouth, she launches in again.

"You know, I've never flown first class before. Well, I'm guessing you know that since I already said I've never flown *at all*, but let me just say, I feel like after this, I'll be sorely disappointed when my regular ass is flying economy. I can only imagine how squished the seats are." She shakes her head at me then gives the flight attendant a big smile as he hands over a new drink. "Thank you!" she chirps, taking it and placing it on her tray.

"Thanks," I say when a new whiskey is settled on mine.

I appreciate when the flight crew refills my drink without me having to ask, regardless of what time of day it is. Less chance for me to get judged for drinking hard liquor before noon.

"And I guess that means I'll basically never fly ever again since I would never be able to afford a first class ticket on my own." She scoffs as she butters her toast. "The fact that I'm even flying first class today was a huge shock. Well"—she tilts her head left and right—"maybe I *should* have realized Ken would buy me the fancy-schmancy ticket." Then she bites off a piece of her bread.

"Who's Ken?" I ask, suddenly wondering if she has some rich boyfriend in California who is paying for her to fly out.

And why does that thought make me feel like someone has poked a hole in my chest?

"Ken's my 'dad,'" she says, using air quotes that have me pausing with my drink halfway to my mouth.

"What's with the air quotes?"

"Well, far be it from me to claim I'm the knower of all, but it's my opinion that if you want a title, you have to actually do the job," she says, her tone coming out a little intense.

My eyebrows rise at her statement, and I watch as Ruby takes a deep breath in and exhales a long, slow breath out.

"That was mean-spirited of me. I shouldn't have said that."

She spends a minute poking at the last few blueberries in her bowl then turns her head to eye me.

"You don't have an opinion?" she asks.

I lift a shoulder, knowing this is way outside of my comfort zone. Besides, whatever is going on between Ruby and her 'dad,' the last thing I should do is form an opinion with almost no information.

"Well, *I'm* a firm believer that I shouldn't jump in with judgments about something when I don't know the story," I reply.

"You *would* be the levelheaded type," she says back, and I smile at how quickly she's been able to peg me.

"What gave me away?"

"Oh, you know…all the…levelheadedness," she says, wiggling her spoon at me.

I shake my head and bite back another grin, eyeing the whiskey in my glass. "Tell me about Ken," I say, realizing I'm not just willing to *endure* Ruby's chatter—I'm eager for it.

She sighs and leans back, grinning at the flight attendant as he takes our first-course plates away.

"He's just the typical dad who leaves his family behind. Left when I was a kid and I haven't seen him since I was six, so it feels like I'm going to meet him for the first time. He lives outside of Sacramento, and…" She shakes her head, her smile slipping slightly. "I'm not even sure I want to see him, but a few months ago I decided it was time to figure out who he is and either get some closure or try to bridge things between us. When I contacted him and he offered me the ticket, I thought, *Why not?*"

I've always known I was lucky to have the parents that I

do—two people who love each other immensely, always put our family first, and would never think of leaving one of us high and dry.

The idea that a dad could just leave? Mark Mitchell would *never* do something like that, let alone disappear. I'm pretty sure my dad would show up and beat my door down if I ever went longer than a few weeks without talking to him. I can't imagine having nearly twenty years without him.

"Either I meet him, realize he is exactly who I think he is, and I get some closure, or he pleasantly surprises me and I get a dad. It's a win-win, I guess, even though I'm crazy nervous and totally regretting this trip altogether." Ruby pauses then looks at me with a pinched expression. "Sorry to dump this on you," she says. "I tend to ramble when I'm nervous, and talking is helping me not think about the fact that we're flying thirty thousand feet in the air. My mom calls me Ruby Rambles for a very legitimate reason."

"It seems like a fitting nickname."

She blushes and shakes her head but doesn't say anything in response as the attendant brings out our next course.

"You're close with your mom?" I ask, picking up my utensils and cutting into the egg white and spinach dish that is probably going to taste nowhere near as good as it looks.

"Careful, Boyd. If you ask me questions, you'll make it seem like you actually want to have a conversation."

I can tell her tone is teasing, but I'm still a little embarrassed. Normally, I can't be blatant enough about the fact that I don't want to talk to someone. Now that I actually *want* to talk to Ruby, I feel a little bad about how standoffish I was earlier.

Thankfully, she doesn't keep the spotlight focused on me for long, instead launching into sharing about her mom and what it was like growing up as just the two of them.

She talks about the struggles—like moving around a lot, having a hard time making rent, and watching other kids with dads have fun doing things together—but also the good things, like getting all of the attention, having slumber parties together in the living room, and getting a lot more freedom and independence than her peers.

"She's my best friend," Ruby says, finally pausing to take a bite of her own eggs.

"How does she feel about you going to visit your dad?" I ask.

I can tell almost instantly that I've struck a nerve. She sets down her knife and fork and takes a sip from her drink.

"I didn't tell her," she says, her voice quiet and, if I'm reading her right, a little ashamed. "I just…didn't think she'd approve, so I told her I was going to hang out with friends for a few weeks."

Her nose scrunches up, and I can tell even talking about this is making her emotional.

"Part of me thinks she knows what's going on, though. She didn't ask who the friends were, and it's not like I've got tons of friends from all walks of life, you know? Why would I suddenly have a group of friends from California that my mom has never met or heard me talk about before?"

She takes a bite of her eggs and follows it up with a bite from her toast.

"You don't have friends from college she hasn't met?" I ask, trying to think about how well my own mom knows my friends. She's heard me talk about them, sure, but if I were to bring up someone new, she wouldn't bat an eye.

Ruby snorts and lets out a laugh. "I definitely didn't go to college," she says. "A few classes at the community college when I was fresh out of high school, but nothing that stuck. Besides, you don't need a college degree to be a massage therapist, and I've always known I wanted a nontraditional job. Formal education doesn't really help when all you want is a certificate you can earn in less than a year."

I bob my head but allow myself a moment to think about her perspective.

College was never an option for the Mitchell kids. It was an expectation, a given. Junior high, then high school, then college. After that, it's up to you. Sure, grad school was optional, and my guess is I'll be the only one of my siblings who actually has a need for postgraduate education.

Ruby's perspective is…different than I'm used to.

I had it hammered into me for so long that college is the only way to go, and I didn't even consider what it would be like to have a different mindset, didn't consider that anything else would even be a realistic option.

I can't help but wonder what kind of stability comes with giving massages. Is it set hours? Do you have to find your own clients? Does she work at like…a spa or something? In general, it seems a little flighty.

But I guess when you've grown up the way Ruby has, bouncing between apartments and couch-surfing with a mother who has to work several jobs to make ends meet, maybe this is a step up for her.

As I watch her reach over to touch the window shade then pull her hand back again with an irritated little huff, I smile, realizing there are a lot of layers to Ruby. And for the first time in my life, I'm desperate to explore more than one.

chapter four

ruby

When the attendants finally come around to collect our trays, I feel thankful to stretch out a little bit again. I grab the blanket that was sitting on my seat when I first boarded and unfold it, tucking the soft fabric around my legs.

I've always been one of those people who gets cold no matter what. I'm like a walking ice cube most of the time. It frustrates my roommate because I always keep the temperature in our apartment at about 75, and she's one of those people who hates the sun. In her ideal world, she'd be living in the snow year-round.

"So what takes you to California?" I ask, curling up slightly and resting my back against the wall of the plane. "You said you live in Boston, so…are you visiting someone?"

Please not a girlfriend.

Please not a girlfriend.

He nods, something like happiness coming onto his face.

"Yeah. Heading back to my hometown to stay with my family for a couple weeks. I do this every year. All of us do."

I smile. "All of us? Sounds like you have a big family."

I know I'm prying, pushing my luck with this man who seems to constantly battle with whether or not he wants to talk to me, but he's been indulging me so far—hesitantly at first, but with more interest as time has gone on. I give myself the excuse that I'll quit talking to him when he asks me to.

"It doesn't feel big to me, but I guess it's all based on what you know. I have four siblings—three sisters and a brother."

My eyes widen, the idea of that many people in one house completely outside my realm of understanding.

"I bet the wait to use the bathroom in the morning was crazy."

Boyd laughs. "You have no idea."

"How was that growing up? Did you ever get time alone?"

"Well, no, actually. I have a family who likes to get into each other's business, whether I like it or not, and I don't know if you can tell, but I'm a man who likes his alone time."

I blush slightly at his vague insinuation that I'm interrupting his quiet time on the plane, but thankfully he doesn't dwell on it.

"Having four siblings was a little rough when I was going through my moody phase."

"Is that why you've never grown out of it?" I tease.

He shakes his head but doesn't lose the smile at my joke. "You make a habit of poking most bears you come across?"

"Come on. You know most bears are big softies."

Boyd chuckles softly before continuing.

"I'm the oldest, which was the only thing working in my favor since I was able to leave for college first. The next oldest is Briar. She's 27, two years younger than me. Bishop and Bellamy—they're twins—are 21, and Busy is 19."

"Your family went all in with the B names, huh?"

He rolls his eyes. "Yeah. It's always been our least favorite thing. Some people think it's so cute—like my mother—but it gets really confusing for people who aren't in our family."

"So you're going to visit them for the end of summer?" I ask, resting my head against the seat.

He nods. "Yeah. It's tradition. All the Mitchell kids go home for the last two weeks of August."

"That's really cool," I say, realizing with a wistful kind of wonder that I've never had something like that in my life before. "I'm assuming you guys are all really close if you get together?"

Boyd's head bobs. "We are. We get on each other's nerves a lot, but that's just sibling stuff. My sister Briar and I are really close. Always have been."

"And your other siblings?"

He grins. "They're the three musketeers, and also absolute menaces to society. The twins are constantly bickering and finishing each other's sentences, as you can imagine twins would do, and Busy is this really flamboyant artist who has taken her newfound independence as an adult *very* seriously."

The look on his face is so sentimental and sappy, I almost can't believe it's him I'm looking at.

The frowny-faced Mr. Gruff from the beginning of the flight has stepped aside, leaving room for this genuine guy with a heart for his family.

I can probably credit the two glasses of whiskey that are now running through his system with why his defenses seem to have dropped so much in the past hour, but I'll take what I can get.

My mind wanders as I try to picture Boyd, this introverted stud sitting next to me, surrounded by a bunch of siblings who give him a hard time and poke him like the big bear that he is.

41

I can just imagine him being so intent on his quiet, alone time and this brood of others trying to talk to him and make him laugh.

It makes me smile just imagining it, especially because I don't have any true context for what that kind of life would be like, having grown up as an only child.

"What?" he asks after I stare at him silently for too long.

"Sorry." I shake my head but keep the smile on my face. "I'm just trying to picture you with a big family and a bunch of menacing siblings annoying the shit out of you."

"You can't see it?"

I giggle. "Actually, I *totally* can."

"I love them. Even when I don't," he says, taking another sip of his drink.

"I always wanted siblings. I didn't need as many as *you* have, but I'd love to have a confidant. My mom was amazing—*is* amazing," I amend. "But even though we're so close, I would have loved to have someone I could have been friends with growing up, someone to get irritated with because I love them and hate them at the same time."

"I think the last part is the most accurate, definitely. My brother and sisters drive me absolutely insane. Some of their decisions are just...so..." He shakes his head, not really able to finish.

But I can still see it on his face—how much he loves them, even if they drive him nuts.

And I've always wished for that, right there...that love that riles you up but brings you home at the same time.

"Are you nervous?" he asks, bringing the conversation back to the original reason we started talking about families. "About seeing your 'dad'?"

He uses the air quotes, his question hitting at something inside of me. I haven't really talked with anyone about this trip, haven't taken the time to really analyze how I feel about it.

Am I nervous?

I turn that thought over in my mind for a little bit before responding.

"I'm terrified, actually," I say, giving him what I am sure is far too much honesty for a stranger on a plane. "He has a whole other family…a wife and two kids." I shake my head, my eyes zoning out as I focus on the blank screen in front of me. "It just makes me wonder what could possibly be different now."

Boyd is quiet for a minute, and I can't tell if he's just being polite and doesn't have anything to say, or if he's intuitive enough about me already to let me collect my thoughts.

"Sorry. Didn't mean to get that dark and broody about it."

But he shakes his head. "Don't apologize. How you feel is how you feel. It just seems like a really complicated situation," he admits, letting out an awkward laugh. "And you seem to be processing a lot."

I nod and let out a long sigh. "Yeah."

A flight attendant loops over and asks if we'd like anything to drink. When Boyd orders a third whiskey neat, I decide maybe I should allow myself to have a drink, too.

"I'll have a vodka and cranberry, please," I say when she looks to me. Then I take a look at Boyd. "You're three drinks deep, mister. I don't wanna see any judge-y eyes from you."

Boyd lifts both hands up. "I wasn't. I just think it's safe to assume you've never experienced the joys of day drinking on a plane before. I'm glad to know you're gonna give it a shot."

A few minutes later, the attendant brings us our drinks. Once we both have them in hand, I turn to Boyd.

"Let's cheers," I say, giving him a big smile and holding my drink out. "To hoping we both have a great little summer trip, huh?"

He nods and we tap our cups together before taking sips.

I wince, the burn of alcohol hitting me right in the back of the throat. I'm surprised I don't hack anything up.

"Too strong?"

I nod. "Yeah. I drink pretty much never, so even a drop of alcohol is usually too strong for me." But then I take another sip, remembering that it gets easier to drink the more you drink.

I wince again and he laughs, but almost immediately I can feel the warming effect of the liquor as it slithers through my veins.

Alcohol does two things to me. It makes me tired and very honest, a dangerous mix, which is why I rarely drink.

But the curiosity I've been feeling about Boyd seems to crawl forward and take control of my mind, and within just a few minutes, I can't help myself when I lean a little bit closer to him and decide to dive into more personal questions.

It's time to shift the attention to my handsome new friend, find out a little more about what makes him tick.

"So, tell me, Boyd: What's life like for you back in Boston? You've got a fancy job, right? You have a fancy dog and apartment and girlfriend, too?"

I know I'm not slick when I ask that question. It's blatant fishing, and I've never been good at luring anyone in, but I want to know. Our conversations might be all over the place, but I do enjoy a chance to flirt, especially with a man as handsome as Boyd.

In the bright light of a few sips of vodka, I can definitely say my interest in him has not waned over the course of our conversation or time together on the plane, and I doubt it will.

But if he has a lady? I'll make sure to move myself into more neutral, friendly territory. I like to flirt, but not with someone else's man.

"Yes to the fancy apartment," he says, drawing me back to the fact that I asked him a question. "I live in Cambridge."

"Ooooooooooh, so fancy-schmancy," I say, taking another sip of my drink.

"But no dog. I travel too much for work."

There's a pause, and I lean forward just a little bit, waiting and hoping he answers the last part of my question.

"And no girlfriend, either."

"A handsome guy like you?" I scoff. "I'm shocked. You should have women lining up around the block."

His mouth twists and his eyes twinkle as he watches me.

"You think I'm handsome?"

I'm sure I blush, but the alcohol loosens my tongue and has me sailing right past embarrassment and over the hill of nerves, straight into Confidence Town.

"Absolutely. You're an eleven for sure."

He lets out a reserved chuckle but continues to watch me.

"Most of the guys in my wheelhouse are in the seven or eight category, like me. You know, guys with a job and enough good looks and charm to make you think they've got their shit together. And usually, that's enough. I don't have crazy expectations or want anything long-lasting from them, so good enough is good enough, you know?" Then I wave a hand out in between us. "But I bet you put all those boys to shame."

Boyd continues to smile at me, but now he's biting his lip and watching me like I'm fascinating.

"Is that so?"

I nod. "Yup. Those boys…well, they're boys. Just in it for a hookup and a chance to get off. I have no problem with that, not by any means. I am the queen of casual hookups. I think dating is best when you're a person who likes dating but not relationships, like me. But it would be great if, just once, a guy was able to manage to make it as worthwhile for me, you know?"

Boyd leans closer, his brow furrowed. "What do you mean?"

I follow his lead and lean closer too, enjoying being a little bit closer to him and taking in that delicious smell of his.

"I'm saying the guys I've been with are fun, but they don't know how to deliver. Like, I get that something inside me might not work correctly, but if you're going to take me out to dinner and then we go back to your place and I give you 'the best head of your life'"—I use air quotes to prove that was *his* statement, not mine—"the least you can do is work your butt off to make sure I enjoy myself, too. But of course, it never happens. Though I guess I can't blame them entirely. Like I said, maybe something inside me doesn't work right."

When I look back at Boyd, my body feeling warm and snuggly and heavy in my seat, I realize he's staring at me with an intensity I haven't seen from him before.

Granted, we've only been on this flight together for a few hours so far, but still. It's a new look, focused entirely on me, and I like that.

"Sorry. I'm just going to back you up here a little bit. Are you saying…" He pauses, almost like he isn't sure he wants to say whatever is on his mind. "Are you saying you've never had an orgasm?" he asks, his voice dropping low and his face close enough to mine that I can see the flecks of gold in those beautiful browns.

I'm so distracted by his face being so close to mine that it

the trouble with wanting

takes a beat or two for me to realize what I've said, and I cover my face with my hands.

"Oh my god," I whisper then peek at him through my fingers. "I can't believe I said that."

Mortification seeps into my body, eliminating the little buzz I was enjoying and replacing it with a cold discomfort that makes me want to hide.

I keep my eyes closed and slump as far down in my chair as I can go, lifting my blanket so it's covering my head and I can wallow underneath in my absolute shame.

What the hell?

The only person I've ever talked to about the fact that I can't seem to orgasm is Fiona. Not my mom, not any of my other girlfriends.

Definitely not random fucking strangers on a plane!

Shit.

Shit, shit, shit.

Before I can burrow down any farther, the blanket is tugged off of my head and a sweet-faced Boyd is peering down at me, a smile covering that handsome face of his.

"Ruby," he says, pulling on the blanket as I try to cover my face again. "Come on, I was enjoying our chat. Don't hide from me."

At his gentle cajoling, I right myself in my chair, the sobering effect of having bared a very embarrassing secret to him taking hold of me.

I'm quiet for a minute, peeking over at where he sits next to me, his attention lasered in on my face.

"So…" he starts. "Have you *never* had one before?"

My whole face flushes. In my entire life, I never thought I'd be facing a man like Boyd and having a conversation like this.

"You don't have to be embarrassed about it, you know." His words come out as a statement, and I turn to look at his earnest expression. "It's *their* fault, not yours. They're the ones who should be embarrassed."

I let out a half-laugh, wishing that were actually how it worked.

"Can we talk about something else?" I say, suddenly wishing I were anywhere but here. "This is not where I was hoping this conversation would go."

Boyd pauses, and when I look into his eyes, I see that he wants to keep talking about this. I can't imagine why. Maybe just sheer fascination with the idea that he's looking at a girl who hasn't ever reached the pinnacle of sex before?

But I also see the moment he takes pity on me and changes the subject.

Instead of talking about my orgasm-less sex life, he tells me a little bit more about his job. It's full of concepts I'm not entirely familiar with, but I get the idea that he works for a company that purchases and repurposes apps and software, and Boyd's job is to then meet with startups planning to use those apps and software and help them integrate the technology completely.

It really is interesting hearing about what he does, and any other time, it would have been stimulating enough for me to ask questions and really follow along.

But the effect of the alcohol is slowly wearing me down, and it isn't long into his story that my eyes start to droop.

"You getting sleepy over there?" he asks.

I nod. "It's not because I think you're boring." I want to make sure I clarify. "I barely slept last night because I was nervous about this trip, and alcohol makes me sleepy."

"Why don't you take a nap?"

"But I wanna keep talking," I say, already snuggling up with my back against the plane wall and my head leaning against the seat. "I like the way your voice sounds."

He laughs. "Don't worry, Ruby. We'll talk again soon."

I nod then, tucking my little pillow into a comfortable spot and closing my eyes.

Then I pop one back open.

"Promise?"

He gives me that panty-dropping smile, and something lights up inside of me. "Promise."

"Miss. Excuse me, miss?"

My eyes open a tiny bit at the sound of the flight attendant. I glance around blearily and realize with dawning clarity that the plane has landed and I'm the only person still on board, apart from the cleaning crew that's starting to wander through the cabin.

"Sorry to wake you, but we've landed and it's time for you to disembark."

My eyes widen in shock and I wipe at my face. "Shit, are you serious?"

When she nods, I start apologizing and grabbing my things.

Then I stop, look around again—as if doing another perusal will somehow conjure Boyd into existence.

"Is something wrong?" she asks.

I shake my head. "No, I just... The man I was sitting with—

I'm assuming he already got off the plane?"

She gives me a sympathetic look that I don't like very much.

Listen, lady, I don't need your pity.

"Never mind," I mumble, grabbing my notebook and phone from the seatback pocket and shoving them into my bag. Then I'm scrambling out of my seat and off the aircraft.

I don't know why I'm surprised Boyd took off. Boyd Mitchell with the big family and the awesome life. I rambled on like an absolute idiot, like I always do, and he was probably glad to be shot of me.

Sometimes, I wish I could just have a normal conversation with a man for once. Like, I was nervous on the plane, sure, but I was babbling on about all my personal problems, just dumping them all on his lap and...

I wince.

And I told him I've *never had an orgasm!?!*

Jesus. Talk about mortifying.

So yeah, it would be great if I could talk to a man and not make myself sound like an absolute crazy person, but I guess I'll have to try to learn how to do that another day.

I mean, it's not like he would have asked for my number or...I don't know.

But it doesn't matter. It doesn't matter how he made me feel on that plane. What happens on a plane stays on a plane. I know that's not the saying, but I'm sure it applies. It's like a different world up there, after all.

He was probably just indulging me out of boredom.

I slowly wander out to the pickup area, stopping to look at souvenirs in a few shops before heading to baggage claim, my eyes peering around to see if I spot my seat neighbor, but to no avail.

It isn't until I'm standing at the curb, checked bag in one hand and backpack over my shoulder that I realize I have no idea how I'm getting to Ken's house. I don't even know where I'm going, don't know whether it's close enough that I can just catch an Uber or if I'll need to rent a car.

This is one of those other things my mom says is so endearing about me, even though I know she can't stand it. I'm not a big planner. I don't know what I'm doing for the entire time I'm here. 12 days of spending time with Ken and his family at some house on a lake.

I shake my head as I pull my backpack around to the front of my body and dig around for the address. If I remember correctly, I wrote it down in my notebook.

I keep rummaging while I move over to a bench and take a seat. Finally, my hand grips the book and I pull it out, flipping quickly through the scribbled notes and doodles until I find the address I highlighted in pink. I take a picture for easier reference then flip it closed to shove back in my bag.

But my eye catches unfamiliar handwriting scrawled on an unused page. I quickly open it back up and take a look at the note.

Ruby, I'm sorry I didn't wake you to say goodbye. I fell asleep myself and didn't wake up until just as our feet touched the ground. I enjoyed chatting with you. I don't know if you can tell, but I'm not much for small talk. Thanks for showing me that it can be worthwhile.

I hope you have a lovely vacation and time with your 'dad.' If things fall apart or you're looking for something to do, give me a call. I have plenty of family members I'll happily pawn off on you.

Happy travels,
Boyd (Mitchell)

Underneath his name is his phone number and an arrow pointing at it that says *Use it.*

A smile breaks out on my face and I clutch the notebook to my chest.

Maybe this trip will have an upside after all.

chapter five
boyd

The drive from the airport is everything I remember it being, both from my time growing up in our small town and from each of my visits home over the past decade.

Cedar Point is a community of about 2,500 people during most of the year, though that number swells up significantly during the summer. Named for the incense cedars that grow in a cluster along the south bank, it's tucked away in the Tahoe National Forest and serves as a midway point between Sacramento and Lake Tahoe.

I'm sure there are plenty of kids out there who would much rather grow up in a larger city or in the suburbs of a metropolis, but I was never one to complain about growing up in Cedar Point. I loved waking up early and going for a swim or jogging the lower trails between the ponderosa pines and Douglas fir trees that line the banks of the lake.

In my opinion, we had the perfect setup: access to city life down the hill whenever we wanted it while still getting the quiet calm of a small town. It's a beautiful place to live, to grow up.

The only reason I knew I couldn't stay in Cedar Point forever was the fact that everyone was in everybody's business, especially my family's.

Sure, small towns are like that in general, but the Mitchell family goes back several generations in Cedar Point, to the mid-1800s, our great-great-grandparents being the original founders of the small community that surrounds Cedar Lake.

When the small downtown intersection is Main Street and Mitchell Road, there isn't really anywhere to escape to if you're a teenager wishing people weren't watching your every move.

But it's one of those things we just had to accept. You take the good, you take the bad, and all of that.

When I pull up in front of the home I grew up in, an overwhelming sense of calm fills me.

I always forget it's like this. I put up a fight every year about coming home for the last two weeks of August, telling everyone and their mother I don't have enough time and taking vacation from work is inconvenient and unrealistic.

But, like clockwork, the minute I arrive and see the wind chime my father made for my mom for her fortieth birthday hanging in the same spot on the porch facing the grassy yard, I'm flooded with a million memories.

Like the year we spent eleven hours setting up Christmas decorations for the annual lights competition only to completely lose power because we didn't consider the fact that five thousand lights might overwhelm the generator.

Or the time my dad convinced our entire family to be the Kardashians for Halloween then spent the entire night scaring kids away while dressed up as Khloe.

All the years we spent sunning on the deck during summer

or hanging out on the boat. Even now, as adults, kicking back with a beer in front of the fire pit during the sunset.

There's something special about Cedar Point, something that can't be recreated anywhere else.

Not for the first time, I feel thankful that my mom is such a hard-ass about us returning home for a couple weeks every summer so we can create new memories to mix in with the old.

"Anybody home?"

My voice echoes through the house, and I'm not surprised to find that nobody is here.

Briar and Busy aren't due in until Monday morning, and since it's late on a Saturday afternoon, the twins are probably grabbing a drink at one of the two bars in town. My mom let me know she and my dad would be over at the Perrys' house for a monthly game night until around eight.

So, that means I have the whole house to myself for a few hours to possibly grab a little nap after my long flight. The jet lag is always rough coming east to west. Going back to Boston is never an issue, but without fail, the first few nights in California are always rough.

Dropping the keys to my rental on the little table near the front door, I lug my bag up the stairs, walking down the long hallway to my bedroom at the end.

There's the same blue B on my door that was there in high school, a funny joke Bishop thought of when he was in the third grade, deciding we should each have our first initial on our bedroom door. We all got a good laugh, though at the time, Busy was a little too young to understand why it was so funny.

Maybe it's weird that I still have a room at my parents' house when I'm 29 years old, but when I open the door and step in, I know any kid who says they don't need a room at their childhood home is lying.

It looks significantly different than when I was younger. As the only two fully independent adult children so far, Briar and I have been told we can keep our rooms as long as they also function as guest rooms, so the posters are long gone and the walls have been repainted.

In truth, my mom completely redid this room, leaving only my favorite color—blue—as the marker that it belongs to me when I'm in town. She did the same with Briar's room as well, but Bishop, Bell, and Busy still have actual bedrooms because Cedar Point is still their primary home. Bishop is off at college but only an hour away, so he's home a lot. Bell never moved away, opting to do her coursework online, and Busy just finished her freshman year at a little college in southern California, way too young to give up her childhood bedroom.

I used to love to hang pictures on the walls, and while my mural of photos has been replaced by a beautiful painting of the view from Kilroy, my mom salvaged some of my better pictures and placed them prominently along the window sill and along the wall with the closet in fancy frames of different sizes and shades of blue.

It really does feel like an adult Boyd bedroom, and I love her for knowing how to make me feel at home in a way nobody else could have managed.

I set my suitcase on the bed and begin to unpack.

When I was younger, I used to just live out of the suitcase, but a few years ago, my mom unpacked all my clothes for me when I was out with friends, and it was so nice to have things put away. Now I do it everywhere I go.

After I'm done, I head to the kitchen to grab a quick snack. I'm poking around in the fridge to figure out what I want when my phone vibrates in my pocket.

When I look at the screen, I see a new message in our family group text, The Bitchells. Leaning up against the counter, my fingers fly over the screen in reply.

Dad: Boyd, you home yet?
Me: Yup, got here about 30 minutes ago.
Dad: Great. Looking forward to seeing you, son.
Bishop: Ah the prodigal child. Welcome back, loser.
Bellamy: Yay, you're here!
Bishop: Go away, Bells. No one likes you.

I roll my eyes. They're a mess. I settle on warming up a piece of pizza and pop it into the microwave as my phone continues to ping with message after message.

Bishop: If you're hanging out at the house by yourself, you're an idiot. Come out with us.
Bellamy: Yasssss come drink with meeeee
Mom: You two better make good choices tonight. We are taking our family picture tomorrow and I don't want anybody looking hungover.
Briar: How are you doing the picture tomorrow if Busy and I are not getting into town until Monday?
Mom: What? Since when?
Briar: That was always the plan.
Busy: We both told you Monday.
Mom: It absolutely was not the plan. You told me you were driving home Sunday morning because Chad had some event he wanted you to go to on Saturday night.

I groan, locking the screen and putting my phone on silent. The minute Chad gets mentioned in any conversation is the minute I exit.

Any text, any FaceTime, any room—it doesn't matter.

Briar is marrying a dickbag and our whole family knows it. The last thing I feel like doing when I'm exhausted from flying is reading their bitchy back and forth about when my sister is getting to town, because I know my mom is going to make everything Chad's fault.

I finish off my piece of pizza then flop down on the couch, wondering if I have it in me to get back in the car in a little bit and meet the twins in town.

There are only two options for adult drinks in Cedar Point.

The local townie bar is called The Mitch, originally owned by my dad's older brother, though he ended up selling to someone else when he moved away a while back. The place is a total dive, complete with half-illuminated neon lights that encourage patrons to *Drink Up* and an old-ass jukebox that only ever plays Red Hot Chili Peppers.

The tourist bar is called Dock 7, though the locals have nicknamed it Lucky's since it's the best place to go if you're looking for an easy lay who will be heading out of town soon.

Both options sound kind of miserable right now, if I'm honest. I'm pretty sure the twins went to The Mitch, and knowing they're probably mingling with old friends from high school and, if I go, I'll *also* be mingling with old friends from high school, I just can't seem to muster up the energy to get up and head that way.

There are definitely people in town I will want to see while I'm here, but thinking about facing some of the people I can't stand exhausts me. So, instead of taking a nap on the couch, I dig out my phone, intending to let the twins know I'm not interested in grabbing a drink.

That's when I see a message from an unknown number that came through in the middle of the back and forth textapalooza between my mom and sisters.

Unknown: Hey. it's Ruby.

I smile, glad she decided to send me a message.

I waffled on whether or not to wake Ruby up before I left the plane, feeling oddly like I was sneaking out of the house after a one-night stand, even though it wasn't close to the same.

I fell asleep, too, and when I woke, I felt stiff and cranky and ready to get off the damn plane. Then I looked over at Ruby and smiled at the way her body was tucked into the corner, her mouth slightly open.

On that plane, I might have started off as distant, but by the time Ruby fell asleep a few hours in, I was charming and friendly—conversational, even. It was a new side of me, and something in my mind wasn't ready to think that over or try to understand the significance of the way talking to Ruby made me feel.

I left a note instead, making sure to add my number under where I signed my name, the idea of never speaking to her again not something I was prepared to consider. Though it wasn't something I was prepared to examine, either.

Me: Hey. Did you leave any drool marks on the plane window? I hear they charge extra for that kind of thing.

I don't know where my teasing behavior is coming from, but I can't seem to help it. I go into my settings and update her information, putting Ruby Rambles as her name.

> *Ruby: Did Mr. Serious make a joke? I think I just fell off my chair*

I smile at that, stretching my long legs out on the couch and settling in to have a conversation with the beautiful girl from the plane. I try not to focus too much on the fact that we spent all that time talking and I'm already eager for more.

Or on how quickly she's managed to bring a smile back to my face.

> *Me: I've been known to make a funny here and there*
> *Ruby: Did you get home okay? Is your entire family there waving flags to welcome you home?*
> *Me: Nah. I walked into an empty house. Nobody cares that I'm back. They're all too busy having fun with their friends.*
> *Ruby: Is somebody feeling neglected?*
> *Me: Hardly. I was just about to take a little nap when you messaged me, try to take advantage of the fact that it's so quiet.*
> *Ruby: Oh, well I don't want to keep you if you had plans to get in some rest*

I didn't mean to cut things short by referencing the nap, and I scramble to find something to talk about so she doesn't put her phone down.

> *Me: How about you? Did you get home okay?*

> *Ruby: Yeah*

That's all she says, no additional bubbles popping up to indicate that she has more to say. It's surprising, considering the fact that Ruby is very clearly an over-sharer. I think I can safely assume that if she isn't giving specifics and details, she's feeling reluctant to talk about it.

While I might have allowed that to fly by unnoticed with just about everyone else I know, I can't seem to reconcile it in my mind when it comes to Ruby. I like that she rambles and shares too much.

So instead of texting her back, I do the very unusual thing for me and dial her number.

"You know, I'll be honest, you don't strike me as the *I love to chat on the phone* kind of guy," she says when she picks up.

I laugh. "That's because I'm not. But I wanted to hear about your dad, so I decided to make an exception."

Ruby hums softly into the phone, and again I get the distinct impression that she doesn't want to discuss this.

"What happened?" I prod.

She lets out a long, quiet sigh, something I can barely hear from my end, almost like she's gearing up to tell me.

"He's not here."

My brow furrows in confusion. "What?"

Another pause. "His wife is here, and so are their two kids, but apparently dear old dad had a last-minute business trip he had to take and he won't be back until Thursday."

I remain reclined on the couch in the living room of the home I grew up in, a place where I've made a million memories surrounded by the family I love so much, and I wonder what could possibly be going through Ruby's mind right now.

To travel across the country in the hopes of building a relationship with her father only to arrive and have him not even be there?

It must feel like a slap in the face.

"So, I'll be spending the first half of my twelve-day trip by myself."

I wish there were something I could say to make her feel... anything other than what's probably going through her mind right now, but I stay silent, letting her figure out what else she wants to say about it.

She lets out a humorless laugh. "Like, if I'd fucking known he wasn't going to be here, we could have rescheduled, you know? But instead I'm just going to be stuck in this little town all alone and I just..."

She pauses, and I can tell she's trying not to let her irritation overrun her. I can tell just from the short time we spent together that Ruby isn't the type of person to let things get her down, and to hear her so frustrated and dejected makes me sad for her.

"I'm so sorry, Ruby."

She huffs. "I'm fine. Linda clearly doesn't want me here, but there's nothing to be done about it. I've been relegated to their guesthouse where I can sit out on the porch and look at the lake, so I'm just gonna go to the little store I saw as I drove into town to grab some snacks then I'll sit outside and watch the sunset. It's not anything too horrible."

"That sounds like a great night," I say, suddenly wishing we could sit out on her porch and watch the sunset together.

"What are *you* up to this evening?" she asks, and I can hear her tone turn teasing. "Your family suiting up to play the 49ers tonight?"

I roll my eyes, holding back the bit of laughter that bubbles up. "Okay, my family isn't *that* big."

"Meh," she says, and I just shake my head. "I can't imagine

having so many siblings. Have you ever seen those shows where families have like, twelve kids? I remember the first time I saw something like that my mind was absolutely blown right out of my skull. I mean, here I am, me and my single mama, just the two of us barely making rent in a tiny apartment in Chelsea, and these families have literally *fifteen fucking people* living in one huge house." She laughs. "That's totally how I picture things where you are, some gorgeous mansion and everyone posing for a huge family photo like the Kardashians. Ugh, this is what I get for allowing myself to watch reality TV when I'm on my period and too exhausted to go spend time outside."

I'm just about to tell her about our infamous Halloween costume when my mind rewinds to something she said earlier, about the house she's staying in and the view.

"Wait, back up a second—did you say you have a view of a lake?" I ask, my heart slowly increasing in tempo, the thud of it echoing slightly in my ears.

"Not just a view of the lake—I'm literally *on* the lake. There are people out there right now tubing and partying and having a good time. I'm kind of in a quiet corner, though, which is nice. I probably won't have to worry about a group of college kids parking their pontoon out front and blasting music until I want to strangle them."

There's no way. Right?

No way she's…

"I should have asked you if you'd heard of it since you grew up in California. Have you ever been to a town called Cedar Point?"

The pulsing beat in my veins throbs to life so all I can hear is the sound of my own heartbeat in my ears and the sound of her voice telling me she's…

"It's super cute, and the way it smells here is amazing, like nothing I've ever experienced before. I mean, I love going out in nature back at home, but these pine trees smell like the most delicious, mountainy goodness. The air is so crisp and clean…"

Before she's even finished talking, I'm getting up off the couch and walking across the living room, sliding open the door and stepping outside onto the large deck that leads to our lake-facing lawn and private dock.

I look out across the little bend in the lake, to the house that's three football fields away—the house where Ken Bellows lives with his wife and two kids. My eyes focus on the little guesthouse they usually rent out during the summer that we've used once or twice when we couldn't accommodate all of the Mitchell family in our own home.

"I'm thinking about walking into the little town and grabbing a bottle of wine and some cheese and grapes then maybe I'll crack open a book or something. I've been reading this romance, and the idea of sitting out and looking at the lake while I dig into it makes—"

"Ruby," I interrupt.

"Sorry, I was rambling again," she says, and I hear the telltale sound of a screen door opening and closing.

Sure enough, I can see movement on the guesthouse porch at the Bellows' house. We're not close enough for me to make out her face. If we weren't talking on the phone and I hadn't put it together, I could never have guessed that the girl from the plane and the girl on that porch are one and the same.

"No, it's not that," I finally respond. "I actually have another idea for tonight. For you, I mean."

"Oh really? You wanna help me make plans that are more fun than drinking wine and reading romance?"

"If you drink that wine, you'll fall asleep ten minutes into your book," I say, eliciting an unladylike snort from Ruby that has a shit-eating grin crossing my face.

"Touché. So what are these wonderful plans?"

I bite the inside of my cheek for a second, wondering what the hell I'm doing. I'm in town to see family, and the last thing I'm looking for is starting something up with anyone, let alone a girl I met on a plane.

But something inside of me has decided to sit up and take notice, and it's hard for me to let something go once I've set my sights on it.

Without realizing it, I've set my sights on Ruby.

God, what are the chances? Not only that she'd be here, in Cedar Point, but also that she'd be right *there*, just a little ways away when there are dozens of guesthouses scattered around the lake.

I should be taking a nap, or connecting with my siblings, or even *working*, which is normally the first thing I do when I get to town.

But instead, I decide to allow myself this little distraction, and I say five words that I have a feeling are going to completely change this trip home.

"Have a drink with me."

chapter six
ruby

"Have a drink with me."

I feel a little confused at his idea. Didn't he *just* point out to me that having a drink tonight would make me conk out on the porch and get eaten alive by mosquitos?

"A non-alcoholic drink," he amends.

"Like, over the phone? Do you want to FaceTime or something to keep me company?" I'm already shaking my head, though I know he can't see me. "I don't want to take up your time. You're visiting your family and your mom probably has a million things planned for you to—"

"Ruby," he says, interrupting me again. "Do you see the green house across from you? The one with the massive deck and the L-shaped dock?"

Something strange stutters its way through my body. My eyes flick up and across the little cove where Ken's house is tucked away, instantly finding a massive green home, just like Boyd described.

"Uh huh," I manage to say, though I can't really seem to say anything else.

That's when I see movement on the deck. A single body, a man, standing at the railing and lifting an arm to wave.

At me?

I stare straight ahead for a good ten seconds before all the pieces fall together and I suck in a massive breath.

"Is that you?" I ask, needing confirmation before I allow my excitement level to shoot up like a firework.

"That's me."

"What the fuck?" I say, my crude language much louder than I intended. But seriously…

What the fuck?

Before my mind can try to figure out a way that this is possible, I'm pulled back into the conversation by the sound of something I haven't really heard from Boyd.

Laughter.

And not the quiet chuckles from the plane. This is a deep rumbling laughter that barrels through the phone and hits me square in the stomach, making me wish he wasn't all the way across the water.

"How the hell did we sit next to each other for that whole flight and not talk about the fact that your dad lives in Cedar Point?" he asks.

I put a hand on my hip. "Because *someone* let me fall asleep then never woke me up again." My tone is sassy, though there's no heat behind it.

How can I be irritated at him for earlier when *he's here! Right there!* Right across from me.

"Your dad is Ken Bellows," he says. "I don't know him that well, but my parents are friends with him. What a small world."

Yes, it is. A very small world. A wonderful world where sweet baby Jesus has blessed me with the fortunate luck to be just a few houses away from the most handsome man I think I've ever seen in my life.

Though wrapping up all of Boyd into just his looks isn't fair. He's charming, too, and a secret softy, though he'd never admit it.

"So," he continues, "have a drink with me. A vodka-less cranberry juice or sparkling water or something."

My heart pounds in my chest.

Our interaction during the flight was flirtatious, but there wasn't anything solid behind it. How could there have been? We were strangers who met on a plane.

But now, he's right there. *Right there.* And he's asking me to go get a drink and I just…

"You're serious."

"As a heart attack."

I'm suddenly thankful for the few hundred yards of space between us as my cheeks flush and my smile grows.

"I'd love to."

"Good," he says. Then he pauses. "That's good."

"How crazy is this?" I whisper, still watching him across the water and wishing I could see his face even though I don't want him to see mine.

"Very."

We're both silent for a moment, a lull in the conversation that isn't unpleasant, just silent. I wonder if he's feeling as overwhelmed as I am.

This is unexpected, but in a good way—at least for me.

I hope it is for him as well.

"I'll pick you up in an hour. I just need a chance to shower off the plane ride."

"Sounds good. Me too."

"See you soon, Ruby," he says, his voice sounding so much closer now that I know he's at the house across the water.

"See you soon, Boyd."

We get off the phone, and I watch as Boyd gives me another wave then turns to walk back inside.

I take that as my cue to get my butt in motion, spinning on my heels and darting inside the little bungalow I'm calling home for the next week and a half.

I didn't take a good look around the place when Linda first dropped me at the front door like a sack of potatoes, happy to be rid of me.

"No parties," she snipped before hustling back to the behemoth of a home she, Ken, and their two boys live in.

I wondered if the best thing I could do for myself was to head straight back to the airport and catch the next cheap flight back to Boston.

Now, feeling a lot more encouraged about the direction this trip could possibly be headed, I'm looking at my little abode with fresh eyes. It's an absolutely adorable place I would love to book on a vacation with my mom, if there were ever a chance to do such a thing.

It's three rooms. A kitchen, a living room, and a bedroom with white shiplap from head to toe. The floors are a soft cream carpet that feels amazing beneath my feet, and there's a beautiful white tile in the kitchen and bathroom.

It's filled with romantic touches, like an antique chandelier in the living room, barn doors to close off the bedroom, and an old-fashioned clawfoot tub in the bath.

The deck outside has a handful of Adirondack chairs and a

little shed off to the side with towels and sunscreen, as well as blow-up floaties and rafts. And then of course there's the absolutely breathtaking view of the lake only a few feet away.

In a few words, it's an ideal place to spend the next twelve days, though I can't honestly say it's just because of the sweetness of this little lakeside guesthouse.

The fact that Boyd is so close has my heart fluttering around like a damn butterfly, even though I know catching feelings on a short trip to the west coast is a bad idea.

But he lives in Boston, my mind whispers at me.

Shooing away those thoughts, I make a beeline for the bathroom, hoping to clean myself up a bit more than I did before boarding the plane this morning.

Apparently, some people do their hair and makeup and wear nice clothes on flights, but I can say I am staunchly opposed to such a concept. Every road trip I've ever been on has been firmly in the camp of makeup-free face and comfy yoga pants.

However, when I go out on dates, I like to glam it up a little. Just a smidge. I don't want to look like I have cake on my face, but I do want to feel beautiful, and a hint of makeup goes a long way.

I shower quickly, making a mental note to stand under the rainfall showerhead longer next time, and then I add some leave-in conditioner to my hair to make it extra soft.

As my hair dries wrapped up in a towel on my head, I apply a little bit of this and that to my face. Lotion. A few dabs of concealer to help with the bags from the long flight. A light layer of foundation to minimize redness. And a smidge of mascara to open up my eyes a bit more.

I don't even know what half the things are that people talk about when it comes to doing makeup. Baking. Contouring.

Highlighting. I tried getting into it when I was in high school, but I just never had the money for the fancy shit like my friends had. Then, once I was older and had a full-time job, I realized I didn't want to spend the time it takes to put on a 'full face,' as Fiona calls it.

So my 'signature look' usually makes people think I don't wear makeup but keeps me feeling fresh and beautiful.

When my phone rings, I prance over to where it's plugged in, excited to talk to Boyd.

But my mood sours just a little when I see it's not my very handsome neighbor.

It's my mom.

And then I feel even worse for not wanting to talk to her. She's my best friend, and that's not just lip service.

Michelle Roberts is without a doubt the most amazing person I know, working her ass off my whole life to make sure we kept a roof over our head.

She never relied on a man to take care of us. It meant a harder life for us—for her, more specifically—but it also meant we didn't have to deal with some of the abuse and neglect and substance issues you hear about from so many people in poverty who cling to the first man who claims he can save you.

Knowing she's on the other end of the line and probably just wants to make sure I got here okay, I shake out my hands and answer the call.

"Hey, mama!" I say, giving her my best and brightest.

"My baby," she says, dragging out the long A sound. "I'm assuming you made it safely since I'm not seeing anything about plane crashes on the news."

I groan. "Don't say things like that. That's terrifying."

She cackles. "You know I'm just kidding. How was the

flight? You didn't sit next to anyone smelly, did you?"

My mind recalls the memory of Boyd sitting next to me, that aroma of man and whiskey and something warm stirring my blood.

"Nope. The flight was calm. I was able to sleep for a little bit. Now I'm just…hanging out in the rental." I pause. "I'm the only one here right now, but I'm just about to leave to go out with one of my friends."

I know I'm fibbing. Technically what I said isn't a *lie* lie since I *am* alone at the moment and I'm planning to go out with Boyd, but it isn't completely honest, either, and I hate having that kind of wall between us.

I just don't know how mom would respond to having her only child go across the country to see the man who left us.

Well, I guess I'm not really seeing him since he isn't even here…but that's not the point.

"Oh, how fun. Well you enjoy yourself, now, and make sure you're being safe. Did you pack condoms?"

My cheeks flame and I stutter out an awkward laugh.

Mom and I talk about sex. She always wanted us to have open communication about it because she didn't want me to not use protection and then get pregnant too young, like she did.

But when she double-checks that I have condoms so I can get laid on vacation, I can't help but feel slightly embarrassed. We talk about sex in the general sense, but it isn't like we're exchanging tips on our favorite positions or anything.

"No," I say through gritted teeth. "I didn't bring any."

I assumed I would be spending all of my time with Ken and his family. Why would I need condoms?

Clearly, my forethought was poorly executed, because now all I can think about is the fact that I'm getting together with

Boyd tonight and I don't have anything in case he wants to get physical, which I am so down for.

Right? Am I down to jump in bed with the guy who indulges my ridiculous inability to shut my mouth and has the sexiest voice I've ever heard?

I don't have any rules about sex per se, like a three-date minimum or no hot wax until I know you're smart enough not to burn my skin. Mostly my position on sex and dating is that if it feels right, it feels right.

I might not have been able to enjoy the pinnacle moment of sex with a man, but that doesn't mean I don't enjoy it at all. I can imagine that having Boyd's big body hovering over mine as he moves inside of me would be something spectacular, orgasm or not.

I'm getting ahead of myself, though. Just because Boyd doesn't have a girlfriend doesn't mean he's interested in getting naked with me, and just because he's taking me out for drinks doesn't mean he wants anything more than friendly conversation.

"Well, make sure you stop in somewhere and pick some up. You never know when you might find Mr. Right." She pauses. "Or Mr. *Right There, Yesssssss.*"

I slap my hands over my eyes, feeling the heat of embarrassment rush down my neck.

"Alright, I'm getting off the phone now," I shout over the sound of my mom laughing hysterically in the background. "Loveyoubye."And then I hang up on her before she can make any more sex noises that will haunt me until the day I die.

Pushing away the conversation with my mother—and the bit of guilt I feel at my intentional dishonesty—I head back to my suitcase and dig around, trying to pick out something comfortable and casual that would also be good for a date.

Is this a date?

Do I *want* it to be a date?

I nod to myself as I pull out a pair of skinny jeans and a slouchy tank top.

Yes, I do want it to be a date. A man like Boyd doesn't come around often, so I would be a fool not to take advantage of this absolutely delicious offering that has been placed in my lap.

When I see it's almost time for him to pick me up, I decide to head out to the road to save him from having to walk the long path all the way to my door.

Slipping on a pair of Toms, I grab my purse and take a look at myself in the mirror by the door before I lock up. Then I wander up the small stone path that forks to both Ken's house and the driveway.

The man has done well for himself; there's no denying that. I'm sure houses in tiny towns aren't nearly as expensive as real estate in large cities, but that doesn't take away from the life he's clearly built here.

A lakefront home. A rental property. A wife and two kids.

I'm still angry at him for a lot of reasons, most of them completely justifiable, but at least it seems like he might actually care about this family, enough to give them a comfortable life instead of abandoning them like he did me and mom.

I turn my head away when I walk past the one part of the trail that gives me a view of the inside of the home Ken and Linda live in. I might be here as an unwanted guest on their property, but I'm not trying to intrude on their privacy.

Leaning up against a tree once I'm out front, I pull out my phone from my back pocket, a thought suddenly crossing my mind.

Me: You know, it never occurred to me to ask if you're a serial killer or planning to kidnap me.

Boyd's reply is immediate.

Boyd: I promise I'm not a serial killer.
Me: Oooooooh, okay. Now I believe you. Because all of your type are such upstanding citizens, unable to craft lies to accomplish your dirty deeds.
Boyd: My type?
Me: You know, the kidnapper, serial killer variety.
Boyd: I never said I wasn't a kidnapper. I said I wasn't a serial killer.
Me: Oh, so you'll steal me away but won't kill me?
Boyd: Exactly.
Me: Thanks for the reassurance. I feel so safe now.
Boyd: You're starting to sound like you're actually worried I'm a murderer. If you want, you can check my LinkedIn profile.
Me: Hahahahahahahahahahahahahahahahahaha
Boyd: What?
Me: LinkedIn. You're harmless.

Boyd sends me a GIF of someone sticking their tongue out and then tells me he's leaving his house and will be pulling up soon.

My stomach fills with the fluttering of a million butterflies, my sudden nerves catching me off guard.

It worries me a little bit that I'm feeling this emotional rush, this sudden flickering anxiousness at spending the evening with Boyd.

In real life, I date for fun. For the enjoyment of going out and flirting and being at the center of a man's attention. I can't remember the last time I was actually *nervous*.

I guess it's because all of my previous dates were with men I knew would be fun for a little while, people I could enjoy for a few hours, maybe a few dates, and that's it. No emotions, no drama, no disappointment at the end.

But Boyd's the kind of man that makes a woman think about the future, think about *more*, think about *wanting*. In my experience, those are dangerous feelings, risky in a way I've never thought was worth it.

Which is why I'm startled by the fact that, as overwhelming as this feeling is, I'm not willing to push it to the side just yet.

chapter seven
ruby

Only a few minutes go by before a beat-up blue truck stops in front of me, Boyd at the wheel with a huge smile on his face.

"Hello there, Miss Ruby," he says, flashing me that gorgeous smile. "I'm here to kidnap you."

"Mr. Mitchell," I reply, giving him a big smile as I climb into the cab, my arms and legs working together to hoist me up and onto the bench seat. "Consider me held hostage."

He lets out a laugh, and I love the way his voice sends a zing through my body, lighting my veins on fire.

"Fancy seeing you here."

"Fancy, indeed." His eyes sweep me up and down. "I didn't realize how long your hair is," he says, reaching out and touching the ends of the long tresses that hang in soft waves around my shoulders.

"Much better than the messy bun, huh?"

He shakes his head. "Not better, just different. You look beautiful, by the way."

I blush, enjoying the way his eyes take me in before I can't handle his full attention and turn to grab my seatbelt.

Boyd pulls out of the front drive and turns onto the one major road that seems to loop all the way around the lake, though I'm not sure it should be called a 'major road' since it's a single lane each way. Trees go up into the hills that circle Cedar Point on one side, and there's a flat dip into the lake on the other.

I pretend to watch as the houses to the left pass us in a blur, the lake in the background, but really, I'm looking at Boyd.

I don't think I've ever pinpointed the mountain man type as something that does it for me, but holy goodness. Boyd's relaxed posture and this flannel shirt, one hand on the steering wheel of his scruffy truck—it's like something out of a Hallmark movie, and I am so here for it.

"I really like your truck," I say, my eyes roving over the tan interior that has clearly been treated with a combination of love and abuse over the years.

"Thanks." Boyd runs his hand along the wheel, a tender gesture. "Hank was my baby in high school, but I left it here when I moved to the east coast. I always hijack it from my dad when I'm in town."

I laugh. "Hank? Where does that come from?"

"Hank McCoy? The Beast?"

I just watch him with confusion in my eyes.

"You're breaking my heart right now, Ruby," Boyd says, clutching at his chest like he might collapse at any moment.

Which, of course, only makes me want to giggle even more.

"Your dad doesn't mind being carless while you're in town?"

"Nah, I leave him with the keys to my rental, and I always get something fancy so he can enjoy himself." Boyd shrugs a shoulder then looks at me with a smile. "He pretends to hate it, but it's all bullshit. Besides, there's no way I'm coming to town and spending my days driving around Cedar Point in anything other than Hank."

I've never owned a car in my life, and I only got my driver's license a few years ago when my mom insisted I learn. I can't picture having a vehicle I love enough to name, but for some reason, the sentimental warmth of it rings true for the kind of person Boyd seems to be.

"You settling in okay?"

I tilt my head from side to side. "Yes and no. I mean, the guesthouse is great."

"Yeah, I've been in there before. Linda redid it a few years ago and my mom can't stop raving about how she wants us to update our guesthouse to the same style."

"Oh, you've been in it?" I ask, wondering how I feel about Boyd knowing more about Linda and Ken than I do.

He nods. "We've used it a few times for family when our house couldn't fit everyone."

My eyebrows fly off my face. "Your house is monstrous—how does it not fit everyone?"

That gets me a laugh.

"Well, there are a lot of Mitchells," he says. "My siblings and me, my parents and grandparents. My dad's two sisters and brother, and my mom's four brothers. They're all married and have kids, and some of my cousins are married with kids of their own."

He lifts a shoulder as if he hasn't just described an entire clan of people cramming in under one roof.

"Usually, people visit here and there, taking a guest room or staying in the guesthouse, but sometimes we do family reunions and it's packed. When we can't fit everyone, we borrow cabins or guesthouses from our neighbors."

"People in this town must really like you," I say, trying to figure out which of my neighbors would allow me to use their open guest rooms for visiting family.

I'm unsurprised when my mind comes up blank.

Boyd gives me a wink. "You could say that."

We drive along for a few more minutes, my eyes looking out my own window to take in the mammoth trees and beautiful scenery.

"I can't believe you grew up here. It's such a cute place to live, all the trees and the adorable cabins and houses. What was it like living on a lake?"

"It was pretty much exactly like most people imagine," he says, looking over his shoulder as he makes a left to pull into a parking spot outside a small building tucked away on the side of the road. "A mountain town where everyone knows the gossip. Lots of time on the water. High school kids getting up to no good at late-night bonfires."

"Sounds amazing." I hop out of the truck. "We got here so fast."

He shrugs a shoulder. "Small town, not a lot of places to go. The twins are here, and I'd much rather us have a drink with them than try to find a spot at Lucky's on a Saturday night."

I only understand some of what he said, but I follow along as we cross the dirt lot to what looks like a quintessential small-town dive bar.

All-wooden exterior, weathered from years of sun and lake water. A few windows, though you can't see through them because there are neon signs hanging in the center of each one, boasting the exotic tastes of Coors Light and Budweiser. A sandwich board outside says *Give in to beer pressure*, and a small sign hanging above the front door says The Mitch.

Something about the name feels familiar, but before I can ask about it, I hear a curse to my left. Three men smoking off to the side of the entrance turn toward us as we approach. One of them chucks his butt on the ground and stomps it out, pushing away from where he's leaned against the wall, a smile on his face.

"Fuck, man. I didn't even realize what time of year it was."

He strides over and pulls Boyd into a big hug, each of them patting each other on the back in that very manly way.

"Good to see you, Car," he says, though his expression doesn't look as easygoing as it did a few minutes ago.

"You too. Do you see this, boys?" he calls out to the other two guys. "Mr. Mitchell is back in town."

They lift hands and give Boyd waves but don't move from their smoking spot a dozen or so yards away.

Boyd turns to introduce me. "Carson, this is Ruby. She's…" He pauses, his head tilting to the side as he struggles with his words. "She's staying on the lake for a little bit. Ruby, this is Carson Dillard. We go way back."

"Yeah, we do." Carson eyes me then slaps Boyd on the back. "This guy was my biggest competition. We fought it out in the pool, we fought it out on the field, and we fought it out with the ladies."

He draws out the word ladies in a way that makes me want to wrinkle up my nose, but I manage to keep a neutral expression on my face when I give him a hello.

The two of them talk for a few minutes, referencing a few people who are in town and agreeing to see each other at some sort of end-of-summer festival. I listen politely, trying to remember the names and information in case we talk about it later.

It's hard to focus, though, because my mind struggles to

move past the strange way he introduced me.

Did he not want to say I was his friend? Or his date for the evening? Maybe I'm overreacting or overanalyzing—something I'm very prone to do—but it seemed a little weird. He said he doesn't have a girlfriend, but what if he's trying to keep his options open? It sounds like he was a guy who got around when he was younger; maybe there are other girls in town he wants to see and saying I'm his date will screw things up?

Ugh. I don't like any of those possibilities. None of them sit well with me, and I wonder if I jumped too quickly at getting together when I don't really know that much about him.

I don't want anything serious, obviously, but I don't want to be one of many, either.

Before I can fully form my thoughts about whether I'll ask Boyd about it, Carson says he'll see us later, giving a brief nod to me and heading back over to smoke with the guys who are still hanging outside.

Boyd turns and extends his arm.

"Shall we?" he says, opening the front door and ushering me through in front of him.

It's dark inside The Mitch, and Boyd bumps into my back when I come to a halt, worried I can't see anything and am going to end up knocking over a waitress with a tray full of drinks.

"It takes a minute for your eyes to adjust," he says, that sexy voice rumbling close to my ear and sending a shiver down my spine.

It's hard to hear him over the noise of what I'm assuming is a packed bar, but I can still feel him all the way down in my toes.

"We're over in the corner."

Boyd takes my hand in his and leads the way, past the bar and the tables clustered in the middle, past the small stage and even smaller dance floor off to the side, past the pool table and jukebox.

As my eyes begin to sort things out, I see dozens of people scattered through the room, sitting at tables and standing at high-tops, chatting and laughing and drinking. There's still a hazy quality to the air, almost like the days of indoor smoking left behind a permanent cloudiness.

Eventually, I spot where we're going: a high-top table tucked between a massive bear made entirely of wood and a dartboard, currently occupied by a man and two women around my age with big smiles on their faces.

"Oh shit. He's home, everybody!" the guy shouts, cupping his hands around his mouth. "Boyd Mitchell has returned to the homestead!"

Suddenly, the whole bar starts cheering, a raucous hollering of hoots and hell-yeahs and welcome-backs.

Even in the dim light of the bar, I can still see a faint blush creeping up Boyd's neck, and he glances back with pursed lips and raised shoulders as if to apologize for the craziness.

Before we take even another step forward, the shouting guy rounds the table and wraps Boyd in a bear hug like none other. This one Boyd returns a bit more enthusiastically than the embrace with his friend outside.

"Missed you, Bam," Boyd says, pulling back and looking at the guy with a satisfied smile. Then he lifts a hand and taps his cheek in a gesture that's equal parts affection and irritation.

"What about me?" comes a sassy voice from my right, one of the other two at the table.

"Shut up, Bells," the guy says. "Not everything is about you."

"Um, have you met me? Of *course* everything is about me," she sasses back, a wide smile on her face.

The loud guy—Boyd's brother, Bishop, I'm assuming—and the sassy girl—who I'm guessing is his sister Bellamy—both wrap Boyd in a group hug. Boyd pretends to not want the embrace from either of them, his vocal protests not matching the expression on his face that says he's loving every minute of his siblings' attention.

"I'm glad you decided to join us instead of staying home to do something lame like nuking pizza and napping on the couch."

Boyd chuckles then turns his attention my way.

"Guys," he says, stepping back to my side and resting a hand at the base of my spine to urge me closer to the table, "this is Ruby. Ruby, these are the twins, Bellamy and Bishop. They're pure trouble, and you're much better off not knowing them."

"Hey!" Bellamy protests as she returns to her seat.

"That is completely false, Miss Ruby. Don't believe a word he's said about us."

Bishop steps forward and extends a hand to me, and when I take it, he kisses the back, giving me a mischievous grin.

"And the ladies call me Bam."

I laugh, loving the teasing interaction and understanding what Boyd meant on the plane when he said his siblings like to poke at him all the time.

"Nice to meet you both."

Boyd clears his throat, his attention shifting to the other woman at the table, a beautiful blonde with big breasts and a sultry stare.

"And this is Corinne, an old friend of the family."

"Oh, come on, Boyd—we're much more than that," she says, her voice thick with something that causes my spine to straighten.

Corinne hops up from her stool next to Bellamy and rounds the table to wrap her arms around Boyd, her hands flattening against his back and stroking up and down in a way that's more than a smidge over the line of friendship.

Boyd hugs Corinne back, but there is a stiffness to his body that reflects his discomfort.

"Boyd and I were high school sweethearts back in the day," she says to me, keeping her hands on his waist as she looks up at him with a dreamy expression.

I'm a little surprised at her nerve, especially when she doesn't know who I am. Not that I'm Boyd's girlfriend. For all I know based on the way he introduced me outside, I'm not even his date, but Corinne probably doesn't know that.

The entire interaction strikes me as odd. Maybe it's the desperation rolling off of her? Or the overly seductive attitude that doesn't seem to fit? I don't know enough information—any information, actually—to make any judgments.

Corinne looks in my direction and gives me a smile that doesn't quite reach her eyes then rounds the table and sidles back up next to Bellamy, taking her tall cocktail in hand and sipping slowly from the straw.

There's a silence that lingers just a few seconds too long until Bishop and Boyd start talking about the flight into Sacramento. Boyd pulls me up next to him, probably trying to include me, but my eyes and attention stray away from where he's talking with his brother, drawn over to where Corinne sits staring at me.

Even when Bellamy says something in her ear, she only nods, not responding and keeping her eyes locked with mine.

It feels like a challenge, somehow, like a dare. It picks at the insecure part of me, the bit of me that never feels like I amount to enough in the eyes of others, the part of me I've been working really hard at letting go.

I knew a girl like Corinne when I was younger. A little bit bitchy, a lot self-centered, and ridiculously beautiful, she made life difficult for many girls, including me.

I might be older now and have a better understanding of what drives women like her—insecurity, fear, loneliness—but knowing those things doesn't fix the way her targeted animosity makes me feel.

Lacking.

When I notice silence around the table again, I look up at Boyd, finding him watching me with a furrowed brow.

"I'm going to show Ruby around," he says, giving the table a tight smile. "We'll be back in a few. Bam, order me a beer and grab a cranberry juice for Ruby, yeah?"

Without waiting for his brother's reply, he slips his hand into mine and leads me outside.

chapter eight
boyd

I only have one thing on my mind when I lead Ruby to the outdoor deck at the back of The Mitch, and that's getting her away from Corinne Paulson as quickly as possible.

My sister likes to play matchmaker, and I'm assuming if she's inviting me out to drinks when she's with Corinne, she has it in her mind that the two of us should get back together. It's an idea that has absolutely no merit, seeing as how anything that involves me and an ex-girlfriend from a lifetime ago rekindling things makes my entire body want to hightail it back to Boston.

But that's Bellamy: a little bit of meddlesome and a whole lot of love. She means well, though in the case of myself and Corinne, her efforts are severely misguided.

Ruby and I were only inside for a few minutes, but stepping back into the light of the cooling August evening still has me squinting and holding my hand up for a moment to ease the glare.

Not letting go of Ruby's hand, I continue to lead her through the groups of people outside and over to an open space at the railing that has a decent view of the lake. Once we settle in, both of us leaning against the barrier and looking out at the water, I realize I'm not quite sure what to say.

Saying Ruby has nothing to worry about where Corinne is concerned makes a pretty big assumption regarding the state of things between the two of us, and I'm not sure how she'll take it.

And really, I guess that's the question of the night, huh? How deliberate do I want to be when it comes to Ruby?

Do I want things to be relaxed? Maybe friends, maybe more?

Do I want her to get a really good sense of the way her smile seems to wrap itself around my ribs and squeeze tight until I can barely breathe?

Maybe I should find a healthy medium between those two.

Putting parameters on things isn't something I'm too familiar with, so I don't know exactly how to move forward, especially considering my intentions with Ruby are still up in the air.

The only thing I *do* know for sure is that the girl I met on the plane, the one standing before me, is someone I want to get to know better.

So maybe I start there and see where it goes.

"Just to be clear," I say, looking at Ruby's profile as she watches a truck back an empty trailer into a nearby launch, "my plan tonight was to introduce you to Cedar Point, and for you to meet Bishop and Bellamy. I don't know why Corinne is here, but if I *had* known she'd be here, I would have chosen to do something different."

Ruby gives me a small, unsure smile, but her nose wrinkles and she looks down at a blue ring she wears on her thumb, twisting it around and around.

"The last thing I want to do is put pressure on you to hang

out with me when you have family and…friends to catch up with," she says. "I'm happy to go back to my night of snacks and sunset on the porch if you want to spend time with them."

I'm already shaking my head.

"I don't, though. I mean, yeah I want to hang out with my brother and sister, but I'll see them tonight at the house. Corinne is just…" I wave a hand around, trying to find the right words. "A part of the past. Trust me when I say I am not interested in spending time with her when I'm in town."

"I just don't want to get in the way." Ruby glances up at me then looks back at the water. "We've only been here a few minutes, and it seems like you don't really know what to do with me."

She says the last part with a little bit of a laugh, though it doesn't sound like she thinks her words are funny.

I'm confused, not understanding where this discomfort is coming from, whether it's about Corinne or the bar or my siblings or something else.

"I feel like I'm missing something here, and I need you to fill me in."

"It's stupid, and maybe I'm overanalyzing, but the way you introduced me to the guy outside, and even now inside…" She shrugs a shoulder, her words trailing off like even *she* doesn't understand how she feels.

The pieces click in my mind, Ruby's discomfort suddenly making a little more sense.

"If you're talking about Carson, it's not my place to say you're in town to see Ken. I don't know if he's told anyone he has another daughter or if that kind of information could cause a problem. The last thing I want is to have something I say make life difficult while you're here, and trust me when I tell you small-town tongues are a lot more vicious and quicker to move than in other places."

Whatever clouds were covering the bright sunshine of her face seem to part instantly with understanding.

"And with my brother and sister, I've never introduced them to a woman before, so every detail I give them is going to be dissected to within an inch of its life. Not only do *I* not want to deal with that, but I doubt you want them to ask you a million questions about whether or not you and I are getting married."

Ruby bites her lip, and I can see a blooming blush of embarrassment spreading on her cheeks.

"I never thought of it like that," she says. Then she shakes her head, her long hair falling forward and partially covering her face. "Now I just feel stupid."

I reach forward on instinct and tuck some of those soft, chocolate waves behind her ear so I can see her eyes again. I don't want her to hide away from me.

"I'm an honest guy," I tell her. "I asked you to come out because I want to spend time with you."

I step closer so I'm nearer to the space her body inhabits, enjoying how I can catch that same jasmine scent wafting off of her skin.

"Because I'm interested," I say, my words coming out low but clear. "There's something about you that just…I don't know. I don't want to miss out on a chance to get to know you."

Her gaze is snagged on mine, and I take advantage of the moment, allowing myself to really look at her.

I don't date often, and I prefer simple relationships. My interactions with women are either platonic or sexual, and there isn't usually too much room for anything in between.

But in less than a single day, stretching from one coast to

another, Ruby has convinced me that maybe I've gotten it all wrong so far. Maybe I've been doing myself a disservice by not searching for more beneath the surface with women in the past.

Or, maybe fate has just finally revealed something to me in the right moment, with the right woman.

I can't say for certain what will happen moving forward with Ruby, but I do know, without a doubt, that I want to know everything I can about her, from the way she'll moan my name to the way she likes her coffee and whether or not that pale skin of hers will tan in the sun.

It should be something that scares me, this big feeling that hasn't ever taken root in my body before, but it doesn't. I'm going to make sure I don't let it pass me by.

"One shitty beer and one cranberry juice, as requested."

Two drinks appear in between us and I turn my head, finding Bishop hovering next to me with an irritating smile on his face.

"Thank you," Ruby says, flashing him her own smile, though I definitely don't find hers irritating. Sexy as hell is more like it.

"So your name is Ruby?" Bishop asks, failing to recognize that the two of us are in the middle of a conversation.

"Yup. Ruby Rae Roberts, at your service."

"That is, like, the cutest name in the world," Bellamy says as she pops into our conversation.

My eyes glance around, and I see that Corinne is nowhere to be found. Thank god.

I don't harbor any feelings toward her, bad or otherwise, but I've definitely moved on from the relationship we shared during our high school years. It's been over a decade since we broke up, so I don't understand what she could possibly think would happen between us now.

And that little show earlier, calling us more than friends, giving me a stare she thinks is sultry, wrapping her arms around me in what was much more than a friendly hug—what *was* that? I don't know what is going on in Corinne's mind, but we are definitely not on the same page, that's for sure.

"Thanks. My mom loves alliteration, and she fell in love with the name Ruby after reading *Anne of Green Gables*."

"Oh, hey—that's a Netflix show," Bellamy says, her eyes lighting up. "*Anne with an E*, right? I've been meaning to watch that."

"Trust me when I say you should watch the old Canadian version from the 80s instead of the Netflix one. It's amazing."

Bellamy nods then glances my way before returning her attention to Ruby. "So, you two are friends?" she asks, her expression open but clearly curious.

Ruby giggles, my earlier prediction that my siblings would want to know more about our relationship coming true.

I get it, though. I can't remember the last time any of my siblings saw me with a woman at my side, platonic or otherwise. Most of my friends are guys, and the few women I've spent my time with are definitely not meeting my family.

The curiosity on Bells' face is warranted.

Though not entirely appreciated.

"Well, Boyd and I aren't really *friends*," she answers. "We just met. Today, actually, on the plane, and it's just a coincidence that I ended up being here in Cedar Point."

"Sounds like he's trying to make you a booty call, not a friend," Bishop says, giving her a wink right before he winces from where Bellamy slaps him on the back of the head.

"Rude, much?" she says, completely unapologetic as Bishop rubs at the spot she smacked. "Sorry about that. I can promise you the *being an asshole* thing isn't genetic."

Ruby waves them off. "I'm not worried. Besides, if Boyd had any intention of getting a booty call tonight, he is sorely out of luck because this girl didn't shave her legs."

She winks at me then takes a sip of her drink as Bellamy laughs and Bishop grins at her.

She figured out how to play along with the twins quickly; I can give her that.

"So, you said you met Boyd on the plane?" Bishop asks, taking a sip from his beer as Ruby nods. "How'd that happen? I've known Boyd my entire life, and I can assure you he isn't the type to chitchat with strangers."

Ruby lets out a peal of laughter, setting her drink down on the railing before covering her face with her hands.

"Oh my gosh, you guys. I feel so bad about it."

She focuses all of her attention on Bellamy and Bishop, like I'm not even here. Maybe some guys wouldn't appreciate it or would feel neglected or ignored. Not me. I just lean back against the railing and sip at my beer, watching this bombshell as her energy ricochets slowly through my family.

It's a sight to behold.

"Here I am, first time flying in my whole life, and I just keep rambling on and asking him questions even though he's clearly not into talking to me." She shakes her head. "You'd think I would have caught on at some point, but I guess this mouth has a problem staying shut because I just kept going."

Ruby finally looks at me, a little bit of endearment in her eyes.

"He put up with me, even indulged my desire to chat and helped distract me from my fear of flying."

"You act like you seriously put me out," I finally interject, realizing I can't let her go on any longer thinking I just *indulged* her on that flight. "My siblings can attest to the fact that I would not have talked to you if I didn't want to."

"Truth!" Bellamy says.

"Truer words have never been spoken." Bishop leans forward. "Boyd has no problems being an asshole if it means people will leave him the fuck alone."

"That's a little harsh," I say, rubbing at my chest with my free hand as if his words wounded me.

They didn't. They're pretty accurate, but he doesn't need to be a total prick about it.

"So, we talked for a while until I fell asleep for the second half of the flight. He gave me his number, and we realized later that we were just a few houses away from each other."

Her story glosses over the fact that I left her on the plane without saying goodbye, and I don't know if she's doing that for her or for me. Either way, I appreciate it. Something about having just left her behind doesn't sit well with me anymore, and I'm glad I don't have to face my siblings' criticism.

Because they *always* have something snarky to say.

"It sounds like something out of a movie," Bellamy says. "Are you sure Boyd didn't hire you to pretend to be his girlfriend because he's too stubborn to admit he's a lonely old man who doesn't have anyone to bring home?"

Ruby lets out an awkward giggle and shakes her head. "That is definitely not what happened."

I cross my arms and purse my lips, though Bellamy waves off my glare like it means nothing.

"Don't give me that face. You know I'm kidding." She pauses. "About the fake girlfriend part, not the lonely old man part."

Then she gives me a wide smile that reveals almost all of her teeth and makes her look like a monster.

"You're a little shit, you know that?"

Bells laughs. "It's why I'm your favorite."

The four of us stay out on the deck for a while longer, the twins answering all of Ruby's questions about what it was like growing up with someone sharing almost all of your DNA.

It's the normal questions people ask twins when they've never met a pair before.

Do they finish each other's sentences?

Do they have their own secret language?

Have they ever switched places?

Ruby burst into laughter after asking the last one, belatedly remembering they're brother and sister, not identical.

"You know, we actually get that question more than you'd think," Bellamy says. "Normally we don't share the real answer, but maybe today we can make an exception?"

She asks the last as a question, her eyes looking over at Bishop like she's seeking his permission.

He sighs and scrubs his hand through his hair as he thinks something over, looking far more serious than he normally does.

"Yeah, I think we can trust Ruby with the intel," he finally says. Then he crosses his arms and gives Ruby an intense look. "But just know, if you decide to share this, you'll be banished from Cedar Point for all of eternity."

Ruby looks like she might burst out of her skin with how

she's practically vibrating in place. Her excitement is palpable, and it makes her eyes glitter in a completely new way.

"Oh my god, cross my heart and hope to die," she says, actually using her finger to make an X over her chest.

"Bishop, do you want to tell it, or do you want me to?"

"You tell it," he says before tilting his head back and finishing off the remainder of his beer in one long pull.

"Alright, we are going to call this story *The Day Bellamy Interviewed For Her Internship.*"

She launches into the story I've heard a dozen times, though never outside of our family, about how she was hungover on the day of her interview with the place she wanted to intern at. Thankfully, the interview was online via teleconference, and Bishop rushed to her rescue, dressing in full Bellamy extravagance and completing the entire interview for her over the camera on her laptop.

"I was lying on the bed in the same room listening to the entire thing, and I have to say, he did an excellent job."

"Yeah, I did," Bishop asserts. "You got the internship, didn't you?"

Bellamy rolls her eyes and ignores him. "The best part was when I finally moved to Texas for the job over that summer, my boss said my voice sounded completely different in person."

She lets out a cackle of a laugh and Ruby follows along, the two of them leaning their heads close as they both enjoy the end to Bellamy's story.

"Yuck it up, ladies."

"You should have seen him in lipstick and a wig," Bellamy wheezes, laughing just as hard about it now as she has every other time I've heard this story.

"Hey," he says, irritation coloring his words, "I have friends who do drag. It's an art form."

"Yeah, you're just the Monet of the bunch," she says.

We all laugh at that, even Bishop.

God, I love my family. They're weird and ridiculous and we are all *so* different from each other, but hell if they aren't the best people to have a drink and a laugh with.

And that's really all you need at the end of the day.

When I glance at Ruby, I see her watching the twins with this strange mixture of happiness and adoration in her expression. I like seeing her enjoying the time with them, though I know we need to get going if I want to whisk my girl away to watch the sunset.

I swallow thickly at my own words.

My girl.

You could have asked me that question every day for the past decade and I never would have thought I'd legitimately have that phrase in my mind regarding a woman, especially not one I just met.

I've only had a few relationships since moving to Boston over a decade ago, short little nothings that wouldn't be a blip on most people's radar, and each of them ended because there was always a wall in place that was keeping them at a distance.

Now I'm calling Ruby *my girl* when I met her literal hours ago? Jesus. I need to slow my fucking roll here and soon or I'm going to be declaring my love when I take her home.

Eventually, we all agree it's time to head out, the rowdier bunch of townies arriving in waves and escalating the noise out of conversational level and into shout mode.

"It was so great meeting you both," Ruby says, giving both Bellamy and Bishop hugs as we stop at the side of Hank. "I hope I'll get to see you again while I'm in town."

"Oh you can bet on it," Bellamy says. "We're having a bonfire tomorrow night at Forks if you wanna come."

"I don't know what a Forks is, but I'd love to join," Ruby says, but then her expression drops slightly as she looks at me. "Sorry, I should have asked you first. I don't want to intrude."

"I was going to invite you," I say, giving Bellamy a look, "before the little monster swiped the invite out from underneath me."

My sister gives me a look that says she enjoys my irritation. "Hey, man, if you see something you like, you gotta jump on it fast or someone else will yank it from your hands." She swings an arm around Ruby's shoulders. "Which is why Ruby, here, is going to be *my* date tomorrow—not yours."

Even though my sister bugs me and her little games are more than obvious, I let it go, seeing the clear enjoyment on Ruby's face at being on the receiving end of Bellamy's attention.

"Well if you're stealing her for the bonfire, don't take offense when I tell you two to fuck off so Ruby and I can finish our evening without you," I say, causing both girls to giggle and Bishop to let out a harsh laugh.

Ruby and Bellamy exchange numbers and hug again before she walks over to where I've pulled the passenger door open.

"Bye guys!" Bellamy says before she and Bishop walk over to his Bronco parked in the corner.

"See you," I call after them as I round the hood.

Once I'm inside, I look over at Ruby, who is still beaming.

"You look so pleased." I turn my key in the ignition and turn to look over my shoulder as I back out. "I'm assuming you had fun tonight?"

"Oh my gosh, *so* much fun."

Ruby turns to the side and presses her back against her door, looking at me straight on.

"Those two are hilarious. Thank you so much for inviting me out, seriously. I wasn't expecting to have any fun on this trip at all, and you guys have turned that all around on the first day."

Something solidifies in my chest at her words, the knowledge that I improved her outlook on the trip feeding this desire to make her smile that's taken root inside of me.

"I'm glad. The twins are a mess, but they're good people. I think you and Bellamy are really going to like each other."

"I think so, too."

We drive in silence for a little bit as I take the same road back to the Bellows' house. Ruby and I never talked about what this evening would look like, and I feel like I got to spend time with her, but not enough.

When we pull up in front of her dad's, I'm still working up my ideas for how we can hang out for longer without making it seem like I want her to *invite me in*.

"I know we missed the sunset, but do you want to sit out on the deck for a little bit?" I ask.

When she hesitates, I know I've pushed too quickly.

"Or if you're sick of me, I can leave you alone," I joke, trying to make sure she doesn't feel guilty about turning me down.

"It's not that I don't want to hang out with you. I'm just still really tired with the jetlag and my bad sleep last night," she says, and when she looks at me, I can actually see the exhaustion in her eyes.

"No, I totally understand," I say. "I'm usually up way before the sun, so it's getting a little late for me, too."

"But I'll see you tomorrow?" she says, though I hear the hint of a question in her voice. "I'm excited about the bonfire. That will be fun."

My heart sags just a little, realizing she's talking about seeing me there, not about spending more time together during the day.

"Yeah. It'll be a good time."

We both get out of the truck and I walk her down the little pathway to her door, battling with myself on what to say when we say good night.

It's the weirdest sensation, trying to come up with excuses to hang out with her. I've never had to think things over like this. When I've wanted to spend time with a woman, it was usually for one purpose, no complicated or messy emotions involved.

Now that I'm here, in this place where I want to spend time just hanging out and shooting the shit with Ruby, I realize how floundering I feel hoping she wants the same.

She's verbalized a few times that she doesn't want to impose on me or my family, so I decide to take a risk, hoping her mention of the bonfire was her way of not trying to dominate my time and not her lack of interest in hanging out with me.

"So, listen, I know you'll be at the bonfire tomorrow night, but maybe I can make you breakfast in the morning?"

Ruby eyes me as she bites her lip, seeming to mull something over in her mind.

"Any interest in doing morning yoga with me? It's my routine and I like to—"

"Absolutely," I interrupt.

I don't care if she wants me to learn how to swallow fire. I'll do whatever she asks.

Ruby beams at me with tired eyes as we come to a stop in front of the door to the guesthouse.

"Sunrise yoga and breakfast?" she says, reaching forward and playing with a button on my shirt. "My kind of man."

I bite my lip at the blush on her cheeks, enjoying the way her soft, pale skin looks slightly pinked up under the porch light.

"I'll see you in the morning, then."

She nods, and I take her hand in mine, kissing the inside of her wrist, enjoying the little shiver that seems to race through her at my affection.

It's a first for me, not trying to kiss her up against her door or convince her to ask me to stay.

But I don't want a quick fuck with Ruby Rae Roberts. I want something different.

I just hope I figure out what exactly that is. And soon.

chapter nine
boyd

"She's cute."

My brother plops down next to me on one of the other deck chairs then props his feet up on the footrest before sticking his beer bottle out to clink with mine.

"She is."

"No bullshit—did you two really just start chatting on the plane? Doesn't seem like you."

I roll my eyes. "Like you're an expert at knowing what I would and wouldn't do."

He smirks. "I know you pretty damn well, Boy," he says, chuckling when my irritation shows on my face. "Well at least enough to know how to rile you up, that's for sure."

Ain't that the truth.

I take a swig of the IPA dad likes to get from the local brewery, my eyes on the little guesthouse across the water.

The lights went off only a few minutes after I came out here to relax after the long day, confirming that Ruby probably dropped into bed like dead weight right after I dropped her off.

Not that I'm keeping tabs or anything. She'd have every right to get rid of me and stay up all night.

Still, it feels good knowing she only begged off because she was tired and not because she was trying to avoid any more time with me and my annoying siblings.

Bishop and I sit in silence for a while, long enough that I realize something might be wrong. A glance over at his face confirms it, his expression distracted, his eyes off in the distance, the rim of his beer bottle resting against his lip as he thinks over whatever big thing is on his mind.

"You know I love you, right, Bam?" I say, using the nickname I've had for him since he was a wild little baby. It fits him perfectly, a mixture of his intense personality as a kid, smashing into things and cackling hysterically, as well as his initials.

I don't know why I feel the need tell my brother I love him, but I do. When Bishop reaches over and pats my hand a few times, I know I've said the right thing.

He might act like he's full of swagger and charm 24/7, but my only brother has a big heart and big shoulders, big enough to carry quite a burden on his own without asking for help.

"I'm gonna head to bed," he says a few minutes later. "I'm meeting up with Andy Marshall tomorrow to help with the buildout at the store."

I nod, knowing Andy's dad had heart surgery not too long ago and can't do the same heavy lifting he used to. They planned to expand the store and started construction a while back, but it was knocked off course by Willy's heart attack. They put up some plywood to block off the wall they'd already dropped and said they'd get to it later.

Now that I've made plans to do yoga and have breakfast

with Ruby, I feel a little bad about doing something so self-in-dulgent when someone in our community is clearly in need.

"What time are you heading over?" I ask, wondering if I can make it work. "Maybe I can help, too."

"Around 7, but I'll be there all day if you want to swing by. I'm sure Andy would appreciate another set of hands."

I nod. "I have plans in the morning, but count me in."

Bishop smiles at me then ruffles my hair a bit. "Sounds good. Night Boyd."

My brother heads back inside the house, the sound of the screen door squeaking lightly behind me. Then I'm alone again, taking another sip of my beer and turning my eyes back to the lake.

I really do love Cedar Point. There's something about grow-ing up in a small town that just creates a different type of person. When you're encouraged to get to know your neighbors, you care about what happens to them.

It's the reason my dad and I helped search for Roy Grove when he went missing on a hike when I was in high school. The reason my mother spends her Wednesday mornings at the elderly home on the south bank, teaching the ladies to knit or playing board games. Why my brother is going over to help the Marshalls finish building out the grocery store.

To some degree, we're all family, and family is there for each other, whether times are good or hard, in feast and famine.

It's also why Ken Bellows is such a confusing thing for me. I've never been particularly close with him, but I know his wife and kids and we always say hello when we pass each other in town, stopping for the surface-level chitchat acquaintances ex-change.

So, to find out he has another kid, one he has largely ignored and then basically abandoned…it strikes me wrong. It feels like it doesn't fit into the picture of what I assumed Cedar Point citizens are like.

I guess that's another part of growing up that adults don't warn you about.

The older you get, the less certain you are that people are who they claim to be. You find out the nice guy hits his kids, or the happy woman at work struggles with depression. There are all these layers to people, things that make them go much deeper than you'd guess at first glance.

With people like Ken, I start to wonder if there's something a little less sincere than I was expecting underneath all those layers. But there's also the flip side.

Like with Ruby.

She has this pure energy that radiates out from her core. It shoots out of her through every move she makes. Her smile. Her laugh. The way she looks at me. Her teasing attitude.

I thought about it earlier today, and I can acknowledge it now. The girl has many layers, some of them going deep.

And I want to take my time exploring each one.

When my alarm goes off at 6am, I'm rolling out of bed with more energy than I can remember having in a while. I might be on east coast time, but I should be jet-lagged, especially considering the fact that I didn't knock off until after midnight.

I grab a quick shower, dress in some loose basketball shorts and an athletic tee, and then head down into the kitchen to snoop through what's available for me to make for Ruby after we yoga. Hopefully, mom stocked up and I won't need to make a trip to the store this early, but if I need to go, I will.

"Morning, baby."

The sound of my mother's warm voice both startles and soothes me, though I should have known she'd already be up and on her second cup of coffee.

I definitely got my early-riser tendencies from her, and it was both a blessing and a curse. I got time with her all to myself growing up, time I still get with her even now as an adult.

But it also meant I never got that morning time all to myself, and as a self-proclaimed introvert, having alone time in the morning is as essential to me as breathing.

Back home, I wake up every morning by 5am, usually heading to the gym nearby to get in laps at the pool, though I've recently been getting into running as well. I eat breakfast once I'm home and showered, and then I spend some time reading or listening to NPR while I do some kind of housework, like dishes or laundry.

This morning, though, seeing my mother for the first time in months, I let go of my desire to be by myself and try to revel in the joy of being with my favorite woman on the planet.

"Hey, mom." I wrap my arms around her and give her a tight squeeze, letting her give me a kiss on the cheek before backing away to head over to the coffee maker.

"I thought I'd get to see you last night, but when I got home from the Perrys', you three were still out." She takes a sip of her coffee then sets it back down, both of her hands wrapped around the mug. "You were with the twins?"

I nod as I pull down my own mug—the blue one that says

I don't want to talk to you even after I drink this, which my sister Busy bought for me as a Christmas gift when I was in college. I purposefully left it here and make sure to drink out of it while I stare at her.

It always makes her laugh.

"We went to The Mitch," I say, lifting the old-school coffee pot from the cradle and pouring myself a steaming cup almost to the top. "It was fun."

"Heard you had a girl with you."

My mug hovers in front of my mouth as I blow on the scorching hot liquid, realizing without any surprise that the Cedar Point tongues are already wagging.

I probably didn't even need to keep Ruby's stay at Ken's to myself when I was talking with Carson. Surely mom has already heard about the pretty little brunette staying at the Bellows' place. The blend of tourists starts to fade as summer comes to a close, making new faces easier to spot.

And a face like Ruby's isn't going unnoticed.

"Am I going to have a half-naked woman prancing through the house in one of your shirts in a little bit?" she asks.

I snort and finally take a sip of my drink. Then I set my coffee down and pin her with a glare that contains no heat.

"In what world have I ever done something like that?" I ask, feeling some righteous indignation at what she's implying.

"Never, but big city life is very different than things are here."

"Exactly." I shake my head and cross my arms. "Even if that was something I was doing at home, there's still a level of respect I have for my mother, okay?"

She nods and takes another sip of her drink, just watching me over the top of her mug.

"What brought that on?" I ask, knowing there has to be something more than what she's saying.

"Oh, it's just something stupid Margie said last night about her *own* damn son." She waves a hand between us as if to brush it away. "I should know better than to lump you in with LP."

I let out a laugh at the idea that mom could ever put me in the same boat as Linden Perry, Margie's younger son who went to school with Busy and is all kinds of trouble. But I decide to just move on from it instead of wasting my mental energy.

Turning my attention back to the breakfast I'll be making for Ruby, I open the fridge and begin to take mental notes of what we have, what we don't, what I could make, and what I can't make unless I decide I want to go to the store.

"So who was the girl?" I hear from behind me.

When I glance back, I find my mom with a mischievous twinkle in her eye.

I return my attention to the fridge, deciding to indulge her. I might not tell my mother *all* my secrets, but I don't mind her knowing who Ruby is and the story behind how we met.

"She's Ken Bellow's daughter."

"Ken doesn't have a daughter," she interjects, and when I turn to give her a look, her mouth drops open. "Shut. Up."

I laugh at her very youthful reaction.

"You can't say anything—to *anyone*. I don't know who knows, but it seems like it might be a secret. She's staying in their guesthouse for a little while."

"Oh, yeah. I won't say anything."

I believe my mother when she says that. As much as the woman enjoys the local gossip, she knows when something is important enough to keep to herself, especially when it isn't her secret to share.

"So you just met her in town?" she asks.

I close the fridge, having a pretty good idea of what I'm going to do food-wise, and turn back to my mother, taking a seat across from her on a stool at the bar.

"No. I met her on the plane actually."

"And she's here in Cedar Point? What are the odds?"

I take the next ten minutes to fill my mom in about our plane ride and how I left her my number, finding out she was at Ken's, and then our 'date' at The Mitch.

"She's coming over this morning, just so you know. She's going to lead me in a yoga lesson on the deck."

My mother pins me with a look. "I'm sure you've always wanted to do yoga, too. It doesn't happen to have anything to do with the fact that she'll be wearing tight clothes and getting all bendy?"

I let out a somewhat embarrassed chuckle, my hand on my face at my mom saying 'getting all bendy.'

I could lie down and die right here.

"You said it yourself—you don't know what life in Boston is like for me. I could be a closet yoga enthusiast."

"Son, the minute you become a yoga enthusiast will be the day I shave my head," she says.

We both share a laugh at that image.

Looking at the clock on the wall, I realize I only have a few minutes before Ruby gets here, and I still need to find Briar's old yoga mats, which I think are in the garage.

"I'm gonna be honest, honey," my mom says, before I can leave the room. "I've never seen you talk about someone like this before. Do you think you're getting a little too intense about it when you've known her such a short time?"

My mom's question isn't anything I haven't already thought

about myself, though hearing it from her directly has me retaking my seat at the counter.

"I just don't want you to get overly involved with someone you might not ever see again after this little trip of hers, you know? This might be her...what do kids call them? Bangcations?"

I bark out an uncontrollable laugh at my mother's choice of words. She is a serious spitfire once she's had her second cup of coffee.

"Mom, I appreciate the concern—really—but you'll meet Ruby when she gets here and you'll really like her." I lift a shoulder. "Besides, if both of us want to enjoy each other while we're on this trip, why not?"

Her hands fly up and she closes her eyes. "Okay, that might have been a little more information than I needed."

I hop out of my chair and round the counter, wrapping her in my arms and placing a big kiss on her temple.

"Don't worry—you'll always be my favorite mom."

"I'm your only mom," she sasses.

I kiss her head again before heading out to the garage. It takes a few minutes of digging, but eventually I find the yoga mats stuffed behind some fishing gear that has seen better days.

Tucking them under an arm, I click off the light and head back inside, where I find my mom and Ruby chatting animatedly in the kitchen.

"There he is."

Ruby looks over her shoulder at me and smiles, and just like yesterday, that simple look about knocks me off my feet.

"I thought you might have overslept," she says. "Or changed your mind about doing yoga."

"Not a chance. I was grabbing mats from the garage. Don't

write me off so fast, missy. I'm all in."

My mother steps up next to me and pats my shoulder, her eyes connecting with mine. There's a look there I recognize from when I was younger, this specific way she'd purse her lips and wrinkle her nose when she thought I was getting myself into a bit of trouble.

Be careful.

That's what she's saying.

"Have fun, you two. It was nice to meet you, Ruby."

And then my mom is shuffling out of the kitchen and over to the den, where she's likely going to turn on the morning news and play on her iPad.

I look back at Ruby and grin. "Let's head outside."

Thirty minutes later, I am having serious regrets about agreeing to do yoga with Ruby this morning.

It's not because I don't enjoy it—I'm actually surprised I'm liking it as much as I do. I've always been a solo-sport kind of guy. Swimming. Running. I learned to play tennis and golf in college. Something like yoga *should* be on my radar, whether or not it's labeled as a fairly feminine exercise.

So it isn't that I'm not enjoying the yoga. It's that I've been forced to watch Ruby 'getting all bendy' in front of me for the past thirty minutes and fight off the arousal that is simmering on low at the base of my spine.

"Keep your shoulders over your hips and bring both arms

up," she says, her voice like butter, calm and soothing. "Bend your right knee a little bit and stretch out that hip. Inhale deeply and stretch, and then as you exhale, open to Warrior Two."

I follow her motions, even if my body does feel—and look—significantly more clunky than hers.

Everything about the way she leads me looks like waves, fluid and undulating without any strange hitches or trip-ups. I can't say the same about myself. I might like the workout and stretch I'm getting right now, but that doesn't mean I'm very good at it. I'm man enough to admit that.

I'm also man enough to readily welcome the way Ruby helps to gently correct my mistakes, sometimes with a soft direction, sometimes by exiting out of her own stance and coming over to shift my hips one way or tilt my head another.

It really is amazing how different my body feels once she helps me make those little adjustments.

I also don't mind her hands on me in the slightest.

We continue on for another ten minutes or so before she has us shifting into cooldown positions and lying flat on the mats, making me thankful that I brought us off of the wooden deck and down to the soft, grassy area that leads to the water.

As we lie in what Ruby called Savasana, she asks me to gradually relax every single muscle in my body. We start with toes and ankles then move up the legs. She takes a while to go through the cooldown, a component of exercise I'm prone to move through rather quickly, and I'm shocked to find just how relaxed and mentally calm I feel once we're done, like I could literally melt into the ground.

"So what did you think?" she asks as we roll up our mats.

The smile on her face is tentative, almost like she's worried I hated it and might shove her down the bank and into the water.

"I'm going to be honest," I say, dragging it out a little bit and watching as she bites her lip, waiting for me to spit it out.

Then I return her smile. "I loved it."

"Did you really?" She almost goes up on her tiptoes with excitement, her expression morphing into one I wish I could kiss right off her face.

I nod. "Really."

Ruby does a little hop-skip as we head back to the house, practically radiating joy.

"I might even make it a new part of my workout routine. Normally I swim, and I mix in running here and there, but occasionally adding in a yoga class could be really fun."

"Yay!" she squeals, pulling open the sliding door and stepping into the kitchen. "You should check out the studio I go to when you're back to Boston. The teachers there are amazing."

It's the first time either of us has made reference to the fact that we don't live far from each other back in New England. Sure, it's a nugget of knowledge we both have—that we flew here together and will both wind up back in Beantown in the next few weeks.

But our friendship so far has felt rooted in Cedar Point, like it wouldn't have bloomed past that in-air flirtation if we hadn't been fortunate enough to be staying in the same town.

I'm surprised by how it feels, knowing I like her comment. It takes those little roots and begins to measure them to see if they'll stretch out to grow something along the shores of the east coast, too.

"Good morning." Bellamy's husky hello from where she sits drinking a cup of coffee at the counter has both Ruby and me turning to take her in, in all of her hungover, not-a-morning-person, pajama'd glory.

"Morning!"

Bellamy winces. "I don't know how you're this chipper this early when I would kill to crawl back into bed."

"Why *are* you up this early?"

My sister normally isn't up until at least ten, so to see her down here at—I glance at the clock on the stove—just after eight is unusual.

"I promised Bishop I'd help him and Andy with that stuff at One Stop," she says, yawning and then resting her head on an arm she has splayed across the countertop.

Crossing the kitchen to pour myself another cup of coffee, I let out a snort at the fact that my brother has managed to rope in additional bodies to assist the Marshall men with their buildout.

"Funny. I promised him the same thing."

She groans, rolling her head to hide her face. "Well then what the hell am I doing getting up this early? I could be snuggled in bed right now." She lets out some dramatic fake tears that have Ruby giggling from where she's taken a seat next to her.

"What's happening?"

I set a cup of coffee in front of Ruby, along with a little cup of creamer and a bowl of sugar, before opening the fridge to start pulling out the breakfast ingredients.

"The owner of the grocery store had a heart attack a while back and his son is struggling to finish an expansion they'd started working on."

I chuck a package of bacon onto the counter, followed by a carton of eggs and the last few slices of bread.

"Bishop's helping him and asked us to help, too. I'm such a sucker for the locals," Bellamy says. Then she breaks into fake sobbing again. "I wish I'd said no."

"Speaking of locals," I say, bracing my hands on the counter and glaring at my sister. "Since when are you and Corinne making nice?"

Bells drops the sobbing bit and tries to smile at me. "I'm sorry, okay? She's been around all summer and you *know* shit gets boring around here sometimes. I was desperate for a friend."

"You couldn't have found anybody else? Or, at the very least, not brought her out when you knew I was going to be around?"

My sister groans. "I get it, okay? Besides, after seeing how icky she was last night when you got there, I can certainly confirm that I have no intention of watching her act like that again."

Then she fake gags. So dramatic.

I glance over at Ruby, who is watching us with a soft smile on her face, sipping her coffee and holding her mug in both hands. God, she's adorable.

"But back to the *real* travesty of the day." Bellamy begins to fake sob again. "Doing construction work on a Sunday morning in this heat."

"I can go in your place."

Bellamy's ridiculous faux-wails stop again and she perks up, looking at Ruby like the woman has saved her life.

"Come on," I interject. "Bellamy, don't guilt Ruby into helping in your place."

"I'm not!"

"She's not!"

They turn and look at each other with a laugh.

"What else am I gonna do?" Ruby adds. "Sit out on the porch and read all day?"

"Oh my god that sounds amazing." Bellamy draws out the last word, stretching back out along the counter, likely envisioning curling up on the porch and digging into the next thriller on her Kindle.

"I'm here for another eleven days and I'm all by myself until Ken gets back." Ruby looks at me, almost like she's asking permission. "I'll get bored if all I'm doing is reading and trying to tan my pasty skin."

"And it'll give you guys some more time to hang out," Bellamy offers, a shit-eating smile on her face.

I look her way with an expression that tells her to cut the bullshit. She doesn't give a damn about me spending time with Ruby. She just wants to curl back up in her nest and fall asleep.

"I'm a good helper, I promise."

"Yeah, Boyd, she promises."

I narrow my eyes at Bellamy, my unspoken words clearly having no effect on her as she continues to smile at me. She knows she's won, knows Ruby is going to come with me to One Stop and help with the buildout.

As much as she's able to, anyway. I don't want to make quick assumptions, but Ruby's tiny. It's hard to picture her lugging wood or hoisting beams.

That said, I'm sure she's the type of person to always find a way to make herself useful, maybe in ways one wouldn't entirely expect.

"Alright, Ruby, if you want to gear up and spend your day sweating and doing construction work on your vacation, I'm not going to be the one to stop you."

She gives me a big cheesy grin and does a wiggly little dance on her stool, as if I've given her some amazing gift.

Who knows? Maybe by giving her something to do with her free time and distracting her from the fact that her dad's an asshole, I *am* giving her a gift.

Inviting her along is completely selfless, really.

It isn't about the idea of her dressed in construction gear, maybe one of the sexist things I've ever imagined. And it isn't because the idea of spending the whole day with her sounds like the best plan in the world.

It's because I don't want her to be alone all day. Because she needs to be distracted and have a little fun.

I'm doing this for Ruby, not for me.

Hopefully if I repeat that to myself enough times, I'll eventually believe it's true.

chapter ten
ruby

The town grocery store—One Stop Shop—is a lot smaller than what I pictured when Boyd told me we'd be working at the only grocery in town.

It reminds me more of the bodegas scattered on corners through the city and near my apartment than what I would consider a full-sized store.

It's hard to imagine an entire community relying on this one little place to get all of their food, year-round, but I guess that's what life is like when you live in a small mountain town. You make do with fewer amenities because that's your only choice.

When we round a corner at the back, I see what Boyd meant when he said the guy with the recent heart attack wouldn't be able to help with the expansion. The only thing in place is the concrete foundation.

I kind of assumed the framing would be done and that we'd be helping put up things like drywall and finishing touches, things I can help with. Clearly, I was mistaken, and I'm worried

I'm just going to get in the way.

Hopefully, I can make up for my lack of knowledge with enthusiasm. I'm great at that.

"I'm glad you're here, guys," says a man around the same age as Boyd as we approach. "We are just about to put up the framing, and it would be amazing to have extra hands."

"Put us wherever!" I say, clapping my hands together, my excitement about helping this family probably overwhelming to him since he has no idea who I am.

When he looks at me, I see that little bit of charm pop out that men usually put on when they talk to me.

I'm not an idiot. I know I'm nice-looking. That's why my mom and I have had the sex conversation so many times. We both know there are plenty of guys who want what I'm putting out into the world.

"I'm Andy," he says, taking off a glove and sticking his hand out for me to shake. "I know we haven't met before—I would have remembered a face like yours."

I blush and choke back a laugh, unable to help my reaction to his flirtation. "I'm Ruby."

"And what brings you by today?"

I lift a shoulder, realizing I don't really know what to say. Am I here to hang out with Boyd? Am I here to help just because? How do I explain who I am? Am I Ken's daughter? Boyd's friend? *Are* we just friends?

Ultimately, I settle on a vague version of the truth.

"Just vacationing in town and thought I'd tag along with Boyd, here, to help. If you need me, that is."

"Oh, without a doubt, Ruby. We can—"

"Is Bishop here?" Boyd's voice cuts into whatever else Andy was going to say, his tone gruff enough that I turn to look at his face.

He's looking at Andy like...well, like Andy punched him in the face or something. Where did this irritation come from? Aren't they friends? Yes, he said that during the car ride over, said he and Andy were really good friends from way back in kindergarten when some "little shit" made fun of his ears.

I don't see anything wrong with his ears, though he probably grew into them as he got older.

"Yeah, he's over helping Greg with the unload."

Boyd nods his head and stalks off in search of his brother, leaving me wondering if I'm supposed to follow in his wake or stay here with Andy.

My eyes follow Boyd until it's clear he doesn't plan to give me any instructions, then I turn back to look at Andy. I'm a little surprised to find a smile on his face.

"Interesting."

"What's interesting?"

Andy shrugs a shoulder then waves for me to follow him. "Boyd getting jealous. I don't think I've ever seen that before."

I almost laugh, replaying the interaction in my mind, wondering what he could have been jealous of. I'm here with Boyd, right?

"Jealous of what?"

Andy shrugs again, looking back at me. "Me, most likely. We're friends, but we also have a bit of history when it comes to women—though that's the first time I've seen a look quite like that," he says with a chuckle.

I look in the direction Boyd went one more time, wishing I could reassure him, but I don't know what I'd reassure him of. That I'm here with him? That I'm not interested in this Andy guy? That he doesn't need to get grouchy just because someone flirts with me?

All those things feel much bigger than the casual kind of thing we seem to have going on, so I decide to let the thoughts drift away, knowing I can always revisit them later. Instead, I refocus my mind on the task in front of me.

I assumed I'd be relegated to some menial bullshit task like handing nails to someone with a hammer or passing out waters, but Andy blows my mind when he has me working alongside the small group of men as they lift up the first walls to do what they're calling rough framing.

As the day progresses, I spend my time holding walls in place with Bishop and another guy named Greg, helping to hoist up heavy beams and lugging newly cut wood from the saw to the concrete slab where the exterior walls are being constructed.

I've never done such intense manual labor before, most of my sweat equity coming from yoga, gardening, or cleaning, but it feels amazing.

I'm thankful that Bellamy let me borrow a pair of boots and that Boyd stopped by my house so I could change first; otherwise I would have been way out of my depth in comfy sneakers and yoga pants.

When we take a break for lunch, I realize I've hardly talked to Boyd at all, most of my attention lasered in on not being the one girl on site who screws something up.

"Ham and cheese," he says, passing a sub sandwich my way once we finish for the day around lunch time.

"Thanks!" I say, beaming at him.

He grins, though something seems slightly off about it.

"You look like you're having fun."

I nod, taking a much-needed sip from my water bottle before answering.

"A blast. I actually helped. The last time I offered to help with something like this, I was stuck off to the side at a table checking tools in and out."

Then I point at the unfinished structure, the exterior frame in place though still missing a roof, which is what Andy's roofer friend will begin working on this afternoon.

"Look at that bitch! I helped with that!"

This time, when Boyd smiles at me, it feels more genuine, and I revel in his attention.

It's weird realizing we haven't talked in only a few hours and I already started to miss his eyes on me. That look of his has become familiar and wanted in such a short period of time.

"Thanks so much for your help, guys," Andy says, walking over to where Boyd and I are seated on a shaded set of steps off the back of the original One Stop structure. "Seriously, I never imagined all the walls going up in one morning."

"I had a blast," I say before taking a massive bite of my sandwich.

"If you need more hands with any of the next steps, count Bishop and me in again," Boyd says.

"What if I want Ruby to help?"

I freeze, mid-chew, the food in my mouth keeping me from saying anything in response, though I'm not sure what I'd say anyway.

Why would he want *me* to help again?

When I look from Andy, who has a smile on his face, to Boyd, who is glaring at Andy with that same look from earlier, I realize this is something else entirely.

I frown.

Andy's comment about him and Boyd having history rings through my mind, and my frown deepens.

I don't like feeling like Andy is using me to make Boyd jealous, and now that I'm taking the time to look, it seems like that's exactly what's going on.

Maybe I'm not the fastest mind in the mix, standing next to a business owner and an MIT grad, but I'm not stupid.

"I don't like that you're talking about me like I'm not here," I say, pulling Andy's attention away from Boyd and over to where I'm glaring at him. "Or how you're intentionally baiting someone you're supposed to be friends with, a guy who took hours out of his vacation and family time to help you do backbreaking work."

Immediately, Andy's expression morphs into one of contrition. I don't know him well enough to be certain of whether or not it's genuine, but I also know it doesn't really matter.

Andy isn't really my concern. Boyd, though…he has quickly become someone I want to spend my time with, and the last thing I want to do is make him think I'm playing some sort of game.

Andy lets out an uncomfortable laugh and palms the back of his neck, the hat on his head shading his face as he looks off to the side.

"You're right." Then he looks back at Boyd. "Sometimes I forget we're not in high school anymore."

Something unspoken passes between them before they shake hands and Andy wanders off to do something construction-y.

When I look up at Boyd, I find his eyes on mine, and they're scorching, though laced with something that looks like humor as well.

What's that called?

Humorlust? Like wanderlust but funny? I don't know if that's a thing, but it should be.

We don't say anything else, each of us finishing up our sandwiches and waters before saying our goodbyes and heading over to where Hank is parked along the side of the road.

He opens my door for me, and I hop in, pausing with my seatbelt when I realize he isn't moving to close the door.

Before I even know what's happening, he's stepped forward and slipped a hand around the back of my neck, pulling me forward so he can plant a kiss on my lips.

It's chaste. Soft. So delicious I wonder if I might be dehydrated from all that time in the sun because damn if I don't feel a little dizzy when he pulls back and looks at me

I wonder what he sees as I sit here, dirt and sweat covering so much of me, my body emitting that smell that comes along with too much time in the hot sun.

Whatever it is, it must work for him, because he places his lips back against mine for another kiss. And then another and another, first sucking on my top lip and then the bottom.

I can feel his kisses in my toes, along every single inch of skin he's touching with his work-roughened hands, in the warm space between my legs.

When he pulls back and looks at me again, I feel a thrilling little shiver race along my spine as I see how heated his eyes are.

"Let's get you home," he says, finally moving back and closing my door, rounding the front to the driver's side.

The ride back to the guesthouse is a loud mess of silence. All I can hear is the sound of his breaths and the beating of my heart in my ears.

When was the last time I was kissed like that?

Like it was just as much simple as it was spectacular?

Like it was the only thing that mattered?

If it's ever happened before, I certainly can't pinpoint when it was, none of the boys I've kissed before popping into my mind.

"We're here."

Boyd's voice cuts through my internal musings, and I look out the window to see that we have, indeed, pulled up in front of Ken's house.

"Thanks for your help today. It made a big difference."

I blush and wave a hand at him. "I hardly did anything."

"You did, though. You really were helpful, and I know it meant a lot to Andy to have us there."

I grin at him, wishing I could sit and stare at him for a little longer instead of going back into the guesthouse where I'll be all alone.

Sure, I need to shower, but that only takes 15 minutes. If Boyd's dropping me off now, I probably won't see him until later tonight when we go to Forks for the bonfire.

I still don't know what a Forks is, but I figure it will be more fun if I'm surprised later.

"Bellamy said she was commandeering my afternoon," I say, referring to a text I received from her while we were at One Stop letting me know she'd be coming over around 4. "But I'm assuming I'll see you at the bonfire tonight?"

He flashes me a grin that has that same feeling rushing through me and makes me wish, not for the first time, that I could just drag him into my little house and have my way with him.

"You will *definitely* be seeing me tonight," he says.

I slip out of the truck and give him a wave before walking down the path to my door.

And if I happen to sway my hips a little bit more in the hopes that Boyd's watching?

Well, that'll be our little secret.

"Bitch, this place is *gorgeous*."

Bellamy slips off her shoes and wanders around, taking a look at everything she can see, even poking her head in the bathroom before she looks at me with wide eyes.

"I haven't seen it since Linda redid everything a few years ago. It's amazing. They must rent this place out for a fortune."

I swirl my sparkling water and lime in a glass but refrain from saying anything, unsure if Bellamy and Linda are friends, or how well she knows Ken.

I might have a tendency to ramble, but I have made enough snafus in my life to know when to keep my mouth shut.

"It looks like something out of a magazine," I say. "My favorite part is the clawfoot tub, though I haven't used it yet."

"Soaking in that thing with a glass of wine and a good book? Ohmygod girl…you need to get on that *immediately*."

Bellamy yanks the cork from her bottle of wine then carries it and a single glass with her out to the guesthouse porch that looks out to the lake. And to the Mitchell house.

I can't help but wonder what Boyd's doing, if he's over there eating dinner or getting ready for the bonfire, or maybe even looking out the window over here to see what *I'm* doing?

"So you don't drink?" she asks as we each take a seat in the surprisingly comfortable Adirondack chairs.

"Not really. It makes me pretty tired. Some people drink and become the life of the party, but it just makes me want to curl up and take a nap."

Bellamy laughs and pours the merlot into her glass, filling it a little more than halfway.

"It's why I drink sparkling waters and juices when I'm out. It looks like a cocktail, so nobody bothers me about it."

She bobs her head and swirls her wine around with the grace of someone who has been drinking wine for a long time. Then she takes a long sip, letting out a low hum of enjoyment before settling fully into her chair, her glass hanging elegantly from her fingers as she focuses her attention on me.

"My brother is absolutely bananas about you."

The skin on the side of my neck heats up at her words. Even though I know he's interested, hearing it from someone else based on their own observations is a different thing altogether.

"You think so?"

She nods. "Absolutely. I've never seen my brother the way he is with you, like he can't get enough. How long have you known each other? 24 hours?"

"I think 36, but that's splitting hairs."

"He really likes you, and in that very grown-up way my college ass still hasn't ever found."

At that, I laugh.

"At my age, the boys don't want to take you out for drinks to meet the family. They want to shuffle you around and screw you behind the bar where nobody can see."

There's an edge to her words that I'm not expecting, but when I glance over, she still has that same pleasant expression.

"What was he like with Corinne?" I ask, unable to keep myself from asking.

For a second, I worry I'm being too nosy, but Bellamy doesn't seem to have any problems sharing.

"Corinne is not even in the same league as you—let me just start off with that," she says, taking another sip of her wine before setting it on the side table and adjusting to get more comfortable in her chair.

"How do you mean?"

"Well, they dated when they were teenagers. You don't really know what you want when you're that young, and I've heard from more than one person that the two of them only stayed together as long as they did because Boyd didn't want to hurt her feelings. He thought it would just be easier to have a clean break when he left for college."

My nose wrinkles, picturing a young Boyd, fresh off of a breakup and heading off to college. I think of all the sexy co-eds who must have been just waiting for him to have a good time with.

"Obviously, I'm a little younger than my brother so I don't know everything that happened except for what I've been told over the years, but Corinne and I have been spending a lot of time together this summer, and she is definitely not over him." She pauses and then rephrases. "Well, according to her."

I laugh. "You think she's wrong? Wouldn't she be the best person to know how she feels?"

Bellamy waves a hand, like she's swatting something away. "Corinne is just feeling lost and focusing her attention on the one that got away. It's easy to romanticize something from over a decade ago when you were probably a completely different person. Living it in real life is another thing altogether."

I nod, surprised by the wisdom of her observation. Bellamy might be young as a 21-year-old going into her senior year of college, but she talks about love and life as if she's been through quite a bit. I'm a firm believer that if you're going to take someone's advice, it should be based on scars from battle, not just hypothetical situations and possibilities.

"You have nothing to worry about—that's what I'm trying to get at," she finally says. "Boyd is into you. If you're one of those girls who struggles with exes or jealousy, don't waste your chips on Corinne."

I nod, feeling thankful that Bellamy is so forthcoming. It's helped soothe some of my irritation toward Corinne from last night, as well as a little bit of residual nerves that maybe something really *is* going on between her and Boyd.

Now, I feel like I can be fully excited about spending time with him at the bonfire tonight. Maybe he'll open up a bit and I can get a better understanding of what makes him tick.

I'm realizing with belated certainty just how much I want to know all the little pieces that make Boyd the man he is.

Hopefully, under the moonlit sky and next to the undulating flames of a fire, I'll be able to gather the courage to invite him over tonight.

I would be lying to myself if I didn't acknowledge the way he makes me feel, like I'm a bonfire in my own right, my fires stoked and fueled and steadily building, like just the right moment with Boyd might set everything ablaze.

I have to be careful, though, because even the headiest of bonfires have a tipping point where things can go one of two ways.

There's a moment when there's a risk of the fire burning too hot or being extinguished completely.

chapter eleven
boyd

It was the seniors a few years before me who began the tradition of Sunday-night bonfires at Forks during the summer. I don't know exactly what it was that drove that specific custom, why Sunday evenings and why never during the school year.

All I knew as a sophomore in high school was that going out to have a few drinks at one of the campgrounds with my new girlfriend sounded like the best time I could ever imagine.

Corinne and I had been dating for a few months during that first summer when Peter Gillis and his buddies started rounding up all the cool kids, inviting us to the most epic party we could imagine.

I lost my virginity to Corinne in the back of her dad's truck at one of those bonfires. It was clumsy and awkward and I'm pretty sure I wasn't very good at anything I was doing. Eventually it got better, but all throughout our time dating, we liked to drive out to Forks together and recreate that night, both of us pretending it was our first time so we could get a do-over.

It took me a long time to understand why we used to do that, why we couldn't seem to move on from that first sexual experience. It finally occurred to me when I was in my twenties that we kept trying to make it better because we wanted so desperately for *something* between us to make sense.

We didn't like the same things. We hardly ever had conversations about anything that mattered. We pretty much dated because she liked me and I thought she was pretty and that should have been enough at sixteen years old.

So we kept going back to the thing that *should* have made us feel inextricably connected to each other—being each other's firsts—and trying to recreate some sort of spark or connection that just never seemed to pop up between us.

Then when it was time for me to leave for college, I broke up with her. All I could picture was her being jealous of other girls, us arguing on the phone, coming home for the summer and being back in that *same* relationship again. The idea of doing long-distance with Corinne created visions of an endless cycle of all the horrible things to come, and I didn't have it in me to even try.

It's one of the reasons I've never really tried to have another relationship, instead choosing to enjoy the casual sex that's so common as a college student, as a new professional, and then as a bachelor.

It didn't ever occur to me that things didn't work in that relationship because things weren't right between *me and Corinne*. I just assumed it meant relationships weren't for me, thought it would be the same with *any* woman, so why bother? Why not just enjoy the one part that was almost always great?

Sex.

I preferred the somewhat transparent component to casual

sex. Meeting women on hookup apps and in bars meant they were usually interested in the same thing I was: a good time. There weren't hidden emotions or secret feelings or any sort of chance that either of us could be in it for anything other than getting off and having a little fun while we did it.

Sure, there were a few women in there who were interesting enough to hold my attention for a bit longer than one night, but those fizzled out fairly quickly once the word *more* came into play.

Now, in my late twenties, my mindset is starting to shift away from that place it's been locked up in for so long. It's like a layer of grime and filth that was caked on something beautiful for a long time has finally been wiped away, revealing something completely different than what I thought it would be.

And that beautiful thing is Ruby.

Ruby Rae Roberts and her ridiculous laugh and silly ramblings and smile that makes me unable to do anything but smile back.

She's something else, and watching her walk toward me across the campground, the red and orange flames lighting up one side of her face, I know without a shadow of a doubt that the last thing I want with her is casual.

Is a single day too soon to realize something like that?

Maybe.

Maybe I'll fuck this all up by allowing my emotions to grow roots too quickly.

Or maybe I won't.

And *that* is the key difference between Ruby and the only other serious relationship I've had: I'm willing to accept that there might be something shitty in the future, that things with Ruby might not end up working out. We might try to take this back to Boston and eventually watch it collapse into a rubbish heap of misery.

I'm willing to accept those things as a possibility, and yet I'm still wanting to move forward anyway, still want to get to know her anyway. Because the idea of not getting that, not understanding her at her most base level, not sharing with her the things I didn't even know I wanted to share…that sounds far more horrible than any kind of breakup could ever be.

"Fancy seeing you here," Ruby says as she hops up next to me on the back of my lowered tailgate, bumping me with her shoulder.

"Fancy indeed," I reply, calling back to our meeting in front of Ken's when I picked her up yesterday.

Bellamy gives me a little wave then walks straight past me, heading over to a group of her old high school friends parked a few vehicles away.

"So what is this place?" Ruby asks, her eyes searching the area, though it's too dark for her to really see anything that would tell her where she is.

"Smith Campground."

"It's just a campground?"

I nod. "It's a closed campground, though, has been for about fifteen years, and the park service hasn't ever come through to do the repairs needed to get it back in working order. So, the hooligans have taken it over."

"Why is it called Forks?"

"Ah, local nickname. It's a small-town thing. We nickname everything so when we're talking about spots with friends and tourists overhear us, we don't actually give anything away."

"So sneaky," she jokes. "Does everything really have a nickname?"

"Not everything, but a lot of places, yes."

"Will you tell them to me? Even though I'm a tourist?"

I pretend to mull it over for a second. "I'll tell you, but you should know that failure to keep these secrets will result in a swift and untimely death."

Ruby bites her lip to keep from laughing then marks an X across her heart like she did last night with Bishop.

"Well, the tourist bar is called Dock 7, but we call it Lucky's."

She tilts her head to the side and thinks about it for a second. "Because locals get lucky there?"

I hold up my beer bottle as if to cheers her. "Bingo."

"Does the grocery store have a nickname?"

I shake my head. "Nah. Everyone needs groceries, so there's no fun in giving that spot a secret name."

Ruby nods.

"Smith Campground is Forks," I continue, "because it's at the spot with the fork in the road, between the lake and the exit out of town. The resort on the south bank has a road behind it that leads up to a lookout over the water, and we call that Easy Street, because that's where a lot of high schoolers drive to when they want to hook up."

"Really?" she says, her tone conveying her skepticism. "I would have assumed bonfire nights would be a better choice. Drinks, music, a glowing fire." She shrugs a shoulder. "Sounds like the best place to hook up to me."

Even though the light from the bonfire is glowing with varying hues of red, I can still see the flush that creeps from her cheeks down through her neck.

"I…I mean…like, for high school kids, you know?" She bumbles her words and puts a hand over her face.

"*Just* high school kids?" I ask, knowing I'm poking at her

when she's embarrassed but not wanting to let this slide.

The woman has teased me more than enough times for me to make sure I return the favor.

She narrows her eyes and glares at me, her lips pouted and her body leaning toward mine.

"I thought you didn't like to be teased."

I take advantage of her position and shift my own body closer to hers.

"I don't like to *be* teased, but I *love* teasing you."

"Well that's not very sportsmanlike."

"I can play fair when the occasion calls for it."

"And now isn't a time to play fair?"

I shake my head, my eyes dipping to her lips, enjoying the little shiver that runs through her body at my attention.

"When it comes to you, Ruby Rae Roberts, the *last* thing I want to do is play fair."

"And why is that?" she asks, her words coming out in a little bit of a whisper.

I lean in farther, until my mouth is right by her ear. "Because I'd much rather play dirty."

Ruby lets out a long, tortured breath as I pull back, our faces inches from each other. My eyes zero in on her lips again, the ones she's licked a few times since we've been sitting together.

They drive me crazy. Plump and full and soft.

That kiss earlier today was more than I imagined and yet not nearly enough. I didn't plan on kissing her since we were both sweaty and gross and covered with dirt, but then I couldn't help it. Couldn't imagine another moment going by without connecting myself to her in some kind of tangible way, and holy hell was it a thing of beauty.

It might have been the most innocent kiss I've had in over a decade, but it still lit a fire inside of me that I know only Ruby will be able to manage.

I have that same feeling now, our faces close, our breaths intermingling in the dry mountain air. My nose is touching hers, and if I just shift a little bit closer...

She closes her eyes, all but begging me to kiss her.

"Well, well, well, what do we have here?"

I close my eyes in irritation and let a long, controlled breath out of my nose before I pull back and take a look at the woman standing in front of us.

With her back to the fire, I might not have noticed her here, but I'd know that voice anywhere. And it's the last one I want to hear.

"Corinne," I say, bobbing my head in greeting then glancing at the women standing next to her. "Jen, Keegan. Good to see you both."

That's a straight lie. Jen has always been an annoying pain in my side, and Keegan cheated on a friend of mine during our senior year. The only person I want to see *less* than them is the one who brought them over to talk to me.

"Judy, right?" Corinne says, looking Ruby up and down with an attitude she should have left back at Cedar Point High.

"Ruby, actually." She gives Corinne a surprisingly friendly attitude considering their very short, very awkward encounter yesterday at The Mitch. "But you remember my name. You're just pretending not to because you want to make me feel small."

Corinne's face freezes. I almost want to let out a small laugh at the way Ruby is handling herself, but I manage to hold it in—barely.

"Whatever," she finally says. "I didn't come over here to talk to you anyway."

"Then why did you come over here, Corinne?" I say, my tone curt. "You can probably tell that I'm busy."

Her eyes narrow for a split second before she puts on a smile. "I came over to say hello, of course. I've missed you since you've been away, and I was hoping we could get together soon." Then she lowers her voice. "You know…catch up?"

I purse my lips, mulling over what I should say to her that isn't mean but still conveys that I have no intentions of *catching up*, especially when she's over here trying to stir up trouble.

"Can I ask you a question?"

The sound of Ruby's voice is almost jarring, except for the fact that I love the way it sounds. I doubt the same is true for Corinne, though, because she and her two friends turn their eyes to look at Ruby almost in unison. She's sitting next to me in a pair of jeans and a loose sweater with almost no makeup, and the differences between the two women couldn't be more obvious.

Corinne crosses her arms. "What?"

"I'm just wondering what exactly your goal is. With Boyd, I mean," she says, gesturing to me. "I've been wondering since yesterday, when you watched him walk in with a girl on his arm and you tried to give him an oddly sexual hug, and I'm wondering now as you pretend not to remember my name and hint at giving him sexual favors later. I'm just curious what your end goal is."

Ruby glances over at me then back at Corinne.

"Boyd and I aren't dating. We met yesterday. You have a lot more history with him than I do, and honestly it seems like you *should* probably get together to catch up since you appear to be on very different pages. But, like I said, I'm just wondering what your aim is in trying to make me feel uncomfortable. It would seem, to me at least, like you want me to assume you have something going on with Boyd so I'll leave and you can try to get back together with him. Correct me if I'm wrong."

It's work for me to keep my mouth from hanging open, but I do. I can't say the same for Corinne, though. She looks like she could catch a whole lotta flies with that mouth of hers and the way she's gaping at Ruby.

There's a long silence as Ruby waits for Corinne to respond, and the longer it goes on, the more I can see Corinne scrambling for something to say.

Ultimately, she ignores Ruby and looks at me.

"This is the kind of girl you're into now?" she asks, one lip in a kind of snarl.

"You bet your ass."

It's out of my mouth in a second, before I can even think about the words, a knee-jerk reaction.

Because I'm abso*lutely* into Ruby. The type of woman she is, the way she handles herself—all of it.

Even the way she handled Corinne.

I think most girls would have either sat next to me and stayed silent or allowed Corinne's catty attitude to lure them into some sort of chick fight.

But not Ruby. She stated a truth about the way Corinne is talking to her in a manner that completely laid Corinne out on the mat without even really having to throw any punches.

She introduced a sweeping kick into boxing and knocked Corinne's legs out from underneath her in record time.

It was amazing.

Corinne rolls her eyes and huffs out a "*Bitch*" before she and her two minions storm off to another part of the bonfire.

I can only hope Ruby's words have done enough to keep her away from me for the rest of my trip, though if I know Corinne at all, I don't think I'll be so lucky.

Next time I see her—though hopefully there isn't a next time—I'll be sure to let her know I don't appreciate her attitude or thinly veiled agenda.

But right now, all I can focus on is the woman sitting next to me.

"Sorry if that was too much," she says, looking at me with a twinkle in her eyes that says she's not the least bit sorry. "But you know how you always look back on conversations you have with people and you're like, dammit, I could have said *that* and it would have been perfect and totally made them regret being a bitch? I've had to deal with so many people in life who want to talk down to me or around me or about me like I'm not there. They think they're so sly, making other people feel bad or uncomfortable or unwanted. I've always wished I could force them to acknowledge how bitchy they're being without being a bitch myself, and tonight the words just came to me. I'm sorry if I overstepped or if I shouldn't have said it, but oh my gosh it felt so amazing to just—"

I can't wait any longer for her to finish her monologue. Instead of allowing her to continue explaining to me why she handed Corinne her own ass in spectacular fashion, I press my lips against hers, slipping my hand into her hair behind her neck so I can hold her against me.

Because watching her ramble was making me want her even more. I like just about everything that comes out of Ruby's mouth, including the sass, and I couldn't let another minute go by without tasting the place all her words come from.

Unlike the chaste kiss in my truck earlier, both of us open our mouths, tongues seeking, exploring. Warmth and wetness and a hint of cinnamon explode on my tongue as I kiss her exactly the way I've been wanting to since the minute she smiled at me in the terminal at Boston Logan.

Her hand circles my wrist, and I worry she's going to pull me away. Instead she squeezes, just a single pulse, but it communicates to me that she doesn't want me to stop, further confirmed by the tiny moan I hear right before she nibbles on my bottom lip.

She makes me want to throw her down on the bed of my truck right here.

But even that thought calls back the nights I came to the bonfire with Corinne. I never cared if anyone knew what we were doing, whether or not anyone could see us as we parked off to the side.

Just the idea of someone seeing Ruby in anything less than what she has on now, though…it makes my blood boil, a fierce protector threatening to break free from chains I didn't know existed.

So instead of doing what my baser instincts might have directed me to do in my youth, I pull back, enjoying the way her mouth follows me to steal another kiss.

"Ruby," I say, lifting my hands so they're both on her face, calling her eyes up to mine instead of where they're focused on my lips.

When she looks at me, I smile. That's all I want to do every time her eyes meet mine.

"You ready to go?"

It takes her a minute to understand what I'm saying, but I see the heat blazing in her eyes when she nods.

We both hop off the bed of the truck and hustle to climb inside the cab.

"See you in the morning, Boyd!" someone calls out to me as

I'm scrambling to get my key into the ignition.

The sound of my engine muffles a few laughs coming from the group of guys who I know are just some old friends trying to give me a hard time.

But that lustful energy bubbling up inside of me starts to simmer and cool as we drive back to Ruby's guesthouse.

It only takes us about ten minutes to get back to the other side of the lake, the late hour making the single-lane drive a breeze, but it's more than enough time for my mindset to shift.

Ruby spends the ride with one foot up on the dash and the window down, looking out at where the moonlight reflects off the lake, a smile on her face.

God, she's beautiful.

As we pull up in front of Ken's, I park and turn off the engine, wondering what I should say to communicate to her the thoughts on my mind.

Before I have a chance to say anything, she's sliding across the bench seat and straddling me where I sit.

Her warm body presses against mine and her lips follow, sucking the breath straight out of my lungs. It's everything I could imagine, her curves soft beneath my hands as I grip her hips and lick deeper into her mouth.

Ruby is the sexiest woman I've ever had the pleasure of having in my arms, and as she shifts her hips and grinds against me, I worry I'm going to embarrass myself by coming in my jeans right here.

Her fingers are in my hair, the slight scratch against my scalp making me groan as shivers ripple beneath my skin.

"Boyd," she whispers, biting my lip just a little bit, "do you want to come inside?"

I want to—*badly*. I seriously consider it as her mouth drops to suck at the skin on my neck, her hips shifting back and forth in maddening little circles that have me wanting to crawl out of my skin.

But I hear the call-out from the bonfire again. I know people will see Hank parked outside the guesthouse. Some sort of sleazy hookup on the mouths of Cedar Point residents isn't what I want to happen between the two of us.

So, as much as I know I'm going to regret this later as I lie in bed with a massive hard-on and a wish that I was wrapped around Ruby's body in her bed, I say the thing I know I *should* say instead of what I *want* to say.

"I wish I could, but I have to get up early to pick up Busy from the airport tomorrow morning."

Ruby pulls back slightly, confusion marking her eyes with something that looks markedly like rejection.

"Can I take a raincheck for another night?" I ask, hoping that by mentioning another evening together, she doesn't feel like I've shut her down completely.

I watch as she swallows and then shifts off of me with a smile that doesn't look entirely sincere.

"Sure."

"I really do wish I could come in," I tell her. "But there's no rush, right?"

She nods then opens her door and slides out. I follow, making sure to take her hand in mine as we walk the little path down to the guesthouse.

She unlocks the door and then pauses. "I didn't upset you with what I said earlier?" she asks, her eyes flitting up to mine. "To Corinne?"

Barking out a laugh, I shake my head. "Not in the slightest. I thought that was…brilliant, actually. It's why I needed to kiss you so bad once she finally walked away."

Ruby's expression eases slightly, but I can still tell she's a little confused by my heat earlier and the shutdown now that I've brought her home.

My mother told me once that women are conditioned to believe men only want one thing from them, so it makes sense that my refusal of Ruby's offer tonight would make her feel less certain of my interest.

"I meant it when I said I wish I could come in," I say, my voice gruff as I shift our bodies so that Ruby's backed up against her door.

"Then why don't you?" she whispers, the moonlight glinting in her eyes, and damn I could drown in those baby blues.

"The real reason?" I ask, and she nods.

I pause, hoping I'm able to pull up the right words to make sure she walks inside tonight knowing she'll see me tomorrow, knowing I'll still want her tomorrow.

"I don't want people to see my truck on the road and talk. I don't want to hook up with you on a night when we were catcalled on the way out of the bonfire. We don't have to jump straight into bed, right?"

Ruby nods, her face flushed.

I can tell I'm not convincing her, so I lean in close and press my lips to her forehead, trying to show her the tender affection that feels so new to me.

"Besides," I add, my voice dipping low, "once we do crawl into bed together, I don't want to have to leave in the middle of the night. I don't want to be rushed."

I take a single finger and trace it down her neck and along her collarbone, feeling Ruby's body shiver beneath me, watching the goose bumps as they race across her skin.

"I want to take my time with you," I whisper into her ear.

Ruby takes a deep breath then releases it, long and slow. "Damn," she says.

I nod, grinning. "Damn is right."

And then I kiss her again, just to drive the point home.

chapter twelve
ruby

When I wake up Monday morning, I find a text on my phone from Boyd.

Boyd: My family is going to do a brunch for our family and some neighbors if you want to come. It starts at around 10.
Boyd: I'd love for you to join. If you want to

I smile and stuff my face back into my pillow, enjoying the simplicity of Boyd's words and the major effect they seem to have on me.

Maybe it's just because Boyd is a bit older than the guys I normally date, or maybe he's just a little more of a straightfor-ward person; either way, I love that he doesn't play games.

When I was in high school, guys seemed to want to bounce from girl to girl, whichever one was going to put out or suck them off or make them feel like a peacock as they strutted through parties or school dances with someone on their arm.

After I graduated, I assumed the world would be different, assumed *men* would be different, but they just seemed to be the same, only with a little more money and a lot more freedom.

The only guy I ever really found worth my time was Evan, my one long-term relationship and the man who ended up hurting me more than anyone else.

We met through a friend of mine, a girl I'd known since elementary school, at one of the bars I was hopping through on my 21st birthday. He bought me a shot and slipped me his number, telling me he wanted to take me out for brunch the following morning to help me get over my inevitable hangover.

I remember thinking that was the most charming thing I'd ever heard, and I hardly had any drinks that night, not wanting to get messed up only to feel too shitty the following day and be unable to go out with him.

I fell hard for the college man who was so smart and gave me so much attention and made me feel like I was *so* important to him.

And then, at some point, things changed.

My rambling mouth was no longer cute, but rather an embarrassment or a waste of time, my quirky personality a bore. When Evan started making me feel like I was the one thing I couldn't bear to be—an inconvenience in his life—I pulled the plug.

Fiona told me it was for the best since I dated him for over a year and he wasn't able to get me over the tipping point in bed, but I try not to dwell on that part. It doesn't feel fair to focus on something neither of us could seem to control.

His attitude, though? His slow shift into a man who treated me with disdain instead of adoration?

That he had complete control over. And so did I.

I decided to never give a man that kind of power again.

I swore off anything serious, knowing the longer a man is in my life, the more chance he has of letting me down or leaving me behind.

Instead, I focus on work, on spending time outside, on going out with friends or hanging with my mom.

I date, sure. That beginning part is always so magical. The sexual tension, the flirtation, the dreaminess and curiosity. I might not have rules about sex, but I do have a few rules about dating.

I have to be able to count the total number of dates on one hand (i.e. no more than 5 dinners or movies or hikes or picnics or whatever things he comes up with). The conversation topics have to stay light and flirtatious, and definitely no talk of the future unless it's individually.

Maybe I'm too rigid about it, but why should I allow anything outside of those rules when the only time a guy really treats you right is in the beginning? Flowers, romance. Opening doors and sexy kisses. Staring at you across the dinner table at a restaurant, their attention solely on your face as you talk.

Those things fade. Men don't know how to be selfless over the long haul. Eventually, they want their life back, their freedom.

They don't want to be faced with having to care about a woman's feelings, her wants, her needs, especially when those things directly contradict their own.

Ken did it to my mom, Evan did it to me, and countless other men have backed out on women, just proving my point.

I'd rather keep it casual and loose and fun and then have us each happily move on to the next person. No harm, no foul. No hurt feelings or expectations unmet.

Which is why Boyd scares me a little bit.

This twelve-day fling—or whatever it is—certainly feels a lot less flingish than I intended for it to be. We've already broken one of my rules, each of us talking about things that are much deeper than I normally go.

I'm well on my way to breaking the other two as well, imagining the fun things we can do together while I'm in town, which would constitute way more than five dates, and thinking about ways we can make it work for real back in Boston, which is absolutely a focus on the future.

I'd continue doing massage and he'd work for his company, and the two of us would enjoy our evenings and weekends together exploring the city or going on road trips. Maybe I could travel with him for work, and maybe he'll join my yoga studio.

Snuggling farther into my pillow, I give in to the fantasy for just a few minutes, of a life with a man like Boyd.

No.

Not a man *like* Boyd.

Actual Boyd.

Boyd Mitchell, the endlessly sweet, family-focused, friend-helping, secret softy and yoga convert who makes me laugh and smile and sizzle in my boots in equal measure.

He makes me feel…different. New things I didn't realize I was capable of. Emotions that are much bigger than I even felt with Evan back at the beginning.

It's a beautiful image, the two of us, and I wish with everything inside of my soul that I could give in to it and believe it's something we could make real.

I guess that's the trouble with wanting something you know you can't have.

Because even if we *could* make it real, I know how things

would eventually go. The relationship would sour, grow cold. We'd grow apart, me and my verbose curiosities never truly meshing with his introverted gruffness.

He'd be the stoic man who moved on, and I'd be left behind to pick up the pieces.

When it finally rolls around to brunch time, I leave my rental car parked outside of Ken's, opting to walk the road around the bend to the Mitchell house.

When I get there and see dozens of cars filling the drive, I know I made the right choice. I wouldn't have been able to find somewhere to park anyway.

I knock on the large, dark blue door with the white trim, admiring the summery wreath hanging in the center. I hear people and movement on the other side, but the door stays closed.

Maybe I should just…go in?

I rock from foot to foot, ultimately taking a deep breath and pushing the door open.

Poking my head through, I see crowds of people outside on the deck facing the lake and a few handfuls spilled through the center of the home.

Once I accept that it should be okay for me to walk in, I quickly close the door behind me and head for the outside, hoping I'll be able to find Boyd quickly, or at least someone I've met already.

"What are *you* doing here?"

My head turns at the sharp question, my eyes widening when I see the last person I would expect to be here—although they *are* neighbors.

Linda walks over to me, her surprise at seeing me etched in almost every frown line on her face.

Her expression demands an explanation, but my own surprise at seeing her has me wanting to retreat inside of myself, my normally extroverted persona identifying Linda as a real threat and scrambling to hide.

If only this were one of those moments when I was able to find just the right thing to say.

"I…well…um…" I stumble over my words, unable to settle on anything solid.

"Oh, Ruby! There you are."

The sweet voice of Patty Mitchell behind Linda helps ease my discomfort significantly, but I probably still look flustered as I try to give Mrs. Mitchell a smile.

"I'd wondered when you would get here, especially when Linda showed up without you."

The smile on her face looks genuine and welcoming, but my eyes flit to Linda's briefly. Hers have remained narrowed, but the loathing rolling off her body has dropped a notch or two.

"Oh, I just…thought I'd walk over."

"Well, we just set out all the food, so come on in. Boyd's helping his dad with something boat-related that I do *not* understand"—she laughs—"but he should be back soon."

Patty waves a hand out to encourage me to head outside before scurrying off, likely to handle more hostess duties.

Linda stays standing next to me, her arms crossed, and it takes everything in me not to skitter away from her. But she's Ken's wife, and even though she clearly hates me for whatever reason, I'm not trying to get into a war with her.

"How are you, Linda?" I ask, once Boyd's mom is out of earshot.

Her eyes scan up and down, like she's expecting me to be covered in dirt or fleas or something. I don't know what she's expecting, really.

"Fine."

And then she turns and stalks off in the same direction Patty went, leaving me to stand alone in the entry.

I haven't interacted with Linda since my arrival on Saturday. She made it pretty clear that she didn't want to talk to me, and that she didn't want me talking to her kids, either.

Even though they're my little brothers.

Technically.

Elliott and Nathan Bellows are ten and eight years old. They have Linda's dark brown hair and tan features. By all accounts, nobody would ever guess we were related.

Except for their eyes.

They have the same baby blue eyes that I do.

It was the one good thing my father gave me, and it makes me happy knowing I share it with the two boys, even if I'm the only one who enjoys it.

I take a few moments to collect myself before walking through the house and out to the deck behind the Mitchell house. My eyes survey the crowds of people, wondering if I misunderstood Boyd's text somehow.

He said family and a few neighbors, but there are easily fifty people in the yard enjoying a massive spread of breakfast goods, mingling on the deck and the dock, and playing bag toss in the grass.

"Ruby!"

I turn and find Bellamy walking toward me with a huge smile on her face and her arms wide. Before I can say hello, she's wrapped me in a tight hug and squeezed me half to death.

I like how quickly she's welcomed me into the fold.

"Boyd said you might be coming to today. I'm so glad you're here."

She steps back then loops her arm in mine, designating herself in charge of our twosome as she leads me across the deck and over to look out at the lake.

"Yeah, he texted me this morning. I thought it was going to be mostly family, though. I had no idea it would be such a big party."

Bellamy laughs. "Well, there's definitely a lot of family here. A lot of Mitchells do live in Cedar Point, but in a small town like ours, the word family takes on a different kind of meaning, I guess. Neighbors and friends fall into that category, too."

I nod, my lips tipping up at that concept. I assumed when Boyd said family, he meant his siblings and parents, but thinking back to our conversation on the plane, he *did* say he has a really big family.

What must that be like? Having a family big enough to throw a party like this? Caring enough about the people around you to consider them family, too?

It makes me yearn for something intangible, something I can't quite put my finger on.

I've always taken pride in the fact that it was just my mama and me, the two of us against the world, not relying on anyone but ourselves. Then I took that mentality and applied it to my life as well, opting out of most relationships that would result in something significant.

Maybe there is something to be said for leaning on someone

every once in a while, for believing that the people in your life will come through for you.

Maybe I've been wrong.

Bellamy and I shoot the shit for a little while longer before she runs off to help her mom with something and I'm left to my own devices.

Even though I was here yesterday, I allow myself a chance to appreciate the Mitchells' beautiful home.

The partially covered wooden deck leads off of the living room and kitchen, and there's a built-in outdoor kitchen area with a barbeque and countertop space that Boyd told me they use to clean up the fish they catch each weekend.

Right now, everything is out of the way to make room for the crowd, but when I was here yesterday morning, they had a massive table right in the middle with twelve chairs around it. Potted plants are strewn along the edge of the wooden deck, giving visual separation between it and the half-step down to the grass.

The yard space is slightly inclined and rolls down to the long, L-shaped dock that stretches out into the water. A boat has just come to a stop at it, unloading a group of men. I can see Bishop and Boyd in the mix, and I smile knowing he's here.

Maybe I should play harder to get, but I can't help but watch Boyd as he makes his way to the house from the dock, a big cheesy smile on my face. He moves slowly through the crowd, his attention constantly distracted by another person saying hello or giving him a hug or handshake. I wonder if he knows I'm here until I see his eyes flit up to mine, like he knew exactly where I was standing and waiting for him all along.

In that very moment, I decide to rationalize breaking some of my rules for Boyd Mitchell.

What happens on vacation, stays on vacation, right? I should be able to spend all the time I want with him, should be able to talk with him about whatever comes to mind and daydream about this continuing in Boston.

I can deal with the consequences of it later, when I'm heading back to the east coast alone.

Right now, I'm just focused on him and the way my heart rate picks up as he steps onto the deck, walking straight toward me.

When Boyd gets to me, he wraps his arms around my waist and I lift mine to circle his neck, allowing him to squeeze me tightly against him and tucking my face into the crook of his neck.

I take in a deep breath. There is nothing headier than the way Boyd smells, something woodsy and manly and hinting at some sort of clean soap scent.

Suddenly, I'm glad I'm not the type of girl who plays hard to get. It's overrated.

"There you are." His voice rumbles in my ear.

I pull back to look at him. "Here *I* am?" I ask, still smiling. "How about there *you* are? I've been here for a while just hanging out all alone like a loser."

His brow furrows. "I'm sorry, I didn't know what time you were going to get here or I would have—"

"Boyd," I interrupt, squeezing his biceps. "I'm teasing. I was chatting with Bellamy and enjoying myself. Promise."

"Did someone say my name?"

Bellamy prances over, returning from wherever she was helping her mother.

"You're not Beetlejuice," Boyd grouses, keeping his arms around me and tucking me into his side. "You're not supposed to just *appear* when your name is used."

"But I'm magic like that."

Boyd rolls his eyes and looks down at me. "I'm glad you came," he says.

"Me too."

I reach up and touch the scruffiness on his chin, biting my lip at how prickly it is on my skin. The last few days, Boyd has always been clean-shaven. The tiny bit of stubble around his jawline is new. "I like this."

He grins, something kind of devilish flashing in his eyes before he tucks it away. "Then I'll leave it."

"Just like that?"

Boyd nods. "Just like that."

"Alright, you two—get a room."

I blush and try to take a step away from him, but his grip tightens, keeping me tucked in at his side, an arm resting around my waist.

He seems so relaxed, so comfortable with the two of us standing here together, looking so much like a couple in the middle of all his friends and family.

It's unlike what I was expecting from him, and yet I can't help but enjoy it. That little space in my chest that fantasizes about something real with Boyd revels in the way he stands with me proudly at his side, unconcerned about the people around us and what they might think.

"If you're just going to be annoying, you can go do it to one of the few dozen other people that are here," Boyd says.

Bellamy smirks at him. "The last thing I want to do is spend time with you anyway, so I will take the directive. Adios."

She wanders off into the crowd, greeting family, friends, and neighbors as she goes.

Speaking of neighbors...

"Did you know Linda was going to be here?" I ask, trying to keep my tone light and conversational even though bringing up my dad's wife who hates me isn't exactly a jovial talking point.

Boyd's neck does a weird jerky thing that says he's just as confused as I am.

"I didn't know she was invited, but it doesn't surprise me that my mom extended the olive branch if she knows you're staying there," he says, his eyes focused on mine. "I know she wasn't that nice to you when you got here. Are you okay?"

I stroke my hand softly against Boyd's back where my hand is resting, appreciating his concern.

"I'm fine."

He searches my expression for a minute before nodding, apparently finding whatever he's looking for.

With anyone else that I'd only known a few days, I wouldn't necessarily read into it so much, but with Boyd, I relish his focus. He's a man who pays attention, so it doesn't surprise me that he thinks he can read my emotions just based on a look.

"Have you eaten yet?"

I shake my head.

"Well then, let's get you a plate."

Slipping his hand into mine, Boyd leads me over to the buffet table, handing me a plate before grabbing one for himself. We each take a little of everything, and by the time I've finished putting everything together, my mouth is watering at how many delicious things I'm about to stuff into my tummy.

We end up taking our food inside, finding the spot we ate at yesterday at the counter. Everything is delicious, and I make sure to share my enthusiasm with Patty when she walks in carrying an empty water jug.

"Everything tastes so amazing," I tell her. "Is this your cooking?"

She laughs, her attention on where she's filling up the container with water and ice in her large basin sink.

"Honey, I wish I could cook like this. When we do family brunches, I always order from Jersey."

I glance at Boyd. "Is that a…person?" I ask, not wanting to sound stupid enough to ask what I really wanted to ask.

Like, *New* Jersey?

"Jersey Park is our resident chef," Boyd offers. "She went to culinary school and worked in a big-deal restaurant in New York before moving back here with her kids. I swear, mom orders enough food from her throughout the year to keep her business in business."

"Well, regardless of who made it, everything was so delicious. Thanks for inviting me, because it might be the best breakfast I've ever had." I emphasize the statement by shoving another bite of delicious French toast into my mouth.

"Better than *my* breakfast?" Boyd asks, placing a hand against his chest as if I've severely wounded him.

My eyes widen. I know he's joking, but I don't know whether I should tease more and dig the knife in farther or stroke his ego a bit.

"Loads better," is what I settle on. Clearly, I prefer the knife.

Boyd smirks and takes a sip of his orange juice.

157

"Ruby, I wanted to say…" Patty sets the now full container of water on the counter and leans over the island so her face is closer to mine. "I am so sorry if I made things awkward between you and Linda." She shakes her head. "I assumed you would come along with her and the boys, not that she would come without you."

"Elliott and Nathan are here?" I ask, my eyes wide. I still haven't seen them in person, only knowing what they look like because Ken sent me a picture of the four of them over text when we were discussing me coming out.

It was perfectly posed, their perfect little family at a perfect lake on a perfect day looking just…perfect.

I step slightly away from the counter and over to the window to look outside, my eyes searching the crowd to find Linda, or two little boys with brown hair and blue eyes.

"Mom, maybe next time, ask first."

Boyd's tone with Patty is calm but firm, a reprimand she doesn't deserve.

She was trying to be helpful, friendly. If only Ken could have married someone more like Patty, someone welcoming and caring.

Instead he married a snotty, angry woman hell-bent on keeping me away from her, her boys, and her life here in Cedar Point.

"I tend to butt my nose in where it doesn't belong a little too often," Patty says. "But I promise my intentions are always in the right place."

I turn back to where the two of them stand together in the kitchen once I've determined that Linda has probably left. Patty is looking at me with apologetic eyes.

"You didn't do anything wrong, Patty," I say. "Linda hasn't

been that welcoming, but there's no way you could have known."

She tilts her head to the side and gives me a look of pure empathy. Then she widens her arms and envelops me in the kind of hug only a really kick-ass mom knows how to give.

"Everything will work itself out," she says, rubbing my back.

I smile, enjoying her hug and wishing I could be as optimistic as her.

chapter thirteen
boyd

A few hours later, most of our brunch guests have returned home, leaving just my immediate family sitting around our sunken entertainment room like slugs with full bellies.

This is one of my favorite spaces in my parents' home. They added it on to the main house when I was a junior in high school, and I was always a bit jealous that I didn't have it for longer like my siblings.

The cream walls and dark blue bookshelves give it a blended look of both masculine and rustic that matches with the rest of the house. There's a projector hidden in the ceiling that shoots out anything we want to watch on the massive screen in the center of the room, and there is a fireplace in the corner and oversized couches with enough room for a family of seven plus guests.

In essence, it's the best room to hang out in when you're a teenager and have a bunch of friends over, or when you're an adult and the whole family is home at the same time.

When Ruby and I walk in after saying goodbye to the last few people, all eyes turn to look at us, including the curious gazes of the two sisters who have yet to meet her.

I picked Briar up from her house this morning since she had a last-minute issue with her asshole fiancé and their car, and then the two of us picked up Busy from the airport.

Next I suffered an hour-long car ride home with the two of them peppering me with incessant and overly nosy questions about 'the girl from the plane.'

Apparently, my siblings have been texting in a little group chat without me, and their primary topic of conversation has been Ruby, though none of them will tell me what it is they're actually saying about her.

My assumption so far is that the conversation is leaning positive since the questions my sisters were asking me sounded oddly like they were approving of something serious blooming between us.

For anyone who knows Briar and Busy, the two of them actually agreeing on anything is almost impossible.

"So this is her."

Briar's words aren't said loudly, but they sure do fill the room when she says them.

Thankfully, I can see that my sister has her normally prickly guard down when she approaches the two of us, extending her hand with a smile on her face.

"I'm Briar."

Ruby gives my sister a warm smile in return.

"It's so great to meet you," she says. "And damn do I love your name. It's almost as beautiful as you are."

Briar actually blushes, something that rarely happens, though she tries to hide it by turning around and returning to

161

the massive beanbag chair she was flopped in when we entered the room.

Sinking back into it, she thanks Ruby then asks the question I specifically told them they're not allowed to ask.

My sisters are nothing if not nosy.

"So…what's going on between you and my brother?"

Ruby bites her lip and lets out an awkward laugh, her eyes flitting up to mine as if to ask for direction on what to say.

"Stop snooping," I say, deflecting so as not to put Ruby on the spot. "Or would you like me to turn the tables so we can talk about Chad?"

Briar's eyes narrow and she crosses her arms.

It might have been a low blow to bring up the chode, but the last thing I need is for my sister to poke her nose into my relationship with Ruby—if I can call it that—especially when I don't have any answers, either.

"When are we doing the family photo?"

My sister Busy lies lengthwise along one sofa, stretching out and taking up a ton of space in a way only she can seem to get away with as the youngest.

"Right now!" my mother says, her voice overflowing with excitement as she bustles into the room with my father in her wake.

He comes to my side and plops a hand on my shoulder, giving it a squeeze before walking over to lean against the back of the couch.

"But we haven't even picked out our outfits!" Bellamy's widened eyes and absolute shock are par for the course. "Why didn't you warn us earlier?"

Bishop snorts. "She's been talking about this picture for *weeks*, Bells. Literal *weeks*. It's not our fault you didn't listen when she told us we'd be doing it the day Briar and Busy got to town."

My sister huffs and crosses her arms but doesn't say anything else.

"This year, I've decided we're finally doing the lake shot."

Bishop groans. Busy scrambles up to sitting and begins to clap her hands excitedly. Briar and Bellamy stay in their seated positions with arms crossed.

I, personally, don't care what we're doing. I just want to get it over with, stat.

"Where do you normally take pictures?" Ruby asks, confusion marring her brow.

I lift my thumb and smooth it down, making her smile.

"Mom has been telling us for years that we're going to take a family picture of all of us jumping off the dock and into the lake, but each year, she chickens out and ends up just having us take a posed picture instead. She likes to pretend we're well-adjusted."

My mom swats my arm.

"So you're all going to jump into the lake?" Ruby asks. "Oh my gosh, that sounds so fun!"

"Yup." Mom steps forward, a camera in her hands and a mischievous smile on her face. "And *you're* going to take the picture."

Ruby's eyes widen as she glances up at me then looks back at my mom again.

"Huh?"

Watching Ruby climb into a rowboat and slowly make her way a safe distance away from the dock where my siblings, my parents, and I are lined up, I can't help but think she looks perfect on the water.

A little nervous, sure, and clearly struggling as her rowboat spins slowly in a circle she can't seem to figure out how to stop, but still.

Perfect.

"Normally, I'd give you shit about a girl," Busy says, arms crossed as she stands next to me on the dock. "But I'll give you a pass this time."

Glancing down, I take in the fierce expression on my sister's face and decide to humor her.

"Oh, and why is that?"

She lifts a shoulder in that way only teenagers can manage to pull off then looks up at me, her punkish little attitude taking a back seat for a minute. "Because I've never seen you look at someone like that before."

My smile dips slightly, my whole body seeming to sober at her words.

Part of me wants to deny it, wants to insist anything happening between myself and Ruby shouldn't be taken for much. It's too fast. Too different. Too outside of my comfort zone.

But really, it's the fact that my sister can read me that has thrown me for a loop. Busy has always been kind of lost in her own world, so if there is something on my face for her to see, something about the way I look at Ruby...it means everyone can see it.

Maybe even the sweet girl in the boat.

"There's nothing wrong with wanting a real relationship, Boyd." Her voice is low as she slips her hand into mine and gives

164

it a squeeze.

It's crazy how just a few softly spoken words from my sister can bubble up crazy emotions inside of my chest, creating an almost overwhelming feeling that I'm not entirely sure how to manage.

So, I do what makes me the most comfortable.

I take all those emotions and feelings and I package them into a box and set them to the side for now, where I can choose to ignore them or examine them at a better time.

Right now, I need to be focused on taking this picture for my mom, and she doesn't want to see me staring awkwardly at the camera once she has them printed.

Wrapping an arm around Busy's neck, I tug her close and plant a kiss on the crown of her head.

"You're getting far too old, Little Bee," I say, using the nick-name I've had for her since she was a baby.

She snorts but doesn't pull away. "You have no idea."

"Alright everyone, I think Ruby is about set up." My mother's voice echoes out to Ruby, even though it's meant as a cue for us to shut up and pay attention.

Looking back out to the water, I see she has finally stopped spinning, though she's still seated very rigidly inside the boat, holding my mother's camera like it's a bomb about to go off.

They spent a good fifteen minutes going over what my mom wanted Ruby to do while she was on the boat taking pictures, Ruby repeating over and over how nervous she was to hold such an expensive camera on a small boat in the water.

"Nonsense," my mom said, waving her hand. "If you drop it in the water, I'll just make sure to hold it over your head until the day you die."

Ruby's eyes widened as my mom burst into laughter and

assured her she was joking.

Her eyes have that same wideness now as she lifts the camera to look through the viewfinder.

"Alright, Ruby is going to take a few group shots first, just so we have a backup in case we don't like the jumping one."

Bishop and Busy groan but shuffle closer to one another, knowing no amount of protesting will change our mother's mind.

Once we've all snuggled close, my mom tells Ruby to start taking pictures.

"Boyd, can you move a little to the left? I can't see your face," she calls from the water.

I shift, following her directions.

"Gotta make sure Boyd looks good in the photo," Bishop teases quietly through his smile, a few giggles coming from my other siblings.

Ruby gives some more instructions then offers to take pictures of just my parents, just the siblings, just the boys, just the girls. I hope these come out okay because it sounds like she's doing a great job, and my mom is very excited.

When it comes time for us to do the lake shot, my mom calls out a few last-minute instructions to Ruby as a reminder of what they already talked about. Then we all line up for the picture.

"I'm going to start taking photo bursts, and once I do, I'll do a countdown," Ruby calls over. "It'll be 3, 2, 1, jump. And don't forget to smile at me as you're jumping. Are we ready?"

A beat passes before Ruby finally yells out the signal, and all of us do as she says, jumping into the air and off the dock then falling into the lake with loud splashes.

When my head pops back up, I hear the laughter and squeals

from my family as they adjust to the cool lake water.

"I think I got it!" I hear, and when I look over, I see Ruby has taken her seat again and is looking at the display on the camera, beaming.

"Good, because you couldn't pay me to do this again," Briar grumbles.

"Oh come on, you prissy bitch."

Bishop lets out a loud laugh at Bellamy's insult, the sound echoing across the lake.

"Prissy!?" Briar shrieks, sounding a lot more like she did when we were kids than she has in a long time. "I'm not the one who sits in front of the mirror for two hours doing makeup every morning."

"Yeah, and those bags under your eyes are saying maybe you should," Bellamy fires back.

"Alright, let's not get into a fight, girls. It's just a little water."

My dad floats over to where Bellamy and Briar are treading water, clearly hoping to be a voice of calm and reason.

That hope is very quickly demolished.

"Stay out of it, dad."

Both girls glare at each other after saying the exact same words at the exact same time.

"Just a little water, huh?" Bishop says, swimming into the fray. "Maybe you'll like some of it in your *face*."

And with that, Bishop shoves an armful of water at all three of them.

Both girls scream, as if they weren't already soaking wet to begin with. My dad and Bishop laugh. Busy paddles over quickly and shoves another wave at her sisters.

Within a few seconds, it's a full-on water fight.

"Sometimes, I wish I had grown up with siblings," comes

from my right, and I turn to find Ruby has slowly rowed herself over to where I float next to the wooden dock. "And other times, I'm glad I never had to fight over stupid shit."

I snort, understanding the sentiment. I'd never trade my siblings for anything, obviously, but that doesn't mean I haven't wished more than a handful of times that I didn't have to deal with all their squabbling.

"Thank you so much, Ruby," my mother says as she walks down the dock, already wrapped in a towel. Clearly, she had the foresight to get out of the water quickly and not deal with the impending complications of a bunch of waterlogged Mitchells.

She reaches over to where Ruby's boat is floating next to the dock and takes her hand, helping her step up onto the wooden platform. I float at their feet, watching as my mom and Ruby look through the images on the camera together.

"Obviously they're really small right now, but it looks like these are going to be perfect," my mom says, squeezing Ruby on the arm. "Thank you so much for your help."

"It was fun. Thanks for asking." Then Ruby's eyes drop to mine. "You gonna float around for a while or are you going to get out of the water?"

"I'm gonna get out," I say, hoisting myself up onto the dock, my still-fully-clothed body dripping with water as I come to stand next to her. "Can I borrow your phone really quick?"

Ruby pats her pockets. "Oh, I left it inside."

"Perfect."

Her brow furrows for a split second before her eyes widen, understanding hitting her like lightning as I grab her and pull her back into the water with me. I only hear a little bit of a squeal before we're both submerged.

When we come soaring out from beneath the surface, Ruby

is spluttering and coughing and wiping water from her face. Maybe I should have given her a little more warning so she didn't inhale as much lake water, but then she'd have had more time to get away, and where's the fun in that?

"I can't believe you," she shouts at me, breaking into a fit of joyful laughter and shoving a small wave of water in my direction.

"You *just* told me earlier today you'd been here two days and hadn't gotten into the lake yet. I was simply granting your wish."

Ruby rolls her eyes but fights back a smirk, though her attention drifts over to where my sister Briar is storming out of the water at the shore. My dad, Busy, and Bishop are in a little circle looking at Bellamy with narrowed eyes.

"Uh, oh," I say, realizing something more serious went down and wondering what exactly it was.

Normally, our family has little tiffs then jokes around until everyone lets things go. Clearly that is *not* what happened this time around with Bellamy and Briar.

"Go inside and fix it."

That was from my dad, his voice firm as he points in the direction Briar just went.

Whatever happened, when my dad gets involved with a tone like that, none of us back down, even though all of us opted out of obeying our parents' every request long ago.

"Let's all go in, and I can make us some dinner?" my mom says, ever the host and always the mother.

Ruby starts to float forward as my dad, brother, and sisters begin heading for the shore.

"We're gonna pass," I call after my mom.

If we go inside, it'll be nonstop with all of my siblings for hours. I want alone time with Ruby today, so I'm going to have to yank her away to keep her all to myself.

"We are?" Ruby whispers, her eyes glancing between me and where my mom is giving us a little wave before heading up the dock back to the house.

I nod, taking her hand in mind and pulling her with me farther out into the water. "Let's float over to your house," I say, "and we can just enjoy the outdoors for a little bit."

Ruby's face lights up, and I know I've said the right thing. She flips onto her back, keeping her body buoyant so she floats along the surface. Her hand never lets go of mine, our fingers twisting together as we float away from the dock and out toward the middle of the cove.

"Did you enjoy yourself today?"

It takes a few seconds for Ruby to respond, but when she does, she's a lot more honest than I would have expected.

"Yes and no. I really did enjoy spending time with you and your family, but Linda being so…dismissive of me is just really frustrating."

"What's the deal there?" Turning to my side, I swim a little bit, pulling a floating Ruby along with me as I edge us closer to her guesthouse.

Ruby sighs, and I can hear the true sadness there, along with a host of other things as well.

"I don't really know for sure, but I can guess, and my guess is that she doesn't want me here to mess with things. She has a happy life with a man and they have two kids, and now some woman is coming into town claiming to be her husband's daughter?" Her eyes connect with mine. "I feel like I'd be wary, too."

I shake my head. "Nah. I don't think you'd ever handle things the way she does."

"Really?"

"Yeah. You're too caring, and I'll be honest, people don't become assholes because of circumstances. You're either an asshole or you're not. Your circumstances just reveal who you *really* are underneath who you *pretend* to be."

She's silent for a minute, taking that thought in.

"I guess I can just acknowledge the fact that my presence disrupts her life."

"And it's really wonderful that you can put yourself in her shoes and understand where her feelings are stemming from, but she doesn't have to be a bitch to you—especially when you're here alone and your dad fucking bailed."

I wince, realizing the harshness of my words.

"Sorry, I didn't mean to be so callous about it. I just—"

"No, it's true. He bailed when I was a kid, and he bailed now." She pauses. "I don't know why I was surprised. He's proven to me that I can't trust him, you know? That wanting him to be a dad is too much. He doesn't want me here, not really. I'm not even sure why I came."

I squeeze her hand and she flips over so she's floating on her stomach, looking at me with a sad expression.

"Sorry. I know you were probably hoping for a fun float back to my place and I turned it into—"

"Don't apologize. How you feel is how you feel, and you shouldn't ever apologize for it."

There are so many thoughts and emotions on her face. I wish I could say something…anything to make her understand that she doesn't have to allow this shit to get her down.

"What do you think happened between Bellamy and Briar?" Ruby asks, changing the subject with all the stealth of an elephant.

I puff out a breath and stroke my arms through the water,

thinking it over. Really, I haven't seen that kind of anger from one of my siblings directed at another in a long time.

"My guess is it's about Briar's fiancé, but I could be wrong. It might be something else."

"You guys don't like him or something?"

I shake my head. "Not at all. I mean, we try—for the most part. We don't want him to think we *hate* him or anything, but he's a prick, and in my opinion, he doesn't treat my sister very well. So, we typically just don't talk about him."

"Sorry. That must be hard, especially since all of you seem to be so close."

"The good news is that nobody is in a fight with me," I joke. "Usually, I'm the one pissing everyone off."

"Oh, and why is that?"

I snort. "They like to tease me a lot, like to dissect my life and judge my decisions. Normally, it drives me insane. I don't like to share a lot about my life with people. I'm a pretty private guy, but none of my siblings care how I feel and just do it anyway."

Ruby's silent for a second. "Well, maybe I'm overstepping, but I'd love for you to share about yourself with me."

My lips tilt up at the sides.

I don't think Ruby realizes it, but I've shared a lot more with her than I have with anyone in a long time. I thought about this last night as I lay in bed, wishing I'd stayed at Ruby's instead of going home and taking a cold shower.

The things I've shared with her—mostly my family and my life in Boston and in Cedar Point—it's a lot for me.

I can't pinpoint why, exactly, I feel comfortable talking to Ruby. All I know is that I do, and I want her to know it.

"Maybe it doesn't seem like it, but I've shared a lot more

with you than I do with other people—with anyone, for a long time."

"Really?" she asks, and when I look her way, I see she's watching me with a laser focus.

"Something about you, Ruby…" My voice fades as I try to put it into words for her. "You make me *want* to share. To talk. About anything."

She blushes and looks away, but I still see the smile on her face and love that I'm the one who put it there.

Her hand slips back into mine, and we keep floating in silence, just enjoying each other's company as we get closer and closer to Ken's property.

A few minutes later we're both trudging out of the water and toward the house, our shoes making slurpy, squelching noises as we walk up the banks of the lake and across the grass.

Once we get to the deck, she grabs towels from the outdoor cabinet stocked with summer lake supplies and hands me one, each of us taking a moment to dry off most of the way.

Ruby toes off her sandals then wraps the towel around her hair for a minute to get it dry before draping it around her shoulders and tugging it in tight over her arms. She looks so snug, and it makes me want to kiss her.

So I do.

I startle her at first when I step so close, my towel left in a heap on one of the Adirondack chairs. But when she sees me looking at her mouth, my head dipping closer to hers, she tilts her head slightly and closes her eyes, encouragement emanating from every single cell of her body.

It makes me smile, enjoying how quickly she's wanting to give in to me, to this thing between us.

Taking her face in my hands, I kiss her gently on the forehead. Then once on each eyelid. Each of her temples, her cheek-bones, her nose.

I can feel her twitching, her body beginning to fidget with each moment I let pass where I'm not kissing her lips.

Finally, when I can't bear it any longer and I don't think Ruby can either, I lower my mouth to hers.

There's nothing timid about the way she kisses me. Some sort of flip has switched inside of Ruby Rae Roberts, because she opens her mouth for me and tangles her tongue with mine without any kind of flirtation or preamble.

And damn does she taste good.

chapter fourteen
ruby

God, I love the way he tastes.

My entire body trembles, both from the cold lake water and from the feeling of him wrapping his arms around me and holding me close.

I nip at his lip, suck on the soft flesh to soothe it, and then lick into his mouth again.

He's like a drug.

One I will happily get addicted to.

Boyd slows our kiss down, pressing his forehead against mine, both of us breathing hard.

"You make it hard to resist you," he says, his voice sending shivers down my spine, making me more wet than the lake water ever could have.

I bump his nose with mine. "What if I don't want you to resist?" I ask.

Even in my relationship with Evan, when it was at its steamy beginning, I never craved him like I do my next breath. Just three days into knowing Boyd Mitchell, I feel more hooked on him than anything I've ever known.

"Come inside," I whisper, tugging him with me to my door.

I'll admit, there's something a little bruising about having to push Boyd a bit before he seems fully on board with it, but that thought quickly flies away once we're both inside the house.

Once I close the door behind us, the lack of sound—no rustling water, no birds chirping, no wisps of wind—makes it seem like I can hear my own heartbeat.

Boyd and I look at each other for a long moment, and then I reach over and latch the lock on the door. Suddenly, his mouth is on mine and his hands are in my hair. I wind my own arms around him, enjoying the feeling of his strong body beneath my hands.

It's like locking us in gave him permission to let go, and instead of moving at the slow and steady pace he was wanting us to proceed at, he's put the pedal to the metal.

He walks me backward, the two of us bumping into things as we stumble toward the bedroom. I'm so focused on his mouth on mine, his hands gripping me tight, that not until we're standing next to my bed do I realize I'm still dripping lake water—only now, it's on Linda's nice guesthouse floor.

I pull back from Boyd's kiss, sliding my fingers in his belt loops and giving him a knowing smile.

"Come with me," I say, my voice quiet.

With Boyd following behind me, I lead us into the cute little bath off the bedroom. White tile floors, white marble countertops, white clawfoot tub, white subway tile in the shower—white, white, white everywhere, giving the room a bright and clean feeling. Everywhere in this guesthouse looks like it could come from an HGTV home makeover, and I love it.

Right now, though, I'm not focused on the fancy bathroom or the unique décor. I'm focused on Boyd, on stripping us both down and getting us into that shower so we can get nice and clean and nice and dirty.

Thankfully, he doesn't seem like he wants to pump the brakes any time soon if the size of the bulge in his pants is anything to go by. I press my hand against him and he moans, something low and tortured.

"We need to shower," I say, stepping over and rotating the handle so the water turns on.

And then I lift my arms, looking straight at him and waiting for him to take the hint.

His expression sobers slightly, and just as quickly as we sped up a few minutes ago, each of us takes a deep breath and decides to slow down. Chooses not to rush. Takes a moment to appreciate what comes next.

Boyd's hands drop to my waist, slipping under my knit top, his warm fingers scorching me as they touch the skin around my belly. My stomach dips and I giggle, the ticklish part of me unable to be put on pause.

"Ticklish?" he rumbles with a small smile on his face, lifting my top slightly, grazing up my sides and sending shivers rolling through my arms.

I nod but stay silent, allowing him to pull the shirt over my chest, my neck, my shoulders and head.

Once it's off, he takes in the tiny white bralette I have on. I might have been given curves in the hips and ass, but I'm a little smaller up top.

You wouldn't be able to tell from the way Boyd's eyeing me, though, nor from the way his fingers trace the fabric like he's savoring the moment. One finger drops down and circles my puckered nipple through the material, the darkness of my areola visible through the light fabric. He traces it around and around, the tiny little motion making me clench my thighs together.

Then he surprises me, dropping his face to my chest, sucking one of my nipples into his mouth through the damp cotton. My hands fly to his head, threading into his hair as I tip my head back and let out a soft cry of pleasure at the sensation.

His hands move, shifting the scrap of fabric down and out of the way so he can latch onto me, skin to skin, his impatience overtaking his desire to move slow. The wetness of his tongue, the heat of his mouth, the stubble on his jaw—it's too much, so much, and I love every second of it.

That original pulsing energy seems to overtake us both again, and we become a flurry of motion, each of us tugging at our clothing to get it off as quickly as possible.

Once we're both naked, we climb into the shower, the rainfall showerhead soaking us both all over again. Boyd's eyes never leave mine, even as he closes the glass door behind us and I stand completely naked before him, pushing my hands into my hair to help the warm shower water replace the damp coldness from the lake.

My own eyes dip, taking in the magnificence of Boyd's body, appreciating the hard, lean muscle and toned chest before dropping down to the thick shaft between his thighs.

Which he currently has gripped tightly in one of his hands. He strokes it a few times, finally allowing his gaze to drop and rove over my naked body.

I've said it before and I'll say it again: Being the recipient of the full force of his attention is unlike anything I've experienced before, an aphrodisiac that has me lighting up inside and desperate for more.

He steps under the water with me, pressing his lips against mine. My hands caress his hard, naked body, enjoying the firm muscle and warm skin. He does the same, his hands dropping to squeeze my ass, his mouth moving to kiss along bare flesh.

"Time to get clean," he finally says, something wicked in his tone as he steps back and reaches for a bottle of bodywash.

He squirts a dollop into his hand and then some into mine before he puts the bottle back. Then he's rubbing his hands together and scrubbing all over his body.

I bite my lip as I watch him, momentarily distracted. Then I jump into motion, rubbing my own soap all over, taking my sweet time and making sure to give Boyd a show.

I start at my arms and then slick up my chest, making sure to apply the suds liberally over my breasts and enjoying the pulse in my belly when I tweak my own nipples.

All the while, his heated stare follows my hands, his mouth slightly open and his own movements stalled.

It's when I dip between my thighs, my small hands stroking intently against my pussy, that he breaks from his motionless stance and steps into me, pushing me against all that white subway tile and pressing his mouth to mine again.

The way his body feels against mine—hard, wet, slick with soap—is unreal. When he dips down so his dick is pressed between my legs, rubbing back and forth between my lower lips and putting friction and pressure against my clit, I can't help but let out a deep moan.

God, it feels so good, the way he just keeps stroking and stroking, over and over.

I told Boyd I've never had an orgasm before, and it's true. I've also never felt this keyed up before, never felt like I'm a cord pulled taut and ready to snap at any second.

"Boyd." I breathe out his name, unable to say anything else.

"You gonna come for me?" he asks, his mouth dropping to suck on my neck.

"I don't know."

It's the only thing I can say in response, because I really don't know. This feels so much bigger than the meager little tremblings I've felt at my own hands in my bed as I've tried to figure out my orgasm in the past. It's like I'm chugging up the ramp on a roller coaster, getting ready to crest the top and fall over.

It almost feels *too* big. Too much. Too deep, even though he's not even inside of me. I keep squirming, my breaths coming faster and my cries harder to hold back.

"Boyd, I can't," I say, realizing with desperation that I probably won't ever reach the top.

His motions stutter at my words and his head comes back so we're looking at each other.

"You can."

I shake my head and close my eyes.

It still feels so good, but I can't look at him while I'm like this, wound so tight with nowhere to go.

"It's okay," I say, my hands halting his motions between my legs, his body coming to a standstill.

Boyd's brow furrows as his eyes take in the expression on my face. The last thing I want is for him to turn this into something where he focuses on trying to get me off when I know it's not going to happen.

Other men have done that in the past, and it does the exact opposite of what they want it to do. Instead of making me feel good, it sucks away the good I've enjoyed so far.

So, instead of allowing him to focus on me, I take his dick in my hand, stroking him. His eyes shut and his jaw tenses as he lets out another of those moans I'm quickly becoming addicted to.

I keep him like that until he's thrusting into my hand, the overhead water washing the soap off of us. Then I drop to my knees, intent on him remembering this as the time he got sucked off in the shower and *not* as the time he couldn't make Ruby come.

His eyes fly open and he looks down at me, his jaw slack and his breathing heavy as I suck him between my lips and stroke him with my tongue. I use my hand to wrap around the part of him I can't fit into my mouth, pumping him as I lick and suck, never letting my eyes look away from his.

"Fuck, Ruby," he moans, his hand resting on the side of my face, his thumb stroking my cheek.

It's when I use my other hand to tug on his balls that I feel him wobble a little bit on his feet, and I use that knowledge against him. I fondle his heavy sac, rolling him in my hand, never letting up on where I'm sucking.

Until his head tilts back and he tells me he's coming.

I pull my mouth off, watching his entire body tense, his hands bracing against the shower walls as he comes hard. The evidence quickly swishes down the shower drain, but I'll never forget the look on Boyd's face as he rests his forehead against his bicep, his breath coming in pants.

I stand, my own desire still buzzing in my lower stomach, the space between my thighs aching at how sexy he looks when he comes.

"I can't remember the last time I came that hard," he says, finally standing up straight and looking at me with a smile. "Shit, Ruby."

Then he steps closer and pulls me in for a deep kiss.

181

I could quickly become addicted to these, to the feel of his warm mouth and slick tongue, the pressure of his lips against mine.

But the longer we kiss, the more I can feel his hands shifting toward my center again, and I know he's wanting to return his attention to my body. To my ache, my need.

Stepping back, I smile at him. "Now that we've gotten a little dirty, let's get *actual* clean," I say with a smile, trying to redirect as I spin around and focus my attention on the bottle of shampoo in the corner.

Boyd doesn't take the hint, stepping in so his front presses into my back.

"We're not done, though." He places a kiss on my shoulder, his hands wrapping around my waist.

If I didn't know any better, I'd think he didn't come at all with the way his dick is pressed against me, still hard.

"I'm okay," I say, giving him a smile over my shoulder then beginning to shampoo my head.

He takes a step back, and the silence behind me fills the shower with something more tangible than the steam from the hot water. Once I've foamed up enough suds on my head and turned around so I can rinse it out in the water, I see him leaning against the glass stall with his arms crossed.

Something inside of me flickers with irritation that he won't just let this go. I can see it in his eyes.

It's the same look Evan used to give me when I couldn't come for him, either, the frustrated irritation I've gotten from several men who didn't like when I wouldn't let them keep trying.

As much as I think Boyd likes me, I know what that look *actually* means. It isn't about the fact that I'm not able to have an orgasm. It's about the fact that I'm not able to have an orgasm *with him.* The blow to his ego is too much.

That's what it was with Evan, and surely that's what it is with Boyd, too.

"What's the issue?" he asks me, his voice low but still echoing off the tile.

My hands still where they are in my hair.

"What's the *issue*?" I reply, trying to give him the benefit of the doubt. "I've already talked with you about this. I've never been able to orgasm before. It's not a big deal."

"It is, though."

"No it isn't."

"It is."

"Not if you don't make it one," I sass back, dipping my head under the water to rinse the shampoo out.

He glares at me, all the tenderness between us from earlier seemingly evaporating.

"Why won't you let me keep trying? It felt good, right? I mean, you're probably just—"

"What?" I interrupt. "What am I, Boyd? Please, tell me what I'm doing wrong with my body."

His shoulders drop. "Ruby..." His voice holds an apology, but it's no different than the other times I've heard the same thing.

"You wanna know why I won't let you keep trying? Because of *that* face," I say, pointing at him. "Right there. That face of you being disappointed that *you* did something wrong. It's not about you, Boyd. *I'm* the one with the problem. *I'm* the one who can't seem to figure it out, and trust me when I say I've tried—over and over again. I'm sorry you weren't able to step in and solve a problem I've had for years in only a few minutes."

With that, I push out of the shower, closing the door behind me and leaving him alone.

I yank a towel out of the basket next to the shower and leave the bathroom, not wanting to have to stand naked in front of him as I dry off. Once that's done, I pull on some clothes and wrap my hair up in my towel on the top of my head.

Only a few minutes pass before I hear the shower water shut off and the door open again.

By the time Boyd steps out of the bathroom, a towel wrapped around his waist, I'm fully dressed except for the socks I'm tugging onto my feet.

When I'm angry, I need to exercise, and even though I just took a shower, a nice hike will probably be just what I need to calm the irritation in my chest.

"Ruby, I'm sorry," he says, standing at the threshold between the bathroom and the bedroom. "I didn't mean to imply anything or hurt your feelings or whatever I made you feel in there. Really."

I finish tugging on my second sock and then look up at him.

"I just wanted to make you feel good. Is that so bad?"

Letting out a sigh, I tilt my head from side to side, stretching out the muscles and trying to let go of some of my frustration.

"It's not bad, Boyd," I say. "The problem isn't that you want to make me feel good. It's that by focusing on how *you* can make me feel good—or the fact that you couldn't make me orgasm—you did the exact *opposite* of make me feel good."

His face falls, the hopeful expression he was wearing withering away as fast as my looming orgasm.

"Do you know what it feels like to have *every* sexual experience in my life result in an argument like that?" I say, pointing at the bathroom behind him. "To have every man I've slept with look at me like you did, like you still are?"

Instantly, he wipes his face clean.

"It wrecks something inside of me. I'm not a broken toy for you to fix. I'm fine just the way I am. And when all you can focus on is the fact that you haven't made me orgasm, it makes *me* unable to think about anything else. It takes away the things I *can* enjoy about sex because all I can think about is the idea that I'm letting you and your precious ego down."

Boyd doesn't say anything after that, his nostrils flaring as he tries not to show me how upset he is.

I sigh again then unwrap my hair from the towel, wishing I'd followed Boyd's lead about taking things slow instead of pushing for us to move faster.

Maybe then something like this wouldn't have happened.

Or maybe it would have been just the same.

"I'm gonna go on a hike, and I'll be gone for a while." I tuck my hair into a messy bun. "There's a dryer in the closet next to the kitchen if you want to throw your clothes in there. Take your time."

Giving him a sad smile, I grab my keys and watch off the dresser, pull my walking shoes from my suitcase, and then walk out the door.

chapter fifteen

ruby

Washburn Trail isn't particularly steep, stretching in switch-backs from the road near Ken's house through the tall pines that surround the lake. It still takes me over an hour to get to the spot I'm searching for, and when the clearing finally breaks free, the view does not disappoint.

I found this outlook last night, my online search for hiking trails one of the things I did to keep my mind off of wishing Boyd had stayed. Ironic that the search for the trail was what I did to distract me from a man, and now the actual hike itself is doing the same.

California mountains are different than what I've seen in the movies and on TV. Maybe it's just this specific area, but I always assumed there would be higher peaks. Most of the terrain surrounding Cedar Point is kind of flat, the tree-filled expanse around the small town providing elevations that are more like hills than mountains.

It isn't until I look from my slightly elevated viewpoint at the end of Washburn that I can see real mountains off in the distance, the summits high enough that they're covered by a ring of clouds.

I hike a lot back home. I'm sure a city girl like me might not *look* like I spend that much time in nature, but the beauty of the Massachusetts outdoors can't be beat.

Though, now that I've hiked along this trail and I have enough elevation to see a good portion of the woodlands surrounding Cedar Point, I might be able to agree that California forests can *rival* the beauty of my favorite Bay State spots.

I take a seat on an old tree stump that was cut away at some point, just enjoying the view.

Something inside of me enjoys this quiet town much more than I ever expected to. I'm not sure what it is exactly that makes me feel like my rambling soul has found a place to rest. Maybe it's the crisp mountain air. Maybe it's the quiet, something I'm not as familiar with being a Chelsea girl, born and raised.

Or maybe it's none of those things.

Maybe it isn't the place. Maybe it's the people.

Or the *person*, rather.

One person.

Boyd.

As much as I'd like to say I walked this trail and really enjoyed nature and my surroundings, I was so much more distracted than I want to admit.

I spent the—I glance at my watch—eighty-minute hike up here going over my conversation with him back at the house, where I had a complete meltdown because he didn't know how to handle things.

It was so unfair to him.

Boyd didn't do anything wrong today. The things I said to

him were valid, sure, but did he deserve my irritation and frustration simply because he was unfamiliar with the hurdles I face on the sexual highway?

He wasn't an asshole about it, and I *know* what that looks like after an absolute mistake of a sexual experience with a guy who works as a bouncer at the one nightclub I went to with Fiona last year. He was the quintessential hard-bodied security type, and I swooned over those big biceps and perpetual frown.

Unfortunately, he was also the kind of man to shame me when I couldn't crest the top of the peak with him. Trust me when I say hearing the words *What the hell is wrong with you?* after sex is not something forgotten easily.

The only thing Boyd did was try to get me to try again. It isn't his fault that he doesn't understand why *trying again* is a mood killer for me, and instead of explaining it to him, I shut him down, shut him out.

I treated him like he was a disposable dick I could get away from and never have to see again, running out of the guesthouse like it was on fire.

He might be a guy I've only known for a few days, but I don't like to make a habit of treating anyone the way I just did with him. If I still want to spend more time with him on this trip—which I definitely do—then I'll need to figure out a way to explain myself.

So, after I take a few more minutes to appreciate the view, wishing I'd had my phone so I could take a few shots of the lake and surrounding hills filled with beautiful trees, I make the long trek back down the trail.

I can only hope my immature storm-out hasn't made him feel like his time would be better spent somewhere else.

Like with Corinne.

Okay, that was a stupid thought. He already made it clear that she isn't the person he wants to spend time with, that he'd basically rather shove bamboo under his fingernails than be around her on this trip.

Still, that insecurity inside of me, the one that says he could have sex with her and not feel as shitty as I probably made him feel, worries anyway.

I'm so distracted by my thoughts on the walk home that when I get there, I don't notice the shoes outside the door as I kick off my own.

It isn't until I open the door and walk in that I realize I'm not alone, my body coming to a dramatic halt when I find Boyd, fully dressed, seated at the small round table and drinking a glass of water.

"You're...still here." My words come out choppy, mostly because I feel confused.

Why is he still here?

Boyd rises from the table, his big body moving gracefully even though he dwarfs the tiny table and chairs, and then he strides toward me with purposeful steps, his eyes never leaving mine.

"I'm sorry," he says, his eyes holding a sincerity I've not seen from a man...ever. "I didn't mean to upset you or make you feel like you're broken. You're perfect."

My mouth drops open, the seriousness of his statement and the honesty in his eyes too overwhelming.

He lets out a sigh, one hand rising and holding the side of my face, his gaze scanning my features.

"No, I'm sorry," I finally manage to say. "I shouldn't have laid a lifetime of shit on your shoulders and stormed out."

It's amazing to me that he's still here. When Evan and I

fought and I'd take a walk, he was always gone when I got home. I'm just surprised that he...stayed.

"I wasn't expecting you," he whispers.

I nuzzle my face into that strong hand, knowing exactly what he means. I wasn't expecting him either.

Boyd bends and places a soft kiss on my lips, chaste and sweet. Then he pulls back, his eyes staying intent on my face, tracing over the sweat and handful of freckles.

"Are you hungry?" he asks. "I was thinking we could go into town and grab some dinner."

I nod. "Yeah. That sounds good."

He kisses me again, and I take the moment to breathe in that delicious smell of his, the one that's now mixed with the scent of the bodywash from our earlier rendezvous in the shower.

Boyd is a different kind of man. When was the last time a man apologized to me like that? With sincerity and thoughtfulness leaking from his every pore?

If it's happened, it surely hasn't been recently, or come from a man who mattered in the course of my life.

My father certainly has never done it, his approach more along the vein of excuses than apologies, and Evan wasn't the kind of guy to ever admit when he was wrong.

Clearly, I need to work on not lumping Boyd in with all the others who have let me down in the past.

Easier said than done.

Half an hour later, I've taken a second shower to scrub off the hike, thrown my hair into a loose ponytail, and changed into some jean shorts and a loose cotton tank.

"You look beautiful."

I roll my eyes but have to fight to hide my smile as I climb into the cab of Boyd's truck.

"I'm serious," he insists, passing over the phone he ran home to grab for me, then pulling away once I've buckled my seatbelt. "When I saw you in the terminal at the airport, you looked like this—fresh, clean, sweet."

Snorting, I glance over at where he sits, wearing a pair of cargo shorts and a black polo, looking like a delicious mix of city boy and mountain man.

"I'm not sweet."

"That is such a lie."

I cross my arms. "Okay, I'm sweet, but you don't have to build up my ego. I don't need lots of compliments."

"Maybe you don't"—Boyd looks over at me—"but that doesn't mean I'm going to stop giving them to you. And I'm not lying when I say you look beautiful."

I've never been the person who fishes for compliments from a man, but damn if Boyd doesn't make me want to keep poking around so he can say more in that sexy voice about how he sees me.

A few minutes later, we walk in the door to Dock 7, and I can immediately see the marked differences between this place and The Mitch.

While both are on the water and have outdoor spaces over-looking the lake, The Mitch has a decidedly rustic feel and looks like a dive that hasn't been updated in a decade or two. Dock 7, on the other hand, is clean and contemporary with brick walls and massive windows, giving off a feel that's much more in line with some of the hipster restaurants back in Boston.

"I thought this place was a tourist bar," I say to Boyd as we're seated at a table on the patio and handed menus.

He lifts a shoulder. "It is, but they also have food, including the best burgers in Cedar Point, and I am really in the mood for a blue cheese burger tonight."

I grin, thinking that might sound pretty delicious to me as well.

The server brings out some waters and shares the specials, telling us to take our time.

"It's weird. I always feel like I know everyone in this town, and then I come home and see how much things have changed," Boyd says, his eyes looking around. "Last time I was here, I knew all the servers because they were all Busy's friends from school. Now, I only recognize a few faces."

"You ever think you'll come back?" I ask. "Because you look like you really love it here."

Boyd smiles at me. "I do love it, really, but Cedar Point isn't for me anymore." He pauses. "At least not right now. Maybe someday when I'm older and want to retire or something, but living the same Mitchell life as all my family isn't for me."

I tilt my head to the side. "What do you mean?"

"It's hard growing up in a town where the road is named after your ancestors, you know?"

My eyebrows nearly fly off my face. "What?"

Boyd gets an amused expression. "The main road around the lake—it's Mitchell Road."

"Get out of town," I say, my mouth open as I slap the table. "And take your damn self-named street to get there. Oh my gosh, that's so cool!" Then something else clicks in my mind.

"The Mitch? Is that named after you guys too?"

He smiles at how much fun I'm having with this then launches into a brief overview of how his great-great-grandparents were the original settlers in Cedar Point, and how the Mitchell family has been a big part of changes and expansions over the years.

"So you're like, Cedar Point royalty. Tell me, did anyone ever call you King Boyd when you were in school?"

Boyd just chuckles. "No, but there is a week during tenth grade on local history, and when the entirety of that history is about your own family...well, it's just as humiliating as it sounds."

I burst into laughter, and Boyd shoots me a stare that's supposed to convey exasperation but really just makes him look even cuter.

"I'm going to need to hear all about it," I say, "and please, be as detailed and as graphic as possible."

We spend three hours at Dock 7—aka Lucky's—talking about everything under the sun. Boyd tells me more about what it's like being a Mitchell in a town founded by his family, crazy stories about town politics, and the intensity of the high school rivalry with another mountain town an hour away.

He talks about his job, the townhouse he lives in a few blocks from Harvard, and the weird things that go on living so close to an Ivy League institution. He asks about my mom and my friends, my job as a massage therapist, and how I got into yoga. We talk about my choice not to go to college, Boyd's fears about moving away around the same time his dad was diagnosed with prostate cancer, and what it was like coming home when his dad was fighting through it.

It's an amazing dinner, an amazing date overall, and not just because the food is delicious, which it is, or because I love the view of the lake, which I do.

It's because Boyd has managed to be my *friend* as we sit here and chat. Sure, there's that same underlying buzz of attraction that just never seems to go away when I'm near him, but at the same time, that's not the driving force.

Our focus is on each other, on our conversation, on laughing and enjoying each other's company.

Boyd has managed to, again, demonstrate to me what it could be like to have a deeper relationship with a man, and it is something powerful, that's for sure.

"The twins decided to light up the fire pit in our yard," Boyd tells me as we're walking out to his truck. "And Bellamy said you have to come over for s'mores. Non-negotiable."

"Well, I can't let the girl down, now can I?" I reply, grinning and hopping up into Hank with significantly more ease than the first few times.

And that's how I end up spending my Monday night sitting in a circle around a fire pit in the Mitchell yard, looking out at the lake and listening to Boyd's family absolutely roast him to death with stories about his childhood.

I don't think I've ever truly realized the solitude in which I live my life back in Boston before. Sure, I have a roommate, though she spends most of her time at her boyfriend's, and I have my mom. There's my neighbor Fiona, friends from yoga, and a few girls from high school I still connect with occasionally.

But all in all, I have primarily set up my life to go it alone. I rarely have anyone over or go out with people. My mom is the closest thing I have to a best friend, which—as much as I love her, and I really, really do—is kind of pathetic.

Where is the community? Where is the deepened life experiences from living side by side with loved ones?

I watch Boyd as he jokes about all the memories with his siblings, and I wonder what it would have been like to be able to tease and poke about things like that, to have a larger family, or even a group of friends who know everything about you, inside and out.

It makes me wonder if I've been so busy protecting myself from getting hurt that I've missed out on some of the amazing things relationships bring to your life.

"You've been awfully quiet," Patty says as she takes a seat next to me when Boyd heads inside to use the restroom.

I give her a tired smile and shake my head. "Just thinking. I love your family dynamic, how close everyone is, how much you all care about each other."

She looks at me with something warm in her eyes. "It's not always perfect," she jokes, letting out a hearty chuckle. "In fact, it usually isn't, but there's definitely something special about my kiddos."

"Boyd talks about all of you with this look of complete adoration on his face," I say. "I don't think I've ever seen a man love his family the way Boyd loves you."

Patty's expression gets soft and gooey as she looks across the expanse of her yard as her oldest son crosses the deck and heads our way.

"He's a mama's boy, that's for sure," she says. "I tried for years to get pregnant before we finally conceived. Every single one of my kids is a blessing, without a doubt, but we fought for Boyd. He was my first miracle baby."

I've never been one to think about having a family. I rarely plan more than a few months ahead—if that—and I've never seen myself being with a man long-term. I love my mother so much, but she talks about motherhood like it was the most difficult thing she's ever experienced. Imagining myself with kids? Why would that ever be something I'd want for myself?

The way Patty talks about it, though, makes it sound magical, like it fills a space inside of her chest that is shaped like a baby. I don't even know if that little hole exists inside of me somewhere because I've never taken the time to think about it before.

"What's got that dreamy expression on your face?"

My eyes flit to Boyd's where he's standing above me, and I tilt my head back as he leans down to kiss my forehead.

"Just talking about how you were my miracle baby," Patty answers. "The first little love of my life."

Boyd rolls his eyes but leans over to kiss his mother's cheek.

"You're gonna need to lay off the miracle baby stuff around the others," he says, flicking his hand in the direction of his siblings. "Otherwise they'll know who your true favorite is."

Patty lets out a cackle I bet all the neighbors can hear, the sound echoing across the lake.

"You know what I always say," she responds. "You *are* my favorite—my favorite firstborn."

Our conversation drifts to join in with the others, and I make sure to get in another s'more before all the supplies are gone. Eventually, Patty slaps her legs and excuses herself to go to bed. She and Mark hold hands as they head in, leaving me, Boyd, Bishop, and Bellamy to watch their parents.

"I love that their romance hasn't died," I say. "It's not every day you see a couple like them still holding hands and flirting with each other."

"Don't remind me," Bishop groans, his youthful irritation at seeing his parents be lovey-dovey clear in his tone.

"It's sweet." Bellamy emphasizes her opinion by slapping her brother across the chest. "Don't shit on it. Most kids would kill to have parents like we do."

Her eyes flit to mine for a second but quickly return to the chocolate and graham cracker sandwich she's been nibbling on.

"Sweet, sure—it's sweet as a fucking peach pie until you hear your parents having sex through the walls at night, or you walk in on them groping each other in the kitchen where anyone can see them," Bishop says.

He makes a gagging noise as the rest of us burst into laughter.

"It's funny until it happens to you," he adds, pointing a finger at each of us. "And mark my words, you're going to be coming to me with an apology someday."

Boyd's laugh dies off as he yanks me closer, tugging me to sit on his legs, my own dangling off the side of his chair as he tucks me in against his chest.

It's a snuggly position, and as much as I want to keep my attention on the conversation, it isn't long before my eyes start to droop.

I listen to the twins argue about something that has to do with groceries and a disappearing bag of Cheetos, but the thread of their conversation begins to get muddled as I sink deeper against Boyd.

"You still awake?" he asks, his voice low, the sound of it rumbling in my ear.

"Mmmmm," I moan, pressing my face into him, enjoying the heat from the fire on one side and the warmth of Boyd's body on the other.

"That's not an answer."

"Barely," I mumble, wishing I could just snuggle into his chest and fall asleep.

I know he should take me back to my little house and my own bed right now, know he should say good night and give me a kiss and then leave.

It's the smart thing to do.

But I don't want to be smart.

What I want is for him to carry me up to his room here. I want to stay nestled against him and fall asleep in this home full of happiness and family and love.

Nothing in the world would make me happier, and as I think about how much I'd like that, I eventually drift off to sleep wrapped in his arms.

chapter sixteen
boyd

I probably should have taken her home. It would have been the smart thing, especially after I told my mother the other day that I wouldn't bring random girls to stay overnight.

But Ruby's far from being a random girl, and as much as I'd like to say bringing her to my room is a last-minute decision, that would be a lie. I made the choice in my head as she sat in my lap outside, her body pressed snug against mine, her head resting beneath my chin.

Bellamy was watching us for a while as Bishop droned on in her ear, and when there was a lull in the conversation, she held up her hand, the back of it toward me, then dropped all of her fingers except one.

Her ring finger.

She wiggled it at me, a gleeful smirk stretched across her face.

"Mark my words," she said. "I give it a year."

I don't know how to feel about my sister's declaration. If

she'd done something like that a few years ago—hell, even a few *months* ago—I would have shaken my head in firm protest.

But tonight, I kept Ruby nestled against me and didn't say a word in response. I'm unsure whether my silence spoke for me or whether it was just silence, but I can at least acknowledge to myself that I didn't jump in to deny anything.

It's foolish to allow my mind to take a route like that, though, especially when there are still so many unknowns. More unknowns than knowns, if I'm being honest.

I know she lives in Boston about twenty minutes from me—because yes, I did a little map search on my phone. I know Ruby has a great relationship with her mom and a nonexistent one with her dad, know she gives massages and does yoga and likes her coffee with a splash of cream but no sugar.

The facts of her life have been coming together in little pieces that are helping me understand Ruby, but it would be unfair for me to think those bits of knowledge make up the picture of who she is.

A warm heart. A soft laugh. A positive spirit.

A willingness to talk out miscommunications, a desire to spend time with family, an interest in listening to others.

Those are better representations of who Ruby is than her job or how well she gets along with her parents.

How I feel about her has continued to sharpen with every interaction. Every look and laugh has brought her into focus in a way I never could have imagined just days ago.

But there's also something about her that screams at me to slow down. Not because it's what *I* need, but because it's what *she* needs.

Ruby responds to my physical presence, the touches, the kisses, the flirting.

It's the other things she seems less certain of, like her struggle to accept that I want her around, her constant worry that I see her as an inconvenience, her hesitation to believe that I want to spend time getting to know her and not just the part of her I can slip inside.

I think it's going to take some work to convince her I don't just want to fuck around for a while, but how do you even begin to attempt something like that when you have the limited time we do?

A balance, I think. Finding a blend between what she's expecting from me and what I'm wanting to give.

I need to be less intense about slowing things down, because I know she takes it as rejection, regardless of what my intentions are. I also need to make sure what I say to her and do with her is consistent in bed and out, need to bring the emotional depth into bed and the physical care into light.

We have eight more days with her here in Cedar Point, eight more days for us to explore what's going on between us, to dive deeper, to laugh harder.

Hopefully, during that tiny little scrap of time, I'll be able to decide what it is I want from Ruby, exactly. Because right now, it feels like I want more than just a delicious fling, but I think Ruby might see us as something with an expiration date.

If we don't get on the same page, one of us is going to get hurt.

When I open my eyes in the morning, I find Ruby's beautiful blues staring back at me. With our faces this close, I can see the little waves that make her left eye a slightly lighter blue than her right.

I don't know how long she's been watching me, but the idea that she's been taking me in while I sleep next to her has me pulling her close so I can press a kiss to her forehead.

"Morning," I whisper, not wanting my voice to wake us up fully yet.

"Morning," she says back, her body shifting next to mine as she stretches and lets out a yawn.

She blinks her eyes sleepily then tucks her face into her pillow.

"You're really cute when you sleep," I say, making her grin. "You breathe really deeply. It's like snoring through your mouth instead of your nose."

She snorts and shoves her face farther into her pillow, keeping just one eye looking at me.

"Rude."

Her voice is muffled, but I can still hear her amusement.

"Sorry I fell asleep so hard. Did you carry me up here?"

I nod.

"God, I don't even remember. Maybe it was the swim or the hike or the jet lag or the food, but I was *out*."

I shrug a shoulder, turning fully on my side so my body is facing hers, propping my head up with one arm.

"It gave me an excuse to keep you here so I could wake up next to you."

Her blush starts in her cheeks and creeps down her neck until it booms on her chest. Lifting my hand, I push some of her thick hair out of the way so I can see it better then trace a single finger from her ear, down her neck, to the red splotches above her breasts.

"Kiss me," she says, biting her lip when I immediately move closer to her.

"You sure?" I ask, my mind shifting gears and reprioritizing what I want out of this morning.

Ruby nods and leans closer to me so our bodies are pressed fully against one another. I know she can feel my morning wood poking into her hip, and I can even imagine that she is trying to figure out what she might be able to do about it.

She has another thing coming if she's assuming I'll be the only one receiving pleasure from the physical part of our relationship.

Instead of pressing my lips to Ruby's, which I'm dying to do, I lift off of my side, pushing her to her back so I'm hovering over her. Before Ruby can even react, I'm sliding down her body, my nose tracing over her exposed skin, careful to keep my lips to myself.

"What are you doing?" she asks, her voice low and breathless as I pop the button on the little jean shorts she fell asleep in and drag the zipper down.

I don't answer her, looping my fingers into the belt loops and tugging, my eyes feasting on her exposed skin as I pull them down her thighs, toned from years of healthy living, outdoor exploring, and yoga.

I trace my fingers over the fabric of her tiny panties, a lacy pink pair that rests softly against the prize underneath.

Ruby emits a soft panting sound as I stroke my finger straight down the center of her. She's already getting damp. I can feel it beginning to saturate the material, leaving some bits slightly darker than others.

"Boyd," she whispers as I stroke over her again. "What are you doing?"

I look up at her, across the length of her body from my place between her thighs, and I give her a devilish smirk.

"What am I doing?" I ask, taking each of her legs and propping them over my shoulders so I can settle in properly. "I'm kissing you."

Ruby's eyes flush with lust, but I shift my focus away from her face, tugging her panties aside and stroking my tongue long and deep through the crease of her lower lips.

God, she tastes better than I thought she would, like pure honey dipped in lust and wrapped in greed.

It's the only way to describe what it feels like as I go after her core with long, thick strokes. I am the inventor of lust and the embodiment of greed. I want her taste and her smell and her body overwhelming my every sensation until I can't breathe in anything but her.

A low, desperate wail comes from above my head, and when I glance up, I see she is lying flat on her back with her pillow over her face, her fingers scrunched up tight.

Like she can't take it.

I smirk but don't stop what I'm doing.

That's the edge I want to get her to. I want to nudge her slowly to a point where she feels like it's too big, too much, the words she spoke in the shower yesterday coming back to me.

It's a place other men have probably gotten her to before, the sensation building and building but never cresting. If I had to wager a guess, that desperation with no resolution is what makes her self-conscious, what causes Ruby to wonder things like *Does he think it's taking too long?* or *What's wrong with me that I can't get there?*

As I flick my tongue over her clit and relish the way her thighs are squeezing my neck and ears, I formulate a plan. What I *won't* have is Ruby pushing me away because she doesn't think she's worth the time it takes to figure it out.

I could spend years with my mouth attached to her core, drinking down her soft moans as she tries to muffle her reactions.

"It feels so good," she says, lifting the pillow from her face and whispering to me. "But I want to kiss you, too."

I shake my head, unwilling to let her deter me.

My goal isn't to make her come right now. Who knows how many times we'll need to do things like this before it happens—if it ever does.

But I *do* want her to give over to just enjoying herself, taking from me without the expectation of returning a 'favor' of some kind. She needs to know I want to worship her body, regardless of the raging hard-on that's tenting my sweats and aching for her touch.

"You'll need to wait," I tell her, pulling my mouth off and using my fingers to drag her panties down. "I'm busy down here."

I can see the thread of self-consciousness warring with desire on her face. She loves how it feels—I know it—but she doesn't want to be an *inconvenience*. It's the one thing she can't seem to get past, and the one thing I think gets in the way of her allowing her body to let go.

"It isn't going to happen, though," she tells me, her brows furrowed. "I don't want you to waste your time."

I rest my head on her thigh and just watch her, making sure she has a chance to get her thoughts off her chest. Her hand reaches out and strokes my hair.

"But it does feel really good." Her eyes are imploring me

to understand that she appreciates my efforts, her intentions of stroking my ego clear.

"I'm glad it feels good," I say, grinning at her. "I hope you don't mind, but I plan to be down here for a little bit."

Her head tilts to the side in confusion.

"If you can't come, you can't come, but that's not my goal. I'm down here because you taste better than anything I've ever experienced in my life, and I'm so turned on."

I press an open-mouthed kiss against her thigh, enjoying the way she jumps slightly when I suck on her soft skin.

"There is literally nothing else I want to be doing with my time right now than sucking on your clit."

Before Ruby can say anything else, I put my mouth back on her, focusing my attention on the little nub that rests at the apex of her lips.

I flick it with my tongue, over and over again, loving the way Ruby shoves her face back into her pillow, how her stomach muscles contract and her body rolls as she experiences the slow buildup.

This time, my eyes stay focused on her, making sure I'm observing her every move, every shift and sigh and cry, the soft noises and movements my guide to making sure I know when she's getting close to that peak she never seems to tip over.

And when she does, I pull away, wiping my face on the inside of her thigh and giving her another kiss there.

Ruby looks at me with curious eyes as I rise up and press a kiss to her mouth.

She wraps her arms around my body, kissing me deep, sucking on my tongue as we share the taste of her body, the little move making my dick throb in my sweats. I pull back slightly and press a chaste kiss to her forehead, knowing I need to get out of this room quickly.

"Let's go down for breakfast," I say. "I think I can smell something cooking."

The shock that covers her face is almost comical, but I make quick work of shifting off the bed and heading over to where my clothes are unpacked neatly in my dresser.

It only takes a minute for me to feel Ruby pressed up against my back, her arms wrapping around my stomach.

"What about you?" she asks, kissing my bare skin, her hands sliding along my chest and beginning to make a descent toward where my dick is rock solid and absolutely on board with what she's doing.

But I take her roving hands in mine, kissing the palms before I step away from her, tugging a shirt over my head.

"I didn't go down on you because I wanted you to return the favor," I tell her. "I did it because I've been dreaming about tasting you since our first kiss. Sometimes, the goal is just to have fun."

Ruby licks her lips, her eyes blinking rapidly. She looks adorable when she's confused, but I don't want to let on as to what I'm doing, what my ultimate plan is.

To crank her up so high, so hard, so tight, that she can't help but tip over.

Ruby's problem isn't her body, it's her mind. And I want to get her so blissed out, so frantic, so throbbing with need that she just doesn't have time to worry about anything else but finally letting go.

"Use the bathroom if you need to and throw your clothes back on," I say, pressing another kiss to Ruby's head and then one to her lips. "I'll meet you downstairs."

And then I leave her behind in my room.

When Ruby creeps down the steps fifteen minutes later, the flush on her cheeks is gone, but that hazy lust is still in her eyes.

Thankfully, my mom isn't home, having already gone off to her regular Wednesday morning at The Pines, the elderly home on the south bank of the lake.

It was Briar, surprisingly, who was cooking breakfast, though by the time I got down here a little bit ago, she'd already finished and shot me a glare when I implied she should have made enough to share.

Now, I'm standing over a stove, cooking up a heap of scrambled eggs in one pan and watching bacon pop and sizzle in another.

"Coffee's over in the corner," Briar says, and I enjoy the tiny bit of blush that colors Ruby's cheeks at the fact she's been acknowledged by one of my siblings.

"Good morning," she says to my sister, giving her a small smile before hustling over to pour herself a mug of the brown stuff.

"Morning." Briar's response isn't overly welcoming, but it isn't as bitchy as I was expecting after she stormed off yesterday.

Briar is not one to let go of her irritation quickly and has been known to go for weeks without resolving family drama. Today she seems neutral, level, though there is definitely a consistent bit of bristle that seems to pop up in her shoulders any time I—or anyone else—talks to her.

"I'm thinking about spending a few hours out on the boat," I say to the room. "If anyone wants to join me."

When I glance behind me, I see my sister thinking it over. Ruby, on the other hand, has a big smile on her face and her hand in the air.

"Pick me, pick me!" she says, giggling. "I want to go, for sure."

I nod. "Alright then. Let's plan to head out in an hour? We can eat breakfast then I'll drop you at home so you can get your stuff ready?"

Ruby nods, still smiling, and takes a sip of her coffee.

"You should tell the others," Briar interjects. "Especially if you're going to North Bay. You know the twins will be so in."

I figured as much, but there was a part of me that hoped I'd be able to finagle my way out of taking my siblings. Briar would have eventually declined, but if I bring it up to the twins, they'll jump into the boat without having any supplies. Busy will probably be down as well.

"What's North Bay?" Ruby asks.

"It's a corner of the lake that's closed to non-residents. It's not policed or anything, but you have to have a pass if lake security comes by."

Briar's answer has Ruby wiggling excitedly in her seat. It's one of the things I've noticed about her. She loves to be in the know, an insider, so taking her to The Mitch, Forks, North Bay...any kind of local hotspot is going to make her wiggle around like that.

I love it.

"Hurry up and finish breakfast," Ruby tells me, stars in her eyes. "We've got super-secret Cedar Point things to do."

chapter seventeen
ruby

It's after dinner time when we finally pull the boat back into the dock at the Mitchell house, and I'm exhausted once we've finished unloading and wiping everything down.

Boyd's dad calls us all up to feast on ribs he's making on the outdoor grill, and then I sit down with the whole Mitchell family for a delicious dinner overlooking the water, feeling thankful that they seem to have adopted me into their group for a little while.

"Today was amazing," I tell Boyd as he's driving me home once dinner is done and I've turned down Bellamy's invitation to watch a movie. "It's been a long time since I've gotten quite that much sun, though. I'll need to wear more sunscreen on this trip. My skin can't handle it."

Boyd reaches over and presses a finger into the skin on my shoulder, the faint pink color disappearing and leaving behind a solid outline of his finger.

"Yeah, you got a little color today, huh."

I nod, dropping the mirror on the back of the visor, wincing when I see my face looking back at me.

I've never been particularly vain, but I do fall into that category of women who assumes they look better than they actually do when they've finished a long day in the sun or exercising. I always imagine myself with a glowing sheen and pink cheeks, bright eyes and damp hair pulled back in a tight ponytail.

What I *actually* look like is much different.

My eyes are tired and my nose has a deep red tint to it, a lighter version of the color covering the rest of my face. I'm shiny and greasy-looking, and the fuzzy baby hairs I've never managed to get rid of around my temples are giving me a serious halo as they stand at attention.

I look wiped out. The only good thing is I know most of the pink and red will fade overnight. It'll hurt like a bitch in the shower, though. *That* I am not looking forward to.

Boyd pulls to a stop in front of the Bellows' house, puts it in park, and opens his door. Then he rounds to my side, stopping me as I slide down to the gravel beneath my feet.

His hands are on my waist and his frame towers over me as I lean against the interior of the passenger side, and just that small little thing—his fingers against the skin at my hips—has a shiver racing through me.

The man has been playing me like a fiddle all day, his every movement like a caress along the ridge of my spine that had me brimming with sexual tension.

Every moment he had a chance, his fingers were touching me: playing with the strap of my bathing suit top or letting his hands *accidentally* brush lightly over my nipples, holding my hand and stroking my palm with his fingers, soft kisses when we were alone in the boat or the water.

To anyone else, it would naturally be attributed to our earlier sexploration in his childhood bedroom, his mouth between my legs, giving me the best head I've ever had in my life. For a person with a normal body, failing to get off would obviously keep them on edge all day.

But I never get off. I've spent years in situations like today, where I fooled around or did something sexual and never reached the culmination.

So what was different?

What about Boyd has kept me set on a low simmer all day long, my thighs constantly squeezing together, my core pulsing with need?

I was absolutely aching for him, and now, with his hands on my hips, that same desperate throbbing at my center has returned with a quickness I could never have expected.

"I'm really glad you came with us today," he says, his fingers stroking softly against my skin. "It was a lot more fun with you there."

I shake my head. "Thanks for inviting me. Hanging out with you and your family has been..." My eyes search his, trying to pick the right words. "Well, let's just say your family makes me feel welcome here."

He dips down and presses his lips against mine, our mouths opening so I can feel that slow stroke of his tongue.

Even just these kisses, the little movements of his tongue sweeping in and tasting me, tangling with mine, remind me of what it was like to have Boyd's face pressed against my pussy, his tongue stroking right at the heart of me.

I might not have come earlier, but damn it felt good.

It was a shock to have Boyd shut things down once he was done going down on me. I can't ever remember a man not wanting sexual favors reciprocated, but he talked about licking me as if *that* was the favor, as if it was a gift to him to just get the opportunity to do it for me.

I've thought a lot about that today, trying to reconcile his actions with the things I've always thought to be true about men. Just like the fact that Boyd doesn't play games and really listens to me, his sexual behaviors are just another item to add to the list of what makes Boyd a man in comparison to all the boys I've known before.

Eventually, he pulls back from the kiss and takes my hand in his, leading us down the path to the front door.

"Tomorrow I'm busy all day," he tells me, and I have to put in extra effort to not look too depressed about it. "Every year when I come to town, my dad, Bishop, and I do a guy's day. It's nothing fantastic—fishing, beer, whatever—but I won't be back until after sunset."

I nod, giving him an understanding smile.

As much as I would like it, I can't expect Boyd to entertain me every second I'm here. I brought books with me to read, sudoku puzzles to complete. Maybe I can do some SUP boarding or go on another hike. There are shops in town on Main Street that I can explore.

"I understand," I say. "Besides, I've probably taken up *way* too much of your time since you've been home," I add, laughing and trying to make it okay for him to spend less time with me.

He shakes his head. "Don't let that mind of yours make you believe I don't want to spend every moment with you that I can. The best part about my trip home this year has been you, Ruby."

I bite my lip, blushing at the intensity of his statement.

Boyd Mitchell, everybody. Unlike any man.

"How do you feel about doing a little drive together tomorrow night?" he asks. "There's a pretty great view I want you to see."

I grin and nod, eager to see him as soon as I can. It's unlike me to jump so quickly into making plans with someone I'm seeing. It normally feels dangerous to do so because people so often let you down, but Boyd manages to make me feel like my importance surpasses anything else on his plate or in his life.

It's a heady feeling, and one I don't want to miss out on.

He kisses me again, soft and slow, his tongue licking into my mouth in that way of his that makes me slick between the thighs.

Then he pulls back and places a chaste kiss on my forehead—a signature move of his that I'm beginning to recognize and cherish—before giving me a wave and saying goodbye.

I glance at my watch: only 24 hours until I get to see him again. Let the countdown begin.

Most of Wednesday goes by without a hitch. When I wake up around 6, I take a towel out onto the patio and do an extra-long yoga session since I missed out on it yesterday when I was too busy grinding on Boyd's face.

I shower and change, driving my tiny rental car around to the other side of the lake where Main Street meets Mitchell Road. After getting a coffee from the tiny little coffee shop, I spend a few hours perusing every single shop, enjoying the little tchotchkes and souvenirs.

I buy a few small things—a keychain with trees and the word

Cedar Point on it, a magnet for the fridge, and a screen-printed tee of John Cusack that says *Grosse Point Blank,* but the word 'Grosse' is crossed out and replaced with 'Cedar.' Fiona is *obsessed* with dark comedies from the 90s, so it was quite a find.

Once I get back to the house, I open the little veggie tray I got at One Stop and post up on the deck, cracking the book I started reading a few days before I left. I planned to finish it on this trip, but I clearly haven't been taking any time to get a few words in.

When I'm changing after I get out of the shower, a firm knock at the door draws my attention. At first, I assume it's Boyd. Maybe they got back early and he's coming by to get me. But when I walk over and pull the door open, my jaw drops.

Ken is on the other side. He looks different than I expected him to, and it takes me a hot second to realize why. In the picture he sent to me, he was sitting with his wife and boys, smiling at the camera, not a care in the world.

Right now, standing in front of me, he looks like one of the unhappiest individuals I've ever seen in my life, and it seems pretty clear what the cause of his disgruntled attitude is.

Me.

"Hey," I say, not sure what words to use when greeting my 'dad' for the first time in almost twenty years. "Ken."

It comes out choppy and awkward, his name so clearly said after having to think about it.

"Ruby," he grunts.

And just like that, with just his gravelly voice saying my name with such irritation and displeasure, I'm struck with a memory that I'd long ago forgotten.

I couldn't have been more than five at the time, and I was standing in the doorway of my bedroom. Mom and Ken were in a fight. I don't have many memories of Ken, but in them, the two were always fighting, and my mom was always, *always* crying.

Even at that young age, my loyalty line was clearly drawn in the sand. My mother was my person. Ken wasn't the enemy, but I had little trust in him, especially when all I could see was his gruff face and my mother's tears.

I was supposed to stay in my room. That I remember, but how do you watch someone cry and do nothing? Even at that tender age, I knew I couldn't just stand there, so I went to my mom. I went to her and wrapped my little body around her neck, telling her it would be okay.

"Ruby."

Ken's voice hit me like a slap, his irritation with me clear as day. Then he picked me up, pulling me out of my mother's arms, and walked me back to my bedroom, closing the door on my own tear-streaked face without a word.

Now, as he stands before me, that memory clear in my mind, I wonder what the hell I'm doing here.

Why did I ever agree to come to this place to get to know an angry man who abandoned me? He discarded me and my mother like we were yesterday's trash, and I'm here doing…what? Wanting a relationship? Wishing we could erase it all?

"I was supposed to get back from my trip tomorrow," he says, yanking me almost violently out of the gray-toned pain lurking in my mind. "But there was a change of plans, and they told me I could come home early."

I nod at him, though I keep my mouth shut. The anger that's coursing through my veins feels like it could boil up at any moment.

"Did Linda help get you settled alright?"

My head jerks back, my face surely displaying in every uncomfortable line and irritated wrinkle just how stupid the question he just asked me is.

"Did she *get me settled*?" I repeat, my fingernails digging into the palms of my hands.

The girl my mama raised would normally keep the peace, wouldn't dream of ruffling feathers or causing problems, especially as a guest in someone's home—but that's not the girl I am today. Just as quickly as I told myself to hold in the anger, I also tell myself it's okay to let it pour out.

"She's treated me like shit since the moment I arrived," I bite out, unsure whether or not I enjoy the shock plastered across Ken's face. "She barely spoke a word to me when I got here, made it clear I wasn't welcome in your home, and forbade me from interacting with the boys. So, no, Ken, she didn't help me get settled. What she *did* do was make sure I know how unwelcome and unwanted I am."

He gapes at me, and any other time, I might find the expression funny: a guy in his fifties, mouth wide enough to catch flies, eyebrows high.

Right now, though, it's infuriating. Doesn't he know his wife? Doesn't he know what kind of person she is that she would treat me this way? Like I'm the devil come to ruin her life?

"I didn't..." he starts, glancing behind him as if Linda might appear at any moment to explain herself. "I didn't..." he says again, clearly unable to finish his thought.

Well that's just fine by me. I'll fucking finish it for him.

"You didn't *what*? Know your wife would treat me like I'm worthless? Talk to her about what would happen when I came to town? Prepare your kids for the fact that they'd be meeting their sister for the first time?" I shrug my shoulder sarcastically.

"What, Ken?"

But then his own shoulders drop, and he looks at me with sadness in his eyes.

"I didn't handle this right at all."

"No, you didn't," I snap, unable to let go of my anger just because he actually took responsibility for throwing me to the wolves.

"I was going to ask if you wanted to come have dinner with us so we could all get to know each other," Ken says, his expression looking akin to that of a kicked puppy. "But I think I need to spend some time sorting a few things out first."

I cross my arms and just glare at him, but my expression says exactly what my mouth doesn't.

Ya think!?

"I'm sorry, Ruby," he says. "I truly am. I'll make this right."

Never in my life have I lived on a man's promises, and I don't plan to start today. I stay silent as Ken gives me an awkward grimace and a wave then turns and walks the path that splits off to his house.

Then I slam the door, not caring in the slightest if it makes me seem immature or childish.

I spin around and look at the interior of the picture-perfect guesthouse, wishing for just a moment that I were the kind of bitch who would absolutely trash the place in anger.

But I'm not that girl, and I don't have it in me to go exercise right now, my normal anger processor off the table.

I wander through the house, feeling aimless and irritated for a few minutes before my eyes fall on the clawfoot tub in the bathroom.

I might not want to go on a hike right now to feel better, but I can always do the next best thing.

When I hear Boyd walking through the house, I wonder what his reaction will be.

He wanted to take me up to some viewpoint tonight, and when he asked me yesterday, it sounded fantastic. But after the confrontation with Ken, the only thing that felt like it would make me feel better was a soak in the tub, some relaxing music, and delicious-smelling candles.

So when Boyd texted me fifteen minutes after I crawled into the steaming hot water to say he was on his way to get me, I told him he should come inside because I wasn't ready.

When his face shows up in the doorway, his surprise is evident, but he quickly adopts a wolfish grin, crossing over to where I'm sitting back against one end, covered in a heap of bubbles.

"Well, aren't you something," he says, leaning down to press a kiss to my lips. "I'm gonna be honest, it would be quite the ordeal to get this tub all the way up Easy Street."

I bite my lip and smile at him.

"You were going to take me to high school hookup central?" I ask, my voice heavy with teasing. "And here I thought you were interested in my personality."

Boyd leans a hip against the counter, folding his arms and crossing his long legs at the ankles. "I'm interested in everything, Ruby."

"Really?"

He nods.

"Even interested in taking a bath with me?"

He ducks his head slightly, as if there is any way he'd be able to hide that smile of his.

"You want me to get in?" he asks.

When I nod, he doesn't waste any time pretending to think it over. He strips down quickly, first his socks and then his jeans. His shirt, his boxer briefs, his watch set on the marble counter.

He walks across the small room stark naked and looking every inch the sexually primed male, absolutely no shame in his expression at the way my eyes rove over his body.

Lifting one leg at a time, he steps into the opposite end, the water undulating in soft waves at the movement and change in water level.

It isn't a massive tub and definitely isn't designed to be big enough for two people, so when Boyd is finally settled and comfortable, his legs are pressed against the sides, his feet near my bottom. Then he pulls my feet into his lap.

"How was your day with your dad and brother?" I ask, poking my toes against the hard ridges of his abdomen. "Was it a super-manly day filled with testosterone and blood sport?"

Boyd lets out a soft laugh. "Yeah, if sitting out on a boat trying to catch fish all day is your idea of testosterone-filled, sure."

I smile at him. "What did you do?"

He shrugs, sinking a little farther into the water. "We fished, we talked a bit, we listened to some 80s rock. Once we came in, we went to the grocery store to get fish for lunch since we didn't catch any."

I laugh.

"And then we just kind of hung out."

"Do you like doing that with them?"

He nods. "I do. Bishop always seems like he's just spending

time with us because it makes *us* happy or because we force him to come with us. There was probably a time in my life when that's how I felt about my parents, but…" He shrugs a shoulder again. "The older I get, the more I realize how important those moments are. Someday, I won't have them anymore, so I need to take advantage now."

My surprise meeting with Ken still weighs heavy on my mind, even with a sexy, naked man covered in bubbles sitting right across from me. Even so, I don't want to waste my time with Boyd thinking about a man who doesn't seem to ever think of me.

We sit in silence for a while, just enjoying the little bit of music and the muted lighting from the candles. All we have right now is each other's company, and that's more than enough. I could fall asleep with the way Boyd is using the back of his thumb to stroke up and down the bridge of my foot.

"Feel good?" he asks when I shiver a little bit.

I nod, and Boyd takes my simple agreement as a directive, lifting my right foot and using his thumbs to press on the pads of my toes and massage the arch in a way that is absolutely heavenly.

I can't help the moans I let out at how good it feels.

"God, when you moan like that," Boyd says, his voice rumbling in that sexy way that gets me wet—even when I'm *not* submerged in a shower or a lake or a tub of water. Then he hums deep in his throat. "It turns me on like nothing else."

My heart rate starts to pick up, that same unsatisfied urge from yesterday beginning to thrum through me again.

"You're turned on?" I ask.

He nods, dropping my foot slightly in the water so I can feel his manhood beneath the surface, thick and hard.

I shift, using the side of my foot to brush lightly against him, thrilling at the way his eyelids lower.

"You have a foot fetish?"

I'm teasing him, and he knows it.

"I have a fetish for having any part of you touching any part of me," he says, wrapping his hands around my feet again.

But he doesn't massage them like I expect him to. Instead, he gives them a tiny tug, shifting my body so I'm slightly more reclined. Then he slides his hands along my shins, eyeing me like a piece of meat he wants to devour.

"Your skin is so silky," he tells me, lifting one leg out of the water and running a single finger from ankle to knee.

"It's the stuff I put in the water." I try to keep my voice from sounding too breathless. "A few of these little oil balls that help hydrate your skin. It creates that slick feeling."

He hums low in his throat, continuing to stroke up and down my shin with his hand.

"Slick," he says, stretching the word out so each letter is paid its due. "I like that word."

Boyd adjusts his position, causing the water to slosh a bit, the remaining bubbles foaming up higher on my chest and then receding enough that my breasts are newly exposed to the cooler air above the warm water.

His eyes drop instantly, and I see the tip of his tongue touch his two front teeth, his hunger clear in every small movement.

It's unreal what his attention does to my body, the way his gaze feels like hands caressing my skin as he peruses my exposed flesh—but his restraint is maddening.

I assumed Boyd would climb into this tub and give me a good time the minute he crossed the threshold. Instead, he's been quiet and relaxed, chatting a little but mostly just watching me.

And all the while his hands keep roving and probing, stroking and then massaging.

Like I said, *maddening.*

His every touch seems to rev me up in ways no other man has been wont to do, and it makes me want to crawl out of my skin and burrow into him.

"What's that look?" he asks me.

"What look?"

I'm full of shit. The expression he's seeing is called blatant, unfiltered horniness, unadulterated lust. There's no way I can hide the feelings bubbling up inside of me from his watchful gaze, not that I want to.

It's just not in my wheelhouse to make the first move.

Maybe it makes me a bitch, but I know I'm attractive, and most of the time, attractive women don't have to make the first move. Men are only too happy to take the reins, sexually speaking.

It's not in my experience to have a man make all the overtures of sexual interest and yet not be the one to push us to take that next step.

So, clearly, I'll need to get out of my comfort zone. If anyone is worth putting myself on the line for, it's Boyd.

"*That*—that look. I like it, but I haven't figured out what it means yet."

I lick my lips and push my hands through the water, bringing some of it up to wash over my cooled skin and rinse away the bubbles left behind.

Boyd's eyes again drop to my chest, to the nipples that are hard little points begging for his attention in the cold air.

Moving my body slowly, I push away from my side of the

tub, coming up on my knees in between his thighs.

"It means…" I say, wrapping my arms around his neck and moving one leg at a time so I'm straddling his naked body. Then I bring my mouth to his ear and whisper. "It means I want you inside of me."

I notch myself against his hardness under the water and begin undulating my body so the head of him is rubbing up against the spot that's aching the most.

Boyd shivers, an almost violent tremble that wracks his entire body. It's intoxicating, seeing the way my actions impact him.

He wraps his arms around me, grabbing handfuls of my ass and using his strength to overpower my movements, adjusting my motions so that just the tip of him is pulsing in and out of me.

Just like that, he sucks up all the power I thought I would be wielding, taking over in a way that makes me feel small and safe and cherished, even though he's beneath me.

I drop my head, fucking my tongue into his mouth the way I wish he would fuck into me, and he returns my pressure and aggression in equal force.

"God, Ruby," he groans, tilting his head back and shifting lower in the tub, changing his angle.

We continue like that for who knows how long, alternating between focus on my clit and the sensitive tissues right at my entrance.

All the while, Boyd's focus stays zeroed in on me, his mouth slightly open, his breaths as heavy as the lust in his eyes.

As much as I love this feeling, I start to worry about the fact that I know my body won't give Boyd what he's looking for, that he'll start to…

Boyd adjusts his grip on my ass, one finger grazing my backside in a way that has every hair on my body standing up straight. My core clenches and a shiver rolls through me, the forbidden nature of his attention bringing my mind right back to where it was before.

Observing my reaction and seeing my body set ablaze, Boyd strokes his finger against me again. And again. And again.

Until I can't handle looking into his eyes anymore.

Slamming them shut, I bite the inside of my cheek, trying to distract myself from my body feeling like this massive, throbbing thing. I feel dirty in the best way possible.

Suddenly, Boyd's notched dick against my center probes deeper, and my eyes fly open.

Then he lets go of where he's been controlling me with his hands and arms, finally allowing my body weight to drive me down onto him.

I cry out in pleasure and pain as my core envelops him, the slow seating seeming to go on and on and on. His thickness and length fill me with warmth and a fullness I've not experienced before.

"Oh my god," I whisper, my eyes closed again and my head tilted back. "You're too big," I say.

I keep my body frozen once he's all the way in, allowing myself a moment to adjust to the sensation of my body trying to fuck a tree trunk.

Boyd's hands massage soothingly over my hips, run along my back, and trace soft nothings into my stomach, making me giggle then cry out again when the laughter unexpectedly shifts him inside of me.

"Don't make me laugh."

Of course, Boyd begins chuckling himself, and I drop my

gaze back to his in a glare, which only makes him laugh harder. His body moves slightly, the broadness of his dick pushing ever so slightly more inside of where he already rests, too deep, too big, too much.

A deep moan falls unbidden out of my mouth, the sound echoing off the walls.

"I've never laughed during sex before," he tells me, his grin wide. "Maybe before or after, but not while I'm inside of someone."

"Does that mean I can say having sex with you was a joke?"

His eyes narrow. "You teasing me?"

I nod. "I love teasing you," I whisper.

Boyd moves his hands so one rests on my hip, the other stroking down my belly toward where we're connected.

"And I love teasing *you*," he replies.

Then his finger swirls around my clit, the tiny ministration drawing every ounce of my attention right to that impossibly small bundle of nerves.

I moan, my body moving of its own accord when my hips begin to rotate in slow circles. It only soothes the ache inside me for a moment, though, eventually only serving to stoke the fire blazing under the water.

"You're so tight," he tells me.

"Does it feel good?" I whisper, loving the way his eyes roll back and his mouth falls open as I lift the slightest bit off of him and then drop back down.

The movement makes me pant out a harsh breath, an unfamiliar feeling suddenly and swiftly spreading up to my chest.

"So fucking good." He moves his hands back to palm my ass cheeks, taking control of the motion of my hips.

My fingernails dig into the skin of his shoulders as my movements become harsher, harder. Up and down, up and down, the water beginning to swirl around us. Then that single finger is back again, stroking against the dangerous spot that has me filled with confusion and feeling like I might burst out of my skin.

There's no way I'm stopping, whether I can come or not. The way this feels, this slow burn that's turned into a brush-fire, the way Boyd's eyes stay attuned to my every movement…I wouldn't give this up for the world.

We've graduated from humping against each other to full-on fucking, my body smacking against Boyd's as he helps lift me up and slam me back down, his dick pounding into me hard, again and again and again.

"I'm going to come," Boyd says, the cords in his neck straining as his body surges him on a train toward a pleasure I wish I could experience *with* him.

But I still get joy out of watching him hit that peak, knowing I brought him there.

His eyes roll back in his head, his jaw grinding as he groans in pleasure, and I squeeze my internal muscles as much as I can, reveling in the little jolts his body gets as he comes down from the summit.

"That was…" Boyd doesn't use words to describe it, instead letting out a moan I've heard people emit when they taste something delicious for the first time.

"For me, too," I say, dropping my mouth to kiss him, wanting to reassure him that even though I didn't come, I still enjoyed every minute.

He hums and kisses me then pulls his head back. "Even the butt stuff?"

I burst into laughter and watch as Boyd convulses under me, his softening dick still inside me. I laugh even harder as he pulls out of me, my vagina becoming a weapon of torture now that he's not hard anymore.

Pressing a kiss against his lips again even though it does nothing to mask my continued giggles, I answer his question.

"Even the butt stuff."

chapter eighteen
boyd

"We're hiking Kilroy tomorrow," I tell her as we lie in bed together the following morning. "We leave at 7am."

"Mmmmmm."

I snicker at her nonanswer then realize she probably has no idea what I'm talking about. "It's an overnight hike. We leave early, hike most of the way up, set up camp for the night, and then keep going to watch the sunrise the following morning. Do you want to come with us? Wait, let me rephrase that—I want you to come with us. Will you?"

Ruby peeks an eye open, probably to gauge the sincerity of my invitation. Just that little look is a reminder that the two of us have a long road ahead when it comes to teaching her that her presence is desired, not an imposition.

She rolls onto her back without answering me, her eyes focused on the ceiling. A long minute goes by before she replies.

"Let me think about it," she says. "I love spending time with you and your family, but I don't want to intrude."

"You wouldn't be intruding."

She turns and snuggles her face into my chest. "You know what I mean. You should have at least *some* family time without me."

I kiss the top of her head, appreciating the sentiment. I want to push her harder, but what am I supposed to say that doesn't make me sound like a crazy person? What I *want* to say is that she fits perfectly into my family and she should get used to being around us, but that's insane.

"What are your plans for today?" she asks.

I trace a finger along her collarbone, enjoying the way her skin pebbles with goose bumps at my touch.

"Mostly preparing for the hike and hanging around the house," I answer. "Nothing too spectacular. Why?"

She shrugs a shoulder then turns and snuggles her body into mine, pressing a kiss against my bare chest. "I was thinking about renting a jet ski. I saw some info about it when I was in town yesterday and it sounds so fun, but it would be *more* fun with a friend."

I snake my arms around her waist and tug her back slightly so I can see her face. "A friend, huh?"

Ruby blushes, and I watch as it spreads from her cheeks, down her neck, across her chest. "You know what I mean."

Nudging her onto her back, I lift myself so I'm hovering over her then I rub my hard dick against her thigh.

"I know exactly what you mean," I reply, pressing an open-mouthed kiss against her neck then sucking on the area until she squeals and giggles. When I pull back to look at her, I revel in the smile on her face. "I also know I've been having some thoughts about you that don't feel very…" I rub against her again, "… *friendly.*"

Ruby bites her lip, her eyelids lowering, but before anything can come from our little bit of flirtation, there's a knock on the door.

Her eyes widen, and in less than ten seconds she's out from underneath me and yanking on a pair of shorts and a loose shirt.

"I'll be right back," she says, stepping out of the bedroom and closing the barn door that separates the bedroom from the living room.

I doubt she'll be *right back*, and when she does return, it won't be to snuggle up in bed again, so I roll out of it and head to the bathroom, taking a piss before donning my jeans and shirt from last night.

When I'm finished, I wash my hands and face, grab my watch and wallet from the counter, and head out to the living room to join Ruby and see what's going on.

I can tell instantly I've made a grave error.

While I haven't had any intention of keeping my relationship with Ruby a secret, I didn't fully think through the ramifications of walking out of her bedroom in the morning to face her father at the door.

I don't have a lot of experience with meeting fathers—any experience, really—but I can tell by the look on his face I was absolutely the last thing he was expecting to see in his guesthouse.

"Boyd," he says, his eyes widening slightly.

He takes me in as I walk across the room, and I have a split second to decide how to handle myself.

Ultimately, I go with the thing that feels right: *boyfriendly*.

"Hey, Mr. Bellows," I say, giving him a smile as I come up behind Ruby and drop an arm around her shoulders. "Good to see you," I add, extending a hand to him.

Ken's eyes bounce between the two of us for a second before

he does the polite thing, taking my hand and giving it a firm shake.

"Surprised to see *you*," he responds. "I didn't realize Ruby was…friends with anyone in town."

"More than friends," I reply, giving him an easy smile before I drop my eyes down to look at Ruby.

Her somewhat shell-shocked expression is mixed with something that looks oddly like…delight?

"We met before she got here. I live in Boston, too."

I'm aware what I'm saying to Ken is a misdirection, but the last thing I want to do is make him think I've turned his daughter into a booty call. I don't know what their dynamic is or what his values are, but I *do* know I don't want to make things more difficult for Ruby, especially when how I feel about her can't be summed up in just the one week we've known each other.

"Small world," he says, looking back at Ruby.

"Yep," she says, a smile finally stretching across her face. "So small."

"Well, I'm glad we'll be getting together tonight." Ken shuffles his feet a little. "It'll give us a chance to talk…about everything."

Ruby nods but doesn't say anything in response.

"I'll see you at 6?"

"Sounds good."

Then he's waving goodbye and heading back to his own home, likely still trying to figure out what's going on with me and his daughter.

Ruby closes the door, inhaling long and exhaling slow.

"Everything okay?" I ask, moving behind her to massage her shoulders.

Her head falls forward, a soft hum coming from her mouth

as I roll my thumbs over her muscles.

"Yeah," she finally says. "I'm having dinner with him and Linda tonight."

My hands stop moving. "That's good, right?"

I can tell from the tension in her body that my question was stupid.

"He came by yesterday," she says. "And it was...not a good conversation." She launches into what happened last night before I showed up, detailing her interaction with Ken when he popped over, having come back from his trip early.

I'll be completely honest—the more I'm learning about Ken Bellows, the less impressed I am.

"I can't believe he was so clueless," I say, shaking my head once she's done and the two of us are seated on the couch. "What the hell did he tell Linda before you got here? *Did* he even tell her about you?"

She shrugs a shoulder.

"I have no idea, but part of me doesn't really care. What matters is that he hasn't seemed to do anything right. He didn't care enough to make sure things went smoothly for the estranged daughter he abandoned two decades ago."

I purse my lips, trying to come up with anything that might make her feel better, but before I can say anything, Ruby takes in a deep breath and speaks again.

"I feel like...I need to stay here and get to know Ken," she says, returning her gaze to mine. "He might have done things wrong, and he might be an asshole..."

I grin.

"But the masochist in me wants to give him a chance to do it right. If he's having discussions with Linda before coming to invite me to dinner...I don't know, it seems like he's trying."

Then she shrugs a shoulder and snuggles farther into the couch. "I mean, he has his faults, but he seemed sincere yesterday, so…"

There are a million things I've yet to learn about Ruby, but something I'm quickly picking up on is her desire to give people chances. She is a benefit-of-the-doubt kind of person, the type who will never write someone off completely.

What a wonderful thing to be in a world full of judgmental assholes, and yet what a difficult way to live your life when so many people look for any opportunity to take advantage of others.

"I understand completely," I say, even though I selfishly wish she'd give him the boot and come on the hike with us.

I could never ask her to do that. She's supposed to be here to spend time with him, though his own actions don't necessarily reflect that he's taking it seriously. If she feels like skipping out on the hike means she'll get more time with the man who left her behind, possibly giving them an opportunity to reconcile, the best thing I can do is be supportive.

Ruby suddenly pops up from the couch. "I don't want to think about it," she tells me. "What I want is to go jet-skiing with my more-than-a-friend, Boyd."

I bite my lip, loving her little joke and completely on board with helping distract her from the more intense issues at hand.

"I'll go with you, under one condition."

"What's that?"

"You don't need to rent jet skis. It's a waste of money when we have some."

Her eyes widen, her excitement growing.

"Well that's even more awesome because it means I can save that money and use it toward buying more ridiculous souvenirs to take home with me."

"Oh my god, tell me you didn't just say *more*. What did you already buy?"

She bounces up and down, still wrapped around my waist, shaking me with her.

"The cutest things *ever*, duh. I like to support small businesses."

I roll my eyes, pretending I don't find her excitement about cheap tchotchke bullshit endearing when I totally do. I also don't have the heart to tell her all the little things she's purchased were likely made in China and not here in Cedar Point.

When she drags me behind her through the house and over to where she has her prized new possessions sitting out on a side table, I make sure to compliment each one.

Because seeing her face light up is quickly becoming the best fucking part of my day.

"I'm moving home."

My head jerks to the side when I hear my sister's words, shock and confusion rippling through my body.

We just got done with dinner, all of us sitting down for a big pasta dish my mom made after we spent a few hours getting things ready for the hike tomorrow. It was our first family-only meal since all of us have been home, and everyone shared their life updates.

Busy talked about the summer job she had as a camp counselor a few hours away and Bellamy lamented her fears about not knowing what she wants to do when she graduates next year. Bishop shared his excitement about possibly getting picked up by a triple-A team after his final season playing college baseball. I talked briefly about my possible upcoming promotion, though I leave out the fact I've been mostly ignoring work since coming to town which I'm sure isn't doing me any favors.

Briar was noticeably tight-lipped, though she *did* share how things at her shop have been going. She's been working as a florist at a boutique down the mountain, and as far as I'm aware, she loves her job.

So her words right now are nothing short of confusing.

"You're moving home," I repeat, staring at her as we both enjoy the warmth of the fire pit.

It's just the two of us out here. Everyone else is inside watching a movie, and for once, I'm thankful that my sister decided to intrude on what I was hoping would be some quiet alone time.

Out of all of my siblings, Briar and I are the closest, which is why her distance since she arrived a few days ago has been noticeable—though I'm sure my near obsession with spending time with Ruby was a factor as well.

"Yeah," she says, her face remaining stoic and emotionless. "I need a break from...everything."

There are unspoken words there, and I wouldn't be a good big brother if I didn't address them. "Chad, you mean."

She continues to stare at the fire, almost unblinking. "And other things."

We sit in silence for another moment as I scroll through all the questions I have for her. I have to be careful. Regardless of how close we are, Briar has always been a closed-off person. If I come at her with a million questions, she'll shut down and not talk to me. I have to pick the ones I think she might answer and make sure I say them in the right way.

"Have you told mom and dad yet?"

She shakes her head, her hair moving in the light breeze. "I know they won't mind, though."

"They won't mind, sure, but they'll care," I say. "About whatever the *reason* is."

I mention it but don't ask. Whatever the reason, my sister isn't going to share it until she's good and ready.

"Did you tell Chad? Or your job?"

Briar blinks, and I see a single tear make a slow trek down her face. My entire body goes on red alert.

"Yeah, I told them," she whispers.

I feel stricken by the fact that I just saw her cry. I have only seen my sister cry three times in our entire lives that didn't have to do with being a little kid or serious injuries.

The first time was when our family dog died. She loved Shep more than anyone else. Even though German Shepherds are supposedly guard dogs, we wound up with the one that was afraid of everything. But he was my sister's best friend, sleeping in her bed every night. She was devastated when he was gone.

The second time was when her high school boyfriend broke up with her. She vowed to never allow a man to make her cry again, and as far as I know, it's never happened.

The third and most recent time was when we found out my dad was in remission from his prostate cancer, though it was only a misty eye, and she'd deny it if anyone asked her about it.

So this tear, while seemingly small to anyone else, feels like a blow to the chest. It means, at 27 years old, Briar is finally crying about a guy, which means whatever happened before she made the decision to move home is seriously serious.

I get out of my chair, suddenly feeling like the distance between us is too much, and I crouch next to her, putting a hand over hers. Then I reach out and wipe the single tear away.

She clenches her jaw, and I know that's her internal frustration with having been 'caught' being emotional, but I need her to know I see her pain.

"I'm not going to ask you what happened," I say, keeping my voice low. "I know you well enough to know you might not ever tell me."

She blinks, her eyes taking on a sadness that makes my big brother genes want to grab my baseball bat, drive down the mountain to find Chad, and fuck shit up.

But I know that won't solve anything, so I keep that angry pest locked up tight.

"But I just want you to know I'm here for you. Whether I'm physically here by your side or you need someone to talk to over the phone in the middle of the night, I'm here for you."

Briar gives me a jerky nod, and I can tell that's the most I'm going to get out of her.

I pat her hand and return to my chair then take a long pull of my beer, draining the rest of the bottle in just a few seconds.

"I've always thought Chad wasn't good enough for you," I tack on. "I've always kept that to myself, and if you decide to get back together with him, I'll love and support you no matter what, but the man isn't your soulmate."

I pause, thinking back to all the things I dislike about him and zeroing in on one in particular, hoping to make Briar laugh.

"I mean, he has shirts with deeper V-cuts than you do."

Briar lets out a choked sound before she throws her head back and laughs, her throaty voice sending a howl into the night air that makes me smile. My sister needs to laugh like that more often, and it makes me sad that I'm just now realizing how long it's been since I've heard it.

Her laughter dies down slowly, and she wipes under her eyes, looking at me with gratitude. "Thanks for that. I needed it," she says.

I nod. "Any time."

We sit in silence for a little longer before I can sense her looking at me. When my eyes lock with hers, she asks me a question I should have expected.

"Do *you* believe in soulmates?"

I don't know how to answer her, because anything I say will sound too cliché for someone as thoughtful and logical as my sister.

The truth is that if she'd asked me this question a week ago, I would have shrugged it off with a snort and an eye roll. I've never been the guy to believe in soulmates, destiny, true love, happily ever after. Those things are for fairy tales, not real life.

And yet just a short while into knowing Ruby, I'm completely changing my tune.

Maybe that's the thing about soulmates. I don't know if you can ever really believe in them until you find one yourself.

I don't get a chance to answer Briar's question, though, because the screen door squeaks as it opens, and I hear my mother calling my name.

When I turn and look over my shoulder, my eyes widen when I see Ruby standing next to her, her eyes and nose red like she's been crying.

I fly out of my seat and go to her, immediately pulling her into my arms, wishing with every fiber of my being that I could take her emotional burden and strap it to my own back.

"What's wrong?" I ask, even though I'm pretty sure I know the answer since she was just at her dinner with Ken and Linda.

She doesn't answer me, just shakes her head and wraps her arms around my waist, and I take solace in the fact that I'm able to give her comfort when she so clearly needs it.

"Can I still come on the hike tomorrow?" she asks, her voice muffled against my shirt.

I bring a hand to her head and pull her in even tighter. "Of course you can. Absolutely."

"Thank you," she whispers.

I don't say it aloud, but she doesn't need to thank me. She doesn't need to feel gratitude for the fact that I want her around, that I'm ready to include her on my list of priorities.

Right now, she doesn't need someone to give her any kind of advice or critique.

As the brother of three sisters and the son of a mother, I've had it drilled into my head many times that when women are upset, they want someone to listen to them, not someone who assumes they can fix the problem.

I know my place tonight will be to provide Ruby with a shoulder to cry on and an ear to vent to.

I just hope whatever it is that happened isn't something that's wounded Ruby in a way that's impossible to repair.

chapter nineteen
ruby

I'm nervous when I make the short walk across the stone pathway that leads from the guesthouse over to Ken and Linda's.

I spent a few hours with Boyd, goofing off on the jet skis and lying out on the dock—this time with significantly more sunscreen. It was a struggle to keep my mind distracted from the looming dinner, but Boyd did his best to keep me laughing and smiling all afternoon.

Eventually he needed to start getting ready for the Mitchell family hike up to Kilroy, and I said goodbye, knowing it would be a good idea for me to get in a little nap and shower before going over to have dinner with my 'dad' and his wife.

The nap went slightly too long, leaving me with that deer-in-the-headlights feeling and mental fog that are difficult to shake off. Thankfully, I still had time for a quick shower. Nothing like a blast of cold water to wake up every nerve and neuron in your body.

Ken answers the door when I knock, his face looking as uncomfortable and awkward as I feel.

"Ruby," he says, giving me a small smile. "Glad you could make it."

I want to roll my eyes. *Obviously* I could make it. I literally came here to see him, not that he cared enough to be around when I arrived.

But I swallow those feelings down and return the sentiment. I can't let my irritation be on the tip of my tongue all evening or else I should just turn around and leave now.

Politeness will get us much farther than anger.

"Me too."

He waves me in and I cross through the doorway, my eyes taking in the inside of Ken's lakeside home for the first time.

It's just as beautiful as the guesthouse I'm staying in, maybe even more so.

The white rustic theme is continued from one to the other, though the living room at Ken's leans much more country club than fancy barn motif. A large patterned area rug lies over hardwood floors, and elegant striped couches and antique armchairs square off with a stone fireplace that reaches all the way up to the top of the high ceilings.

Along one wall is nothing but square blocks of windows with thin trim, providing a breathtaking view of Cedar Lake.

There's a stuffiness to everything, though, and it makes my skin itch, like I've been placed in an uncomfortable outfit and can do nothing about it.

"Your home is beautiful," I say, unsure of what topics are right for our first real conversation in my life.

Ken nods, giving me a real smile, though it's still small. I'm starting to get that he might not be that comfortable with showing his emotions on his face, or maybe he's one of those levelheaded types—like I thought Boyd was when I met him on the plane—and he just doesn't have a lot of emotions to express.

It would explain his lack of wrinkles, that's for sure, but that could just be Botox.

"Linda dabbles in interior design," he tells me. "She got her bachelor's degree and had a business for a while, but ultimately she wanted to be a mother. So now, it's all recreational."

I bob my head, my eyes still tracing over everything I can see, trying to drum up something else to say.

When my eyes land on a family picture over the fireplace, I head there, wanting another chance to see the boys.

It's another version of the photo Ken sent to me in his message, though this one is a lot less posed. Instead of all four of them smiling at the camera, this one looks to be some kind of blooper where they're laughing at something unseen.

When I feel a bubble of happiness in my chest, I let it simmer there for a moment, feeling thankful that even if I don't know my little brothers, they look to be having a good life.

"They're 8 and 10?" I ask, even though I already know. Maybe the boys are a safe subject we can discuss while we're still getting our feet wet.

"Yeah. Elliott turns 11 in October, and he'll be going into junior high in a few weeks. He's very excited."

I smile, my mind scrambling to create a picture of my younger brother with only the handful of things I know about him.

"What are they like?" I say, turning and walking over to the least ostentatious chair in the room to take a seat.

Ken scrubs at the little bit of stubble around his jaw with the back of his hand, taking a moment to think it over.

"Elliott is rambunctious. Very sporty. He loves to snowboard and has been working with a private instructor, hoping to compete professionally once he gets a little older."

My eyebrows rise, and I can't help but wonder what the cost of something like that is, though I guess I shouldn't be surprised considering the size and style of their home.

Immediately I feel petty. I shouldn't be comparing what he spends on his boys to what he spent on me. I should feel happy that they're getting the awesome experiences Ken has been providing for them.

"Nathan wants to be like his brother, but he's not as outgoing, so he's just now learning how to kind of be his own kid. He loves kayaking and hiking, but more for the views and chance to explore nature. He's really into frogs."

"They sound amazing," I say, and I absolutely mean it. "Do you think...I mean, is there a chance I'll get to...you know, meet them? While I'm here?"

Ken made it clear that it would be just him and Linda at dinner tonight, saying the boys already had plans to do a sleepover at a friend's house.

I call bullshit, though I've kept that opinion to myself. I think Linda doesn't want me around them for whatever reason, and she's made it her goal to make sure it doesn't happen. Maybe that's judgmental. Maybe I'm jumping to conclusions. Or maybe I'm just hitting the nail right on the damn head.

Regardless, I've been wondering whether or not I'll get to meet them since I found out they existed, and I'm hoping Ken is going to be willing to give me the one thing I'm eager for.

As much as I'd like to have some kind of a relationship with Ken result from this trip, I can only hold out so much hope for things to work out well.

Knowing the boys—having *brothers*—is something I can actually see happening at some point.

"Elliott and Nathan?" he asks, almost surprised, as if we weren't just talking about them.

I nod, unable to hide the eager expression on my face.

He opens his mouth then closes it again, shifting where he stands.

Before he can say anything, I hear the clacking of heels on the hardwood, and when I turn my head, I see Linda walking into the room.

"Did I hear you talking about the boys?" she asks, giving Ken a tight smile, her eyes straying to mine for a second before returning to her husband.

"Yes, well...we were just...talking about—"

"Whether or not I'd get to meet them," I say, interrupting Ken's blustering. I stand, giving Linda my full focus, knowing she's the gatekeeper I'll need to get through. "I'd love to get to know them while I'm here."

Something dark flashes in her eyes before she gives me the same expression she gave me the day I arrived: sour discomfort clambering to hide behind a hostess's smile.

"Let's just get through this dinner, shall we?" she says. "Speaking of which, everything's ready if you want to..."

Linda motions in the direction she just came from then heads that way, not waiting for me or Ken to follow.

Get this over with.

Those were her unspoken words.

Everything's ready if you want to *get this over with.*

I glance over at Ken, seeing that his eyes are glued to the space where his wife was just standing. If I'm not mistaken, there's a sadness in his eyes, something that reeks of guilt.

But just as quickly as I see it, it's gone.

Ken turns to me and gives me that same uncomfortably tight expression, waving his hand toward where Linda went.

"Let's get to dinner, then."

"So, Ken said you do interior design?" I ask, spearing my fork into a piece of asparagus then lifting it to my mouth.

Linda bobs her head a few times but stays silent, as she has for most of the dinner so far.

Ken and I have been exchanging brutally awkward chitchat. He's asked me a few questions about work, and we made small talk about the things I've done since I came to town. Other than that, there's been lots of fork and knife clanking and chair shuffling, with Linda staying almost completely silent other than telling Ken she was going to turn up the air conditioning then disappearing for ten minutes.

"What made you want to get into that?"

Ken should be the one I want to talk to, but the hostility in the room is coming from Linda. Clearly, I'll need to break down this aggressive dislike—i.e. hatred—she has for me, or else things are just going to continue on this path. If I'm going to try to engage Linda in conversation, I'll need to ask her questions that force her to actually use her words.

She finishes chewing her mouthful of food then takes a sip of wine…then uses a cloth napkin to dab her mouth before setting it back on her lap.

When she finally looks at me, I see reluctant acceptance in

her eyes.

"I really value a traditional home environment. I used to help my mother rearrange things and decorate in the home I grew up in, so it just seemed to come naturally to me."

"Well, you're clearly very good at it. Your home is beautiful, and I *love* the way you did the guesthouse. Boyd told me you just had it redone?"

Her body shifts slightly when I mention Boyd.

"Yes. About two years ago."

"Well, you'll have to make sure to talk to Patty about it," I say, glad we're finally on a topic that feels comfortable to me. My shoulders lose some of their tenseness and I settle back into my chair. "Boyd said she raves about how gorgeous it is, and how she needs to redo *their* guesthouse in a similar style."

Something akin to moderated delight crosses over Linda's face when she hears that.

"Really?"

I nod. "Absolutely. We've both seen the inside of their home, and Patty clearly has a very specific taste. It's gorgeous, no doubt, and a really warm place to spend time. But the guesthouse isn't where *she's* going to live, and there is something to be said about having an actual designer turn a space into something you'd see in a magazine. You should talk to her about it."

Linda nods her head but doesn't say anything else. Maybe it's progress, maybe not, but at the very least, I feel just *slightly* less like the enemy.

Nevertheless, my desire to make this work grows stronger, my discomfort with the extended silence palpable.

"I've never been inside a home that looks as carefully put together and designed as that guesthouse," I say, deciding to stay on that same topic since it seems to put Linda at ease.

247

Who knows? Maybe if I talk for long enough, I'll say something she likes and she can chime in.

"Sure, you see them on HGTV and every so often you'll step into a house where the kitchen has been partially redone or the bathroom has been updated, but that entire place is just... breathtaking. I especially love the chandelier in the living room and the clawfoot tub in the bathroom. That mixture of modern and antique feels soothing. It's very homey, which is a weird thing for me to feel because I never had that whole *home* thing, you know? Mom and I bounced around a lot, and the places weren't nearly as nice, but my idea of home is mostly just where my mom is. So for me to feel *at home* when visiting anywhere without her is definitely new for me."

I take a sip of my water, my mind thinking about where I can lead the conversation next, but when I take stock of the table, I see Linda's expression has returned to that angry, scowly thing from earlier.

"As I'm sure you can understand," Linda says, her voice like acid, "I would appreciate you not bringing up your...mother in my home."

My brow furrows and my hackles rise up. *Excuse me?*

"No, I don't understand. What does she have to do with anything? She's my mom."

Linda's jaw tenses.

"Calm down, honey," Ken says to Linda, his voice low but with a thin layer of pleading in there.

"I will *not* calm down," she hisses.

My entire body goes on alert in response to the venom in her voice, and I know without a doubt that any attempt at having a friendly dinner—while laughable in the first place—is officially nonexistent.

"What's the problem?" I ask, feeling both like I should let the topic drop and also like I shouldn't let it go.

My mother is the most important person in the world to me, and while I might not be someone who instigates fights with others—in fact, it's the exact opposite of the type of person I am—I have no intentions of allowing Linda to say shit.

"The *problem*," Linda mutters through gritted teeth, her anger shifting from Ken over to me, "is that I think it's ill-mannered for you to bring up your tramp of a mother at the dinner table."

I don't know if it's possible, but it feels like my entire body bristles at her words, like I'm a dog catching the scent of something dangerous. My mouth gapes, my body tenses, my hands clench into fists around my silverware.

"Linda," Ken says. But he doesn't say anything else. He doesn't tell his wife she's a bitch or put a fucking muzzle on her for calling my mother a *tramp*.

"Are you fucking kidding me?" I seethe. "Did you really just say that to me?"

"Don't curse in my home. It's inappropriate, though I doubt your mother ever taught you proper manners."

I drop my silverware with loud clanks onto my plate, the clattering sound still not enough to overtake the tension in the room.

"What the hell is your problem?"

"My problem is you—you and your mother. I don't know why you've suddenly decided to pop up in our lives, but I wish you'd leave and go crawl back into the hole you came from."

"Linda." This time, Ken shows a little more disgust at his wife's words, though in my opinion, it's too little too late.

"We didn't do anything to you," I say, my voice beginning

to rise with the level of my anger. "All I did was reach out to the father who abandoned me and my mother, who seemed to love us one day and left us the next. I don't deserve your anger when I did nothing wrong."

"You're right," she says, and my shoulders almost deflate at her words. "*You* did nothing wrong. Your *mother*, on the other hand, is a homewrecking whore, so forgive me for not wanting to discuss anything that has to do with her sniffing around what's mine."

Shock ripples through my body in long waves.

"What are you talking about?" I say.

But I know. I know before she even tries to say anything else.

Every memory I've pushed to the back of my mind, anything at all that had Ken in it, comes flooding back to the forefront, and it's easy to sort through because there's almost nothing there.

A few instances of the three of us going to the beach, mom telling me to get excited to see daddy, the two of them fighting and then him disappearing for long periods of time.

There are almost no memories because he was never there. Even before he left, he was never there.

Which can only mean one thing.

"I'm talking about the fact that I was happily married when your mother set her sights on my husband. She did everything she could to tear us apart, but I won't let something like that happen again, do you hear me? Neither of you are going to be able to sink your claws into our relationship and create pain for us. Not through Ken, not through me, and not through the boys."

I don't remember fully what happens next, everything feeling like a muted, slightly blurry dream.

All I know for sure is that I leave. I walk right out of Ken's fancy-ass home, down the walkway, past the guesthouse, and straight out to the road.

My feet take me on the mile-long walk to Boyd's house without me even realizing it, as if it's something I've done a thousand times before instead of only a few. I walk up the little woodchip path that leads to the beautiful blue door with the white trim, and I stop before I knock.

Is it too much? For me to show up here like this?

I wipe at my eyes, only just now realizing I'm crying. Then I shake my head, thinking maybe it's better if I just go back to the guesthouse and hide away until he gets back from his trip with his family. I don't want to ruin it for him.

But at the same time, I don't want to be alone.

"Ruby?"

My eyes widen when the door opens and Patty stands on the other side of the screen, looking at me with concern.

"Are you okay, sweetheart?" she asks.

Maybe it's because I miss my mom, but I shake my head, allowing the tears to fall even harder from my eyes.

Patty coos at me, pushing open the screen and stepping over the threshold, wrapping me up in her arms. She snuggles me against her with the kind of love and affection only a really great mom can give.

"Oh, honey. Whatever it is, I promise you'll figure it out," she says, rocking us slowly from side to side.

We stay like that for a few minutes, until my self-consciousness takes over and I pull back, wiping at my face and nose with my palm, giving Patty an embarrassed smile.

"Boyd's out back at the fire pit. You wanna come in and talk to him?"

I weigh it in my mind, wondering if I should just go back

the way I came.

Ultimately, I decide to give Boyd the benefit of the doubt. He told me he wants me around all the time, said I should always feel free to tell him what's on my mind and never apologize for how I'm feeling.

And really, nothing sounds better than getting another hug like I got from Patty, this time from the man I'm slowly falling for.

Patty leads me through the house, past some curious eyes from Boyd's siblings as they all sit around watching a movie. I studiously ignore them, focusing only on getting outside, getting to Boyd.

She slides the screen door open to get out onto the deck then calls out for him. I can see him sitting at the fire pit with Briar, a beer bottle hanging loosely from his fingers. The minute he sees me, he's out of his seat and flying across the grass and the deck to get to me.

"What's wrong?"

I want to tell him, but not right here or right now. Not until I've had a minute to get past these tears.

So instead of answering, I just wrap my arms around his middle and tuck myself firmly against him.

The minute I'm in his embrace, the emotions that have been so all over the place feel like they mellow. I can't imagine him leaving tomorrow to go on a hike for two days, so I spit out the first thing that comes to mind.

"Can I still come on the hike tomorrow?"

"Of course you can," he says, tucking me in even more tightly. "Absolutely."

Relief washes over me, both at the fact that I'll get to be with Boyd and that I won't risk bumping into Linda or Ken over the next couple of days.

"Thank you."

Boyd holds me against him for a while longer, the two of us staying out on the deck long after Briar has gone inside to leave us alone.

"I'm glad you came to me," Boyd says, placing a soft kiss against my head. "You can always come to me."

Something in my chest eases, the emotional upheaval that's been dissipating finally coming to the bottom of the hill.

Boyd is very quickly becoming my safe space, a point of refuge in the storm of life.

It both comforts and worries me.

I can't imagine finding another space that makes me feel as happy and whole as Boyd does, and where will that leave me once he's gone?

chapter twenty

boyd

The hike to the top of Kilroy takes about six hours if you're not stopping for breaks or to take in the beauty of nature. Plenty of experienced hikers probably leave before it's light, hike to the top, check out the view, and then hike down, making it back to Cedar Point before the sunset and all the dangers that come along with being in the forest at night.

But something gets lost in that single-day experience. Part of the journey is about slowing down enough to enjoy the little things along the way, not just busting ass to the top, turning around, and sprinting back the way you came. The creeks and streams, the birds, the vegetation and wildlife that are specific to Tahoe National Forest—it's important to stop and smell the flowers, both literally and figuratively. I may have intentionally avoided this hike for years, but that doesn't mean I don't know how to find value in the experience.

Especially now that Ruby is here, experiencing it right along with us all.

She's been mostly silent during our trek, the playful chatter I've come to expect from her noticeably absent. Instead, she's been a sounding board for my siblings as they bitch and moan about life or tell horrifying stories from childhood.

Like when Bellamy and Bishop were in the third grade and got a hold of some wax strips. Bishop didn't have eyebrows for two months, and Bellamy makes sure to keep those pictures in some hidden place in her room, along with embarrassing photos of the rest of us. Ruby laughs in the right places, and she does seem genuinely interested in the things my family members are talking to her about.

But that spunky happiness that usually seems to radiate from her every pore is missing.

It's understandable. She told me about what happened with Linda and Ken as we lay in bed last night. Not only is she dealing with a vindictive, bitchy woman and a shitty, uninvolved father, she's also facing the fact that her mother hasn't been completely honest with her about her life.

About her past, her childhood, her relationship with her father.

My mother offered up the guesthouse and Ruby accepted in a heartbeat, the two of us driving straight over to Ken's to collect all of her belongings.

We returned fairly quickly, but my mother had still found time to spruce the little place up, turning down the bedding, lighting a soothing candle, and leaving a short note for Ruby.

You're always welcome here, it read, and it only took a few seconds for Ruby's tears to return.

Her eyes still hold a little bit of puffiness today, though with the water and the sun and the exercise, she's starting to look a little more like herself the longer we walk.

I love that she asked to come with us on this hike. Before she showed up at the house, I'd been wondering if maybe I should stay to be in town for her in case things went sour with the Bellows, but then I worried my family would assume I was using her as an excuse to skip out on the sixth straight Kilroy hike.

Ultimately, it all worked out. I'm doing the hike my family wanted me to do *and* I'm spending time with the most amazing woman I've ever met.

"The last thing I want to worry about is a possible injury right before getting called to Triple-A," Bishop says to Ruby. "But I promised my parents I would get my degree to fall back on in case things don't work out with the big leagues."

He's been telling her all about his baseball life, from T-ball through pony and getting recruited to play for Whitney College, a Division 2 school outside of Sacramento that has one of the most phenomenal baseball programs in the state.

"Whit might be D2," he continues, "but plenty of amazing players come from smaller institutions. Not everyone who makes it big is coming out of a Pac-12 or Big 10 school."

"What's a D2?" Ruby asks. "Isn't that the name of the *Mighty Ducks* movie?"

I chuckle from where I'm hiking at the back of the pack, listening in as my brother launches into an overly detailed explanation of how schools match up, what divisions mean, how schools might be in a certain division for one sport and another for a different sport, and blah, blah, blah.

Part of me thinks Ruby made a mistake by asking Bishop questions like this, but there's also the strong possibility that it's an intentional diversion tactic designed to keep the attention off of her.

She couldn't have picked a better person to talk to if that

was her goal. Bishop—the most self-absorbed out of all of us—is more than happy to talk about himself all day.

Eventually, we reach Kilroy Camp, the small campground that's a little over a mile from the outlook where we'll enjoy the sunrise and view of Cedar Lake and all of Cedar Point tomorrow morning.

My dad leads us all over to site three, the one he reserved for us online. Even though this spot isn't particularly busy since not everyone wants to hike up a mountain to camp, it's still a good idea to reserve a spot in advance.

Thankfully, we are greeted by a completely empty campground, and my family makes no bones about setting everything up with quickness and efficiency.

It's been a long time since I've come up, so it's a bit surprising to watch all of them move in this well-oiled manner that I'm not as familiar with. My dad begins unpacking his travel cooking supplies. My mom and brother set up one of the two big tents while Briar and Busy set up the other. Bellamy begins yanking out the lightweight chairs from each of our packs, setting them around the fire pit.

"I want to help," Ruby says, her eyes taking in their movements.

"Help me find wood for the fire."

She nods, and once I call out to dad to let him know what we're doing, the two of us wander out of the campground clearing and back into the wilderness in search of logs and sticks we can use for a fire tonight.

"I'm glad you're here," I tell her.

Ruby smiles. "You've told me that five times already."

"Well, it's important to speak the truth, right?"

It takes about an hour, the two of us mostly wandering

257

around in silence, but we end up bringing back three bundles each of small logs, wood pieces, and big sticks that will be more than enough for us to have a nice long fire this evening.

"I thought you said you don't like to go on this hike," Ruby says on our final scavenge through the trees.

"I don't. I mean, most of the time, I'm too busy with work, so it just doesn't fit in my schedule."

Ruby eyes me. "Too busy with work? I haven't seen you work once on this trip."

I nod, knowing what she's said is true, much to the irritation of my employers.

I've been working for SolvTech since a year out of grad school. Normally, they allow me to take the two weeks off in August without issue because I'm fairly accessible while I'm traveling.

For many reasons—one of which is the petite brunette walking next to me—the emails from my boss have sat unanswered in my inbox. I know it's an immature way to handle a problem. I shouldn't skirt around it to avoid the confrontation I know is coming, but I just don't have the mental fortitude to deal with it right now.

There's something to be said about shutting out work and just living life for a little bit. My bank account can handle it. My workload might suffer a smidge, but there is nothing on my task list that is time sensitive or needs handling before I return next Monday, promotion be damned.

So the decision to ignore the job-related shit piling up for me at home is an intentional one. Sometimes, avoidance is done in the name of and for the sake of mental health.

"I've been doing things different this trip," I reply. "Better priorities this time around," I add, winking at her as we come through the trees and back into the clearing where my family has mostly finished setting up camp.

"Boyd, which tent should I chuck your bag in?" Bishop asks, holding my pack in his hands.

The choice he has presented me with is to either sleep with mom, dad, and him in one tent or my sisters in the other.

Thankfully, I had enough foresight to avoid this.

"Neither," I reply. "I brought my own."

Busy giggles, and when I look over at where she stands next to Bellamy, I see them each giving me wiggly eyebrows.

"I don't wanna hear any sex noises tonight," Bishop grunts, dropping my bag back on the ground and giving me a glare.

Ruby dumps her stack of wood in the pile near the fire pit, her face bright red, and not from the exertion.

"I can't believe he said that in front of your mom," she whispers to me.

I laugh. "You wouldn't believe the things he talks about in front of my mother," I reply.

She wiggles her nose and shakes her head. "I'm just going to pretend this conversation isn't happening." And then she wanders over to where my sisters are taking seats in their chairs, presumably to talk about whatever girls talk about.

"I'm not kidding," Bishop says, coming up next to me, his voice dipping. "It's bad enough that I've had to deal with mom and dad before. Do you know how horrible it would be for me to be sharing a tent with them and hear you two assholes moaning?" He makes a gagging noise.

"Yeah, yeah. Don't worry," I tell him. Then I give him a little grin. "I'll make sure she's quiet."

Bishop laughs and gives me a shove, then helps me set up my two-person tent.

"I think this is the most s'morey week I've ever had in my life," Ruby says, her hands on her tiny little belly once she's finished off her third graham cracker, marshmallow, and chocolate treat of the night.

"If you get sick tonight, just make sure you get out of the tent first," Busy warns her. "We had an incident two years ago, and let me promise you, lugging a tent that reeks of vomit down the mountain as it bakes in the sun tomorrow will *not* be a fun thing to do."

Everyone laughs except for Bellamy, who sits with her arms crossed and a glare on her face.

"*You* try not getting sick after eating Bishop's undercooked brats," she declares, eyeing our brother. "I still think he did it on purpose."

It takes only that little memory to stir up one of the twins' arguments, and I take that as my cue to take a leak before we all start rolling off to bed.

We had an amazing time this evening, much better than I can remember on the few times I did this hike years ago. Campfire games like Winking Assassin and Charades become surprisingly more ridiculous when you're an adult, and we had a great time playing Bullshit with the decks of cards Busy brought along.

My favorite, though, was a new idea Briar had about having to earn your s'more. All of us wrote funny little tasks on pieces of paper and put them into dad's hat, and then we each drew one out and had to do what it said before we were allowed to have dessert.

Busy had to pretend to Riverdance for twenty seconds and mom had to create a tower out of playing cards that wouldn't fall over, but nothing was more satisfying than seeing Bishop pull out the slip of paper he himself had added to the pile.

I won't ever forget what it's like to listen to him sing Whitney Houston's *I Will Always Love You* at the top of his lungs.

When I return to the fire after going to the bathroom at the little outhouse stationed up here, I find everyone packing up and tucking things away in their tents to head to bed.

"It feels early to go to sleep," Ruby says, looking at the time on her phone.

It makes sense that she's confused—it's only eight—but we're heading out for Kilroy Peak at four, and that's *after* we've packed everything.

"Gotta get up crazy early," I tell her, wrapping my arm around her shoulders and kissing the top of her head. "But we don't have to go right to sleep. This isn't sleepaway camp—there's no designated lights out."

Ruby giggles.

It's amazing how quickly that sound has become intrinsic to my very being, how imperative it is for me to hear that tinkling fall from between her lips.

Unable to help myself, I dip down and kiss the laugh right off her, loving how it feels when she opens her mouth, her little tongue stroking soft and wet against mine.

"Alright, you two. Time for *bed*."

I flip Bishop off then follow everyone else's lead, packing up my chair and helping to do some of the harder cleanup work tonight so we aren't trying to do it all in the morning.

Once the entire campground is picked up with only a few items left outside the tents, we all turn in for the night.

The tent I'm sharing with Ruby is small, but that's ideal for the two of us. We took a moment earlier and zipped our sleeping bags together to make one large bed big enough for two.

Slipping our shoes off and tucking them into a corner pocket, Ruby and I stretch out on the somewhat comfortable softness of the sleeping bags, the warmth of the late summer evening lingering enough for us to lay on top. I click on the tiny battery-powered light that hangs down from the middle.

"Are you sleeping in your clothes or stripping down?" I ask.

In the past, I've just slept in what I wore for the hike, figuring it can't hurt my body to wear the same thing for two days.

"Um...stripping down?" she replies, the words coming out as a question. "Or should I not do that?"

"You should *absolutely* do that."

Ruby hears the teasing innuendo in my voice, and instead of taking her clothes off, she flops down and stretches out, gazing up at me with adoring eyes.

"I'm so tired though," she says, her voice low. "I might need some help."

I chuckle, enjoying her little game and quickly seeing how I can work it to my advantage.

Well, I guess it's *her* advantage since so much of our sexploration has been to help her get more comfortable with how her body reacts to stimulation.

She bites her lip and watches me with hooded eyes as I slowly undress her, pulling off her leggings with slow intentionality and leaving hot, wet kisses on her skin as I go.

Every time we're together, I want to take my time revving her up, though not because I think it will get her off—that's an issue that rests exclusively inside of Ruby's head, and she'll have to work through that herself.

I do it because I want her to get accustomed to the idea that placing my mouth and hands on her skin is a gift to me. I want her to understand that I enjoy worshipping her body, regardless of whether my own rocks get off. I want her to learn how to enjoy the slow build, not getting so focused on the climax at the end that she can't take in the joy of the journey to get there.

Working over Ruby's body is like this hike to Kilroy. Every step up to the top matters. Enjoying the scenery and little things on the way matters. The view at the top matters, too, but we slow ourselves down to make sure we take everything in. If you don't enjoy the entire journey, that experience of reaching the peak doesn't feel like it means as much once you get there.

Ruby squirms as I divest her of her clothing, protesting in a quiet whisper as I'm tugging off her panties, saying she hasn't showered and probably smells bad, saying she's too dirty for me to put my face between her legs.

I simply shake my head at her, though, and reach up to click off the light hanging above us.

I know for a fact that if I came back from a run or some kind of outside activity that had me sweaty, Ruby wouldn't hesitate to suck me off, because she feels exactly the way about my body as I do about hers.

Like it's never enough.

Her smell, her taste, her soft cries.

It's never enough.

I want them all, and I want them all the time.

So I ignore her last few comments as I take off her last stitch of clothing, and then I dive down into the valley of my goddess, spending quite a while worshipping her body the way she deserves. Nothing goes unexplored, my head between her thighs, my mouth on her tits, my tongue swirling with her own.

She tries to turn the focus on me a few times, letting out little huffs of irritation when I thwart her efforts.

"Why won't you let me get you off?" she asks, her voice still a whisper even with the woven-in irritation. "Is it not good enough?"

Even in the dark, I can hear the insecurity, and I immediately stop where my mouth is sucking on her swollen tips to give her my full attention.

There was an error in my planning, something I didn't think all the way through when deciding on my single-minded focus to teach Ruby that her pleasure isn't a waste of time, and that's how my redirections would make her feel.

So, I make sure I clarify what I'm doing—what I've *been* doing—all along.

"Everything you do to me is more than good. It's amazing," I tell her.

I can't see her completely, but my eyes have adjusted enough that I can see where the light from the moon coming through the thin layer of tent reflects in her eyes.

"The only reason I've been focusing on you is because you have this idea that time taken to pleasure your body isn't worth the effort simply because you haven't been able to get off."

Her swift intake of breath and widening eyes proves I've surprised her. Maybe it's something she hasn't thought through all the way, or maybe she has and just didn't realize I could see it. But I do. I see it, and I want to be the man who helps her get over that impression, because it's a lie.

"And that's just not true," I whisper. "Do the things I do to your body feel good? Do they make you squirmy and horny?

Make you feel like your body is being lit on fire?"

She nods, licking her lips.

"Then that's enough. If you want me to stop because you're not enjoying it, I will. Otherwise, you should just assume I'm having fun with your body because I know it makes you feel amazing, and making *you* feel amazing turns me on like nothing else."

Ruby lifts a hand and strokes it through my hair, the tenderness in her caress cracking something open inside of me.

"I couldn't have dreamed you up," she whispers, looking at me like I hung the fucking moon.

It makes me want to pound on my chest, knowing she sees me that way, but instead, I drop down and press a kiss to those delicious lips I can't get enough of, reveling in the way she kisses me back.

And then I spend a while longer proving to Ruby that every word I just told her was true.

chapter twenty-one
ruby

The sunrise at the top of Kilroy is unlike anything I've ever seen in my life. The entirety of Cedar Point stretches out before us, giving us a breathtaking view of Cedar Lake surrounded by trees and forest in the distance that lead off to Yosemite.

I asked Boyd yesterday why the hike took so long since the view doesn't feel like it's high enough to warrant a six-hour ascent to the top. Apparently, the trail we took out of Cedar Point loops around to the back side of the peak, adding an additional three-plus hours to a hike that would only take two and a half if we'd driven around to the other side.

"But where's the fun in that?" he'd said, grinning and continuing on the trek.

Sitting here at the top, my legs dangling over the edge of a rock that juts out and away from the ridge, I couldn't agree with him more. The sweat equity of getting up here has made this view all the more magical.

Just like my time with Boyd.

God, I'm falling in love with him.

I'm falling in love with a man I've known for a week, and every single part of me feels on board with this absolutely reckless decision.

I've tried to talk myself out of it, tried to remind myself of the men in my life who have let me down and made me feel like my presence is unwanted.

But Boyd isn't those other men. He's unlike *any* man, and I can't manage to lump him in with the ones who have made me feel so small and unimportant in the past.

We sit together at the top, his front pressed against my back, his legs on either side of mine as we both hang our legs down, his arms wrapped around my middle. It's one of the most amazing feelings in the world.

There's something to be said about protecting your heart, keeping yourself safe, but it feels different when you have a strong man at your back who will tuck you against him to make sure you don't fall.

Falling in love seems unsafe to me.

Trusting a man seems unsafe to me.

Believing in someone other than myself seems unsafe to me.

Somehow, Boyd has taken all those places of danger and wrapped me in a bulletproof vest made of his care and concern. Those things are no less unsafe, but I don't have to be afraid, because I've been enveloped in the safety of his…love?

I'm not sure how he feels about me, entirely. The way he treats me and talks to me sure feels like what I *assume* love is, but I can't be sure unless we talk about it.

Even though I'm feeling a lot more brave than I was even a few days ago, I still have things to work through.

No woman can come out of the things I've experienced with

my ex and my dad and pretend everything is picture perfect, but I at least have someone I'm willing to take a chance on, a man who has said and done some of the most thoughtful and beautiful things to make sure I feel like I matter.

The things he said in the tent last night, the way he's cared about me in the wake of what's happened with my father—those are not small things. I might even go as far as to say that we might be able to take this relationship that has bloomed so beautifully in Cedar Point and transplant it back to Boston.

When we started this little thing between us, it felt much more like a fling, like it would be fun here and then a nice good-bye once I go home. But the more time passes, the more Boyd continues to prove to me over and over and over again that the man he is deserves to be compared to no one else, the more I wonder if he might be the guy who's worth breaking all my rules for.

And not just while we're in Cedar Point—I'm talking in the long run. Maybe I'll bring it up to Boyd when we get back to town and the two of us have a moment alone.

The hike down is a lot less fun than the hike up was, simply because the element of anticipation is gone, replaced with the nagging reminder that we have a long walk ahead to get back.

Eventually, we do finally make it back around two on Saturday, the exhaustion in my body thick and overwhelming. All I want to do is wash the dirt and dust from my body, drink an obscene amount of water, and snuggle up next to Boyd.

I smile, wondering what things might be like back in Boston. Maybe I'm jumping the gun, but I can't help allowing myself to daydream, this new and very trusting part of my persona pushing me to fantasize about the future. Will we spend most of our time at his place or mine? Will he take me on proper dates or will we slip right into something simple and easy? Will my mom like him?

I spend a long time in the shower, scrubbing away all the filth and grime. Boyd told me to just go on to the guesthouse when we got back instead of helping him and Bishop clean up all the gear.

"It's boys' work," he said, swatting my ass and sending me on my way.

Now, I'm showered, changed, smelling delicious, and snuggled up on the little loveseat in Patty's guesthouse, flipping through social media and zoning out.

I hear a knock at the door and drop my phone to the cushion, crossing the small space and yanking the door open with a smile.

A smile that falls when I see Ken standing on the other side.

I can't imagine what he could possibly want from me, not after he brought me here and allowed me to get chewed up and spat out by his wife, not when he threw a wrench into my carefully crafted picture of the world I grew up in—one where my father left behind me and my mother, not one where my mother is a homewrecker who lied to me about what things with Ken actually looked like.

That thought physically hurts as it rushes through my mind, but I push it aside, unwilling to dissect it in this moment when I'm standing in front of the one man who seems to be responsible for all the bullshit.

"What do you want?" I ask, crossing my arms and giving him the unhappiest expression I have.

He puts both hands up, as if to promise he means no harm. It makes me want to laugh. All he's ever done is harm me, even with his inaction.

"I just want to talk," he says.

"You had your chance when I came over for dinner," I say, the residual anger coming back into my body in a tsunami. "Why should I talk to you now?"

He drops his hands and his shoulders, looking every bit the wounded man when he says, "At the very least, because I have answers for the questions you probably have, but also because I know I messed up, and I'm here to see how I can fix it."

It feels too easy, too transparent.

But this new Ruby who's giving people trust isn't able to give Ken the narrow-eyed inspection without seeing how serious he looks.

So I let out a sigh and stand back, waving him in. He takes a minute or two to look around, his eyes examining the space the same way I took in his home when I was in it.

That's when I realize something.

He's nervous.

He's as nervous right now, standing in front of me, as I was standing in that massive living room looking at his family picture. Maybe he was even nervous then, too.

As much as I want to say something bitchy like *You don't get to be nervous when you're supposed to be the adult*, it feels incredibly hypocritical to even think it.

Yes, Ken should have done a lot of things different.

Yes, Ken is one of the parties responsible for the shitty circumstances of my life.

And yes, Ken can be blamed for a lot of the bullshit I've dealt with, both from him and from Linda.

But it doesn't feel fair to place the blame solely at his feet.

Even though I don't have the mental capacity to examine how I feel about my mother lying to me right now, I know she and I will be having a long and probably painful conversation when I get home.

The reality is that Ken is a human, too, an imperfect one who has fucked up a lot when it comes to me, and he should take responsibility for that.

But he isn't an evil person.

He's just a man.

A fallible one, but a man all the same.

So instead of ripping into him with how I'm feeling about what happened at his house, I ask if he'd like a glass of water, which he declines. Then the two of us take a seat, me returning to the loveseat and Ken perching on the edge of an older recliner that's seen better days.

If either of us are going to get anywhere, I can give him one last chance to say whatever he thinks will make a difference. I can at least give him that if he's making the effort.

"I want to start off with an apology—with multiple apologies. I'm sorry for not being here when you got here and for not fully sorting things out with Linda before you arrived. I'm sorry for not being completely honest with you about…anything."

Ken scratches the back of his neck then the front before leaning forward and bracing his elbows on his knees.

"And I'm sorry for not being there for you. I'm sure you can understand why, what with the way things were between me and your mother, and between me and Linda. My relationship with Michelle was a mistake, one that hurt many people, and you were an unintended casualty."

I wince when he says that, my heart sinking when I realize that Ken's apologies aren't going to be the bridge or olive branch I thought they were going to be. Just more empty platitudes.

"But I think if we try again, perhaps we can find some solid

271

footing for all of us," he continues, unaware of my discomfort. "I've talked to Linda and she feels…badly about how things went last night. Maybe we could see about you meeting the boys, too."

Then he gives me a soft smile as if what he's said is in any way enough.

"What do you say?"

I take a deep breath and let it out slowly, trying to sort through the millions of words racing through my mind right now. I'm angry, and it feels like this might be my only chance to ever tell Ken how I really feel.

"What I say is…absolutely not."

His smile slips away, and I can tell he wants to convince me otherwise, so I hold my own hand up, wanting him to stay silent. He got his turn. Now it's mine.

"First of all, there are a handful of things you could have done when you came over here. You could have apologized sincerely for the way your wife treated me. You could have taken the time to explain what happened between you and mom, and you and Linda, that even built up Linda's resentment in the first place. You could have been honest about why you invited me out and then went on a business trip."

I pause, watching as the guilt on Ken's face grows.

"But you did none of those things. You came in here with completely insincere, vague apologies that sweep every possible frustration and letdown of my life into one lump. You're sorry you weren't there for me? Since when? With what actions have you ever indicated that statement is true? You weren't just *not there* for me. You *abandoned* me—without a backward glance, without a phone call or a fucking letter. Look at this life you live, Ken," I say, waving my arms out. "The wealth you have. Not only did you abandon me, you left me behind without a care as to what happened to me when you left. My mother worked her *ass* off to provide for us. Three jobs, long nights and weekends and holidays, and we *still* had long stretches where we slept on people's couches or had to get food stamps. I don't need a fucking private snowboard instructor, but not having to use local food banks would have been nice."

Ken looks down at his hands, the coward unable to look me in the eyes while I flay myself bare.

"And then you want me to *understand* what this is like for Linda because of *the way things are* between you two. As if my pain doesn't matter because you were having such a hard time fucking two women. Excuse me for not *understanding* how hard it was for you, and screw you for calling me an unintended casualty, as if I'm roadkill. Your actions may have only been intended for my mother, but you knew I existed. You spent time with me, and you..." My eyes fill with tears, the memory coming back to me suddenly. "You *sang* to me, as if everything in the world would be alright, as if the fighting would stop or things would get better. And then you left. You *left*. So, whether or not you intended to hurt me or not is irrelevant. In fact, you should care *more* about how much you hurt me. More. I'm your flesh and blood, and you talk about me as if I popped up out of the ground like a fucking weed you didn't realize would grow in your garden."

I swipe a hand across my face to clear away the few stray tears that have fallen as I've poured out my pain.

"And it's *bullshit* for you to bring the boys into this now, for you to dangle my little brothers in front of me like a carrot when I've been *starving* for so long. You didn't come here to make things right—not really. You came here because you want to feel good about yourself, because you want to feel like you did everything you could. Well, I'm not going to let you off the hook that easily. You haven't even *begun* to make things right. So fuck you and your apology, and your bullshit excuses. *That's* what I have to say."

My chest is heaving, the emotional dump not draining away any of the adrenaline that's still coursing through me.

Ken's watching me with an expression that looks pained, but I don't care. Ten minutes ago, I was ready to hear him out, ready to give him a chance to talk to me about life and whatever was on his mind. I was open to him leading the way on us figuring out a way to move forward and build a relationship.

But he didn't come here to really fix things between us. He came here to be forgiven and absolved of his sins. He came here with a bullshit apology riddled with clichés and one-liners he probably put together during the drive over here, and he expected me to just accept him and thank him and pat him on the head because of how hard everything was for him.

Well I say fuck that.

In the grand scheme of things, I don't need a father. My mother was enough—*more* than enough to replace him, to give me the love and attention I needed growing up that he failed to provide.

I don't need a man like him in my life, who still deflects his responsibilities and has no idea how to love me like I deserve.

If he doesn't already love me, he never will.

And I shouldn't have to convince him I'm worth much more than what he's shown me so far.

When he sits there not saying anything, I stand and walk over to the door, yanking it open.

"I think you should go," I say. "I don't think there's anything else for us to discuss."

Ken watches me for a moment, indecision in his eyes, before he finally stands from his spot on the recliner and crosses the room to get to the door.

He looks like he wants to say something when he's right in front of me, and I make sure to stare directly into his eyes.

Out of the two of us, I know who the coward is, and it definitely isn't me.

"Goodbye, Ken."

His gaze drops away and he finally leaves, his feet padding softly along the deck outside before thudding down the stairs and leading to wherever he parked his car.

I move to close the door, but that's when I notice the person sitting on a chair on the guesthouse deck, his elbows on his knees, his hands clasped, his expression soft and aimed at me.

He's freshly showered and looks every inch of the delicious man who has shattered my understanding of what men are supposed to be like.

Ken? He's an example of the expectations I've had in the past.

Boyd is the future.

The good. The kind. The honorable.

At just the sight of him, my shoulders fall and my lip begins to tremble, the armor I wear falling away.

Boyd is up and in front of me in no time, wrapping me in that safe space I've begun to cherish.

"I'm here for you," he whispers.

And then he says something that makes me burst into tears, drawing me back to the first time he comforted me on the plane.

"I can't fix it, but I can be here with you so you know you're not alone."

Snuggling me in tight, he presses a kiss against my head then leads me inside.

"I could hear what you were saying, but I couldn't hear him," Boyd says later, once we're both curled up on the couch and nibbling on a fruit and cheese tray he brought over from his house.

"That's because he wasn't saying anything," I reply drily. "He said a few things before I launched into him, but that was it."

He nods, watching me as he pops a little cube of pepper jack into his mouth.

"Does it feel better, getting that stuff off your chest?"

I stare at a grape I'm holding between my fingers, not entirely wanting to answer his question.

"Yes and no," I finally say. "There's a weight off my shoulders knowing I was finally able to say what I wanted to say, knowing I was able to say *exactly* how I felt in *exactly* the right moment. But at the same time, I worry I was too hard on him."

"Why do you care if you were too hard on him?"

My brow furrows. "Why *wouldn't* I care?"

"Well, it sounds like you're planning to wash your hands of him, so it shouldn't matter whether or not you were too hard on him...unless you're afraid he won't try to contact you again."

I don't like all this internal reflection, not right now when my insides feel so raw and vulnerable.

But I guess that's the best time to see the true damage, right? When the wound has been flushed and is held wide open for examination.

Knowing it doesn't make it any less painful.

"I just don't know how I feel," I answer honestly. "Writing him off completely feels too harsh, but leaving room to hope things will change feels too weak. I don't know what the happy medium is, and I'm definitely too tired to figure it out today."

Boyd gives me a soft grin then leans across the couch and plants a kiss on my forehead.

I let out a long sigh and tilt my head back, closing my eyes and enjoying the warmth of his body next to mine.

"I don't know. Maybe I should change my flight and just go home. Staying here feels pointless now, especially since I basically called Ken a fucking asshole straight to his face. The last thing I want is to see him or Linda around town."

I could never have foreseen this outcome, not in a million years. I really thought the interactions between myself and Ken would just be really awkward and boring and I'd go back to Boston feeling like I'd accomplished my purpose—talk to my dad, decide my life is fine without him, move on.

Now that all this emotional drama has occurred, the idea of going home sounds really good. Cedar Point has been a beautiful place for me as long as it has belonged to Boyd and his family. This fight with Ken, however, has shifted that.

The silence between us is long, so I peek my eyes open, finding Boyd staring at me with a strange expression on his face.

"What?"

He shakes his head, his mouth open as he seems to search for something to say, though I don't understand what the issue is.

"Or you could stay here," he finally says. "You know you can keep staying in the guesthouse, right?"

I smile at him. So thoughtful and so caring, making sure I know I'm welcome in his home.

We really do need to talk about what things will be like once we get back to Boston. I've never felt like this about someone in my life, and just knowing we will get to take this beautiful relationship back home with us makes me so happy.

"Thank you for that. I love being here with you and your family," I say. "I only brought up going home because it feels like...I don't know, like maybe getting back to my life and my mom would help ease some of the shit in my chest. I have a re-fundable ticket, so I can always change the date and just like... fly home tomorrow, if I want."

Again, Boyd looks like he's struggling to find something to say, which I don't understand. Eventually, he just nods at me and pops another grape in his mouth.

That's when a thought occurs to me. "Do you...I mean...do you *want* me to stay, or..."

I trail off, that little bit of self-consciousness I've been trying so hard to push aside rearing her ugly head.

What if this is Boyd's way of helping me decide? I mean, he says I'm welcome at the guesthouse, but does he really *want* me to stay?

Boyd bats my question aside like it's a gnat. "Of *course* I want you to stay," he assures me, his voice filled with sincerity. "The question is whether or not *you* want to be here."

I lean back on the couch, nodding my head. "Of course I'll stay," I reply. "I want to be here with you. Obviously."

And it's true. Every fiber of my being *craves* being around him. All the time, almost to the point of neediness, though I'm trying to be careful not to toe that line too much.

I appreciate how quickly Boyd yanked me out of that place

of self-doubt with his reassurances. It confirms for me that he is probably on the same page as me, that he also sees this as something that will last after we leave this sweet lakeside town.

But even though I believe we feel the same, there's still a little voice inside me that whispers the lies I've been trying so hard to fight.

He's just appeasing you.

He's going to kick you to the curb eventually.

You're such a burden.

When Boyd and I crawl into bed later that night, he spreads my thighs and slides inside of me. It feels amazing. It feels like nothing I've ever experienced with a man before, the way he's able to help me enjoy sex in such a different way, the way he's so attuned to my needs.

Sensing my desire for control, Boyd is a little more hands-off, allowing me to work him over. I love that he lets me, because I'm trying to give him something amazing, something mind-blowing.

Something that will convince him I'm worth the long haul.

chapter twenty-two
ruby

The Cedar Point Summerpalooza is not as extravagant as it sounds. I remember the first year they decided to host a little festival to celebrate the transition from tourist season back to local living, and when the town voted to name it Summerpalooza, I shook my head even as a kid, knowing it was a stupid name.

When people hear 'palooza' tacked on to something, there is a certain expectation of what they're going to get. Things like live music, tons of delicious food, maybe some fun rides or crazy games, large crowds.

If you look it up, it literally says *exaggerated event*.

In actuality, the annual Summerpalooza is a glorified church carnival mixed with a farmer's market held smack in the middle of town, shutting down the cross section of Main Street and Mitchell Road.

Face painting from a few vacation bible school volunteers, live music from my cousin Edmund's band with a single speaker amplifier, a petting zoo that consists of a handful of pet pigs, a goat, and five chickens from Melvin Kinny's unsanctioned farm, and a dozen or so booths from local artists, crafters, and veggie growers who can't afford to have their own shops.

Given that information, it wouldn't seem like Summer-palooza would get off the ground at all, let alone be a treasured, annual event, but small-town people like small-town things, and the little gathering bumbled along for about ten years until a new feature was added.

A beer garden.

Suddenly, the end of summer festival became the hot event every year, all because a little brewery opened up in Cedar Point and decided to sponsor the beer garden.

Now, Cedar Cider is one of the most successful businesses in town and a favorite of my father's, although he wishes they would open up a physical location instead of simply providing beers to purchase from One Stop.

It was a proud moment for my friend Rusty when he launched his business, and I was a silent investor when he bought all the equipment he needed to get things off the ground. When he calls me on Sunday and reminds me that I've been in town for over a week and still haven't gone to see him, I know I need to make the time.

The two of us meet Sunday morning at the crack of dawn for a cup of coffee. Rusty is still the main sponsor for the festival, which starts at noon, so the only free time he has is bright and early. It works well for me since I love to be up before the sun.

"I can't believe you're having to *squeeze me in*," is the first thing he says when I walk up to where he's waiting for me outside Ugly Mug.

I flip him off, but still yank him in for a hug, Rusty patting me on the back a few times before we step inside to grab a cup of wake-me-up.

"Things have been different this trip," I say, tucking my hands in my pockets as I get in line.

"Different how? You've been a workaholic as long as I've known you. I'm not surprised you've been too busy to see me."

I glance Rusty's way and give him a smile. "I actually haven't worked at all since I've been here."

He rolls his eyes. "Don't bullshit a bullshitter, Boyd."

"I'm not," I say. "I've been spending time with my family."

I pause, enjoying Rusty's stare.

"And a woman."

His eyes widen, and a smile stretches across his face. "If this is more bullshit, I'll kill you. I know where you live."

I shake my head and step up to the counter, ordering a drip coffee and ignoring my friend's empty threat.

Once we've both added our cream and sugar preferences to our cups and taken a seat at a table in the corner, Rusty demands to know everything.

"It's only been two weeks since we last talked," he says. "Where did this even come from?"

I tell him everything. Well, within reason. In the past, I might have spilled some dirty details about a hookup here and there, but for some reason, the idea of telling Rusty what happens between me and Ruby in bed, or even specifics about her body, feels oddly like an invasion of privacy.

I do tell him about how we met and the time we've been spending together, trying to be specific enough for him to understand that I feel this is serious without spending hours dissecting every interaction we've had.

Rusty and I are close, but we don't need to waste time on reviewing dialogue and facial expressions.

"I gotta be honest, man—I'm surprised," he says. "Happy for you, definitely—sounds like you found a great girl—but I thought I heard through the grapevine that you had something brewing with Corinne again."

My head jerks back, confusion marring my previously happy demeanor.

"Where did you hear that load of nonsense?" I say, almost wanting to laugh at how much I'm starting to sound like my dad.

"From Corinne."

"Wait, since when do you hang out with her?"

He sets down his coffee and crosses his arms. "I don't, but she's been hanging out with Abby." Rusty's younger sister. "She and Abby and Bellamy have been running around town together all summer like they're back in high school. Drinking behind One Stop late at night, hooking up at bonfires, flirting with tourists for free drinks."

"Why is Corinne even here?" I grumble, wishing she would leave my family alone. "I don't like that she's been hanging out with my sister, or yours. She's not a bad person, but her attitude is toxic."

Rusty nods. "Can't say I don't agree with you," he says. "Corinne came back to town because her parents said they wouldn't pay for her life anymore."

"So now she's just…living in Cedar Point again?"

"Yeah, and she's been talking about you. A *lot*."

I groan, dropping my head and scratching the back of my neck. "You know, it's days like today when I feel thankful that I live all the way on the other side of the country."

He narrows his eyes. "But you miss your best friend, of course."

I chuckle. "Obviously."

Taking another sip of my coffee, I lean back in my chair, my mind trying to think over what the hell Corinne could possibly be thinking, spreading rumors that we're getting back together, or that we've even been talking.

The last time I saw her—other than the night at The Mitch and the following night at the bonfire, each of those being occasions when I barely said a word to her—was six years ago.

I was back in town for Christmas, actually, not summer. My parents had a Christmas Eve dinner, which they normally do for a lot of friends and families in town every year, and Corinne came with her parents.

By that time, I had graduated college and moved on to my graduate program. I'd secured my job at SolvTech and was feeling on top of the world. It'd been over five years since Corinne and I had broken up, so when I saw her, I thought we'd be able to be amicable, maybe friendly.

But she gave me attitude, that Corinne Paulson sass returning with a vengeance.

I don't think we've talked since.

So the idea that we might start something up again is just... ridiculous, on so many levels.

The fact that she's talking about it with people is what's irritating. Some other time in my life, I might not care, might not have an opinion—but this isn't another time in my life.

This is the first time I've had a...well, a girlfriend, for all intents and purposes. Ruby is important to me, and it bothers me that Corinne not only treated her like shit but is also spreading things around that could possibly damage things between me and Ruby.

"So there's nothing to it?" Rusty asks.

I glare at him. "You kidding me?"

"Hey," he says, putting his hands up with a smile. "I just had to ask."

We move on to other topics, each of us talking about work and family. In reality, Rusty and I talk a few times a month. We know what's going on with each other, so our meeting is mostly about giving each other a few back taps and a little bit of shit.

Eventually, we say our goodbyes, him promising to save me a bottle of his most recent draft and me promising to come bug him for it at the festival.

"Everybody knows you're not old enough to drink, Little Bee," I say. "It won't matter if we give you a bracelet."

Busy crosses her eyes, her irritation at being the last of us to be of drinking age evident in the nasty glare she's sending to each of her siblings.

"Yeah. We've all been in your shoes, okay?" Bishop says. "You'll live. Just suck it up and go find some friends to hang out with."

She lets out a groan then storms off into the crowd, leaving me, Ruby, and the twins where we're standing in line to get our beer garden bracelets from Sheriff Perry.

"I'm so excited," Bells says, talking to Ruby. "Abby told me Rusty has a new batch of beer he's said is his best yet, and he's debuting it in the garden tonight."

"I hope they don't run out."

I look to my brother. "Don't worry. He's saving me a bottle, so even if they run out, I'll give you a sip."

He makes an exaggerated face. "And risk getting your cooties?" He gags. "I don't think so."

I shake my head at his stupidity, only staying silent because Ruby giggles next to me.

She's been in low spirits for most of the day, though I can tell she's pushing to swing back to the positive side of things.

When I returned from coffee this morning and creeped back into the guesthouse, I was surprised to find Ruby still asleep since she normally likes to wake up early.

I made sure to kickstart her morning the right way—with my fingers between her legs.

Then we took a drive into town to deliver a dozen tables to the event organizers for the festival, eventually swinging by One Stop when we were done.

Andy gave us a little tour of how things are going with the construction of the addition. The roof is up, the walls are enclosed, and the wiring is done. Basically, the construction part is over, leaving just the interior finishes to complete.

I've been trying to keep her distracted and it's mostly working, but I can still see the moments when her mind wants to focus on the shitty stuff.

"IDs."

I pull my wallet out. "Really? You've known me since the day I was born."

Sheriff Perry smiles at me. "I ask for IDs from everyone, no exceptions Mr. Mitchell." When I'm done, he takes a look at Ruby's. "Well, looky here. Did you bring home a lady friend to meet the family?" he says, giving her a wink. "I've been hearing about a pretty brunette coming and going from the Mitchell guesthouse over the past few days, but I assumed it was a friend of one of the girls."

Ruby giggles, taking her ID back.

"Sheriff Perry, this is Ruby. She's my *more than a friend*. Ruby, this is Sheriff Don Perry. He's one of my dad's best friends."

"One of!?" he exclaims, slamming a hand against his chest. "What did you just say?"

"Sorry, sorry, sorry. He's my dad's only and most superior best friend," I correct myself.

The sheriff smiles at me. "Much better." Then his eyes pop over to Ruby's and back to mine. "And don't think I didn't catch that little *more than a friend* comment. In my day, we used to say *going steady*."

"Well, things are a little more complicated now," Ruby offers, though the smile is still dominating her face.

Sheriff Perry rolls his eyes. "Oh I know, trust me. I have two sons, and my youngest likes to let me know on a regular basis how different things are nowadays when it comes to dating." He chuckles as he wraps each of our wrists with a bracelet then sticks his hand out to take Bellamy's ID. "You guys have fun and be safe."

I nod, taking Ruby's hand and leading her away from the bracelet line and over to the actual garden.

It's a bunch of ten-foot lattices in a massive square, the walls interwoven with fake plants and fairy lights hung from side to side across the top. It's usually stifling during the day, but it gets a little breezier in the evening, the night sky and little lights filling the space with ambiance.

I'll have to make sure we come back at the end of the day so Ruby can see it then.

After we grab our beers, we post up at one of the high-top tables along the wall, each of us sipping on a plastic cup of Rusty's bestselling beer.

"This is really good," Ruby says, passing me her cup once she's tasted it.

I laugh. "Just one sip?"

She returns my grin. "I can drink more if you want me to fall asleep before you have time to get a second one."

Bellamy and Bishop sidle up next to us, and the four of us fall into easy conversation, the earlier tension in Ruby's expressions and body language falling to the wayside.

I enjoy watching her interact with my siblings. It makes me think of things in the future, like holidays and other trips, like the really wonderful possibility that I could end up with a woman who so easily clicks with my family.

"Boyd!"

My head turns when I see Rusty in the distance, waving me over.

"I'll be right back, guys," I say, stepping away from the table, chuckling when I hear Bishop call out from behind me, "You better bring some back for us!"

"Seems like he knows what's going on," Rusty says, slapping my back and leading me out of the beer garden and around to the side, where he has two people in charge of a station that manages the beers going in and out.

"I told him I had a new beer hookup," I say, rubbing my hands together. "And Bishop considers himself to be a beer aficionado, so he'll be peeved if I don't let him try it."

"Well, here you go," he says, pointing at a tray on a little table. "Grab a few and take 'em back to your table."

"Boyd?"

My eyes flick behind Rusty, and I see Corinne standing a

few feet away.

"Can I talk to you for a minute?"

Rusty turns around, looks at Corinne, and then looks back at me with his eyebrows raised. "The tray will be here when you're done," he says, patting my shoulder again before walking off.

I drop my shoulders and step toward Corinne, following her around to the side of the beer garden so we can 'talk,' unsure what it is she's hoping this will accomplish.

She spins around to look at me, a look of contrition on her face. It's a little surprising considering the fact that she's been such a menace over the past week.

"I wanted to apologize," she says, "for how I've been acting."

I cross my arms, watching as her fingers twist together, legitimate nervousness skittering across her features.

"I've just…missed you," she continues. "I've missed what we used to be when we were younger. Don't you miss that, at all?"

I shake my head. "I don't, Corinne."

Her expression falls.

"I'm not trying to hurt your feelings, okay? I'm just being honest. When you and I were together, it never really felt right. And I mean, we were kids. We didn't know who we were or what we wanted. We wouldn't make sense now."

"You don't know that," she whispers.

"Yes, I do."

"How do you know for sure?"

"I know for sure because I know what it feels like to make sense with someone, and it feels nothing like what our relationship was like."

Her eyes narrow, her soft expression clouding. "You're talking about that…Judy girl."

I grit my teeth but decide to let her tone slide.

"Ruby."

"I can't believe you're with someone like her. She was such a bitch to me. What can you possibly see in someone like that?"

Normal Corinne is back, her attitude returning and taking the place of the soft, demure woman who was trying to convince me that anything could possibly happen between us.

"First of all," I say, "Ruby is not a bitch. You're mad at her because she didn't cower in response to *your* bitchy attitude. The way you treated her was completely uncalled for, and I'm only going to say this once—talk to her like that again, and I'll be having a word with your dad."

Corinne's eyes narrow as her mouth drops open, my threat hitting exactly where I had intended, but I don't let her say anything in response.

"Second, I'm with Ruby because she makes me smile and laugh. Because she's beautiful and kind. And because standing next to her makes me proud."

Corinne snorts, examining her nails.

"Sounds boring to me."

"Then it's a good thing she isn't *your* girlfriend," I spit back. "She makes me happy, Corinne, happier than I've ever been in my life. And it doesn't matter how many nasty, underhanded things you say to or about her. That is never going to change."

I pause, giving her a chance to say anything else, but she's silent as she stares at my chest. I think there is a possibility I've actually gotten her to back down.

"Good luck in life, Corinne. I wish you the best, but I can honestly say I hope there aren't any reasons for us to talk again in the future."

And then I spin around and walk away from her, heading back over to where Rusty is still working to prepare his new beers for tasting.

"How was that?" he mumbles, holding up a plastic cup.

"Ridiculous," I grumble back, downing the few ounces of beer in one go. "But needed. I think she might finally leave me alone now."

Rusty grins and hands a tray to me. "Take these in for your table. What did you think, by the way?"

"De-fucking-licious," I say.

He laughs. "I haven't named it yet—maybe I'll use that."

"I'll take my 5% royalty in cash."

"Bullshit!" he shouts, laughing hard and slapping me on the back. "Go enjoy your drinks, you dick."

I give him a wave and head back inside the garden, weaving through the other tables full of people before I set my tray on the edge of ours. My siblings and Ruby lift their drinks up so I can slide it on.

"Here you go, fam. Rusty's new drink, tentatively called De-fucking-licious."

I glance around when nobody says anything, wondering what's going on, and that's when I realize they're all smiling at me.

"What?"

"Next time you have it out with Corinne, make sure you're farther away from the beer garden," Bishop says, biting his lip.

"You were literally right on the other side," Bells adds.

My eyes fly to Ruby's, finding her looking at me with big eyes that are full of sparkle and emotion.

She leans into me and brings her mouth to my ear. "Standing next to you makes me proud, too," she whispers.

And then she kisses me so good I forget all about the beer.

chapter twenty-three
ruby

The rest of Sunday afternoon is kind of a blur, not because I had anything to drink, but because I'm riding on a high of emotional bliss.

Boyd did his best to keep me in positive spirits earlier, using his body to keep me distracted in the early hours of the morning then dragging me out of bed to go drop off tables and check in at One Stop to see the work done on the expansion.

I'm amazed by Andy's progress, and it feels good to know the little bit of support I gave last weekend helped a small business. When you grow up poor, there isn't much room for flexibility on where you shop for necessities. Any supplies we bought were from big-box stores, which I know compete directly with small businesses, shutting many of them down.

I may never have the ability to do most of my shopping from small businesses or local shops, but this trip taught me there's always something else I can do to help. I'll need to take that back with me to Boston and see where I can put that mentality to use.

A little later, we went to Summerpalooza and spent some time in the beer garden. I was still struggling with distancing my mind from what happened with my dad, but all of that fell away when I overheard Boyd talking to Corinne on the other side of the lattice wall covered in fake ivy. He said some of the most beautiful things. First, he went on the offensive, putting Corinne in her place regarding how she treated me. Then he bragged about the things he likes about me and told Corinne to back off.

My dad could take some pointers from Boyd Mitchell on how to handle difficult situations and people.

Now, as we drive back to the Mitchell house, I feel like a swoony mess, unable to look away from Boyd, unable to get this stupid smile off my face.

"I had fun today," I tell him.

"I'm glad." He looks over at where I'm sitting next to him in the beat-up blue truck he loves so much. "You wanna hit up one cool spot before we call it a day?"

I nod, enjoying when he squeezes my hand and makes a turn into a driveway, backing out and heading back in the direction we just came from.

"Where are we going?" I ask.

Boyd just smiles. "You'll see."

It only takes a few minutes since everywhere in Cedar Point is nearby, but eventually I realize we're going to an area of town I haven't been to before.

We drive past South Bank Resort and Marina, the one big hotel in town, according to Boyd. I haven't been to this end of the lake, and I peer out the window at the long rows of docks and nice boats that are harbored along them.

"This place is fancy," I say, staring in awe at the looming structure that has been created to so beautifully blend in with the hundreds of trees surrounding the property.

"Yes it is."

Boyd drives through the parking lot and toward the back, exiting the lot along a small road that doesn't look like it gets much use.

That's when I start laughing.

"What?"

"Are you taking me to Easy Street?" I ask, loving that I know the nickname for the hookup spot.

Boyd shrugs a shoulder and looks at me. "Maybe. It's a great place to watch the sunset."

I grin, waiting impatiently as he drives along switchbacks for a few hundred yards before we emerge along a clearing that provides an excellent view of the lake.

"Fancy seeing you here," he says after parking.

I bite my lip and look his way. "Fancy indeed."

Then he takes one of my hands in his and tugs me across the bench seat so I'm plastered up against his side, dropping a soft, sexy kiss against my mouth.

I assume he's brought me up here for a fun little rendezvous, so I'm surprised when he turns on the radio, loops his arm around my shoulders, and starts humming along as we watch the sun begin to set in the distance.

He is…nothing I was expecting, on this trip or in my life—ever—and yet I'm starting to realize he's exactly what I need.

Maybe I've assumed the physical was the only good part of a relationship because I never had a man like Boyd to show me how wrong I was. The best part of being with Boyd *isn't* the physical part. It isn't that he treats me like I assume most men treat women on first dates.

Being with Boyd is about the quiet laughter, the heartfelt conversations, the sweet gestures. He makes me feel like a painful space in my chest is slowly starting to heal, like at one point I was cut open with a rusty hatchet and now he's here to clean out the wound and stitch me back up.

Sometimes, it doesn't feel real. Sometimes, it feels like too much. Too big. Too fast.

But I'm starting to see that the good stuff is something you have to take a risk on.

For the first time in my life, I've found a man who makes me want to gamble.

The following morning, Boyd enlists his siblings to do a family yoga session out on the grass. I don't know what he bribed them with, but it worked. I couldn't stop laughing at Bishop and his relentless gas every time he bent into a new position, or at Briar when she finally moved her mat because of it.

Afterward, the two of us spend a little while out on the boat just cruising Cedar Point and listening to Boyd's stories about growing up, followed by some time spent rotating between swimming outside of his house and lying out on the dock to dry out.

Eventually, we have dinner with his family and end the evening with a ridiculous round of Cards Against Humanity. Saying I lost would be an understatement. Boyd's family is fucking *ruthless.* A friend of mine from high school told me once that you need to play the game with people you know really well because you don't want to risk hurting anyone's feelings, and also because having shared experiences would lead to funnier card combinations.

She was *not* wrong, but Boyd and his family weren't just intent on poking fun at each other. They also ripped the shit out of me, saving some of their most ridiculous cards for the rounds when I would be the one who had to read them out loud.

It was mortifying.

What gives me gas?
pooping as quietly as possible.

When all else fails, I can always masturbate to
grandpa's ashes.

Next time on Dr. Phil, how to talk to your child about
shutting the fuck up.

I swear, I haven't laughed so hard in a long time. For some reason, I was just horrible at putting together card combinations. I think the most risqué one I even put down was only mildly funny.

What's fun until it gets weird?
menstruation.

I didn't win a single hand, and the Mitchells teased me about it relentlessly. I loved every single minute.

On Tuesday morning, I slip out of bed as quietly as possible, leaving a naked Boyd sleeping on his stomach with a sheet wrapped around his waist. I take a minute to just stare at all that delicious tan skin before I make my way over to the main house.

Patty told me she had my favorite coffee in her kitchen and I should come over to share a mug with her this morning instead of brewing the second-rate Keurig pods she keeps in the guest-house.

When I slide the door open from the back deck, I'm unsurprised to see she is already up and sipping on her own cup of coffee. She gives me a smile as I walk in.

"Morning, sweetheart."

"Morning."

I was hoping her suggestion would lead to a chance to talk to her. I really like Boyd's mom. She's smart and funny and genuine, the perfect kind of person to bounce a few thoughts off of before I make the trip back to Boston tomorrow and have to confront my mom about the fact that I came to visit Ken and lied about it, as well as what he and Linda revealed to me.

"How'd you sleep?" she asks as I pull down Boyd's favorite mug and fill it with the freshly brewed coffee on the counter.

I give her a sleepy smile, crossing over to where she's sitting and pulling out a stool of my own to sit on. "I love that bed. It's magical. I usually struggle to fall asleep, but every night I've been in it, I've completely conked out."

"Good, I'm glad. I know things haven't gone super smoothly for you since you've been in town, so I just want to make sure you know you're welcome here for as long as you need."

I bite my lip to hold back my smile. Patty is such an absolute sweetie, always trying to make the people around her feel welcome.

"Thank you, I appreciate it. My flight home is actually tomorrow morning, though, so you don't have to worry about me taking over your guesthouse."

Patty laughs. "Well, the offer stands all the same." She takes a sip then eyes me. "You looking forward to heading back east?"

I nod, trying to find the right words to explain it. "I am. You know, I came out here to try to figure a few things out, learn a little more about where I came from and the man who created me. I feel like I got my answers."

She lifts an eyebrow. "Oh, and what answers are those?"

"That I know where I came from and who created me. I'm from Chelsea, Massachusetts, and the woman who built me into the person I am today is back there waiting for me to come home."

Patty gives me a warm smile. "Are you and your mom close?"

"Very," I say, my tone firm yet wistful. "She's always been my hero."

There's a long pause, and I can see Patty assessing me.

"Can I ask you a question?" I say, realizing that if I'm going to talk to her about my mom, I need to hit on it now, while everyone is still asleep, and the longer I wait, the more risk I take that someone will come bumbling into the kitchen for some coffee and interrupt us.

Patty nods. "Of course."

I eye my mug, my gaze avoiding hers.

"I lied to my mom about coming here. I was worried I'd hurt her feelings or that she wouldn't approve, but it was something I was doing for me." I shake my head. "Now, I'm mad at her, because I learned some things from Ken and Linda that kind of…change my perspective about my life and my childhood. I'm just nervous about talking with her. It's not only about being honest with her about the fact that I came here anymore.

It's bigger than that, and now I have to confront my mother about how *she* lied to *me*."

I pause, struggling to explain it the right way.

"I guess I'm just wondering if you have any suggestions on how to talk to her. You seem like an awesome mom and…I don't know. I just wanted your thoughts."

When I finally look up, Patty gives me a sad smile, her empathy for my situation rolling off of her and enveloping me in something warm and safe.

"Well, it sounds like the main issue is just reminding yourself of why it's important not to put people on pedestals," she says. "Nobody is perfect, even your mama—*especially* mamas. Almost all of us bust our asses to take care of our kids and give them good lives, but we are human, just like everyone else. We make mistakes, we say things we don't mean, we yell and fight and cry. Every mother has regrets about how she has mothered her children."

Her eyes kind of glaze over and look off to the side as she recalls her own memories of motherhood.

"You know, when we're kids, we see our parents as these perfect, all-knowing superheroes who can do no wrong. Then we grow up and have children of our own and we realize they were completely lost and just making it work, doing their best, and making mistakes. Now, I don't know your mother, but if she raised a woman like you all by herself? I'm going to assume she did a pretty good job."

I blush, my eyes dropping down to stare at my hands wrapped around my mug.

"So whatever it is you two need to talk about…however it was that she let you down or lied to you…just remember that she's imperfect, but she loves you, and you love her. Everything will work itself out. It just might be a little bit bumpy and uncomfortable while you sort through things."

I knew talking to Patty would make me feel better. She just has that warm spirit that resonates so deeply with who I am and how I see the world.

"Thanks for all of that," I tell her. "I especially liked the pedestal part. It's a good thing to remember that nobody is perfect."

Patty nods. "It's not a bad thing to elevate somebody you love or admire," she adds. "But maybe find a way to build a staircase around their pedestal so they can walk down when things go wrong. That way, they aren't faced with a deadly fall from grace when they don't measure up to your expectations."

"I love that."

She smiles. "And that goes for all relationships, not just your mama. Intimate relationships deserve the same kind of care as well."

I chew on the inside of my cheek as I take in what she said, wondering if she's giving me general advice or talking specifically about me and Boyd.

"You mean…" I start the sentence but don't finish it, hoping she'll clarify without me having to actually ask.

"I just mean the beginning of relationships are fun, like what you and Boyd have going on, but if you get too serious too quickly, you risk building somebody up too high. That's just setting them up for a big fall, and like I said, nobody is perfect."

I stare at her for a long moment as I digest what she said, but before I can say anything in response, the sliding door behind me opens up, a sleepy Boyd wandering into the kitchen with a smile on his face.

"Morning," he says, his voice low as he kisses the top of my head. Then he rounds the counter and wraps an arm around his mom's shoulders. "Morning."

"Morning, baby," Patty says, patting his hand twice. "Coffee's on if you want some."

"Yeah, I can smell it. Did you break out the good stuff?"

Patty grins. "When I found out it was Ruby's favorite, I had to yank it out."

I smile at her, even though my insides feel like a roiling mess. Her words scroll over and over again through my mind like the ticker tape on the news.

You risk building somebody up too high.

That's just setting them up for a big fall.

Nobody is perfect.

Is that what I'm doing with Boyd?

All I've been thinking to myself during this trip is that he's too good to be true, that he's too kind. Too caring, too thoughtful, too good. Too perfect.

I've wrapped my thoughts up in the insecurities I struggle with, deciding to try to move past those thoughts to enjoy the man he is, regardless of how things have been in the past.

Now, I'm worried I'm setting Boyd up for a big fall—worried I'm setting *myself* up for a big fall.

If my mother, a woman I've known my entire life, a woman I've looked up to and revered for as long as I can remember, can let me down this badly, imagine what a man like Boyd can do.

A man who makes me believe I'm worth taking his time.

A man who proves to me that men can follow through.

A man who shows me love is real.

That place of safety that felt so good and so warm and so solid as we sat at the top of Kilroy now feels like a trembling house of cards.

How long until something big happens and it tumbles to

the ground?

How long before wanting a man like Boyd creates a deeper pain than I ever could have imagined?

"You've been really quiet today," Boyd says as we sit on the deck and stare out at the lake. We're each settled into an Adirondack chair and sipping on a drink—a local IPA for Boyd, a sparkling water for me—enjoying my last sunset in Cedar Point.

"Just…nervous about going home, I guess."

My response is honest. It's just not complete.

Yes, I'm nervous about going home—but I'm also nervous about telling Boyd I want to cool things off a little bit. The idea of doing it makes me want to scream.

"You sure you don't want to change your ticket?" he asks, a joking lilt to his voice even though he's not entirely kidding.

He's mentioned it a few times, since I told him I have a refundable ticket and it has the financial coverage to change the flight without any fees.

"Change your flight to fly home with me on Sunday morning," he said yesterday while we were lying in bed together. "We can tough it out in economy together."

As good as it sounded, being snuggled up next to Boyd in the shitty seats on a long flight, I knew it was just delaying the inevitable.

The longer I stay in Cedar Point, the longer I let this thing with Boyd continue, the more difficult it will get to call it off. It's better for me to leave now so I don't allow myself to be swayed by his sweet words and kind heart.

"Nah, I gotta get home," I finally say. "Time to get back to normal…the way life used to be."

Boyd is quiet next to me, and when I chance a look in his direction, I see him staring off in the distance, his brow furrowed and his shoulders tense, like he has the weight of the world resting on them.

After we finish our drinks, we spend a quiet evening watching a movie with the twins, Busy and Briar having other plans and Boyd's parents out to dinner with another couple.

Later, when the two of us are alone in the guesthouse, Boyd sits on the end of the bed, his legs spread where I stand in between them, slowly stroking my fingers through his hair and along his scalp.

He groans and shivers, enjoying the sensation.

"It feels amazing when you do that," he mumbles, already looking like he could fall asleep. "I feel like I should have taken advantage of the fact that you know how to give a good massage by now."

I stop my movements and tilt his head up slightly so I can look into his eyes.

"You want a massage?" I ask, realizing this might be my only chance to give him one.

He grins at me. "If you're offering."

Pressing a kiss to his lips, I tell him to strip down and lie flat on the bed on his stomach. I can't help but laugh at how quickly he gets naked and in position.

I pull some lotion out of my bag then climb onto the bed with him, straddling his hips, my butt resting on his bare one. Then I squirt some lotion onto his back and begin massaging his muscles.

Starting with light pressure, I knead the muscles in a circular motion. Then I go back and apply additional pressure in areas where Boyd let out longer groans, making sure to give relief to some of the sore areas that have popped up in the days since our hike up Kilroy.

When I finish, Boyd rolls onto his back, looking like he's high, his expression glazed and satisfied.

"I wish I could make you look like that after sex," I joke. "I don't think I've ever seen you look so blissed out."

He laughs, tugging me down against him, his lips coming to mine. Boyd's kisses reflect his sappy, sluggish energy.

Long licks, low groans. It's a little sloppy and a lot delicious, and I cherish every second. His hands wander and grip and push and pull until I realize he's slowly removing all of my clothing.

A part of me feels guilty for allowing myself to get physical with Boyd when I know things are going to end between us. It makes me feel selfish that I'm willing to take this from him, knowing if he could hear my inner thoughts, he would put a stop to this right now and demand answers.

But another part of me knows this will be the last night I spend in Boyd's arms, the last night he'll work so hard to bring me pleasure, the last night I'll get to see that spark in his eyes as he tips over the edge.

And for that reason, I'm okay with being selfish.

He drops down, pressing his mouth between my legs—clearly a favorite of his—sucking and licking and slipping his fingers in and out of me. At one point, he rubs against a space inside of me that has my body bucking off the bed.

"That's the spot, huh?" he says with a smirk, returning his efforts to that same area and moving his fingers in maddening circles all while he flicks his tongue against my clit.

"Ohmygod," I whisper, the words tumbling out of my mouth on repeat, my eyes clenched shut as I feel pulsing heat pool in my lower back.

For the first time, I feel like I'm letting everything fall away. Every other thought, fear, want, emotion…all of it is gone, my attention homed in on the beautiful man between my thighs. I can't help it. I know this will be the last time I'm with him, and I want to remember everything, absorb everything.

Boyd continues to stroke me for a while longer until I tell him I want him inside me, and then he's climbing up the bed and thrusting his hard length into where I need him most.

"Fuck," I choke out, the pleasure-pain enough to make that pool at my spine heat up even more.

I don't know what's different, don't know what Boyd has done to my body, but the feelings charging through me right now have catapulted me through to another level of bliss.

As he strokes in and out of me, one hand pinching a nipple and the other brushing over and over at my core, it feels like everything in me is bubbling up at once.

"God, Ruby," he says, looking at me like I'm the only thing that exists in the world. "I'm so in love with you."

My shock at his words must strip away something inside me, because within seconds, it feels like I've been lanced through with a firework, every muscle in my body clenching in one massive spasm.

I feel like a coil wound tight, a string pulled taut, like every ounce of my being has been wrenched into a tiny, nearly unbearable ball at the center of my body.

Then suddenly it releases, rushing outward like a wave, rolling through every nerve and cell and pore, thrusting out in fits and sparks along my arms and legs and into my fingers and toes. Every hair stands on end, my body overwhelmed.

I cry out, something long and pained, as if this moment has set me free from the chains that have held me bound for so long.

"Holy shit," Boyd whispers, thrusting into me a few more times, his actions sparking additional pulses of pleasure throughout my body.

Now I get it.

Now I understand why people equate sex to love, talk about orgasms as if they're gold, search endlessly for a man who is able to elicit these feelings the way Boyd has with me.

It's so big, so much, so glorious it's almost indescribable, and I know as I begin to come down from my own rush that I would spend the rest of my life trying to recreate this feeling with Boyd if I could.

My attention returns to where he remains above me, to the way my hands are wrapped around his body, slick with sweat, his eyes like pools I can drown in.

He shouts out his own release, his own body racked with shudders and violent tremors. Mine continues to throb in little fits underneath him, my vaginal walls clenching and unclenching until Boyd is forced to pull out of me.

But he doesn't move. He stays hovering above me, his eyes looking into mine in awe. Then he kisses me, long and slow and lovely. It makes me want to burst into tears.

"That was amazing," he says, kissing down my neck before pulling back to look at me with a smile. "You're amazing."

Instead of responding, I slip my arms around him and hold him to me tight.

I'm not sure what Boyd makes of my reaction, but he doesn't push me. Maybe he thinks I'm overwhelmed by the orgasm, or by his declaration of love. Or maybe he just thinks I'm tired and spent and emotional. Who knows?

Whatever the reason, he allows me to stay silent, the two of us snuggling up together, skin to skin.

Boyd drifts off quickly, his soft breaths warming my neck, but I stay awake as long as I possibly can, working hard to keep my eyes open and my body from falling into the soft lull of sleep it so wants to rest in.

If these are my final moments with Boyd—these absolutely magical moments full of love and tenderness—I want to remember every single one.

chapter twenty-four

boyd

Something is different in the morning.

When I wake up, I stretch my arm out, finding an empty bed and cold sheets. It's the same as yesterday, when I found Ruby inside drinking coffee with my mom.

But today, she's not inside with my mom. She's sitting on the loveseat across from the bed putting her socks on.

A quick glance around confirms that she's showered and changed and has already packed up her suitcase, even though her flight isn't until noon and it's only six.

"I thought maybe we'd get some more time in bed this morning," I say, my words groggy as I shift my body and plop another pillow under my head so I can see her better. "Why are you up already?"

She shrugs a shoulder, her expression neutral. "Just ready to get out of here, I guess."

Something in the way she says those words stings my chest enough that I actually rub a palm across the intangible wound.

Where did that come from?

I try to redirect, thinking maybe she just said it wrong.

"Do you want to make breakfast together in the house before you leave in a bit?" I ask. "My mom will definitely be up already, and you *know* the twins will wake up if they smell bacon cooking in—"

"No, I don't think so."

Her swift cutoff confirms it.

Something is different this morning.

"What's your deal?" I ask, having no clue where this attitude of hers is coming from.

"No deal," she answers, rising from the loveseat and beginning to collect her last few belongings: phone and plug from the nightstand, wallet from the top of the short bookshelf. "I'm just ready to go."

I feel like something is happening right now, but I can't for the life of me imagine what it is.

Last night was the best, most amazing night I've ever had with a woman in my entire life. For me, sure, but seeing Ruby finally let go enough to hit that peak she's struggled so hard and so long to climb?

It was incredible.

To wake up to her irritable attitude this morning feels... wrong. In many ways.

Especially since I told her I love her last night and she didn't say it back.

I figured she was overwhelmed by the moment. I decided to accept that her orgasm in the wake of my words was answer enough at the time.

Now, watching as she dithers around the room, looking for little things to keep herself busy, so clearly desperate to get out of this house and on the road to the airport, I wonder if…maybe her lack of response was her actual response.

Maybe she doesn't feel the same way about me as I do her?

It doesn't seem entirely possible given the way things have been between us during the last week and a half. The intimate moments, the deep conversations, the way we both broke down walls with each other.

I mean, I can't even remember the last time I was a cranky asshole to anyone. That has to count for something, right?

In this moment, I'm not so sure.

"I think I'm going to leave early," she says as she tucks her stuff into her little backpack.

"Ruby."

"Avoid the traffic and make sure I have time to return my rental."

"Ruby."

"I don't know the area very well, and flying is already stressful enough, so I should really—"

"Ruby!"

She finally stops talking and looks at me, but her eyes drop to the floor again.

I want to say something that will get her to stop shutting me out right now, but I don't know what the hell I could possibly say that I haven't already said before. I don't know what has actually caused her to retreat into herself and scramble to get away from me.

"What the hell is going on?" I finally ask. "What happened between last night and this morning that has created this… weirdness?"

Ruby shakes her head and finally looks at me. "Nothing happened. Nothing's different. I just…think…" She sighs and shifts

310

on her feet. "I just think maybe we should pump the brakes a little bit, you know?"

My mouth falls open, shock ricocheting through my body. "No. I *don't* know. Where is this coming from?"

"It's coming from a place of reality, Boyd. We hardly know each other. Is this really something we can make work back in Boston?"

"Well apparently not if you aren't on board," I say, feeling incredulous that this is the conversation we're having on the morning she leaves.

I regret the words as soon as I say them. They're a heated, off-the-cuff remark in response to what I'm feeling, the first angry thing I've said to her, ever.

How am I supposed to respond, though? How am I supposed to feel in this moment when she's shutting down something beautiful we've created because of some twisted narrative she's created in her own mind?

"I think I should just...go," she finally says. "It'll be easier if I leave now instead of dragging things out."

It feels like someone has wrapped a belt around my chest and cinched it too tight, the pressure caving in on my heart enough to wonder if it's going to burst.

Or if it already has.

But instead of saying anything else, instead of trying to convince Ruby she's making a mistake, I follow in her wake, carrying her suitcase as we make our way out to her car.

This is too fast.

It's all happening too fast.

I woke up less than fifteen minutes ago, feeling in love and happy and like I was floating on a cloud.

Now I'm sending Ruby off to the airport in an entirely different kind of cloud, one that's gray and storming and filled with strikes of lightning and rolling thunder that is enough to rattle my bones.

"Don't go," I say once she's shut the trunk and stands before me, shuffling back and forth on her feet and looking anywhere but at my face. "I don't know what happened, Ruby, but we can fix it. Don't leave like this."

She bats away a tear and gives me a sad smile before wrapping her arms around my waist and squeezing me tight.

"Thank you for making me feel like I'm not alone," she whispers. Then she's pulling away and turning to get into her car.

"Ruby, wait."

I grab her by the arm and yank her back, crushing my mouth to hers.

It feels desperate, but I don't have the right words. I don't know what to say or do to convince her of how I feel. Clearly telling her I love her wasn't it.

So I pour every ounce of the love and pain I feel into that kiss as I lick into her mouth, trying to prove to her that we are meant for each other, that she's safe in my arms and this is where she belongs.

Her kiss back is painful, especially when I can feel the streaks of her tears as they hit my lips.

She finally wrenches away from me, gasping and upset, bringing a hand to her mouth and watching me with watery eyes.

"I have to go," she says, yanking her car door open. "Good-bye, Boyd."

Her car starts up and backs out of the driveway, and I watch in horror as the love of my life drives away from me with no intention of looking back.

It's Briar who finds me later that day, drunk as a skunk and lying on my back in the heat of the sun on our dock.

After Ruby left, I decided it was time to enjoy the bottle of whiskey that has been sitting unopened in dad's liquor cabinet. Normally, dad, Bishop, and I drink it together on trips home, but I guess I've been a little distracted this go-round.

Now, the expensive bottle rests on the dock next to me, half empty.

I can't remember the last time I got drunk because I was upset. It had to have been in college sometime.

No—it was when I found out about dad's diagnosis. I felt so helpless, like there was nothing I could do, no way for me to solve anything. I was handcuffed by my own ineptitude, and it felt only right that I drown my problems.

Today, I feel the same.

I don't know what I did, what I can do. I don't know if I really fucked things up or if this is just how life works, but I feel so angry at my inability to *do* anything. It's that same feeling of being shackled to something…my own incompetence, maybe.

I just stood there. I just stood there and let her go.

But she also chose to leave.

Both of those truths hurt me on a visceral level.

"You're a fucking mess," I hear from my left.

I turn my head to the side, my eyes falling on a pair of black sandals before I look up and find my sister hovering over me, her

313

long hair hanging around her face like a curtain.

"Yup," I reply, emphasizing the P before I break into laughter.

"What's so funny?"

I shake my head, though I regret the movement immediately, the heat from the sun and the shift of my inner ear making my stomach roll.

And then I'm rotating onto my belly and heaving the entire contents of my stomach over the side of the dock, into the lake.

When I'm done, I let out a long sigh, wiping my mouth with the back of my hand.

"Nothing is funny," I finally say, rolling onto my back again and resting my head against the hard wood.

"Then why were you laughing?"

I shrug. "I'm drunk, Briar. I'm laughing so I'm not crying."

She lets out a sigh then sinks down to sit next to me, resting her palms on the wood behind her and stretching her legs out in front of her.

"Ruby left?"

I don't say anything in response, just continuing to stare up into the blue sky. I feel like every movie about heartbreak has rain on the day things fall apart. Why couldn't Mother Nature have been on my side today?

"I'm assuming things didn't end well?"

"No," I reply, closing my eyes and throwing an arm over my face. "They didn't."

"Was it your fault or hers?"

I glare at my sister. "Does it look like I want to talk about this right now?" I say. "While I'm out here drowning my sorrows?"

"No, but when I'm upset and want to hide away, you always

do your best to pull me out of it, little by little. I might not be doing a very good job, but I don't have a lot of experience being on this side."

I'm silent for a minute, mulling her words over.

"I don't know what went wrong," I tell her honestly. "But I know I let her go without a fight, and that's my fault."

"Should you *have* to fight for love?" she asks me. "Seems like a lot of work for someone you have to convince to love you."

I wince, but I know I need to answer her question. I can't let her go on believing you shouldn't fight for someone you love.

"You're right," I say. "You should *never* have to convince someone to love you. The thing is...I know Ruby loves me. I *know* it. In my bones, I know it's true, and I should have fought to prove that *I* love *her*, and that the hard things that come with a relationship are worth it."

Briar watches me with furrowed brows, and I know I haven't convinced her. I know it will take more than a few words from a drunk man to make her believe in love, especially in the wake of her own issues with her ex.

She sits with me for a few minutes before she stands and dusts her hands off on her jean shorts.

"You asked me if I believe in soulmates," I say, shielding my eyes from the sun. "Do you still want my answer?"

Briar crosses her arms and looks at me, debating for a minute before she nods.

"If you'd asked me a few weeks ago, I would have told you no," I say in response. "I thought people made up the idea of soulmates to justify getting rid of someone when they're not perfect."

"And if I ask you now?"

I look her straight in the eyes and give her a sad smile. "Now, it's not a question of whether or not I believe in them," I say. "I know they exist, because I found mine."

Briar lets out a long sigh before she reaches a hand toward me. I take it, allowing her to help me stand up. Instantly the world starts to tilt, but Briar holds me against her and helps get me back inside.

The last thing I remember her saying before she drops me off in my room is, "You're going to have one hell of a sunburn."

When I finally wake up, my head is pounding and my entire body hurts. Thankfully, Briar took pity on me and left a bottle of ibuprofen and a glass of water next to my bed, along with some aloe vera.

Use liberally is written on a sticky note.

I smirk, then wince.

Reaching out for the bottle, I see the redness on my arms: not bad enough to last more than a few days, but bad enough to sting for a little while.

A look at the clock says I slept through the night, the liquor and the sun enough to have kept me in bed for over 12 hours. What I need is a cup of coffee and some greasy breakfast food, and by some miracle, when I get out of the shower and head downstairs, I find my mom at the counter with a full plate of bacon, sausage, eggs, and toast waiting for me.

Her narrowed eyes reflect the knowledge of a woman who has dealt with more than one Mitchell child hangover throughout the years.

"Morning!" she declares, her voice loud and bright.

I wince, jerking my head to the side, the noise causing an additional, unwelcome throb in my head.

"You're mean," I whisper, wishing I could roll my eyes at her cackling laugh but choosing not to because it will do nothing but worsen the pounding at my temples.

"Yeah, well, sometimes being a mother is about tender sweetness, and sometimes it's about driving a point home."

"What point?" I ask, searching the cabinets for my mug and coming up empty.

"That drinking to the point where you don't want to see or hear anything the next day is a dumbass move."

She laughs again as I open the dishwasher then close it, settling for grabbing one of the dozen other available mugs to drink out of. I fill it up to the brim with black coffee and suck some down without care for if I'm burning my mouth a little bit.

"So, what happened?" my mother asks, her voice lowering slightly and shifting into mom mode. "You've been bounding around town looking lovestruck for the past two weeks. I can't believe something actually yanked you down from that cloud you've been on."

I blow on the brown liquid in my mug and glance at her. "Well, believe it."

She sits silently, waiting.

My mother knows me well. Out of all her kids, I'm the one who takes the longest to open up to her. It's not because I don't want to get her advice, but because I don't want to let her down.

She has also learned over the years that if I'm going to say anything, she needs to sit silently and wait.

"Ruby left."

I stare at the coffee instead of at my mother.

"I don't know what happened, but one minute we were crazy about each other and having a good time, and then all of a sudden she got really quiet and pulled away and started saying maybe we should pump the brakes. I don't know what happened between two days ago and yesterday to make her change her mind about me, but clearly I did *something*."

Letting out a sigh, I set my mug down and finally look at my mother.

"And I let her go. That was my big mistake. Obviously, I couldn't like...forcibly keep her here or anything, but I let her go without trying to really tell her how I feel."

"How *do* you feel?" my mother asks, her face looking oddly somber.

"I'm in love with her," I say. "I want to marry her someday. I can't believe I feel this way about someone who wants to slow things down, but at the same time, like...I'll slow down if she wants. I'll drop to a snail's pace. I'll crab-walk this whole thing. But she shut it down completely and I just...I don't know what to do."

My mom assesses me for a minute before setting her own glass down and clasping her hands together.

"I feel like I need to tell you about our conversation from the other morning, about something I said to Ruby."

"What?" I ask, confusion rushing through me that my mom has something to add.

"She was talking to me about her mother, how she's nervous about going home and discussing what happened here with her dad. I told her it was important not to put people on pedestals, said we're all human and make mistakes and putting someone up too high sets them up for a fall."

She pauses, and I can see regret in her eyes.

"And then I brought you up specifically."

My face turns to stone. "What *exactly* did you say to her?"

"I can't remember my exact words," she says, "but I basically said the beginnings are fun but she shouldn't build you up too high because nobody is perfect. I told her to be careful of not moving things along too quickly."

I run my hands through my hair and close my eyes, irritation rolling through my body in wave after wave.

"I can't believe you would say something like that," I say.

"I'm sorry. I didn't think it would be any big deal. I just wanted to slip something into our conversation to make sure she wasn't pushing you along too fast when I know you've never—"

"It *is* a big deal," I grit out, interrupting whatever else my mother has to say. "Ruby has a lot of internal shit that has to do with her dad abandoning her, stuff that has been bubbling over since she's been in town to see him. She was *finally* starting to open up from some of that, and you basically tell her she's making a mistake by dating me because I'm going to let her down, too. Of course it's a big deal."

"I didn't say she was making a mistake," my mother replies. "Not at all. I never used those words."

"How would you feel?" I ask her. "If you were at Grandma's when you were younger, and she told you to be careful you're not moving too fast with her son because he's probably going to let you down? If you'd been faced with a father who abandoned you and previous relationships with partners who never put you first…what would you think?"

Her shoulders fall, and I can see in her face that she hadn't ever thought of it that way.

But it doesn't matter what her intentions were. Ruby heard

my mother's words as a warning, as a reminder that men let you down, and it made her believe the same would be true for me.

Then when she left, I didn't fight for her, further proving those fears to be well founded.

"I'm sorry," my mother says. "This is all my fault."

I sigh and shake my head.

"It's not your *fault*," I declare. "Nobody is to blame, but now I at least know I have a chance at getting her back."

"How?"

I look at my mother and cross my arms.

"By fighting for her the way she deserves."

chapter twenty-five
ruby

"Look at *you!*" my mom exclaims when I show up at her apartment two days after I return from Cedar Point. "I don't think I've ever seen you so tan in your entire life, not even that one summer when you went and stayed with the Clarks."

She's talking about the three weeks I went with my childhood best friend and her family out to Plum Island to stay in a beachfront house. I got burned on the second day and spent most of the trip inside, returning home weeks later even paler than I'd been when I left.

"Well, as an adult, I've finally learned how to properly alternate between sun and shade, and I use the right amount of sunscreen," I reply, slipping my shoes off and wrapping my arms around my favorite human in the world.

"I missed you, baby."

"I missed you, too."

She pulls back and looks at me, hands on my shoulders, then gives me a squeeze and heads into the kitchen.

"I made dumplings," she calls over her shoulder. "I've been working my way through this book by one of those women on the cooking shows. It has about a million different types of dumplings, and these are my favorites so far."

"Before we eat, can we talk?" I ask.

"If you just wait a few minutes, we can sit down and eat and talk. I have so many questions about your trip."

She disappears into her tiny kitchen, and I decide ripping off the Band-Aid is the best approach right now to make sure this conversation happens.

"I went to see dad."

The little sounds of movement from the kitchen stop, and a whole minute goes by before she rounds the corner and looks at me, her eyes wide and her skin pale.

"What?"

"My trip…it wasn't to go to California with friends, even though that's what I told you. I lied about that. I don't have friends from California. Well, now I do, but I didn't when I left. I flew out to visit Ken. I reached out to him online and told him I'd like to meet him, and he bought me a ticket, so I flew out there to try to get to know him. He lives in this little lake town called Cedar Point, and that's where I've been. I'm sorry I lied to you about it, I was just nervous that you'd be upset with me for wanting to meet him when he abandoned us, and I didn't want to let you down."

My mother raises her hand, our agreed-upon symbol that means I need to actually take a breath and give her a moment to process everything I've said.

She's been through quite a few of my rambling stories, some more serious than others. When I'm droning on and on about something stupid, she lets me ramble.

Clearly, this isn't something stupid.

She takes a few steps over to the couch and sinks down, perching on the edge, her hands on her knees and her eyes on the carpet as she digests everything I've just said.

"You went to visit Ken."

I nod.

She nods, too.

"How was it?"

"Horrible."

Her head jerks back.

"But amazing. Well, I guess it was horrible *and* amazing, and then it was horrible again."

She closes her eyes and shakes her head, waving her hand out in front of her. "Wait, start from the beginning."

Instead of confronting my mom about her lie straight out of the gate, I set that pain aside and remember that she's my best friend. She's someone who loves me and cares about what happened.

So I tell her everything, from meeting Boyd on the plane to arriving in Cedar Point and having Linda treat me like shit. Finding out Boyd was *in* Cedar Point and all the time I spent with him, minus the sexy bits. Then I talk about dinner with Ken and Linda, moving over to the Mitchell house, yelling at Ken, falling for Boyd, and leaving him behind.

By the time I'm done with the whole story, I'm crying my eyes out. God, I haven't cried this much in a long time. Clearly, I've been in need of a good purge.

"Oh, sweetie," she says, wrapping me in her arms and snuggling me close. "What a whirlwind this has all been for you."

I nod, wishing I could have been strong enough to handle everything without getting too emotional or too involved.

"Why did you lie to me?" I whisper, knowing if I don't ask my mom this question now, I'll never build up the nerve.

She sighs and pulls back, her hands on either side of my face.

"I made a mistake," she tells me. "When you were little, I didn't know how to explain to you who I had been. You were too young for me to share the fact that I'd had an affair with a married man but old enough to remember your dad and ask questions during the periods of time when he was gone."

Her thumb wipes away a stray tear from my cheek.

"So I told you he'd left us, and then as you got older, I didn't want to change how you saw me. You always said I was this amazing mom who worked so hard for us, and how could I tear that image down and tell you I wasn't the woman you thought I was?"

Maybe Boyd was right, that day on the plane. He told me fear is about a lack of understanding, a fear of the unknown.

My mother lied because she was afraid of what my response would be to her actions. She was afraid of how I might see her, how that might change.

But I was right too. Her fear was also about love.

My mother loves me, more than anything in this world. I'm the most important thing in her life, and she was afraid that by telling me the truth, she might lose me.

"I'm so sorry, baby," she says, wiping away another tear from my cheek.

In that moment, my forgiveness is immediate.

This woman has proven to me time and time again that I can count on her, that I can believe in her, that her love is everlasting.

She will always be the same person I've known my entire life, the same hardworking, loving, loyal badass who took care of me all by herself.

Having a shameful part of her past is her own patch of weeds to work through, not mine, and I could never let something like this come between us.

As we sit at her small kitchen table, she tells me the truth about what happened between her and Ken. About the young college guy in Boston for a summer internship that she had an affair with, even knowing that he had a girlfriend back home. He'd been an escape for her from the hard life she'd been living, and that she knew she would continue to live once he was gone.

But then a baby happened—me. She thought maybe he'd stick around, or that he'd want to be involved. And for a few years, he gave a half-hearted effort by coming to visit and giving empty promises that went unfulfilled.

Eventually, he finally told Linda the truth. That he'd had a child in an affair. My mom doesn't know all of the details, but according to what Ken told her all those years ago, Linda demanded that he choose. Her or us.

So he chose.

It's a hard story to hear, and I'm thankful my mom chose to gloss over a lot of it when I was younger, the brutality of my own father choosing a love interest over his daughter even harder to handle than all the made-up reasons he left us behind.

But I don't cry. I've cried enough tears over a man who doesn't love me enough to choose me.

After dinner, we sit out on her little fire escape, legs crossed and looking out at the sea of houses surrounding us. My mother lives on the fourth floor of one of the few apartment complexes above two stories in this neighborhood, so she actually has a pretty decent view, even though she's in a struggling area.

"So, tell me more about this...Boyd," my mom says.

I snort. "What more do you want to know? I feel like I already told you everything."

She shakes her head, grinning at me. "Nah, you haven't told me what I want to know."

"And what's that?"

My mom bounces her shoulder against mine, slipping from mother mode into girlfriend mode with a flick of the wrist.

"Ugh," I say, covering my face with my hands. "I'm not talking to you about sex."

The sound of her cackling laughter echoes across the parking lot and through the open air.

"I'm not talking about *sex*, Ruby. I'm talking about *love*."

My expression sobers and my shoulders fall.

"It sounds like the two of you had something really special, and I'm just wondering..."

"You're wondering if it was love?" I ask.

When my mom nods, I let out a long sigh.

"I thought maybe it was."

Pausing, I rotate my glass of cranberry juice in my hands,

rolling it between my palms and watching the liquid slosh around inside.

"And now?"

I shrug. "If it was love, would I be here bawling my eyes out to you about it?" I joke.

"Oh, baby. I'm not an expert on love, not by any means. You know I've had my faults. But that kind of love where you cry over the idea of losing it?" She hums. "That's how you know it's worth it."

I shake my head, my nose scrunching up in distaste.

"I don't like that, though. I don't like the idea that a love has to hurt in order for it to be real. That feels toxic and unhealthy, and I want to veer far away from that as much as possible."

"I'm not saying real love hurts you," my mom says. "I'm saying the world hurts you. Life hurts you. People hurt you. Real love, though? Real love soothes you, wraps you up and protects you. The crying isn't because someone who loves you has hurt you. It's because you've been hurt, and the person who loves you was there for you. The crying is knowing you have someone precious, and you never, ever, ever want to let them go."

I consider her words, feeling that bubbling up of emotions begin again.

"But what if I already let him go?" I whisper, tears streaking down my cheeks.

"Then you fight to get him back."

I think a lot about my mother's words over the next few days as I get back to work and the normal routine of life. A few times, I even pick my phone up to call Boyd.

But I'm worried about what reaching out will do to him, especially when I'm still not sure how I feel.

I know I'm in love with Boyd. That's not what's in question. I'm just struggling with the idea that any relationship is worth the fear of what happens when it crumbles.

On Saturday morning, I show up at my yoga studio for class, getting hugs from the people I missed over the past two weeks while I was out of town. I go through my ritual, laying out my mat and setting up my yoga blocks, then heading into the corner to grab two blankets out of the closet. I head back to my little nest and get comfortable, lying flat on my back and waiting for Katie, the usual Saturday morning instructor, to begin.

Quiet movement happens around me as others get comfortable in their positions, but I try to tune it all out and focus on the sound of the peaceful music streaming through the speakers.

"Do you take walk-ins?"

My eyes fly open at the sound of a familiar male voice, and I jerk my head to look back at the doorway, my eyes colliding with a pair of beautiful brown ones that I worried I'd never see again.

They look just as beautiful, even upside down.

Katie walks over to where Boyd stands at the door to help get him checked in, and the entire time I lie awkwardly on my back with my neck twisted to watch him.

He's here for me, right?

Right?

I mean, it would be a *huge* coincidence for him to decide to take up yoga upon his return and then come to my studio by chance, especially when I told him the name and that I come every Saturday morning at eight. He wasn't even supposed to be flying back to Boston until Sunday.

He's here for me.

The thought has my chest erupting with both joy and trepidation, because I don't know if he's here to chew me out or kiss me or something in between.

Boyd crosses the room and sets up his own mat, his eyes flitting to mine over and over again.

I lie flat on my back, wondering if he's going to come up to me and say something. But he never does, instead getting settled in his own spot and lying down, too.

I return my eyes to the ceiling, wondering how the hell I'm going to focus or calm my inner self when Boyd is back there. Then class begins, and I go through the longest and least productive yoga session of my entire life.

Every stretch, every movement, every rotation of my hips or my neck or my back has me turning my body to look at Boyd, where he stands on his own mat two rows back and three spaces over. He's slightly less clunky this time than he was during our first session and the one we did with his siblings, even though most of their time on the mats was spent teasing each other and trying to push each other over.

"Distracted today?" Katie asks me with a smile as we finish up at the end. Her eyes glance behind me, and I know she was fully aware of my inability to look away from our guest yogi. "I was distracted, too," she jokes, lowering her voice and giving me a little chuckle before walking off to help with picking up some of the blocks left on the ground.

My eyes narrow, not liking the idea that someone else was eyeing my...

But I stop.

He's not my anything, is he?

I don't have any additional time to think that thought over, though, because suddenly, Boyd is there, standing in front of me, overwhelming me with his tall form and beautiful eyes and sexy, sweaty body.

"Hi," he says.

"Hi."

We stand there for a minute, just looking at each other.

"Can we talk?"

I nod without even having to consider it, knowing that whatever he has to say, I at least owe him a chance to talk.

I follow him through the lingering students and out the door. Boyd leads me over to where a fancy black car is parked a few businesses away, popping his trunk and dropping his stuff inside before closing it and turning back to me.

He leans up against the side of his car and crosses his arms, watching me. I've never felt so thankful to have a pair of eyes on me before. It's amazing what just a few days away from him has made me miss.

"When you left, I thought maybe I had done something wrong to push you away," he starts. "I thought maybe I did or said something that hurt your feelings, or thought maybe that wasn't the right time to tell you I love you."

My heart hurts as I watch him, because I can see him standing in front me, *hurting*. I did that. I made him feel that way. It's the very thing I want to avoid, and yet I inflicted that pain on the man I supposedly love.

"But then I realized you pushing away from me, pushing away from how much I love you…that will be something I experience from you for a long time. The only *mistake* I made was believing that when you left, things between us were over."

Confusion fills my face as I take in and process his words, the direction of this conversation shifting away from where I thought it was going.

"I'm in love with you," he continues. "And you're in love with me. But love scares you, because the men who were supposed to give love to you in the past let you down, made you believe it was something so much smaller than it really is. They made you believe it isn't worth the trouble, and that is a *lie*."

I shake my head, closing my eyes as I feel the first true welling of emotion in my chest.

"Boyd..."

"What you need is a man who loves you enough to never let you go, a man who will continue to show up, time after time, who will continue to fight for you, who will prove to you over and over again that love is *absolutely* worth the trouble."

I don't know what to say to that, don't know how to communicate my fears to him. I don't know how to handle any of this right now.

"Boyd, this is too much. It's too fast."

"Then I'll slow down."

"It's too big."

"I'll start smaller."

I growl.

"I understand why you're fighting this, Ruby, but you can't pretend you don't want this."

"Of course I want you, Boyd!" I shout, unconcerned about whether or not other people walking on the sidewalk can hear me. "But what happens when you stop wanting me?"

Tears well up in my eyes, but I don't move, because this is what I want to hear from him. This is the ultimate fear that keeps me from truly opening my heart to this amazing man.

What happens when the world changes, or life gets hard, and he chooses to leave?

Boyd steps closer to me but keeps his hands to himself, like he knows I need the physical distance to maintain my sanity.

If he were to wrap me in his arms right now, I'd break, and I know Boyd—he wants me to love him because he's everything, not just because he's there.

"Here's the reality, Ruby. The only way I can prove to you that I will never stop wanting you is by waking up and loving you every single day. There is nothing I can do or say to convince you today that I will love you tomorrow. That I will choose you every day. If you're scared, I can work with that. If you want me to slow down, I can, but please don't ask me to stop or send me away, because nothing will ever stop me from loving you. Telling me to stop will only make it nearly impossible for me to *prove* it."

My hand comes to my chest, the beauty and sincerity of his words finally hitting the mark I know they're intended for.

Boyd just might really be as good and true and kind and loving as I think he is. Maybe my issue is in adding the word perfect.

Like his mother said, nobody is *perfect*.

But that doesn't mean they can't be perfect *for me*. It doesn't mean I can't look at Boyd and know in the very atoms of my bones that he is the man I want to spend the rest of my life with.

I watch him standing there, his brow furrowed, his eyes on me, and I realize he has given up a man's most valuable weapon.

His power.

I've always said I didn't want a man to have power over me again because I was afraid they could hurt me too deeply to recover from. In this moment, I can see that Boyd has surrendered every single ounce of his power to me. This man who loves to be in control has given me the wheel, put me in the captain's seat, and told me I'm in charge.

Looking into those gorgeous brown eyes of his, I know I have to do the brave thing. I have to be the Ruby who was brave and strong and who stepped out of her comfort zone in Cedar Point, not the scared one who was never willing to take a risk.

In this moment, I know that I have to be the one who chooses him.

I take a step toward Boyd, and in a heartbeat he's crossed the remaining distance between us, pulling me in against him and wrapping me tightly in his arms.

"I love you," I whisper, feeling his body freeze where he stands pressed against me. "I'm sorry I didn't say it before."

"It's okay," he says, pulling his head back so he can look down into my eyes. "We don't always have to be on the same page, as long as both of us know where we are, okay?"

I nod, and then he dips down and presses his lips to mine.

God, kissing him is like heaven, like a joy I didn't think would ever truly exist again. And yet here he is, in my arms.

My mom told me real love is something you can't imagine ever losing and the tears you cry are because you never want to let it go.

As Boyd kisses me and tears stream down my cheeks, I know that's exactly what's happening. He leans back and looks at me then drops a precious kiss against my forehead.

"Can I take you to breakfast?" he asks me.

"Absolutely."

He slips his hand in mine and the two of us head down the street, side-by-side. Neither of us knows for sure where we're going, but together, we'll figure it out.

epilogue
boyd

...six months later...

"That's the last box."

I nod. "Perfect. Thanks so much for your hard work today," I say, shaking the mover's hand and giving him a wave as he heads out the door.

Then I spin around and look at the stack of fifteen boxes and the handful of furniture pieces in my living room.

"I told you I don't have enough stuff to warrant hiring movers," Ruby says as she strolls back into the living room, her eyes perusing her belongings before she settles on a lamp and a small, empty bookshelf. Picking them up, she returns in the direction she came from, the cord from the lamp dragging along the ground behind her.

"And *I* told *you* hiring movers isn't about the amount of stuff. It's about easing the moving process. You were able to finish up at your apartment yesterday, get a restful night of sleep, and then have your stuff delivered here this morning when you're fresh and in the mood to unpack. And it's Boston in February. It's freezing outside. Did you really want lug everything back and forth in this weather?"

She narrows her eyes at me over her shoulder.

"Besides, doing it this way, I can be here to help."

It was a big argument. Not an angry one, just a debate. The end of her lease was on a Friday when I had a presentation at work, so I wouldn't have been able to take the day off to help her. Paying for movers and one night of storage meant I could be here to oversee the delivery then help her get her things settled in at my townhouse.

Well, *our* townhouse.

I'd been dropping hints to Ruby about us moving in together for over two months. My girl isn't a dummy. She picked up on every one of those hints and swiftly shuffled them to the side, ignoring them completely.

Until I finally stopped hinting and actually asked. I explained to her how important it was for me to have us together, for our lives to be even more intertwined, to take that next serious step. I asked her to be brave and believe in our love enough to give it a chance.

Surprisingly, she agreed, and now she's here, officially moved in.

"That would require you to *actually help*," she jokes as she walks back into the living room, opening her arms to indicate the boxes spread out on the floor.

I roll my eyes. "Alright, alright. I guess it's time to break a sweat, huh?"

Ruby and I spend hours getting her belongings set up in new homes throughout the house. Her toiletries and makeup in the bathroom. Her clothes hanging in the closet and put away in the dresser. Her shoes by the front door. Her books on the new bookshelf I bought for the living room.

Eventually, we get everything done, and I take a box cutter to the cardboard, slicing all the tape so everything is flat and leaning up against the wall next to the fridge for me to take out to recycling.

"I can't believe we live together," she says, giving me a big smile, her eyes wide as she looks around the place now that everything is put away.

"Having second thoughts?" I ask, pulling her against me and looping my hands together around her waist.

That day on the street outside the yoga studio, I didn't know what was going to happen. I didn't know if I would need to try over and over again to get her to give us another chance. I was lucky she was feeling brave that day, lucky she extended her hand to me and took a step forward.

It's been a perfect metaphor for what our relationship has been like as Ruby has struggled to truly believe in the love we share. She takes one step, and I take three.

But I'm okay with that. If she needs to take baby steps, I can do that. If she wants to cling to me while I take larger steps forward, I can do that too.

As long as she never lets go.

As long as she holds on to me when something scary happens instead of pushing me away like she used to.

It's been a winding road to get to this point, mostly amazing moments in the sun but also a few scattered showers here and there, but that's love. That's relationships. There are always storms, but love is about how you weather them *together*.

"Second thoughts?" she murmurs, pressing close and giving

me a soft kiss. "Never."

I grin, enjoying the confidence she has in me now, the confidence she has in us. I hope to only help build on that moving forward, to continue proving to her that I will *always* be here for her, at her side.

"You wanna go christen the bed?"

She rolls her eyes. "We're both gross, and we've already christened that bed."

I press my hips against her so she can feel how much I want her.

"But that was when it was just *my* bed. Now it's *our* bed."

"Ooooooh," she says, sarcasm ripe in her voice. "So it's totally different."

"Totally."

She bites her lip, considering. "Maybe a shower first?"

I nod. "Another place we need to christen."

Ruby bursts into laughter and shakes her head at me.

Sex with the two of us has just gotten better and better. Ruby had her very first orgasm on her last night in Cedar Point, the most incredible thing I've ever seen in my life, and she has had many more since then.

She still gets in her head about it on occasion. On those nights—or days—I work extra hard to help her relax and enjoy herself, to make sure she doesn't feel pressured to come. Usually, that's enough for it to end up happening, although there have been times here and there where that peak is just a little too far out of reach.

The good thing is that sex between us isn't always about the orgasm. We've practiced enough to have created a sex life where we enjoy ourselves regardless of the outcome. Some of the joy is just in the intimacy of being together.

Of course, that doesn't mean I don't love getting her off. God, do I love it. The way she tastes, the way she smells, the way she sounds, the way she looks at me—it's still something I work hard to get to, because she deserves for me to bust my ass to get her there.

"Well, Mr. Mitchell, what are you waiting for?" she says, turning on her heel and sashaying toward the bathroom.

I bite my lip, watching her sexy ass strut down the hall.

She looks over her shoulder at me when she reaches the threshold of our bedroom. "Are you...*coming?*" She winks and pulls her top off, dropping it on the floor and using her foot to fling it across the room.

I chuckle, my dick pulsing in my jeans.

Damn do I love her, and I can't wait to spend the rest of my life making sure she knows how I feel down in the deepest parts of her soul.

I even have a little black box in the back of my nightstand to prove it.

For more stories from Cedar Point and the Mitchell family, including a bonus epilogue about Ruby and Boyd, visit

www.jillianliota.com/cedar-point

jillian liota

acknowledgments
from the author

This book poured out of me, and as much as I'd like to credit my own creativity for the development of Ruby and Boyd's characters, there are always other amazing people that had a hand in the telling of this story.

My first thank you is always to my husband. **Danny**, without you, I wouldn't know what a true hero is. Thank you for your unending patience, your confidence, and for doing the dirty shit while I'm busy writing. You are my real life book boyfriend, and I'm so damn lucky.

I always need to thank my family: my **mom** and my **dad** for their continued belief in me, even when I write dirty things.

And to my siblings: **Caitlin**, **Cheyenne**, **Jordan**, **Mike** and **Kevin**. You crazies make it easy to write families with amazing relationships. I cherish each of you.

To my reader group, **The Jillybeans**, and to my small but growing **ARC Team**, thank you for your involvement, and for the wonderful little community you've made online. I truly enjoy spending time with you.

Thank you to my editor, **C. Marie**, for helping me sound like an actual writer and not a complete mess. You always manage to find the little spots where my words can use a little polish, and it makes all the difference.

To my publicist, **Nazarea**, for helping to launch this book out into the world! So many new readers are going to find this story because of you.

Cam and **MaryLou**: I couldn't ask for better friends. Thank you for reading my books and constantly inflating my ego.

The Kaipii Ohana... **Melissa**, **Kristy**, **Jess**, **Destiny**, **Sara**, **Cam** (again) and **Colene**... our numbers are dwindling on the block, but we will always be a family. Thank you for making the place I live so wonderful, for inspiring too many funny jokes to count, and for being a constant reminder that friendship continues even when we live far apart.

Last, but definitely not least, to each of you who have picked up this book. Thank you for taking a chance on an unknown author, or reading every book I've written. I love writing because I know you love reading. So thank you for giving me something to do with my life :)

Happy reading. I'll see you back in Cedar Point soon.

<3 always,
Jillian

Continue to the next page to read the first chapter of

The Opposite of Falling

chapter one
brian

I stare at the three available jobs advertised in the weekly paper with slumped shoulders, realizing with a staggering clarity just how bleak my prospects are.

I don't even think most newspapers have jobs in them anymore, but when you're looking for employment in a small town like Cedar Point, an online job system just seems superfluous. So, businesses like the craft store and the coffee shop and the grocery store advertise their open positions on flyers in their front windows—generally horribly designed, usually with fonts like Comic Sans or Papyrus—or in ads in the *Cedar Reader*.

Full-time nanny.

Weekend barista.

Grocery store cashier.

Those are my options.

If I'd moved home at the start of the summer, maybe I could have found something else. The tourist season in Cedar Point always tends to provide employment opportunities that at least sound enjoyable.

Lifeguard at South Bank Resort.

Counselor at Cedar Lake Summer Camp.

Bartender at Dock 7.

Back in high school, I worked a catch-all job at the community library, shelving returned books and cataloguing new ones, ordering supplies, leading a weekly class on basic computer skills for seniors. But the little spot at the end of Main Street that served as my haven was torn down a few years ago and replaced with a row of shops that are, admittedly, very cute and probably do good things for locals. A bakery. A cute little art gallery. A rustic home goods store with hand-painted signs and quilts and little tchotchkes that say things like *Life is better on the lake.*

I'm sure if I talked to my dad, he'd have some sort of insider knowledge of a job I could find that isn't listed in the *Reader*, but asking either of my parents for help kind of defeats the point of, well, not asking for any more help. They've already allowed me to move back into my childhood bedroom—a shame I never thought I'd have to face—in the wake of my recent breakup and decision to leave behind the life I'd created down the mountain. I can't *also* expect them to find me a job, too.

I'm back in Cedar Point. Single. Broke. Unemployed. And, if I'm honest, a little lonely and a lot lost. Moving home with my tail between my legs definitely wasn't something I ever could have envisioned, but that's just life. I need to accept the circumstances I'm faced with, no matter how distasteful they might be, and that includes working whatever job will pay me, even if it doesn't sound like my cup of tea.

I cross out the nanny job I'm not qualified for and mark an X through the barista position that won't be enough hours, circling the full-time cashier job at One Stop Shop with a bold red pen.

Truthfully, it's the only choice if I'm going to get some serious hours under my belt, even if it *is* minimum wage.

A job is a job, and money is money. The last thing I want—even less than having to move home—is to leech off of my parents for any longer than I absolutely have to. My mom and dad are two of the most generous and loving people out there, and it wouldn't feel right to take advantage of the fact that they'd be more than happy to take care of me. They usually manage a pretty good balance between nudging us kids out of the nest to face the world and providing a safe space to come home to when that world is as cruel as can be.

Even so, that doesn't mean I shouldn't still pull on my big-girl panties and get my butt to work.

Besides, my younger sister lives at home, too, and Bellamy manages a part-time waitressing job along with a full load of college classes online; she'd never let me live it down if I chose to laze around the house all day for months.

Speaking of my sister…

"Can I borrow your car?"

Bellamy pauses, a tortilla chip with an aggressive amount of salsa hovering in midair as she looks over to me and lifts a brow.

"Where are you going?"

I nibble on the inside of my cheek as I decide what to say.

My younger sister gives off the vibe of a totally rambunctious ball-busting 21-year-old, but she's a lot more observant than she lets on. She's been watching me wander almost aimlessly around the house since I moved home about a month ago, and I'm sure it hasn't gone unnoticed that I haven't gone anywhere in town even once.

Nowhere requiring a car, at least. I don't need to drive if I'm running the trails, which has been my primary method of relieving stress since I was in junior high. Other than that, I've stuck close to the house, preferring to avoid any unwanted run-ins with curious townies who are likely to have questions about why the eldest Mitchell daughter has suddenly moved home.

Regardless, it makes sense for my sister to be curious if I'm wanting to borrow her wheels.

"One Stop. Need anything?"

I know I could tell her I'm applying for a job, but I'm not in the mood for the trail of questions that will come in the wake of revealing the fact that I'm planning on sticking around for a while. Telling my sister I left my ex and my old life behind with basically nothing to my name is a conversation for another day.

Or never.

"Nah, I'm good," she says, stuffing another chip into her mouth and returning her eyes to her computer.

"Okay. I'll be back soon."

She waves a hand but doesn't look in my direction again, her eyes already scanning whatever she's staring at on her screen. "Don't worry about it. I've got my first test tomorrow so I'm not going anywhere. Take your time."

I head out of the kitchen and through the living room, stopping in the entry to nab the last pair of car keys on the little table by the door.

Realistically, I could take the one-mile stretch of road between our house and town and walk to One Stop in about twenty minutes. I don't *need* a car to get there, and since I've never owned my own car—my ex and I used to share his—I'm used to having to walk or bike to get places I need to be.

But as I pull out of the front drive and head in the opposite direction of town, opting to take the longer route around Cedar

Lake with the windows down and the country CD Bellamy likes to keep in her stereo on blast, I decide I need to do this more often. Instantly, I feel like I can breathe deeper, and I take my time enjoying the sun on my face and the wind in my hair.

I don't know why, but visiting my hometown has always made me feel a little itchy, like I'm being shoved into an old flannel shirt that's too small. It makes me feel shitty, especially because I really do love my family, and I know my mom works hard to make my childhood home feel warm and welcoming.

My sister loves living here and never wanted to leave, and I'd bet money that my three other siblings will return at some point, even if they're off exploring and doing other things right now. Me? I've always known living in a small town just isn't something I'm interested in.

Sure, there's something whimsical and wonderful about the small, lakeside town where I grew up. Cedar Point is tucked away in the Tahoe National Forest, a pass-through between the much larger cities of Sacramento and Lake Tahoe. It's a beautiful place to live if you enjoy having to drive an hour to go to the movies, are happy with only having two options for places to go out to eat, and don't mind shitty cell service.

Okay, that's not fair.

There are lots of wonderful things about my hometown. It's a friendly community filled with locals who are legitimately invested in where they live. There's the obvious benefit of living on a beautiful lake, the calming scent of pine and cedar trees, and the fantastic hiking trails and outdoorsy activities you can only find in the mountains.

But there's something about small-town life that's just always felt…well, small, I guess. So the *second* I was able to move away, I was out of here like a shot, off to the bright lights of San

Francisco as fast as my long legs could carry me.

My parents were sad to see me go, but they were much happier with my choice to live three hours away than with my brother Boyd's cross-country move to Boston. Thankfully, he took the brunt of their frustration, and by the time I turned 18 a year after he did, mom and dad pretty much gave me a thumbs-up as I drove out of town to go to college down the mountain.

I just knew getting outside of Cedar Point would finally make me happy. I didn't know who I was or what I wanted to do, but I had lots of ideas. Big ideas and big plans for the big life I was going to live in the big city.

Yeah.

Pretty much nothing has gone according to plan.

As I round the farthest point of the lake and begin to move closer to town, I breathe in the crispness of the late summer air. The first official day of fall is next week, and I can already feel the weather starting to change, which is one of the few things I really do miss about living in Cedar Point.

Seasons.

California is a desert. Everything on TV and in the movies makes it seem like all Californians live at the beach and enjoy sunny weather year-round.

All. Lies.

The summers are dry and hot, with temperatures rising up to 115 degrees on the really bad days, and there's hardly any wind if you live inland and away from the beach cities.

And then there are the crazy dips in temperature during winter, though only at night. During the day, it still cranks up into the 80s and 90s, making it necessary to constantly carry around a backup sweatshirt in case the weather suddenly changes.

Ultimately, California's seasons can be summed up in just a

few words.

Summer. Fire season. False winter. And spring—oh wait, just kidding, it's already summer again.

Living in Cedar Point is unlike any other part of California. It's like a completely different world, which means I get to experience my favorite season.

Autumn.

I love when the foliage begins to change. Even though the majority of trees around the lake and in Tahoe National Forest are evergreens, there are still enough deciduous trees sprinkled in, the ones that get the orange, red, and yellow leaves, to make it really feel like fall.

If I'm going to be back at home for a while, at least I get to enjoy the best time of year. It means I'll get to wear sweaters and scarves and the temperature will dip enough to enjoy coffee on the back patio in the morning. Mom and I can go get warm apple cinnamon donuts like we used to do when I was in high school.

As I pull up in front of One Stop Shop, I admire the way the sugar maple trees lining Main Street are starting to show just the barest hints of orange and red. I take a deep breath, trying to remember that life could be crazier. Things could be worse. I made a choice to leave my old life behind. It's only natural for it to take a while to figure out what's next.

You're not stuck here forever, I remind myself. *Just until you figure things out.*

When I see Andrew Marshall walking toward me from the back, I'm unsurprised by the little shiver that rolls through me when he sends a charming smile my way. Though he's always been an attractive guy, I don't remember him being quite so… muscly. Or tall. Like a slightly younger Henry Cavill.

It's been a while since I've seen the grocery owner's son. He was in the athletic crowd with my brother Boyd, which meant he came over to our house for dinner a lot and ruffled the top of my head like I was a puppy instead of a teenage girl with hearts in her eyes.

Mostly I remember Boyd and all his friends as a group of guys who liked to spend their time in pointless competition with each other over *everything*. Physical activities. Major league sports. Drinking challenges. Even dating was practically a sport, and I can remember quite a few nights when I'd sit at the top of the stairs and listen to Boyd's friends talk about the girls from school like they were playing tug of war.

Andy, though…he was different. Charming, sure, but genuine in a way the rest of their friends—sans Boyd—never were. He always had that kind of warmth to him that was incredibly disarming, and I looked at him like he'd hung the damn moon.

It's hard *not* to notice a guy like Andy Marshall.

6'2" with a swimmer's build and a smile that sends a bowling ball through my stomach. The thing I found most attractive was when he studied at our house and wore a pair of glasses as he read from his textbooks. On days like those, I might have made several trips to the bathroom or kitchen or who the hell cared, just so I could make extra passes by Boyd's bedroom to see Andy hunched over a book with those black rims on—not that I ever let *him* catch on to my observations.

The way I felt about Andy back in high school was this frustrating dichotomy I could never seem to manage. Wishing I had his attention yet fleeing the room any time he came over. Daydreaming about the day he'd notice me then just staring at him blankly when he'd actually ask me a question.

Though it wouldn't have mattered even if I *had* tried to find a way to get on his radar. High school boys go after girls who think flirting is part of the curriculum, the ones who develop boobs early and drive down the mountain to buy makeup on the weekends and know how to throw their hair over their shoulders with a seductive smile.

By the time I hit the ninth grade, I was taller than most of the boys in my class. Nobody teaches you how to be the beanstalk, and I struggled with some insecurities that I dealt with by keeping to the outskirts, choosing things that were a little nerdier and a lot more autonomous.

Working at the library.

Running on the cross country team.

Volunteering at the nursing home.

If nobody looked my way, I could avoid the attention I so desperately did *not* want.

Eventually, I got over that incredibly awkward stage once I left for college. That long-ago interest in Andy, though…it hasn't ever faded away. Not when I had that weasel of a boyfriend in high school. Not when I moved away for college. Not even when I moved in with and then got engaged to my ex, Chad.

Andy might not be a person I think about often, but he can still cause a pretty hefty swoop in my stomach when he comes to mind, that sensation you get when you accidentally step off a curb.

Sometime back in college, after having a few of my own shitty experiences with men and watching many of my friends go through the same, I began to realize I'm not a big fan of that heart-in-your-throat kind of feeling. It always seemed to lead to nothing but heartache.

Unfortunately, that perspective doesn't seem to stop my mind and body from reacting whenever I see Andy Marshall.

Like now, as he walks toward me wearing a pair of well-worn jeans and a dark red polo with the One Stop logo on the left sleeve. Damn if he doesn't look like he could grace the cover of a magazine. Strong jaw, artfully messy hair, and a little bit of stubble. All of that topping off a long, lean frame that looks both strong and soft at the same time.

I look away from him, embarrassed by my train of thought.

Strong and soft? I can't remember *ever* thinking about a man like that before. Certainly not Chad, that's for sure. My ex is a nice-looking guy, but he never elicited those kinds of feelings in me at just a glance, even back in the beginning. And I preferred it that way.

I clear my throat and try to shove my weird thoughts to the side. Ogling Andy is the last thing I need to be doing in this moment. I'm here to get a job, and I'd do well to remember that.

"Briar Mitchell," he says once he's finally a few feet away from me, tucking his hands into the pockets of his worn Levi's. "Long time, no see."

I try to give him a friendly smile that doesn't hint at where my mind was roving just a second ago, though I'm sure whatever expression I'm wearing looks less easygoing and more *What's that smell?*

Relaxed conversation has never been my strong suit.

"Hey, Andy."

"Good to see you. How's the fam?"

I lift a shoulder. "Pretty good. Same old, you know."

"Ah, that's not what I hear," he responds, that grin on his face growing slightly. "Word around town is that you've moved back."

I nibble on the inside of my cheek, wishing people weren't so damn talkative.

"Yeah," is all I offer as an explanation, choosing to sidestep any gossip that might arise from going into further detail. I don't need the town tongues to start wagging any more than they probably already are. "And I'm looking for a job, if you haven't filled that cashier position."

His eyebrows rise and he rocks back on his heels, as if I've stunned him.

"Briar Mitchell wants to work at One Stop?" he says, surprise and disbelief coloring his voice. "Never thought I'd see something like *that* happen."

I frown, his words hitting a place in my chest that I don't like.

"What's that supposed to mean?"

Andy lets out a laugh that's one part humor and much more than a dash of condescension, his laidback demeanor shifting away from friendly as he crosses his arms over his chest. "You don't have somewhere better to be than bagging groceries for the little people of Cedar Point?"

My nostrils flare, but I push back my irritation at how quickly he's decided to put me into a box he thinks he understands.

"I came in here looking for a job," I reply, my voice low even though the store is completely empty apart from the two of us and Lois, the sixty-something-year-old cashier who was reading *The National Enquirer* at her check stand when I walked in the front a few minutes ago. "Is it company policy to mock potential employees?"

He drops his hands down to his hips and pins me with a look that dismisses me outright. "You're not a potential employee, Briar. You're bored and looking for a way to get your parents off your back. I'm not looking to hire someone who will just waste my time, require a bunch of training and handholding, and then quit once she's bored."

My entire body bristles at his words.

I don't know what I've ever done to deserve Andy's ire. As far back as I can remember, he's always been approachable and warm. At the very least, I assumed being the younger sister of one of his best friends from high school would assure me some sort of friendliness, as surface level as it might be.

Clearly, I was wrong on all accounts.

My face is flushed red, and his sharp barbs have lanced me with embarrassment, not only regarding the fact that I've had to move home, but also due to what seems to be his opinion that I'm a lazy snob who thinks she's too good for a minimum-wage cashier position.

I should tell him exactly what I think. I should tell him he should give me a chance before judging me so harshly. That he's wrong in his assumptions. That he has no idea what the hell he's talking about.

But I've never been good with my words, so I don't do any of those things.

Instead, I turn away and march out of the store, flight being my chosen response when faced with the choice between being belittled in the middle of the grocery store or hightailing it out of the line of fire.

I'm normally really good at regulating my emotions. It's rare for me to be in a position that causes me to feel a significant emotional surge—positive or negative—that I'm not expecting.

And because I'm usually really good at anticipating things, I'm able to avoid letting my emotions get the best of me in situations like my interaction with Andy.

But never in my wildest dreams could I have imagined those statements coming out of Andy Marshall's mouth, completely unprovoked.

What the hell did I ever do to him?

When I moved back to Cedar Point, I assumed I'd be leaving my feelings of unhappiness and inadequacy behind, not storming out of the grocery store, swallowing down the same kinds of sensations my ex elicited from me for so long.

Maybe I'm overreacting. Maybe I'm reading too much into what Andy said. But I swore to myself when I moved home not too long ago that I'd never allow myself to feel small ever again.

Oh, how quickly I was proven wrong.

ANDY AND BRIAR'S LOVE STORY CONTINUES IN

the
opposite
of
falling

AVAILABLE ON AMAZON AND KINDLE UNLIMITED

jillian liota

about the author
jillian liota

Jillian Liota is a Southern California native currently living in Suwanee, Georgia. She is married to her best friend, has a three-legged pup with endless energy, and acts as a servant to a very temperamental cat.

Jillian writes contemporary and new adult romance, and has had her writing praised for depth of character, strong female friendships, deliciously steamy scenes, and positive portrayal of mental health.

To connect with Jillian:

Join her **Reader Group**   Check out her **Website**
Sign up for her **Newsletter**   Send her an **Email**
Rate her on **Goodreads**   Stalk her on **Instagram**
Visit her on **Facebook**   Add her on **Amazon**

jillian liota

additional titles
from jillian

Cedar Point
The Trouble with Wanting
The Opposite of Falling
The Start of Someday
The Problem with Perfect

Hermosa Beach
Promise Me Nothing
Be Your Anything
Give My Everything
We Were Something
Nowhere Like This
Anywhere But Here

Sandalwood
Solo
Sure

Like You
Like You Mean It
Like You Want It
A Gift Like You

Keeper
The Keeper
Keep Away

Poetry
This Vulnerable Heart

Printed in Great Britain
by Amazon

29149580R00207